THE

Anne Mather

CONTENTS

FALLEN ANGEL

Jason Tarrant hadn't wanted a teenage ward wished on to him—and he wanted it even less when the boy he had expected turned out to be a girl; an *estancia* in South America was hardly the place for someone like Alex Durham. And when Alex, in her artless way, began to throw herself at his head the situation looked like really getting out of hand . . .

FALLEN ANGEL

BY
ANNE MATHER

MILLS & BOON LIMITED
15–16 BROOK'S MEWS
LONDON W1A 1DR

All the characters in this book have no existence outside the imagination of the Author, and have no relation whatsoever to anyone bearing the same name or names. They are not even distantly inspired by any individual known or unknown to the Author, and all the incidents are pure invention.

First published 1978
This edition 1983

ISBN 0 263 74467 6

09/1183/

Set in 10 on 11 pt Intertype Lectura

Made and printed in Great Britain by
Cox & Wyman Ltd, Reading

CHAPTER ONE

JASON did not like London. He had not liked it when he was a student, and he liked it even less now. The crowded thoroughfares, all confusingly one way, the noise of the traffic, the sickly smell of diesel; all these things combined to make him yearn for the open spaces of his *estancia*; though it must be added that anyone observing his tall, immaculately-suited figure and darkly cynical features would never have suspected he felt more at home on the *pampa*.

It was strange, he reflected, when he had been born and brought up in England, albeit in the care of the local council, that he should feel more at ease in the South American republic where he had his home. The well-trammelled spaces of his fatherland held no interest for him, and as soon as he had obtained the engineering degree he had worked for, he left for more adventurous climes. But building bridges in Australia or pipelines in the Middle East soon began to pall, however, and because the money was good he joined a mercenary force fighting in Central Africa. But even money would not compensate for the lack of self-respect he felt facing a barefoot enemy, equipped with only the meanest kind of ammunition, with weaponry of the most sophisticated kind. He left for America with funds to pay the deposit on some land of his own, and succeeded only in blowing it all in on a speculative land deal that left him broke and jobless.

And that was how he met Charles Durham . . .

Jason moved to the window of his hotel suite now and surveyed the busy street several floors below without enthusiasm. Was it really fifteen years since that bar-room brawl? He could hardly credit it. And yet so much had happened in the years since, he should not find it so difficult to believe.

Durham was an archaeologist, taking a break from a dig he was working on in Mexico. He was holidaying in New Orleans at the time, and his initial encounter with Jason took place in the street outside one of the many bars and taverns. He, Jason, had been rolling drunk at the time, he remembered wryly, and was losing the fight he was having with the burly bartender when Durham recognised a fellow Englishman and intervened. He had settled the bill, which had been the cause of the fight, and the bartender, recognising the fact that sober Jason would have little difficulty in laying him out, had been more than willing to accept the settlement. Durham had taken Jason to his lodgings, sobered him up, and eventually persuaded him to admit to his abortive foray into the real estate business. Subsequently, he had offered him a job working with him in Mexico, and although Jason had known little about archaeology, he had been willing to learn.

He worked with Durham for almost two years before they discovered the ruins of the Mayan pyramid, and beneath, untouched for hundreds of years, the burial chamber. Even now, so many years on, Jason could remember the thrill they had felt upon discovering the necklaces and rings and bracelets that decked the crumbling skeleton the chamber had contained, and the jade mask that hid the hollow eye-sockets and gaping mouth.

With his share of what was left after the government had taken their dues, Durham intended to create a research institute in England, but Jason had decided to spend some time in South America. He lived in Brazil for a year, and then twelve years ago he had bought some land in Santa Vittoria, a tiny country sandwiched between Brazil and Uruguay. Although he and Durham had intended to keep in touch, England was a long way from his home at San Gabriel, and somehow he had never found the time to write letters. He had had much to learn—about growing maize and flax, planting orchards of fruit trees, so that he could harvest his own oranges and lemons, peaches and grapes, but mostly about breeding the horses and cattle which were his real love. It was almost as if he had spent his whole life searching for that one reality, and once he found it, he held it fast. And then, six weeks ago, he got the letter . . .

The ringing of the telephone interrupted his train of thought, and moving lithely across the room, he lifted the receiver.

'Tarrant,' he supplied tersely, and then relaxed when the hotel operator said: 'There's a young lady here to see you, Mr Tarrant. She says you're expecting——'

'That's right,' Jason interrupted the flow. 'You can send her right up.'

'Yes, sir.'

'Oh——' Jason chewed on his lower lip for a moment, 'I'm—er—I'm also expecting someone else. A boy. When he arrives, let me know at once, will you?'

'Yes, Mr Tarrant.'

Jason replaced the receiver on its rest thoughtfully, flexing his shoulder muscles as he contemplated the interview ahead. This wasn't quite his line—interviewing a prospective tutor for the boy, particularly a female one, but there seemed few male tutors willing to abandon the bright lights of London for a remote ranch house in the Sierra Grande. He hoped the woman wasn't too young, although these days appearances could be deceptive, and Estelita wouldn't approve of him taking any female under the age of thirty-five into his home.

As he waited he crossed the room again, catching a glimpse of himself in the long Chinese mirrors that flanked the marble fireplace, an anachronism now in the centrally heated hotel. A wry smile crossed his lips at the image of the dark-suited businessman they reflected, his lean frame encased in the mohair jacket, pants and waistcoat which the tailor in Valvedra had assured him was the latest fashion. Certainly his attire gave the illusion of a man accustomed to city ways, but Jason couldn't wait to don the mud-coloured shirts and Levis which were his usual garb back home. Instead of fine suede, he would wear leather gaucho boots, and his dark hair, so smoothly combed, would be rough beneath the wide brim of his slouch hat. His lips twisted as he wondered what Charles Durham would think if he could see him now. The older man would no doubt have been proud of his success, and he regretted the carelessness which had lengthened the distance between them all these years. Still, it was too late now to feel remorse. Instead, he would do everything in his power to give the boy the home he himself had lacked.

He surveyed the luxurious hotel suite with critical eyes. Was this the most suitable place to conduct an interview of this kind? he wondered. Ought he to have had another woman present? But who? He knew few people in London. The hotel receptionist perhaps. She had certainly shown sufficient interest in him when he arrived, but without false modesty he admitted that the kind of interest she had shown was hardly appropriate to the occasion. No, this was something he was going to have to do alone, and trust his own judgment in assessing the woman's capabilities.

He paced a trifle restlessly across to the fireplace. The two men he had interviewed for the post had both laboured under the misapprehension that because he was a wealthy man he must needs live in Puerto Novo or Valvedra. When they learned that his *estancia* was over a hundred miles from the coast, they quickly lost interest in working in such remote surroundings. So why should a woman feel any differently? His eyes narrowed. Unless she was some dried-up old spinster, who saw this post as a golden opportunity to ingratiate herself with the master of the household. He grimaced. He was cynical, he admitted it. But years of hard living and fending for himself had taught him never to trust anyone's motives at face value. Only Charles Durham had ever helped him, and now he was dead Jason was determined to do what he could for his son—but not at the cost of his own freedom. He had had one taste of so-called connubial bliss, and like the use of methadone in drug addiction, it had cured him of the craving. He liked women, he couldn't deny it. He was like any normal healthy male in that respect. But marriage no longer figured in his plans —a circumstance that fired Estelita's hot Latin blood.

A knock at the outer door of the suite brought him upright with a certain tightening of his flat stomach muscles. Stretching the long brown fingers at his sides, he strode purposefully across the room and swung open the door. Then he stood back aghast as a smiling girl of perhaps sixteen years of age stepped forward and, reaching up, bestowed a kiss on each of his taut brown cheeks. A little above medium height and slender, she was only slightly boyish in her fringed suede pants suit, the long curtains of silvery fair hair which fell from a centre parting easily decrying such a supposition. Silky gold-tipped lashes framed wide eyes of a smoky shade of violet, while the smiling mouth was full and generous.

'Jason!' she said, and her voice was low and husky. 'Yes, it has to be. You're exactly as Daddy described you.'

'Daddy!'

Jason was feeling distinctly confused now, particularly when the girl passed him to enter the suite uninvited, looking about her with evident fascination.

'Look—who are you?' he exclaimed, but even as he asked the question he knew, and a sinking feeling invaded the lower regions of his abdomen. 'You . . . can't be . . .'

'Alex Durham, yes.' The girl turned, unconsciously graceful in all her movements. 'Weren't you expecting me?'

Jason's mouth opened and closed on an ominously thin scowl. '*Alex* Durham?' he repeated tersely, and her smile gave way to a grimace of uncertainty.

'Alexandra, actually,' she admitted. Then, adopting a defiant stance, she added: 'Everyone calls me Alex.'

'Do they?' Realising the door was still standing open,

Jason closed it, albeit reluctantly, with a definite click. 'But you knew I thought you were a boy, didn't you?'

'Did you?' She lifted her shoulders in an offhand gesture. 'I'm sorry. I didn't think it would make that much difference.'

Jason moved away from the door, annoyed to find that it was he who was disconcerted here. The correspondence he had had with Durham's solicitors had not been explicit. Obviously, in the circumstances, they had assumed that he would know the age and sex of the child. Child? His lips tightened. Even after so short an acquaintance, Jason could see that Alexandra Durham was not a child. How old was she? Charles had never mentioned a wife in all the time he had known him, and consequently Jason had assumed he had married after returning to England. That would make the boy—girl!—twelve at most, whereas this girl was obviously fifteen or sixteen at least. A shorter guardianship than he had expected perhaps, but what a complication!

'Do you live here?' the girl was asking now, and Jason forced himself to concentrate on what she was saying.

'No, of course not,' he retorted, rather snappishly. 'You know my home is in Santa Vittoria.'

'I meant while you were in England,' she explained politely, her reasonableness irritating Jason even more. 'I've never stayed in an hotel. The nuns didn't approve of that sort of thing. Some of the girls used to spend holidays with their parents, you know, at places like St Moritz and Chamonix in the winter, or Nice or St Tropez or Cap d'Antibes in the summer, but I've never been to those places. Daddy was always on some dig or other——'

'Just a minute.' Jason halted this monologue with a curt intervention. 'Don't you think you ought to explain why you chose to leave me in ignorance of the fact that you're female, and what the hell you expect me to do about it as you are?'

She frowned then, a furrow appearing on the smooth brow. 'What I expect you to do about it?' she repeated softly. 'What do you mean? You're my guardian, aren't you? Whatever sex I happen to be.'

Jason expelled his breath on a heavy sigh. 'I can't believe you're that naïve, *Miss* Durham. You know as well as I do that I expected a boy!'

'So you keep telling me, but I don't see what I can do about *that*,' she retorted, half laughingly, and her amusement was the last straw as far as Jason was concerned.

'Then I'll tell you,' he snapped angrily. 'Your father was a good friend to me when I needed one, and I've never forgotten it. When I heard that he'd died leaving his—child—in my care, I was prepared to do everything in my power to give the boy a decent start in life——'

'I know,' she exclaimed, covering the space between them and laying a hand on the sleeve of his mohair jacket, but he brushed her away, continuing:

'My correspondence with you was addressed to *Master* Alex Durham, and you know it. All my arrangements, all my plans, have been for a boy of perhaps twelve, thirteen years of age——'

'Well, I can't help that,' she protested now, the movement of her head spilling the swathe of silky hair across the dark green suede of her jacket. 'I didn't ask to be willed to you. I couldn't choose what sex I was. If I could, believe me I'd have satisfied you in every detail!'

'What do you mean?'

'Only that my father never wanted a daughter, any more than you want me now,' she retorted, and Jason felt a twinge of remorse for the pained anguish in her eyes. 'I'd have been a boy all right. Then perhaps Daddy might have taken me with him on his trips to Greece and South America, instead of leaving me in the convent until I thought I should die of boredom!'

Jason's eyes narrowed. 'Exactly how old are you?'

'Seventeen!'

'Seventeen?' He stared at her disbelievingly. 'But—but——'

'Daddy never mentioned me?' She shrugged, but he could tell she was fighting her emotions. 'That doesn't surprise me. He never wanted to get married, you know. He never should have. Then—then when my mother died when I was born—well . . .' She shrugged again. 'He put me in the care of the nuns at Sainte Sœur.'

Jason shook his head. 'You speak very good English. But the convent was in France, I gather.'

'Yes. Just outside Paris, actually. My mother was French, you see. But many of the nuns at the convent were English, and my father insisted that as he spoke little French, I should be educated in his language.'

'I see.' Jason ran an impatient hand round the back of his neck, trying to restrain the sense of injustice that was threatening to erupt once more. How could Durham have ignored his child's existence to the extent that never once in the two years he had known him had he mentioned the fact that he had a daughter? It was cold and callous; and totally out of keeping with the man he had thought he had known. But perhaps that was exactly why Durham had helped *him*, out of a sense of guilt towards this—girl, this child, who could have been little more than an infant when Durham was excavating at Los Lobos. Then: 'You say—your father mentioned me?'

'Yes!' Animation entered the girl's features again. 'I don't know whether he wrote you about his expeditions, but towards the end, when he was confined . . .' she faltered, '. . . confined to his bed, he spoke about you a lot.'

Jason drew a deep breath and gestured towards one of the low comfortable couches that faced one another across the width of the hearth. 'Look,' he said. 'I think you'd better sit down. We have to talk, and I guess—I guess it would be easier if we at least tried to understand one another.'

'Of course.' The girl's smile reappeared, and she subsided obediently on to cushions of dark blue brocade. As she did so, the lapels of her jacket parted to reveal the dusky hollow between her breasts, and their rounded fullness pressing against the soft suede was an added indication of her burgeoning maturity. Jason hesitated a moment, and then, with some reluctance, took the couch opposite her, stretching his long legs out in front of him, his fingers curving loosely over the cushions on either side of him.

'Now,' he said, when she raised inquisitive eyebrows, 'tell me a little about what happened to your father—after he returned from Mexico.'

'Oh ...' Alexandra frowned. 'Well, that isn't too easy. I didn't always know where he was or what he was doing. I think he financed an expedition to Egypt, but I'm not sure.'

'But the institute,' said Jason patiently. 'What about the research institute?' The girl looked puzzled now, and his own frown returned. 'Your father intended to use the money he gained from our successful excavation at Los Lobos to create a research institute,' he explained, but Alexandra clearly had no knowledge of this.

'I'm sorry,' she said. 'If—if you think my father died a wealthy man——'

'I didn't say that!' retorted Jason shortly, stung by the implication, and she went on:

'Every penny he had went to finance his last expedition. It was to Turkey—a remote valley in the Taurus mountains. That was where he was taken ill, you see. A chill, followed by a lung infection. They'd been living in tents at the dig, and by the time they got him down to the hospital in Maras it had developed into pneumonia. He recovered, of course, but he wasn't strong enough to go on, and he was flown back to London. That was when he sent for me.'

'And how long ago was that?' asked Jason, watching the play of emotions across her expressive features.

'Six months, I guess,' she answered at once. 'Perhaps he realised the lung infection had weakened the muscles of his heart, and that he hadn't long to live. Or maybe he just wanted to get to know his daughter ...' The words trailed away as a trace of emotion brought a slightly higher note to her voice, but she controlled it. 'I didn't know he'd written to the solicitor—until after—after he was dead. He knew I wouldn't have wanted him to. I mean—I'm quite capable of taking care of myself, you know.'

'Are you?' Jason's tone was dry, but inwardly he admired her spirit. It could not have been an easy six months, whatever way you looked at it.

'Yes.' She squared her shoulders now and looked at him. 'Well? Are you going to disown me?'

'No!' Jason's denial was abrupt, and pushing himself up with his hands, he stood over her, tall and dark and slightly menacing, although he was unaware of it. 'I just need some time to—to revise my plans.'

She rose too, then, and the scent of some perfume she was wearing rose disturbingly to his nostrils. It was fresh and slightly heady, like the lemon groves back home, and for a moment he looked down at her, his dark eyes mirroring the gentler shade of hers. Unwillingly, his senses stirred at the unconscious allure of those gold-fringed irises, pansy-soft as she gazed up at him.

'Thank you,' she said, and quite unselfconsciously pressed two fingers against her lips before transferring them to his mouth. 'Daddy was right about you. You are a good man.'

What Jason would have replied to this totally unexpected provocation he hardly knew, but a sudden knocking at the door to the suite provided a welcome distraction. Of course, he thought abstractedly, it would be the governess, the woman he had been waiting to interview when this frustrating creature erupted into his life. At least the interruption would give him a breathing space, he thought savagely, furious with himself for allowing a girl—little more than a schoolgirl—to disrupt his normally controlled emotions.

'This is going to be awkward,' he said, putting some space between them as he spoke. 'I imagine this is the woman I intended interviewing for the post of—of governess.'

'Governess!' Alexandra echoed, the violet eyes dancing now. 'For me?' She gurgled with laughter. 'Oh, Jason, did you really think I would need a governess?'

Jason's thinning mouth sobered her however. 'It may surprise you to know that as your father never mentioned your existence, I assumed he had married since our expedition to Los Lobos. Naturally, therefore, I expected a younger child.'

'I'm not a child,' she pointed out, unable to let that go, but he had already turned away to open the door.

The woman who was waiting outside was reassuringly middle-aged. Jason guessed her age to be somewhere between forty-five and fifty, and her dress and appearance were in keeping with her profession. If only she had arrived first, he found himself thinking impatiently. Then perhaps he would have been more prepared to deal with his unexpectedly female ward.

'Mr Tarrant?' the woman was asking politely, and Jason nodded shortly, offering his hand in greeting and gesturing for the woman to come in.

'You are Miss Holland, I take it?' he enquired brusquely, and that lady agreed with his admission.

'I'm sorry I'm late,' she apologised, as he closed the door behind them, and her eyes alighted questioningly on Alexandra. 'I—er—I couldn't get a cab, and then the traffic . . .'

'That's quite all right, Miss Holland,' Jason assured her curtly, his eyes flickering briefly over the slender figure by the hearth. 'As it happens, your being late has precipitated a situation which I'm afraid alters matters considerably.'

'Oh?' Miss Holland's glance lingered once more on Alexandra's slim youthfulness, and a rather worried look crossed her homely features. It occurred to Jason that perhaps getting the job had meant a lot to this rather anxious-looking woman, and his deepening interest observed the faintly worn sleeves of her navy-blue uniform coat, and the neat but unmistakable darns in her woollen gloves.

Now he offered her a chair and after she was seated, he explained: 'I'm afraid the post I advertised no longer exists. The—er—the boy turns out to be a girl, and she——' he turned abruptly and indicated Alexandra, 'as you can see, is too old to require a governess.'

Miss Holland's worn features mirrored her disappointment. 'Yes,' she said. 'Yes, I see.'

'I'm sorry . . .' And he was. Jason cast another impatient glance in Alexandra's direction. Why couldn't she have been the child he expected? Why hadn't Durham told him the truth? He knew instinctively that Miss Holland would have taken the post, wherever it was. She had that sort of defeated air about her that smacked of too many interviews and too many disappointments. Nowadays, people wanted modern young governessess for their children, not middle-aged women, however well qualified. Miss Holland just wanted to work, and he wondered how long it was since she had done so. Still, he reflected wryly, he had enough problems of his own right now. He couldn't be blamed for what was indisputably evident.

The woman rose to her feet again now and faced him with a touching air of confidence. 'I'll be going then, Mr Tarrant. Thank you for seeing me. And I'm sorry things haven't worked out as—as you expected.' Faint colour ran up her cheeks as she realised what she was implying, and she added hastily: 'I mean, of course, *I'm* sorry. You—er—you may not be. I'm sure you're not. That is——'

'That's quite all right, Miss Holland,' Jason intervened smoothly, halting her embarrassed flow, and smiling to remove any sharpness from his words. 'I know exactly what you mean.'

Miss Holland nodded, compressed her lips, offered a half smile of apology to Alexandra, and moved towards the door. Jason strode ahead of her, swinging open the door as she approached, and taking the hand she tentatively offered him in farewell.

'Good luck,' he said, as she pulled on her shabby glove, and her smile was more eloquent than any words.

With the door closed behind her, Jason leant against it almost wearily. What now? What was he going to do with the girl? One thing was certain, he could not take her back to San Gabriel with him. Apart from Estelita, his was a masculine household, and there was no place in it for a provocative teenager just waiting to try her claws. Besides, there was nothing for a girl at his *estancia*. The life he led was almost spartan in its simplicity, and remote from any kind of social gathering. With a boy, it would have been different. He could have shown him the ranch, taught him to ride and rope a steer, taught him to break horses and sleep out under the stars when the yearly round-up was made; treated him like a son, in fact, the son he was never likely to have now. But a girl . . . In God's name, what could he do for her?

As if aware of the turmoil inside him, Alexandra left her place by the hearth to approach him, and he stiffened as she halted some few feet away from him.

'What's the matter?' she asked, and her eyes were guarded now. 'What are you thinking? Do you want to change your mind about me?'

'Change my mind?' Jason frowned. 'I don't know what you mean.'

Alexandra's long lashes swept her cheeks. 'I think you do. You're wishing I was a boy, too, aren't you? Just like Daddy.' Her chin lifted, and her eyes were defiant as they sought his. 'What is it with you two? What's wrong with being a woman? Don't they have their uses, too?'

Jason straightened away from the door. 'All right,' he admitted abruptly. 'I don't deny it. I was thinking along those lines. But only because your being a girl makes everything that much more complicated.'

'Why?'

'Why?' A faintly mocking gleam invaded his eyes. 'Oh, come on, Miss Durham, I don't believe you're that unsophisticated.'

'Will you please stop calling me *Miss* Durham! My name's Alex—Alexandra, if you like, or perhaps not, as you seem to prefer the masculine gender!'

Jason's mouth tightened at the deliberately insolent intonation, but he let it go, saying quietly: 'I was merely going to explain that had you been a boy, you could have accompanied me back to Santa Vittoria, and made your home with me at San Gabriel.'

'San Gabriel?' For a moment, she was diverted. 'What's that? Your house?'

'My ranch, yes.'

'How super!' Her eyes sparkled. 'Oh, yes, Jason, I'd like to do that.'

'Now wait a minute . . .' Jason was finding it increasingly difficult to control this conversation. 'I said—had you been a boy——'

'But what does it matter?' she exclaimed. 'So long as I want to go?'

'So long as *you* want to go!' Jason raised his eyes heavenward for a moment in a gesture of frustration. 'My dear Miss—*Alexandra*! You know perfectly well I can't take you to San Gabriel.'

Her dark brows arched. 'Your wife would object?'

'I don't have a wife.'

'Ah, no . . .' She rubbed her nose thoughtfully with her finger. 'You wouldn't.'

'What the hell do you mean?'

Jason spoke angrily, and her lips twitched. 'Why, nothing. Only that—you're a misogynist, aren't you?'

'No, damn you, I'm not!' Jason found he was unaccountably furious. 'I enjoy a *woman*'s company as well as the next man. I just don't intend taking a promiscuous schoolgirl back to a ranch where the men don't see a white woman from one year's end to the next!'

A gurgle of laughter escaped her at this. 'Make up your mind,' she taunted him. 'Either I'm a schoolgirl or a woman —which?'

'You know what I mean,' he grated severely. 'Now, I suggest we discuss what it is you want to do with your life.'

'I want to stay with you. Either here or at San Gabriel.' She sighed. 'Hmm, that's a beautiful name, isn't it? Is the ranch as beautiful as its name? Or is it an *estancia*? Isn't that what they call ranches in South America?'

'Alexandra!'

The warning note in his voice went unheeded as she smiled impishly up at him. 'That's better,' she approved. 'I like the way you say my name. What sort of accent would you say you have? I think it's a sort of mid-Atlantic accent, isn't it? Neither one thing nor the other.'

Jason turned from her to pace tensely towards the window. This was hopeless. He was getting absolutely nowhere. He half wished he had asked Miss Holland to remain during the course of this interview. Maybe she would have been able to make some constructive suggestion, explain to the girl that what she was asking was impossible. *God*, why had Charles done this to him? Surely he must have known the complications it would bring. What had been his intention? What had he expected Jason to do with her? Surely he could not have wanted him to take her back with him to South America. Hadn't he cared about the dangers—the obvious temptation a girl like her would present to men starved of the company of women? And what of his erstwhile colleague? What had he really known of him, that he should feel able to entrust his daughter to his care?

'Jason . . .' Alexandra's husky voice right behind him made him aware she had moved to join him by the window. 'Jason, please—can't we talk about this? I know I must have been a great shock to you, and I admit, I did leave you in ignorance deliberately, but only because—well, because I was afraid you might—you might not come . . .'

'And what kind of a swine would I have been if I hadn't?' Jason demanded, glancing at her broodingly. 'My God, whatever his reasons, your father has left you in my care, at least until you're eighteen, and I should not have shirked that responsibility.'

'Oh, *responsibility* . . .' She scuffed her toe against the expensive rug with ill grace. 'I don't want to be a *responsibility*! I'm a person, a human being; a living entity in my own right. I don't want to be anyone's responsibility. I just want to be—to be a part of your life, part of someone's life anyway,' she finished a trifle wistfully.

Jason's teeth grated. 'You won't try and understand, will you?'

'What's to understand?' She held his gaze deliberately. 'Are you afraid of me, *Mr* Tarrant? Are you afraid you might be as—tempted as the next man——'

'Don't be so ridiculous!' Jason's rejection of her taunting statement was violent, but she stood her ground. 'I'm simply trying to explain to you that my *gauchos* are not the fanciful gallants you've probably seen on the screen. They're rough men, mestizos and Indians for the most part, for whom an unattached white girl is fair game. Do I make myself clear?'

'Perfectly,' she conceded, without flinching. 'But surely as your—ward, I would merit some respect.'

'Perhaps. But I don't feel like being nursemaid!'

'And that's the truth, isn't it?' she declared bitterly. 'Oh, you're just like my father!'

She presented her back to him then, groping in the bag that hung from one shoulder for the handkerchief she couldn't find. Jason watched her helpless fumblings for several minutes, and then extracted his own handkerchief from his pocket and handed it to her.

But instead of thanking him, as he had expected, she snatched the pristine square of white linen and threw it on the floor, deliberately grinding the heel of her boot upon it. Jason stared, bleak-eyed, as she kicked the now soiled handkerchief aside, and rubbed her nose unhygienically on the back of her hand.

'Why, you——'

'Go on!' she encouraged him, chancing a look at him over her shoulder. 'Say it! Call me names. Better that than ignoring my existence!'

Jason allowed his breath to escape on a suppressed oath, then bent and lifted the grubby handkerchief. He regarded it solemnly for several seconds, then he stuffed it back into the pocket of his jacket. Alexandra was sniffing now, her head bent, but he made no attempt to comfort her. Instead, he drew a case of the long narrow cigars he liked from his pocket, and placing one between his teeth, applied the flame of his lighter to it.

The aromatic flavour was soothing, and he attempted to remain calm. Arguing with the girl was doing no good, he could see that. But somehow he had to make her see reason. A sudden idea occurred to him. What she needed was someone to take care of her, some woman, and almost instantaneously the image of Miss Holland sprang to his mind. If that lady could be persuaded to accept a position as housekeeper-cum-guardian, he could lease a house here in London, and Alexandra could choose whether she wanted to continue with her studies or alternatively find some suitable occupation. He might even permit her to visit him in Santa Vittoria on occasion. If she stayed at the hotel in Valvedra, there was no reason why she shouldn't travel if she wanted to.

'Alexandra ...' His own voice was almost persuasive now, and instinctively she responded to the gentler tone.

'Yes?' She half turned, and he glimpsed the tear-washed brilliance of her eyes, tiny globules glistening like raindrops on her lashes. Unaccountably, he was stirred, and the knowledge brought an impatient hardening in his voice.

'I've come to a decision,' he said, thrusting his balled fists into the pockets of his pants, unaware that the action drew her attention to the powerful muscles of his thighs.

'I shall lease a house here in London, for you—and for Miss Holland——'

'Miss Holland?'

'That's right. The woman who was here a few minutes ago. If I'm not mistaken, she needs a job badly. Maybe she will be prepared to act as your guardian in my absence——'

'No!'

'What do you mean—*no?*' he demanded ominously. 'Alexandra, might I remind you that until your eighteenth birthday, I *am* your guardian. You will do as I say.'

'You can't make me,' she retorted, swinging round to face him. 'Oh, I admit, while you're here, you can force me to stay with Miss—Miss Holland, but after you're gone, do you honestly believe she'll be able to make me do as she says? She can't lock me in my room, you know. I shall have to go out sometimes. And who says I'll have to come back?'

His face was steely hard by the time she had finished. 'Are you threatening me?' he demanded, and she sensed the tautening of his body.

'I—why, no. Not—threatening,' she muttered, resorting to looking for her handkerchief again. 'But . . .' She caught her lower lip between her teeth and looked up at him again, and this time there was only appeal in those drowned violet depths. 'Oh, Jason, *please*! Don't do this. Let me come with you. I'll be good, I promise. I won't go near any of your farmhands—*gauchos*, whatever. I'll do exactly as *you* say. I can cook—and clean—and make beds——'

'No, Alexandra!'

'Why not? Why not?' Instead of spitting at him again as he had half expected, she closed the gap between them and he tore his hands out of his pockets to prevent her from getting too close for comfort. 'Jason, Daddy respected you so much. He wanted us to be friends. Won't you at least try to like me?'

Jason's hands had descended on her shoulders, and the fragile vulnerability of the bones beneath his fingers caused him to hesitate before saying, 'It's not a question of—*liking*, Alexandra.'

'Then why——'

He found he was not immune to those eyes after all. Hurting her was like hurting a wounded deer, a trite observation, but true nevertheless. What the hell, her father had abandoned her, hadn't he? Was he about to do the same? What would happen to her if he did? Who knew what dangers she might encounter in London, particularly in her desire to prove to him that she needed his protection? His fingers tightened so that he felt the bones might crack beneath his hold, but she didn't wince, and with a feeling compounded of sympathy and compassion, and a curious kind of self-disgust, he said:

'All right, all right, I give in. You can come with me to Santa Vittoria. You and Miss Holland both.'

'You really mean it?'

Tears overspilled her eyes as she stared disbelievingly up at him, and almost with revulsion he thrust her away from him. But that didn't alter the fact that by allowing her to accompany him, he sensed he was inviting trouble. What form that trouble would take, he could not foresee, but almost immediately he wished he could retract his words.

It was too late, of course. Much too late. The misty relief that shone in her eyes could not be doused, and far from regretting his submission, she was positively incoherent with delight.

'Oh, Jason!' she breathed, brushing away her tears with a careless hand, and before he could anticipate what she was about to do, she had flung her arms around his neck and was bestowing kisses all over his face. 'Darling, darling Jason!' she was crying exuberantly, while he tried rather unsuccessfully to free himself, uncomfortably aware of those firm breasts pressing against the material of his waistcoat and of the warm scent of her arms wound so closely round his neck. If she was to accompany him to

San Gabriel, they would have to talk about her impulsive methods of expressing herself, he thought dryly. He wondered how she saw him. As some kind of Dutch uncle, perhaps, or the father figure she had never known. Whatever, she would have to learn that young women, however enthusiastic, did not throw themselves into the arms of a virtual stranger just because he had agreed to her wishes, albeit against his better judgment.

Having extracted himself, and with her wrists pressed firmly against her sides, Jason felt more able to speak seriously to her, although the dancing violet eyes were a continual distraction.

'Miss Holland,' he said, 'Miss Holland must agree to come with us, do you understand? If she refuses——'

'She won't,' Alexandra interrupted certainly. 'She liked you, I'm sure.'

'It's you she has to deal with,' retorted Jason repressively, wondering with some misgivings how Estelita would react to two such females in his house. 'And while we're on the subject, you must not be so—so demonstrative.'

'Demonstrative?' Alexandra's brows arched. 'Towards you, you mean?'

'Towards anyone,' amended Jason dryly, but she only smiled.

'Why?' she persisted. 'Don't you like it? Don't you like me to touch you?'

'That has nothing to do with it,' he began, but she shook her head.

'I think it has.' She tried to free her wrists, but he knew better than to let her go. 'I think it has everything to do with it. At the convent—you know, when I was living with the nuns—nobody ever touched one another. We were like—separate species.' She sighed. 'We used to talk together—and smile together—even pray together. But we never touched.' She moved her slim shoulders in a helpless gesture. 'I think people should touch one another. That's what caring is all about.' She lifted her head. 'I like touching people. I like touching you . . .'

'That's enough!'

Abruptly, she was free, but she knew better than to touch him just then. After a moment's laboured breathing, he turned and crossed to the telephone, and while she watched, he asked the operator to get him the number of the agency where he had engaged to interview the governess. It was a brief call, but it served a dual purpose—on the one hand, it accomplished the need to contact Miss Holland as quickly as possible, and on the other it gave him time to realise the enormity of the task he was taking upon himself.

CHAPTER TWO

ALEXANDRA had never experienced such a sense of space and freedom, miles and miles of long pampas grass stretching as far as the eye could see. Acres and acres of land, grazed by herds of shorthorned cattle, that turned wicked eyes in their direction as they passed, making Alexandra, at least, aware of the thin sheet of metal which separated them from those ugly pointed projections. Cattle in France and England never had such beady little eyes, or moved with the arrogance of the beast, untamed and magnificent.

Ever since the powerful Range-Rover passed beneath the crossed strips of wood which had marked the boundary of Jason's land, she had been expecting to see the ranch-house, but mile followed mile and there was nothing in sight but the untrammelled grasslands of the Santa Vittorian plateau. The road, which from Valvedra had been passably smooth, was now little more than a beaten track, and she was regretting her impulse to offer Miss Holland the seat beside Jason in front. As she sat in the back of the Range-Rover, the base of her spine was in constant opposition to the springs of the vehicle, and her back ached from being thrown from side to side.

From time to time, her eyes encountered Jason's through the rear-view mirror, and then she made a determined effort to appear unconcerned, aware that occasionally a trace of amusement lightened their umber depths. But she was here, that was the main thing, she thought with satisfaction, and the awareness of Jason's lean body in the seat in front of her was all the compensation she needed.

It had not been easy, she acknowledged it now, and until the moment she and Miss Holland had boarded the plane she had been terrified in case he should send some message forbidding her to join him. But from the minute her father had spoken of Jason Tarrant, describing the kind of man he was, telling her about their adventures in Mexico, the rough absorbing outdoor life they had led, she had wanted to meet him. All her life she had wanted to do the things her father did, meet the people he worked with, and share in the thrill of his excavations. She would have followed him to the ends of the earth if he had asked her, but he never had. So far as he was concerned, she was a girl, and girls were not welcome in what he considered to be a male province. Her own mother had died in childbirth confirming his belief that females were weak, defenceless creatures, and he had only sent for Alexandra at the end because he had known he was dying, too.

Even then, he had not known what to do with her. Her assurances that she would make out on her own had not convinced him, but his suggestion of returning her to the nuns of Sainte Sœur had filled her with alarm. It was then she had coined the idea of writing to Jason Tarrant, of telling him her father was dying, and putting her future into his hands. She knew her father had helped him when he was in trouble, but Charles Durham would not even consider such a proposition. Instead, he had dictated a letter to his solicitors, giving them the address of the convent, and asking that if—*when*—anything happened to him, Alexandra should return there, at least until she was eighteen.

To her shame, Alexandra had never written that letter. Because his eyesight was failing, she had written all her father's letters for him, and it wasn't difficult to substitute a letter of her own for him to sign. It was possible that given time, the solicitors might have questioned that particular missive, but Charles Durham suffered a massive heart attack the following day from which he never recovered. Alexandra was left, pale and distraught, at the mercy of her own machinations.

Her first meeting with Jason, at his hotel, had not been

exactly as she had expected. Of course, she had expected him to protest about the fact of her being a girl—*didn't everyone?*—but she had not imagined he would be so young. She had been prepared to meet a contemporary of her father's, a man in his fifties, at least, instead of someone perhaps twenty years younger. But that initial hazard had been swiftly superseded by her immediate attraction to the man himself, whose lean hard body and dark-skinned features reminded her vividly of the painting of an Indian the nuns had kept at the convent. Those gentle women would have been shocked by Alexandra's reactions to that particular picture, the baptism to Christianity of a tall bronzed pagan, which had taken on a different aspect in Alexandra's maturing eyes.

Jason himself had been as confounded as her father by his new responsibilities, but in the event it proved providential that he had imagined her to be a boy. Without Miss Holland's intervention, he might never have been persuaded to allow her to go to Santa Vittoria, but she felt now that whatever he had decreed, she would have followed him. It was fate, she decided, which had prompted her to write that letter, and for now, just being with him was enough.

Miss Holland was another matter. That lady had taken her responsibilities very seriously, and seemed to regard her situation as that of a nursemaid, rather than a companion. There were times when she made Alexandra feel like a child in the company of an adult, and those occasions were galling. She was seventeen; granted she had led a comparatively sheltered life, but she had read a lot, much of it books the nuns would have been horrified to discover in the hands of one of their charges. The only thing her father had not kept her short of was money and she had spent it lavishly on literature of all kinds. All her experience of the relationship between a man and a woman had come from books, but she felt adequate to cope should the situation arise. She was a mature and intelligent young woman, or so she believed, and Miss Holland's behaviour was a source of irritation to her. The fact that since their arrival in Valvedra, it was a source of amusement to Jason, too, only added to her frustration.

Miss Holland had proved useful when it came to providing her with a wardrobe suitable to the climate in which she was to be living. Her knowledge of London was extensive, she having tutored the children of a titled family for more years than she cared to admit, and maybe because she regarded Alexandra as little more than a child, she chose those shops where teenage clothes were sold. Once inside those shops however, Alexandra soon made her own wishes felt, and the sales assistants added their encouragement. The fashions of the day—jeans and sweaters, pants suits, and long flowing skirts and dresses—looked good on Alexandra's slender figure, and although Miss Holland looked askance at revealing smocks and skin-tight jumpers, her opinion was overruled. Besides, the ear-splitting music which was an accompaniment to the service in these establishments gave her a headache, and she was obliged to wait outside.

Although Charles Durham had not died a poor man, he had not died a rich one either. He had used most of his capital to finance the expeditions which had become the cornerstone of his life, and sacrificed his dream of creating an institute in the tireless search for knowledge. Even so, the sale of the small house he had owned, though seldom occupied, in Ealing did provide Alexandra with a comfortable nest-egg, but her plans of bestowing it on her benefactor were doomed to disappointment. Before departing for South America, Jason had made it very clear that until her majority, he intended to make himself responsible for her maintenance, and the knowledge that she had tricked him into supporting her occasionally gave her a sleepless night. She consoled herself with the belief, however, that once she was living in his house, she would make herself useful to him in every way possible, and somehow she would repay him.

The days following Jason's departure had dragged. She and the middle-aged lady who was to accompany her were obliged to have jabs for various tropical diseases before their departure, and because Jason could not spare the time away from his *estancia*, he had left within a week of their first meeting. From then on, Alexandra had lived in a fever of anxiety, as much from the knowledge of her own duplicity as from the after-effects of the vaccination serum.

But eventually the day of departure had arrived, and they had left a cold, grey England, recovering from the chills of January, to fly south into the sun. Their overnight stay in Rio de Janeiro had given Alexandra no thrill, although Miss Holland had marvelled at the twin peaks overlooking Guanabara Bay, and the magnificent statue of Christ whose shadow embraced the city. The thrill for Alexandra had come when they landed the next morning at Valvedra's much smaller airport, and found Jason awaiting them in the arrivals lounge. In mud-coloured Levis and a matching shirt, half open down the muscled darkness of his chest, he appeared relaxed and casual, only the guarded narrowing of his eyes revealing the doubts he still possessed about bringing her here. But Alexandra had determinedly ignored his restraint, and much to both his, and Miss Holland's, disapproval she had flung her arms about his neck and greeted him in her usual impulsive fashion. This time, however, Jason had quickly disengaged himself, and the kiss meant for his mouth had slid harmlessly along his jawline. Alexandra had been sad, but unrepentant, despite the effort of Miss Holland to behave as if she was some kind of annoying child who refused to behave with decorum.

Beyond the windows of the Range-Rover, the ground was steadily rising, and she saw to her surprise that they were in rolling hill country now, granite-like ridges casting shadows across the land. In the distance, the purple peaks of the Sierra Grande looked rugged and mysterious, and the whole aspect of the country had changed. It was late afternoon and already the shadows were lengthening, elongating the branches of the wind-torn cypresses that clung to the ridges, and shedding a rippling wave of ghost-like fingers across the land.

Their emergence into a sunlit valley was almost startling, the escarpment dropping away below them where a stream tumbled recklessly down the cliff face. It was then that Alexandra saw him, outlined against the golden rays of the sinking sun on the ridge opposite them, a magnificent black stallion silhouetted by the purplish gold backdrop of earth and sky. Just for a second he was there and then he was gone, plunging into the gully behind him, so that she thought for a moment she had imagined him.

'Oh!' she gasped, the sound escaping from her on a soft sigh, and Jason's response was one of wry satisfaction.

'You saw him.' It was a statement, not a question, and Miss Holland, unaware of the tableau, gave an exclamation of surprise.

'I beg your par——' she was beginning, when Alexandra leant forward to rest her arms along the backs of their seats, saying eagerly: 'Yes. Yes, I saw him! Whose is he? Is he yours? Oh, Jason, he's beautiful!'

Jason gave her a half mocking glance over his shoulder. 'I doubt that brute will ever belong to anybody,' he remarked flatly. 'I suppose technically, yes, you could say that as he runs on my land, he belongs to me, but no one's ever succeeded in breaking him.'

'You have caught him, then?'

'Yes.' Jason nodded, and Miss Holland's expression grew even more confused. 'But he's a proud bastard—excuse me!' This as that lady's brows ascended. 'He considers running my range with my mares and keeping them happy his prime objective!'

Alexandra's low laugh was intimate, and as if realising her bare arm was resting comfortably against the broad expanse of his shoulder, Jason's expression hardened and he moved so that she was not touching him. Fortunately, perhaps, Miss Holland chose that moment to ask a question of her own, and Alexandra sank back against the upholstery as Jason explained what they had seen.

'You breed horses, Mr. Tarrant?' she enquired, her lips twitching a little as if at a rather distasteful subject, and Jason's hard features softened a little.

'Horses are my passion,' he admitted, his eyes meeting Alexandra's for a brief compelling moment. Then, braking as the road took a sharp curve, he added: 'But the production of beef is my primary concern.'

'But this animal—the one Alexandra has just seen—is a wild creature?' Miss Holland persisted.

'I suppose he is,' Jason nodded, frowning as the wheels of the Range-Rover slid across a shingly patch of pebbles dangerously close to the edge of the track. 'But sometimes I wonder if he's not more civilised than we are.' His lips twisted at the older woman's apparent astonishment. 'There's little that goes on at the *estancia* that he doesn't know about. Some of the Indians think he's the reincarnation of one of their gods. To them, he's sacred. To me, he has less saintly qualities.'

Miss Holland shook her head, obviously disturbed by her first introduction to life at San Gabriel, but Alexandra was filled with a mixture of anticipation and excitement. This was what she had always wanted, she thought with satisfaction; travel and adventure, and a chance to live her life instead of just existing. Jason's disapproval did not disturb her, it was a challenge, and something told her he was not as indifferent to her femininity as he pretended to be.

Then her breath caught in her throat as she suddenly glimpsed a building ahead of them. As yet, it was below them in the valley, but the painted tiles of its roof, leaved across a wide verandah, gave her her first sight of Jason's *hacienda*.

Uncaring of his hostility, Alexandra leant forward again, deliberately allowing her slim fingers to stroke the nape of his neck, hidden beneath the over-long straightness of his hair. 'Is that your house?' she breathed, and the scent of her breath mingled with the perfume of wild verbena that drifted irresistibly through the open windows of the Range-Rover.

Jason's hand came up, ostensibly to smooth his hair, but he pushed her fingers determinedly away, as he answered: 'Yes, that's San Gabriel,' and her delight in her surroundings obliterated the coldness of his tones.

'It's rather a large house, isn't it, Mr Tarrant?'

Miss Holland had her own opinion, and Jason chose to tell her that the sprawling outbuildings she could see were the lodgings of the *gauchos* who worked for him. He pointed out the long bunkhouse and the cookhouse where their meals were served.

'I have twenty men who work for me on a permanent basis, and at least twice that number who are employed if and when we need them. Then there's Ricardo Goya, and Andrés Alberoni, who has his own home at the other end of the valley. Ricardo is my foreman, and Andrés is the best herdsman this side of the Andes.'

'Quite a large establishment.' Miss Holland was impressed, although Alexandra guessed she still had misgivings about coming out here. It could only be all too different from what she was used to, and unlike Alexandra she was old to change her ways. But pride, and necessity, had taken the choice of working conditions out of her hands, and she had been prepared to sacrifice her desire to remain in England for the very adequate salary Jason had offered her.

The road widened as they reached the grassy lower slopes of the valley, and now they could see the river that meandered beside banks bright with golden rod and curiously yellow poppies. There were cows grazing beside the river, not the wild-eyed beasts they had seen on their journey, but fat, placid-looking creatures that were more interested in cropping the grass than watching their passage. As they neared the homestead, Alexandra saw the corrals where they kept the mares and their foals, and nearer at hand, shaggy-haired goats and chickens that scuttled out of their path.

But the *hacienda* itself riveted her gaze. Now, she could see that the low-hanging tiles were a deep red in colour, shading a balcony above the verandah, where rattan chairs suggested a shady retreat on hot afternoons. Right now, with the sun sinking lower every minute, the air was comparatively cool, unlike earlier in the day when Alexandra had had to discard the jerkin that matched her blue cotton pants. Beyond the verandah, she could see a shadowy hallway, framed by the sprawling cluster of vines and honeysuckle which had made their home around the pillars that supported the balcony. At the side of the building, a wrought-iron staircase wound, Spanish-fashion, to the upper floor, and along the balcony Alexandra could see long curtains moving in the breeze from open shutters. The shutters were all folded back at present, green slats against a pale-washed wall, as distinctive in their way as the riot of exotic blossoms that tumbled carelessly from urns beside the verandah steps.

Unable to suppress her delight, Alexandra bounced forward again, but Jason was already stopping the vehicle, and as he began to open his door a woman appeared round the corner of the building. She was young, that much Alexandra registered at a glance, tall, with full swelling breasts, and hair as dark as Jason's own. It was long, like Alexandra's, but whereas hers was inclined to curl in the heat, this woman's was perfectly straight, and fell smoothly over one shoulder. Her features were those of the Madonna, calm and impassive, but as Alexandra alighted from the vehicle, too, she felt a wave of hostility emanating from her that had none of the Virgin's compassion about it.

Jason greeted the woman with a faintly wry expression,

turning first to help his other passenger to climb down, before saying: 'This is my housekeeper, Miss Holland. Señora Vargas. Estelita, this is my ward—and her companion.'

'Hello.'

Alexandra stepped forward, holding out her hand, determined not to be daunted by this sloe-eyed female. Close at hand, she was not half as young as she had at first imagined, but she was not mistaken that the faintly contemptuous stare Estelita conferred upon her sleeveless vest and creased cotton pants was intended to intimidate. The woman's attire of long black skirt and loose-fitting blouse was common to women she had seen in Valvedra, but Estelita bestowed a certain grace upon them which was not typical.

Now, she allowed Alexandra to take her limp hand before saying: '*Bienvenida, señorita!*' in tones which said just the opposite.

'*Inglés*, Estelita,' Jason warned in an undertone, and the housekeeper greeted Miss Holland in her own language, showing more enthusiasm towards the older woman than she had done to the younger one.

'Come inside ...' Jason was already mounting the steps, and Alexandra quickly followed him meeting his gaze deliberately as he looked back at them. But he refused to answer the question in hers, and strode ahead into the cool, tiled hall of the *hacienda*.

The walls were plain and adorned with small plaques of saints. There were flowers in a copper bowl, huge lilies with thick creamy petals, and orchids, fragile and exotic. There were jewel-bright rugs and a hand-carved chest, and wind-chimes that whispered in the draught of their passing. No one would have taken it for the home of an Englishman, and yet Alexandra felt a sense of homecoming she had never experienced before.

Gazing at the circular window above the gallery of the first floor landing, whose prismatic light slanted down to the hall below, she hardly realised Jason had left her, or that Miss Holland and the woman, Estelita, had come to join her. Until the housekeeper spoke.

'You would like to see your rooms?' she suggested politely. 'I will show them to you while Pepe prepares some tea.' She addressed herself to Miss Holland. 'You would like some tea, *señora*, I am sure.'

'Tea!'

Miss Holland made an obeisance of the word, but Alexandra suddenly realised that Jason was not with them, and looked about her in faint annoyance. Several doors opened from the wide hallway, and through open doors she could see an inner courtyard, but she had no way of knowing where he had gone. Estelita, taking her silence for acquiescence, was already beginning to mount the wrought iron staircase that circled the hall, and Miss Holland was eagerly following.

It was irritating to have to go with them. Alexandra wasn't tired. On the contrary, she was exhilarated, and all too eager to explore her new domain. Jason! she thought impatiently. He must have known how she would feel, and yet he had left her to Estelita's less than friendly overtures.

Her room temporarily overcame her annoyance. Large, and high-ceilinged, it overlooked the whole sweep of the valley, and although the furnishings were not luxurious, their very spareness was attractive. Long woven beige curtains matched the woven bedspread, and the dressing table and long clothes closet left plenty of room for the velvet-cushioned *prie-dieu* in the corner. Two candles could be lighted on either side of the carved wooden cross, and Alexandra was enchanted to discover that the candles were hand-made, too. Miss Holland's room was next door, very little different from that of her charge, and Estelita explained that there was only one bathroom, unfortunately.

'The men use the showers down at the bunkhouse,' she said, when Miss Holland revealed her dismay, and Alexandra asked who she meant.

'Why—Jason, *sin duda*,' she explained with a slight curl to her lip, 'and Ricardo.'

'Ricardo?' Alexandra frowned, noticing the familiar way Estelita spoke of her employer. 'That would be—Mr Tarrant's foreman?'

'That is correct.' Estelita's black eyes were insolent. 'You will meet him at supper, no doubt. Now . . .' She turned once more to Miss Holland. 'If you will excuse me, I will see about your tea.'

'Of course, of course.'

Miss Holland was only too willing to agree, but she followed Alexandra into her room when the woman had gone, and sank down rather wearily onto the bed.

'Do you think you're going to be happy here?' she asked, as the girl walked rather thoughtfully towards the open balcony doors, and Alexandra looked back at her with some misgivings.

'Why do you ask that?' she exclaimed, trying to subdue the irritating feeling of anti-climax she herself was feeling, and her companion gave a somewhat helpless shrug of her shoulders.

'I get the feeling we're not altogether welcome,' she confessed, taking out her handkerchief and wiping the grime of the journey from her rather anxious features. 'Oh, not from Mr Tarrant, of course. He's been charming. But Señora Vargas . . .'

'*Estelita*,' said Alexandra firmly, more firmly than she was actually feeling, 'Estelita is the housekeeper, that's all. I don't intend to let a housekeeper intimidate me!'

'Do you think that's all she is?' asked Miss Holland doubtfully, unexpectedly voicing those fears which Alexandra had succeeded in keeping hidden until that moment. 'She seems—very much in command to me.'

Alexandra determinedly squared her shoulders. 'Well, maybe she is, at that. But she's not in command of us, Miss Holland, and that's what matters.'

The older woman gave a rueful smile. 'Oh, for the

arrogance of youth!' she murmured, a trifle anxiously, and then started when a male voice spoke brusquely behind them.

'Is everything all right?'

It was Jason, and Alexandra turned to him mutinously, wondering how much of their conversation he had overheard. 'Must you creep up on us like that?' she snapped, thrusting back the weight of her hair with a nervous hand, aware that it must be uncombed and unruly after the journey, and his mouth took a downward curve.

'I did not creep up on you!' he declared coldly. 'I was merely attempting to assure myself that you had everything you needed.'

'Well, we haven't!' said Alexandra childishly, facing him in defiance of her emotions. 'We're short on a host, for one thing, and for another—where did you disappear to?'

Jason's mouth relaxed a little. 'I'm sorry, but I'm afraid this is not a holiday hotel. It's a working ranch, with any number of things waiting to be done. I'm sorry if you think I neglect my duties——'

'Oh, I'm sure we didn't think any such thing.' Miss Holland rose now and after a reproving look in Alexandra's direction moved uncomfortably towards the door where Jason was standing. 'I expect we're all tired. I know I am.'

'I'm not,' declared Alexandra shortly, tipping her head on one side and daring Jason to argue with her, but he was already standing aside to allow her companion to leave the room.

'I suggest you rest for a while, Miss Holland,' he was saying with quiet assurance. 'Supper isn't served much before eight, and there's time for you to take a bath, if you'd like to.'

'Thank you. I may take you up on that,' she agreed, moving along the landing, and presently Alexandra heard the door of her room close behind her.

Only then did Jason step into her room, his face eloquent

with disapproval. 'Do you think you could refrain from embarrassing me in front of Miss Holland?' he demanded, in low angry tones, and her momentary joy that he had chosen to remain was quickly doused.

'Yes,' she declared now, holding up her chin, 'if you can guarantee that—that Estelita won't embarrass *me* in front of her!'

'Oh, God!' He raked back his hair with impatient fingers. 'Now what has she been saying?'

'Saying?' Alexandra's shrug was offhand. 'She hasn't exactly—said anything. It's just—her attitude,' she finished lamely.

'I see.' His lips thinned. 'Is that all?'

'No, it's not all.' Her chin jutted defensively. 'I like my room. It's very nice.' She paused. 'But I don't want to rest. I'm not tired. I want to see the ranch. I want to be with you!'

Jason's features took on the guarded expression she was coming to know so well. 'The *estancia*,' he said, stressing the Spanish derivative, 'comprises some twenty thousand acres. How much do you suppose you could see before it gets dark?' He gestured towards the open windows, where already shadows were falling. 'Tomorrow—or the next day—if you can sit a horse, I'll have Ricardo show you the home paddocks——'

'Ricardo!' Alexandra's chest heaved. 'I don't know Ricardo. I don't want Ricardo to show me the—the *estancia*. I want you——'

'*Alexandra!*' His use of her name cut her off in full spate. 'The sooner you realise your every wish is *not* my command, the better. All right, so I allowed you to come here as you wanted, but so long as you are living under my roof, there are certain things you will have to learn, and the first is that I cannot devote all my time to your entertainment!'

There was silence for a moment after that while they

viewed one another with wary speculation. Then Alexandra spoke, but it was so quietly that he could barely hear the words.

'You want me to hate it here, don't you?' she accused him, in low choking tones. 'You want me to find it so awful that I'll pack my bags and go away again, don't you? Then you won't have to be bothered with me any longer!'

'Alexandra!' With a driven kind of anguish, he crossed the room between them with long easy strides, and grasping her by the shoulders, he shook her until her head felt too heavy for the slender column of her throat. 'Stop it!' he ordered savagely. 'Stop feeling sorry for yourself. Of course I want you here. If I hadn't, I wouldn't have allowed you to come, whatever you said.'

'Is that true?' The long silky lashes swept upward, and the smouldering torment of his gaze was achingly reassuring. 'Oh, Jason,' she whispered, lifting her hand to his face and touching his cheek. 'Jason, you do care about me, don't you?'

'I've said so, haven't I?' he muttered gruffly, but he held himself away from her, and almost instinctively she moved nearer to him.

Immediately she was aware of the tautness of his body, of the moist male smell of him that no written word had ever warned her about. She could feel the hard muscles of his legs where hers were touching him, and longed, with an incomprehensible yearning, for something she hardly understood; for some contact between them that was not compounded of sympathy and comfort.

'Jason . . .'

His name on her lips was a plea for understanding, but when he turned his head and parted his lips against her palm, she fairly snatched her hand away and pressed it tightly to her. Her startled eyes were mesmerised by the probing force of his, her whole body tingling with emotions she was not equipped to handle. She felt her breasts taut against the thinness of her vest, shameless in their eagerness, her head was swimming, and her legs, weak and trembling, scarcely had the strength to support her. Then she glimpsed the dawning cynicism in his gaze, the mocking curve of his mouth—and guessed his intention had been to achieve just this result. With a shudder of reaction, she pulled herself away from him, and his hands fell loosely to his sides.

'Yes,' he said, and his voice was low and angry, 'you are just a child, aren't you, Alexandra? So don't try to play the *femme fatale*. It doesn't satisfy.'

'I—I suppose you think I'm afraid of you!' she burst out jerkily, her arms folding about herself, as if for protection, and he nodded.

'Aren't you?' he demanded, and then, as if his patience had spent itself, he brushed past her and left the room.

CHAPTER THREE

THE mare was a solid little creature, with the gentlest eyes Alexandra had ever seen. Her colouring was not distinctive, a kind of rusty grey with spots of white splashed over her hindquarters, but compared to the horse they had had at the convent, she was a veritable thoroughbred. Alexandra was glad now she had spent so much time with the old shire horse at Sainte Sœur, grooming him and riding him, most times with only a blanket for a saddle.

Not that Ricardo had been convinced of her ability. He had had her ride the mare round and round the paddock until he assured himself that she was able to handle the animal, and her spine, still tender from the previous day's journey, ached from the unaccustomed exercise.

It was the morning after her arrival at San Gabriel, and Alexandra had awakened with a distinct feeling of discouragement. It was unusual for her, she was normally of an optimistic disposition, but she had lain for a few minutes recalling the events of the previous evening with depressing clarity.

After her confrontation with Jason she had felt little like eating supper, but a hasty bath, after Miss Holland had vacated the bathroom, and a change of clothes, had lightened her mood. It was too soon to jump to any conclusions, she had told herself firmly, flicking the skirt of an embroidered caftan down over her hips. Just because she and Jason had had their first row it did not mean that he was regretting bringing her here. They had had a difference of opinion, that was all—but deep inside her she had known it was more than that. At the first sign of his responding to the curious emotions he aroused inside her, she had bolted like a scared rabbit, and she was left with the disturbing evidence of her own immaturity.

Rummaging through her case—which had been brought by the same dark-skinned man who had provided Miss Holland's tray of tea—she had brought out the tattered copy of *Desert Rhapsody*, from which she had gleaned much of her knowledge of the man-woman relationship. It was most explicit in its descriptions of the torrid affair between a fragile English girl and a hawk-eyed Arab sheik, but although the girl shrank from the Arab's passions, the book never actually explained why. Indeed, the passions themselves were described in such a way that Alexandra scarcely understood what was going on. She only knew her imagination ran riot when Tarik 'tore the shimmering gauze from her slender body, and threw himself upon her', and there was an odd sensation in her lower limbs when she contemplated that intimate scene. It was strange, because the girl always gave in to the man, despite constant assertions that she hated him. Yet, as soon as he touched her, 'she was aflame'. Alexandra sighed and put the book away, and went down to supper with a rather thoughtful expression in her shadowed eyes.

They ate in what she assumed to be the dining room. It was a bare room, with a long low dresser set with plates, and an equally long table, covered by a linen cloth. Darkness had fallen, and the shutters had been drawn against the night insects, but their wings were still audible. They fought to reach the lamps that were standing at either end of the dresser, golden globes, that reminded Alexandra of the old oil lamps they used to use in the cellar at the convent. The lighting in the house was electric, however, and she had been surprised at this modern innovation in what was essentially a traditional dwelling.

As well as taking part in the serving of the meal, Estelita also ate with them, along with Ricardo Goya, and Pepe, the manservant who had brought their cases. Meeting Ricardo for the first time, Alexandra was rather intimidated by his enormous frame and grizzled dark hair, an extension of which grew down his cheeks and curled beneath his strong nose in exuberant *mostachos*. But his hearty laughter rang often in the high-ceilinged room, and his teasing baiting of Estelita made Alexandra his friend for life.

Pepe was a different proposition. A rather morose Jason had introduced the thin young man as Estelita's brother, and watching them together, Alexandra could see the resemblance. Both were very dark-skinned, although their features were predominantly Spanish, but Pepe's features were not quite so refined as his sister's. She was the older, too, possibly twenty-nine or thirty, Alexandra estimated, while Pepe was hardly more than her own age. He spoke little throughout the meal, and it was left to Estelita to question Jason about his journey, and Ricardo to make jokes at the housekeeper's expense.

All in all supper had not been a comfortable meal. Miss Holland had not joined them, after all, and Alexandra was very conscious of her own alienation among these people. She spent her time studying the relationships between them, avoiding the most obvious one between the man who persistently parried all questions, and the woman he called his housekeeper. Although from time to time, she sensed Pepe's eyes upon her, they dropped as soon as she lifted her head, and she came to the conclusion that he was intrigued by her pale skin. She had seen few pale-skinned people since coming to South America, but contrarily she admired the brown skins she had seen, envying them their immunity to the sun's rays.

Ricardo spoke to her once or twice, asking her about her father, and revealing that he, too, had known Charles Durham. It was reassuring to hear that her father was not forgotten by these men, but although she would have liked to have asked him questions, she was all too conscious of Estelita's cold dark eyes upon her.

The meal itself was rather too rich for her palate. A casserole of meat and vegetables, very highly spiced and hot with peppers, was an assault to a stomach still not attuned to the change of latitude, and Alexandra contented herself with crumbling the bread which accompanied it, and spreading it thinly with butter that tasted slightly rancid.

'You are not eating, *señorita*,' Estelita remarked once, her lips twisting contemptuously. 'She will never lose that boyish figure if she does not put some flesh on her bones, eh, Jason?'

Ricardo made a comment to this which seemed to amuse him greatly, and which caused the housekeeper's eyes to flash angrily. Her response was a vituperative tirade in their own language, which Jason silenced with a curt admonishment. But Ricardo was unrepentant, and turning to Alexandra, he explained:

'I tell Estelita she does not need any more flesh on her bones, no? I think perhaps she could afford to spare you some, hmm?'

'Ricardo!' Jason's impatient interjection gave Alexandra the chance to avoid an embarrassing answer, but Estelita was not appeased. She spent the remainder of the meal in sullen silence, only responding when Jason suggested she should serve the coffee.

Alexandra, apprehensive of Jason's censure, was glad when, after the meal was over, he disappeared, and making the excuse of seeing how Miss Holland was faring, she left the room. The hall was a silent cavern, and the lamp standing on the chest cast pools of darkness in shadowy corners. The remoteness of their situation was suddenly a tangible presence, and shivering slightly she crossed the tiled floor to the stairs. A shaft of light from an open doorway caught her gaze as she ascended the stairs and dipping slightly to peer into the room, she saw Jason standing behind a square desk. The desk was strewn with papers, and he was presently engrossed in the sheet he held in his hand, a brooding expression marring his lean features. His indifference to the isolation was reassuring somehow, but she went on her way, aware that for tonight at least, Jason's company was barred to her.

In her room, she turned out the light and stepped out on to the balcony. The scent from the passion-flower vine below her windows rose tantalisingly to her nostrils, and she tried to relax. But the starlit darkness was like a wall between her and the life she had known, and succumbing to a ridiculous sense of unease, she closed the shutters and went to find Miss Holland.

Morning had displaced the shadows of the night, and although it was early, even for her, Alexandra was up soon after six. Her system was still adjusting to the time change, and besides, she was eager to dispel her first impressions. She was sure her anxieties of the previous evening had been exaggerated, and the prospect of seeing more of the *estancia* lifted her spirits. She was even prepared to believe that that scene with Jason had never happened, that it had been some figment of her imagination, and she determined to show him that her feelings towards him had not changed. Exactly what those feelings were, she was not quite sure. She felt a sense of gratitude towards him, of course, but it was more than that that made her senses tingle when he was near her. He was much older than she was, even if he was much younger than her father had been, but not old enough to regard in that light. She only knew she liked being with him, better than with anyone she had ever known before, except perhaps her father, but even in her innocence she sensed that the relationship she wanted with Jason was much different from the relationship she had wanted with her father. It was all most disturbing. She had sent herself to sleep trying to imagine how she would feel if Jason treated her as the sheik had treated his fair prisoner, but her inexperienced imagination had been unable to provide any satisfactory answer.

After checking that Miss Holland was still sleeping, she went downstairs for breakfast. It was still barely seven, and she was glad of the warmth of cream cords and a matching long-sleeved sweater. Her extreme fairness was accentuated by the light-coloured clothes, and Pepe, encountering her in the hall, stared with open eyes.

'Good morning,' she greeted him smilingly, but his mumbled response was scarcely audible and she hurried after him, saying: 'Where is everyone? Where's Jason? Is he up?'

'Por favor?'

Pepe was obviously finding it difficult to follow her, and Alexandra nodded her head, repeating slowly: 'Ja-son. Er—*donde es tá* Jason?'

'Jason was up and out an hour ago,' remarked a supercilious voice behind her, and turning, Alexandra found Estelita standing in the shadow of the stairs. 'You will need to rise a little earlier to find him here, *señorita*.'

'I see.' Alexandra glanced back at Pepe and found him shrugging as he went on his way.

'I did not know you spoke our language, *señorita*,' murmured the housekeeper mockingly. *'Deseaba usted algo? Tiene usted hambre, acaso ...'*

Alexandra controlled her temper with admirable restraint. 'You must know I do not speak Spanish, *señora*,' she insisted quietly, but Estelita was not so willing to abandon such a provocative subject.

'But you spoke in Spanish with my brother.'

'A word or two, only. I—well, I've heard Jason use those words—when he asked about our luggage at the airport, that's all.'

'Ah!' Estelita folded her arms across her ample bosom. 'You are very—what would you say?—sharp, no? I shall have to be careful what I say when you are around, *señorita*.'

Alexandra forced a smile, determining not to be provoked, and as if her reaction was not what she had hoped, Estelita's breath hissed a trifle impatiently as she swung about and disappeared down a passage leading to the back of the house. Giving herself a moment to school her features, Alexandra followed her, and saw with interest that the arched hallway overlooked the inner courtyard. A door at the end of the passage was Estelita's destination, and without giving herself time to have second thoughts, Alexandra went through the door after the housekeeper.

She found herself in a huge, old-fashioned kitchen that was unpleasantly hot from the heat that emanated from an enormous open grate. Despite an open door on to a yard where chickens strutted, the temperature in the room was suffocating, but Estelita seemed not to notice it. She scarcely glanced at the girl who had followed her, before going to the oven beside the fire and drawing out a tray of loaves, golden brown and smelling deliciously. She set the tray on the scrubbed pine table that occupied the centre of the room, and then swung the oven door closed again with her elbow.

Alexandra made another attempt to be civil. 'You make all your own bread?' she asked, and the housekeeper bestowed on her a scornful stare.

'We have no shops here, *señorita*. We cannot—how do you say?—go to the supermarket, every time we want a loaf, no?'

Alexandra pushed her hands into the hip pockets of her cords. 'At the convent, we used to bake our own bread, too,' she said. 'We couldn't afford the supermarket.'

'*Convento?*' Estelita echoed curiously. 'You were a *novicio?*'

'Oh, no.' Alexandra's laugh was rueful. 'I just lived there. I suppose it was a kind of boarding school. My father—my father sent me there when I was very young.'

'Your father!' Estelita's moment of interest was gone. 'The man who made Jason responsible for his *son!*'

'No.' Alexandra shifted uncomfortably. 'No, actually, that was me.'

'You?'

Estelita's lip curled, and Alexandra half wished she hadn't been so honest. But it was too late now. 'Yes,' she said. 'You see, my father always wanted a son, so he called me Alex. I—well, I naturally used that name . . .'

'To trick Jason!' Estelita's eyes flashed. 'So you can come here, so you can make the nursemaid out of him!'

'No!' Alexandra was indignant. 'I'm not a child exactly.'

'No, you are not. So why are you not taking care of yourself?'

Alexandra heaved a sigh, looking about her helplessly, wishing Pepe would make a reappearance. 'Look,' she said, 'oughtn't you to take your complaints up with—with your employer?' She refused to say Jason to *her*! 'I—well, I'm hungry, as it happens. May I try some of your delicious-looking bread?'

Silently, Estelita supplied her with bread and butter, and a conserve made with peaches, which satisfactorily disguised the taste—which privately Alexandra thought had to be acquired—of the butter. There was coffee, too, strong and black, and highly aromatic, that completed a meal which, eaten in more congenial company, would have been very enjoyable.

Ricardo Goya appeared as she was finishing her second cup of coffee, and immediately Alexandra sensed the antagonism between these two. Ricardo greeted the housekeeper with a playful slap to her rump, as she bent over the basket of logs that fed the blaze, but her response was another of the vitriolic outbursts which had so marred supper the evening before.

Unrepentant, Ricardo turned to Alexandra, saying: 'So—and how is our visitor today? You did not sleep well, that you should be about so early?'

Alexandra rose to her feet. 'I expect it's because back in England the time would be ten or eleven o'clock,' she explained, rather awkwardly. 'I—er—I gather you've all been up for hours already.'

'Is that what *she* said?' Ricardo jerked his thumb in the housekeeper's direction, and then followed it with a dismissing motion. 'You do not think I would leave the comfort of my bed so early if I did not have to, do you?' He shook his head. 'No, but it is true. Jason and I were down at the stockyards by five-thirty. We are—how do you say? —putting the mark on the beef, no?'

'Branding?' asked Alexandra doubtfully, and Ricardo laughed and nodded.

'*Si*,' he said. 'Like this!' and he thrust a poker into the fire and brought it out smoking to lay across Estelita's back. The housekeeper jumped back angrily, and Alexandra's hand went to her lips in horror, but the foreman was only joking, and his amusement rang out once more.

'*Qué*, Estelita,' he exclaimed mockingly, 'you did not think I would brand *you, mi incendiaria*?'

Alexandra did not need a knowledge of the language to understand his meaning, and she was glad when he turned to her again and said:

'*Bueno*, if you are ready, *señorita*, my orders are to put myself at your disposal, *si*?'

'At *my* disposal?'

Alexandra, still scarcely recovered from his playful attack on Estelita, was taken aback, but Ricardo lounged against the table and said: '*Si*. You wish to see something of the *estancia*, do you not? Do you ride? If not, Jason says I must teach you.'

'You?'

Remembering what Jason had said, Alexandra ought not to have been surprised, but this man was so—overpowering. In leather leggings, and a sheepskin waistcoat over a brilliantly woven scarlet shirt, he was more like a gipsy than a rancher, and she wasn't at all sure she liked him any more than Estelita this morning.

'Come!' he said, and the housekeeper remarked: 'Yes, go, *señorita*. I do not like the smell of pigs in here.'

Ricardo's laughter had accompanied them outside, but once out of earshot of the house, he sobered and said apologetically: 'Do not take any notice of Estelita, *señorita*. She and I are old adversaries, *no*? Her husband was my best friend, but she never liked me. I think perhaps because I always could see the kind of woman she was.'

'Estelita is married?' exclaimed Alexandra, interested in her surroundings, but intrigued by his words.

'Not now, *señorita*,' he denied regretfully. 'Enrique is dead. *She* killed him. Oh, not actually . . .' This as Alexandra turned horrified eyes in his direction. 'But she is ambitious, *señorita*. She wanted money. And Enrique, poor fool, worked himself to death to keep her.'

Deciding this conversation had gone far enough, Alexandra pointed to the long wooden building ahead of them. 'I suppose that is where the men sleep, is it?'

Ricardo shrugged, and his good humour was restored. '*Si*,' he agreed. 'That is the bunkhouse, no? Come, I will introduce you to Chan.'

'Chan?'

'The cook. You did not think Estelita fed the men, too? No. They have their own cook, and a very fine one he is, too. My son lives with the men, and he vouches for his ability.'

He kissed the tips of his fingers as he spoke, and Alexandra felt herself relaxing. He could be so charming when he chose, and it was good to be out in the open air after the stifling heat of the kitchen.

They were crossing the yard that was bounded on two sides by outbuildings, but away to their left the pasture sloped towards the river. Stands of willow and poplar trees grew in clumps along the river bank, and Alexandra could see two riders on the far bank just sitting their horses, apparently lazing in the early morning sun. Beyond, the mist was slowly rising from the hills that circled the valley, and the sky was shading from apricot to palest yellow.

She was unaware of how expressive her features were until Ricardo bent his curly head to hers, and said, 'Is beautiful, *no*?' emotion for once overcoming his mastery of her language. But when Alexandra smiled, he realised his weakness and clapped a hand on her shoulder, almost causing her to jump out of her skin. 'A hat,' he declared gruffly, indicating her bare head. 'With such pale skin, you must always wear a hat. I will get you one.'

Adjoining the long bunkhouse, which lay beyond the storehouses, was the cookhouse. It was a squarer building, built of logs, notched at the corners and painted with creosote for waterproofing; it provided cooking and eating facilities for the men who worked on the *estancia*, with plenty of room for casual workers when they were hired. Most of the cooking was done on a huge, log-fired range, but there was a gas cooker for emergency use. Long wooden tables were lined with benches, and empty now, it smelled of the burnt steaks the men had had for breakfast. It was not an unpleasant smell, mingling as it did with coffee and tobacco smoke, and Alexandra really felt as if she was learning something about her new surroundings.

Chan, as she had expected, was Chinese, but she guessed his parentage had been mixed. He was taller than the average Chinese, and his eyes were not as narrow. Like Ricardo, he had an ample girth, which said much for his own food, and his smile was seldom long absent from his olive-skinned features.

'Miss Tarrant,' he said politely, when she was introduced to him, which evoked another of Ricardo's hearty laughs.

'She is not Jason's daughter, Chan!' he exclaimed with humour. 'Does she look like him, I ask you? No, her father was the good friend to the *patrón, si*?'

'Ah!' Chan nodded. 'Well, I am happy to meet you, *señorita*,' he added, with a distinctly American intonation. 'You think you will like it here?'

'I hope so,' Alexandra smiled. 'I like what I've seen so far.'

'That includes you, Chan,' jeered Ricardo, with his usual humour, but the Chinese cook took it in good part.

'You'd like to stay for coffee?' he suggested, indicating the pot on the polished range, but Ricardo shook his head now.

'The *señorita* is going to show me if she can ride,' he declared, and Alexandra wasn't sure whether he was mocking her or not. 'You can come and watch, Chan. You know a good *gaucho* when you see one.'

'Oh, but . . .' Alexandra licked her lips doubtfully, sure she would make a fool of herself on any horse Ricardo chose to produce, and Chan shook his head.

'Some other time, Rico,' he promised, and with a chuckle, the foreman followed her outside again.

The stables were nearby, and here Alexandra was introduced to the elderly Indian whose job it was to keep the stalls clean and the brasses polished. There were saddles hanging on the walls, big, cumbersome saddles, which she hadn't the first idea how to fasten, but Ricardo ignored them.

The little mare he produced for her was a docile creature, much different from the stallion in the adjoining stall, who whinnied protestingly when they ignored him. The mare's name was Placida, and Alexandra could see why, although she felt her first misgivings when Ricardo threw only a sheepskin fleece across the mare's back before leading her outside. Hanging by the door were several of the broad-brimmed sombreros she had seen men wearing in Valvedra, and Ricardo planted one of these on her head before she emerged into the sunlight.

'I—er—don't we need a saddle?' she asked, as her companion adjusted the bridle over the mare's ears, and he grinned.

'First I see how you sit the horse,' he said. She had told him about the horse at the convent on their way to the stables. 'Then we will see about a saddle, *no*?'

Adjusting the hat on her head, Alexandra accepted his hand to mount the animal, the sheepskin a comforting barrier between her spine and the mare's back. She took the reins he handed to her, dug in her heels, and Placida walked obediently forward. Immediately, her sombrero went flying back off her head, and as she twisted in an attempt to retrieve it, the sheepskin beneath her slid sideways, and she would have fallen to the ground if Ricardo's strong arms had not caught her.

He set her on her feet, rescued the hat, and then directed her to tie the cords beneath her chin. 'Right,' he said, when this was done to his satisfaction, offering his linked fingers for her foot. 'Shall we begin again?'

An hour later he had satisfied himself that she would not fall off again, but Alexandra's legs felt like jellies as she clambered down.

'Qué?' Ricardo regarded her with humour. 'Do you not wish to go riding after all?'

Her spine smarting from the hardness of the mare's, Alexandra regarded him with ill-concealed resentment. 'You know I'm aching all over!' she accused, half tearfully. 'Why couldn't I have used a saddle like anyone else?'

Ricardo's features softened. 'Don't you know that in country like this, it is always best to learn the hard way? To ride without a saddle is an achievement. It means you are controlling the horse from here . . .' He indicated his knees. 'Bodily contact, *no*? Now, you will never forget what you have learned. You know the feel of the animal. The touch, *no*?'

Touching! Again that word, thought Alexandra ruefully. She thought if anyone touched her spine ever again, she would scream in agony.

'So?' Ricardo smiled encouragingly. 'You will forgive the lesson, hmm?'

'Oh, yes. Yes.' Alexandra sniffed, half regretting her anger with him. 'I—I suppose I should—thank you.'

'Thank me?' Ricardo laughed. 'Why? For hurting you? No, no.' He shook his head. 'But look, is not this the elderly lady you brought with you?'

'Miss Holland?'

Alexandra swung round, a finger raised to her lips in dismay, as she realised she had forgotten all about her companion. Miss Holland, ridiculously out of place in country tweeds and stout brogues, was marching across the paddock towards them, and Ricardo bent his head to whisper outrageously: 'Shall we teach the lady how to ride, too? I could lend her some pants, and a shirt, *no*?'

Ignoring him, although her lips twitched irresistibly, Alexandra walked painfully to meet the other woman. Her somewhat mincing steps did not go unobserved, and Miss Holland looked first at her, and then past her to the grinning black-haired giant behind her.

'Alexandra!' she exclaimed in alarm, and almost at the same moment Alexandra realised she probably looked as rough as she felt. The sombrero had slipped to the back of her neck, and her hair was a tumbled mass about her shoulders, her cream cords stained from the sweat of the mare's sides.

'Hello, Miss Holland,' she said. 'I'm sorry if you've been concerned about me. But as you can see——'

'What have you been doing with yourself?' Miss Holland spoke to her, but she was looking at Ricardo, and with his usual showmanship, he swept her a deep bow, stepping forward and saying:

'I have been giving your young friend a riding lesson, *señora*. Regrettably, she has—how do you say?—overdone it, *no*?'

'Overdone it? Overdone what?' Miss Holland was not in a mood to be placated so easily, and Alexandra sighed before explaining that her back was aching from the exercise.

'And in this heat!' exclaimed Miss Holland when she had finished. 'Do you want to be taken ill as soon as you arrive?'

It was only as she said this that Alexandra began to realise how warm it had become, and feeling her damp forehead, she guessed her face was streaked with sweat, too.

'Don't you realise how susceptible you are in a strange climate?' Miss Holland persisted, but Alexandra waved her protests aside.

'Have you met Ricardo?' she asked, knowing full well she hadn't, and their introduction successfully halted any further objections on Miss Holland's part. Instead, Ricardo took his cue and insisted on introducing the lady to the mare, and because she was such a gentle animal, Miss Holland was diverted.

But later, when she and Alexandra walked back to the house together, she returned to the attack. 'I must say, I was surprised to hear that Mr Tarrant had suggested Señor Goya as your instructor. The man looks scarcely civilised. Is he an Indian, do you think? He has a very large nose.'

'Indians don't usually wear hair on their faces,' said Alexandra thoughtfully, remembering something she had read years ago. Certainly, the Indian in the painting at the convent had not had any hair on his face, and thinking of the Indian brought irresistible thoughts of Jason.

Shading her eyes, she looked across the valley, but it was too long and too wide to allow her to see anything more than the sweeping stretch of grassland, and the blue-grey curve of the river where it reflected the arc of the sky. She could see a pall of dust in the distance, which could mean anything, but all she could hear were the domestic sounds of the beasts in the pasture near the *hacienda* and the continual clucking of the hens.

From this side, the house looked different, set about with its pens and outbuildings. The store-sheds, Ricardo had told her, contained everything necessary to a community of this size, including animal feedstuffs, and farm machinery, crockery and leather goods, and dried food and meat enough for a siege. There was a smithy, he had told her, at the stockyards, and sheds for shearing the sheep that ran the high ranges, but the *hacienda* itself was the kingpin by which the *estancia* was controlled, the axle on which the various spokes of life at San Gabriel turned.

She wondered if Jason would return for the midday meal, but in this she was disappointed. The meal which was served, much to Miss Holland's distaste, at the kitchen table, was attended by Estelita, Pepe and themselves, Ricardo having disappeared about his own business. Alexandra guessed her companion found life at the *hacienda* much different to what she was used to, and she spared a moment to wonder what Jason would do should Miss Holland choose to pack her bags and return to England. It was always possible that she might find the heat, or the isolation, or even Estelita's familiarity more than she could take, and decide that however difficult her circumstances, life in England was preferable to this remote valley. Whatever else she was, Miss Holland was first and foremost a gentlewoman, and the crude humour of men like Ricardo Goya could only accentuate the distinctions.

Sighing, Alexandra tried to concentrate on the meat-filled pancake in front of her. She must not think so pessimistically. After all, Miss Holland had been told the circumstances of life out here before she left England. The fact that it was different from what either of them had imagined did not mean it was going to prove unacceptable to them.

CHAPTER FOUR

It was the next morning before Alexandra encountered Jason again.

Following her riding lesson, she found she was very tired, and although she forced herself to go down for supper, the fact that only herself and Estelita were present might have saved her the trouble. The housekeeper took great pleasure in informing her that Jason had sent a message to the effect that it would be late before he got back, and even Pepe had deserted the supper table to join the men in the bunkhouse. Alexandra had seen the men returning earlier in the evening, the thunder of their horses' hooves bringing her to the balcony doors. But straight from the bath, and only thinly clad in a silk wrapper, she had quickly disguised herself behind the curtains, just in case anyone should come her way. She had expected Jason to be with them, and it was with an acute feeling of disappointment that she listened to Estelita's mocking explanation.

Miss Holland had done as she had the night before, and been served her meal in her room. She was feeling the heat and the change of latitude, too, and Alexandra herself had approved her choice. However, when she found she had only Estelita for company, she dearly wished the older woman had joined them, after all.

They ate a concoction of beef, black beans and rice, and Alexandra couldn't decide whether she found its spicy mixture more acceptable because her stomach had adjusted to the flavour, or simply because she was anxious and she was eating to compensate. Whatever, she parried Estelita's more pointed questions, and succeeded in getting the woman to talk about herself. Estelita, it turned out, was of Portuguese extraction and had been born in Sao Paulo. Although she and Pepe were brother and sister, they had had different fathers, Pepe's father having lived in Valvedra all his life. It was there that Estelita's mother had met him when her first husband had deserted her, she said. She didn't say a lot about her father. Apparently, she hardly remembered him; and also, she didn't explain what her mother was doing in Valvedra while her father was reputedly looking for work elsewhere. However, it seemed that Pepe's father's advent had been the turning point in all their lives, and she and Pepe were very close. She did not mention her own husband, or the fact that he was dead.

It was only towards the end of the meal that she seemed to realise she had done all the talking, but by then Alexandra was too tired to respond to her deliberate baiting.

Her offer of help with the washing up being rejected, Alexandra left the room after the meal and sought the sanctuary of her bedroom. During the afternoon, she had explored a little more of the house, and knew that there was a comfortable *salón* adjoining the room she thought of as Jason's study, but this evening it had no appeal. She knew if she sat there in solitary state she would fall asleep, and she didn't want Jason to come upon her snoring or, horror of horrors, with her mouth open. Besides, he would not expect her to wait up, he might not even want her to wait up, and Estelita was waiting in the kitchen, like some jealous spider, in her web.

As if to compensate for her tiredness the night before, the next morning, Alexandra was awake as soon as it was light. Expecting some hangover from the previous day's riding lesson, she was pleasantly surprised to find that apart from a little stiffness, she felt fine, and even eager to get into the saddle again . . . or its equivalent.

Collecting her spongebag, she went along to the bathroom, expecting it to be empty at this hour of the morning, and walked straight in on Jason, sluicing his neck at the basin.

'Oh, I—I'm sorry,' she began, awkward at this unexpected encounter. 'I mean—Estelita said you usually—showered . . .'

Jason had grabbed a towel and draped it round his neck as she spoke. He was bare to his waist, the denim pants he wore hanging low on his hips. But it was the jagged scratch that ran the length of his arm from elbow to wrist that caught her attention as he turned, and her lips parted in anxious question. Seeing her immediate reaction, he pulled a wry face, saying dryly:

'That's why I didn't take a shower this morning. I decided I'd better wash in filtered water until it heals over.'

'But it should be stitched!' she protested, forgetting for the moment that she was wearing only the cotton nightshirt she had worn to sleep in, and going towards him. Her tentative fingers reached out to touch the bruised area around the gash, trembling against his warm flesh. 'How did you do it? It's so deep!'

Jason removed her fingers firmly and finished drying his neck. 'It will heal,' he asserted flatly. 'A rogue steer decided he'd put his own brand on me, that's all. I'll live, I can assure you.'

'Oh, but Jason, it should have proper treatment,' she exclaimed, not responding to the warning light in his eyes. 'Don't you have any medication—bandages?'

Jason reached for his shirt, which was lying on the chair beside the bath. 'Are you a nurse, too?' he enquired derisively, his mouth pulling down at the corners, but she paid no attention to his sarcasm.

'I've treated cuts,' she defended, her lips pursed. 'Do you want to get septicaemia? Would you like to lose an arm?'

'My God, you're a little pessimist, aren't you?' he exclaimed, but he hesitated before pulling on his shirt. It was then she saw the shirt he had discarded, dropped in the bath, caked with dried blood.

'Jason, please,' she pleaded. 'Let me put some ointment on it for you. Surely a bandage won't—cramp your style.'

'I'll get Estelita to do it,' he said, bending to pick up the soiled shirt, and she could have stamped her foot in frustration.

'Why can't I?'

Jason straightened, and his features had taken on a resigned expression. 'I thought we went into all that,' he observed quietly, but she didn't respond. 'All right,' he said, after another moment's silence, 'I'll put some ointment on it myself. I have a case of liniment in my room, and I believe there's some Savlon there, too.'

Alexandra said nothing. She just stood aside when he went past her, and then, putting down her sponge bag, she followed him.

Jason's room was several doors along the landing from her own, above the curve of the staircase. She guessed it was the master bedroom, judging by the size of the bed that occupied the centre of the room. Unlike her bed, it had hanging drapes, and the curtains and coverings were predominantly brown. But it was just as starkly furnished, except for the pictures on the walls.

She was hovering at the doorway when he saw her. He had pulled a drawer open in the chest beside the long windows, and was attempting to wind a length of bandage about his wrist. It was an impossible task, and the words he was muttering to himself were not words the nuns would have approved of.

'What do you want?' he demanded, as she stood there, and she stepped into the room, gesturing that she could apply the dressing.

'And what do you suppose Miss Holland would say if she came by and saw you in my bedroom dressed like that?' Jason asked irritably, making her aware for the first time that she was still in her nightshirt.

Then, determined not to appear naïve, she said: 'I'm adequately covered, aren't I? If I were wearing a bikini——'

'But you're not, are you?' Jason retorted. 'And this is

not the beach. Oh—what the hell, all right. Help me. But be quick about it.'

Alexandra approached him cautiously, but with the roll of bandage in her hand, she felt more confident. However, winding it about his arm brought her close to his lean, muscled body, and every now and then her fingers brushed the skin of his midriff. Although he had smeared some ointment over the cut which had successfully stopped the bleeding, it was still an ugly sight, and she knew the most ridiculous impulse to comfort him. But he didn't want her sympathy, and she had to content herself with making the best job of it that she could.

'You're very efficient,' he murmured, as she reached his elbow and tore the bandage down the middle for a few inches to bind it with a knot. Then, his breath whistling unevenly in his throat, he added: 'I haven't seen you since the night you arrived. Are you settling down?'

Alexandra finished the job, but she didn't immediately move away from him. 'I expect so,' she answered quietly, running her fingers down the ridges of the bandage. 'Does that feel too tight?'

'It feels just fine,' he assured her, and she nodded her head with satisfaction. 'I hear Ricardo gave you quite a riding lesson yesterday.'

She half smiled at that. 'Did he tell you? I fell off once.'

'You did?' Jason's brows descended. 'Were you hurt?' His mouth tightened. 'He didn't tell me that.'

'Oh, it was nothing,' she exclaimed, shaking her head. 'It was my own fault. And he caught me.'

'Did he?' Jason's voice was rough. 'Well, take more care in future.'

'I will.' She dimpled. 'It's nice to know you care.'

'I care,' he agreed curtly. Then: 'I have to go. Estelita will be waiting with my breakfast.'

'Oh!' Alexandra's parted lips revealed her disappointment. 'You're not going down to the stockyards again!'

'Not this morning, no. I want to drive over to Puerto

Novo to collect some stores for Chan.' He paused. 'Why? Do you want to come?'

'Could I?'

Alexandra gazed up at him in delight, and as if regretting his impulsive invitation, Jason grimaced. 'I guess so,' he conceded, reaching for his shirt, but she forestalled him, wrapping her arms around his waist and hugging him.

'Thank you,' she breathed, pressing her lips to the hair-roughened skin of his chest, and then putting out her tongue as the fine filaments tickled her nose.

'Alexandra ...' His impatient protest accompanied his hands gripping her upper arms, pushing her back from him. But the thoughtless action sent a shaft of pain ripping up his arm to his shoulder, and he uttered an involuntary groan, releasing her abruptly.

'Oh, your arm!' she gasped in dismay. 'Jason—I'm sorry ...'

'Forget it,' he gritted, between his teeth, but his face was pale under his tan.

'I can't forget it,' she persisted. 'It—it was my fault. If I hadn't been so careless ...'

'I said it's all right,' he muttered, but there were beads of sweat standing out on his forehead, and she saw the tell-tale stains seeping through the white bandage.

'It's not all right,' she argued. 'It's started bleeding again.'

'God!' His frustration caused a pulse to throb reveal-ingly near his jawline, and Alexandra, thinking his anger was caused by the re-opening of the injury, started to un-wind the bandage. He stopped her with his uninjured arm, grasping both her hands in one of his, and saying tautly: 'What the hell do you think you're doing now?'

'I—I was going to dress the wound again,' she stam-mered, but the ugly oath he uttered silenced her.

'And what then?' he demanded. 'After the wound is dressed to your satisfaction, what then? Will you kiss it better?'

Alexandra caught her breath at the glittering fire of his eyes. 'If—if you want me to,' she ventured chokingly, but he flung her hands from him with such force that she almost fell.

'You—are—a—menace!' he grated, enunciating each word with heavy significance. 'Do you know that? Oh, go on—get out of here. I'll do it myself.'

'But, Jason——'

'I said go!'

She caught her lower lip between her teeth. 'Will you—will you still take me to Puerta Nova?' she ventured, as he regarded her without liking.

'Puerto Novo,' he corrected irritably. Then, with a harsh exclamation he nodded. 'Yes. Yes, I'll take you. And Miss Holland, too, if she'd like to come.'

'Miss Holland?'

Alexandra couldn't hide her dismay, but Jason's hand in the small of her back propelled her purposefully towards the door. 'Yes, Miss Holland,' he agreed. 'Ask her!' And she had no alternative but to obey.

In the doorway, however, his voice stopped her, and she turned eagerly, her spirits lifting, sure he had changed his mind.

But his expression was not encouraging, and his: 'Put some clothes on before you ask her, won't you?' was not what she wanted to hear. Cheeks burning, she walked quickly back to her room.

Puerto Novo was a small town, situated in the mountains, midway between Valvedra and Montesanto, the western state capital. It was accessible from the coast by the railway that had been built many years before, and Jason explained that it was from here that his beef cattle began their journey east. It was half a day's journey from San Gabriel, through some of the most rugged scenery Alexandra had ever seen, but again she was in the back of the Range-Rover and at the mercy of every pothole in the road.

Miss Holland had chosen to join them after all. Privately, Alexandra didn't blame her not wanting to spend the day in Estelita's company, particularly as the housekeeper had made no secret of her dislike of the arrangement. Not that she had actually said anything in Alexandra's presence, but the malevolent looks she cast in Jason's direction were enough, signifying as they did the words that had passed between them.

Apart from holding his arm a little stiffly, Jason showed no sign of his injury, but Alexandra couldn't help but notice how the muscles in his face tautened when they bumped over a particularly rough patch of ground. She was concerned about the dangers of infection in an area like this, but she refrained from voicing her opinion in Miss Holland's company.

For the most part, Jason spoke to Miss Holland during the journey, inviting her opinion of the *estancia*, encouraging her to air any grievances she might be feeling. Was her room comfortable? Was the food to her liking? Did she think she would get used to the remoteness and the isolation?

Miss Holland was reticent. Her room was very pleasant, she said, and the bed was extremely comfortable. But the food was obviously very different from what she was used to, and so far as the remoteness and isolation were concerned, she hadn't yet had the time to come to any decision.

'I'm hoping Alexandra and I will get about a little more freely when she has mastered the art of riding,' she said, causing the girl's lips to part in astonishment, and even Jason glanced at her a trifle disbelievingly.

'You—ride, Miss Holland?' he asked politely, and she nodded.

'Reasonably well,' she agreed. 'When I was tutoring Lord Carleon's children, we spent a considerable amount of time at his estate in Ireland. Naturally, the children learned to ride, it was expected of them, and I accompanied them.'

Jason uttered an amused chuckle. 'Well, well! Hidden talents. My apologies, Miss Holland. I should have known a little thing like sitting a horse wouldn't be beyond your capabilities.' He glanced round at his ward, sitting in glum incredulity in the back. 'Do you hear that, Alexandra? You and Ricardo will have companionship on your outings. I shan't need to feel that I'm neglecting you, if Miss Holland is along.'

Alexandra said nothing, but the challenge in her gold-fringed violet eyes did not go unobserved. However, Jason seemed more interested in finding out more about his unusual middle-aged companion, and for the rest of the journey Alexandra viewed the scenery with a slightly jaundiced eye. She had expected she and Jason would take rides together. She had looked forward to him showing her over the *estancia*. But now, it seemed, they would have Miss Holland's company, too, and like today, Alexandra would be pushed into the background. The fact that this wasn't strictly true, that Alexandra herself had suggested Miss Holland should sit in front, was forgotten. Instead, she stared gloomily out on to rolling plateaux and mountain peaks which had somehow lost their appeal.

Puerto Novo was quite a busy metropolis. As they neared the town, they passed more houses and homesteads, and there was a little traffic on the road, including some of the ox-drawn carts that Alexandra had found so picturesque in the outlying villages surrounding Valvedra. The carts were piled high with fruit and vegetables, no doubt bound for the market, and her mouth watered at the sight of huge peaches, downy-soft and juicy, bouncing along beside oranges and melons, and luscious bunches of grapes.

The town itself was situated round a square where the parish church of St Cecilia faced the municipal buildings. The church itself dated from the eighteenth century, Jason told them after he had parked the Range-Rover in a street close by, and he recommended a visit if they had the time.

But it was almost lunchtime, and he suggested they had

a meal in the hotel before going about their separate pursuits. Alexandra, who had expected to stay with him, suppressed the protest that rose to her lips at this information, and was unusually silent over the meal of *asado criollo*, barbecued meat, which was served with a delicious side salad. She refused anything but fruit to finish, and watched without amusement as Miss Holland ploughed her way through a particularly sticky pastry, coated with raisins and sugar. They drank *mate*, the local tea, and Jason smoked one of his long cigars, and then he suggested the 'ladies' might like to go shopping while he completed his business.

'Does that appeal to you, Alexandra?' asked Miss Holland, turning to her charge, but Alexandra only shrugged. The question was largely academic anyway, as her opinion was not consulted with any real purpose, and she refused to respond to the warning impatience in Jason's expression.

'Is that what you want to do, Alexandra?' he asked, virtually repeating Miss Holland's words, and she raised her shoulders in a gesture of indifference.

'Whatever you arrange,' she said, with pointed candour, and he thrust his hands into the pockets of his pants, as if not trusting himself not to shake her.

'I want to go to the bank, and there are various men I have to see,' he said, speaking through his teeth, for her benefit alone. 'Now if you think standing around listening to me arguing about my overdraft, or discussing the trade in hides, is more interesting than spending a couple of hours looking round the shops——'

'I do!' she declared, overriding him. 'I'm not an inveterate window-shopper. I only go shopping if there's something I want to buy.'

Jason's frustration was evident. 'Well, you can't come with me,' he averred harshly. 'At the risk of sounding pompous, my business affairs are private. I don't want you butting in.'

'You do sound pompous!' retorted Alexandra, hiding the hurt in her voice. 'Pompous and—and dull! I don't want to listen to your stupid old private affairs. I wouldn't know what you were talking about anyway, would I?'

'Then you'll go with Miss Holland, and accompany her on her shopping trip,' commanded Jason coldly, his patience shredding. 'I'll see you both back here at four o'clock!' And he strode away before she could make any further objections.

After he had gone there was an unpleasant silence for a few moments, then Miss Holland said: 'That was rather childish, wasn't it, Alexandra? What on earth possessed you to speak to Mr Tarrant like that?'

Realising Miss Holland was unaware of the development of their relationship, Alexandra sighed. After all, it was hardly the woman's fault if Jason chose to behave as if she was some annoying child throwing a temper tantrum. And it had been childish to behave as she had, she knew that. But—dear God! he made her act that way, behaving as if she was incapable of looking after herself.

It seemed that every time she and Jason came to words, she lost the battle. She didn't have his experience, of course, and he could always patronise her. But there were times when she sensed he enjoyed her company—and resented it. It was as if he had constantly to remind himself that she was only seventeen—well, nearly eighteen, she amended, remembering it was only four months to her birthday. Or maybe she was completely wrong. Maybe he only acted that way sometimes. Was he acting on the occasions when he was nice to her, and not on the occasions when he was brutal? One thing was certain, he had the almost exclusive ability to hurt her, and used it, indiscriminately.

Miss Holland was still waiting for a reply, and pulling herself together with an effort, Alexandra made a moue with her lips. 'He—annoys me,' she said lamely. 'I didn't realise he was bringing us here to abandon us.'

Miss Holland clicked her tongue. 'My dear child, a man with Mr Tarrant's responsibilities can't be expected to take time off to entertain us. You have to remember that we're the outsiders here, that without your father's intervention, you wouldn't even be in Mr Tarrant's care. I think his taking it upon himself to place you in his personal care until your eighteenth birthday is commendable, but you mustn't expect too much of him. He has his own life to lead, and we must just—fit ourselves to his plans.'

The words Alexandra would have liked to have offered in response to that little speech trembled on her tongue, but she was learning caution. Behaving like a shrew was not going to achieve anything. And yet submitting to his admonitions as if they were unworthy of contradiction was totally alien to her beliefs. At the convent, she had been taught that the truth was all, that telling lies or dissembling was wrong. Yet already she had learned that being honest earned one a reputation for childishness, and showing her feelings had aroused anger and impatience.

In the event, the afternoon passed quite pleasantly. Miss Holland was soon bored with the limitations of shopping on the Avenida Central, and instead, they explored the gardens of the memorial erected to a famous freedom fighter, and visited the church. The screens that flanked the altar were exquisitely painted, and there were real gems in the robes of the Virgin, whose statue dominated the Lady Chapel. Saint Cecilia herself was depicted in the panes of the stained-glass windows that distributed the sun's rays in multi-faceted colours across polished wooden pews.

Jason was already waiting for them when they arrived back at the hotel. He had ordered tea, and listened with interest while Miss Holland described their afternoon. Alexandra said little, but she did observe that he was holding his arm more stiffly, and unable to prevent the words, asked how it was.

Miss Holland looked surprised at the question, unaware as she was of the injury, and Jason's mouth turned down at the corners as he admitted that he had seen a doctor and had a couple of jabs. Alexandra, feeling justifiably relieved, couldn't prevent a smug smile from appearing on her lips as he explained to Miss Holland what had happened.

'My goodness!' she exclaimed, pressing her lace handkerchief to her lips. 'You could have been killed!'

'Hardly,' remarked Jason dryly. 'Alexandra exaggerates its importance. It's only a scratch. I stood more danger from the infection than from the wound itself.'

'Even so ...' Miss Holland shook her head, and Alexandra faced him with defiant eyes. After all, he had seen a doctor, as she had suggested, and that proved something, didn't it?

The journey back to San Gabriel was more hairy than the outward journey had been. For one thing, shadows were lengthening, casting veils of shade across the road, and the winking sensation of the sun darting at them between the leaves of the trees had a stroboscope effect. For another, Jason drove more swiftly, not taking his time as he had on the way to Puerto Novo, so that they could enjoy the scenery. It was growing late, and he wanted to get back before total darkness engulfed them. Alexandra could understand that. She had already experienced how total that darkness could be. Nevertheless, she wished she could forget the fact that in places the road skirted stark ravines and precipices, a narrow track winding its precarious way through the mountains.

Both she and Miss Holland breathed a sigh of relief when the lights of the *hacienda* became visible ahead of them, and Alexandra leant forward in her seat for the last few minutes, surprised at the sense of homecoming she felt. Her arm rested companionably on Jason's shoulder and this time he didn't draw away, a fact which made her wish they had more than just a few hundred yards to go.

CHAPTER FIVE

Miss Holland wore jodhpurs for riding, uncomfortably heavy breeches, that looked totally out of place in such surroundings. She also insisted on wearing a riding hat, instead of the sombrero Ricardo offered, and her appearance was not unreminiscent of the final days of the Indian Raj. Nevertheless, her ability could not be faulted, and the protection afforded by the helmet was undeniable. She became quite a well-known figure about the *estancia*, and the men called her *La Mula*, because she was so stubborn. Not that she seemed to object. She had their reluctant respect, too, and the men had names for all of them. Alexandra was always referred to as *La Niña*, and while she didn't care for the childish overtones, she knew it was a form of endearment.

Ricardo mounted Miss Holland on a grey gelding, and Alexandra graduated to a chestnut mare, several hands taller than Placida. She found the more she rode, the more confidence she gained, and during the week that followed the three of them ventured further and further afield. Surprisingly, after their initial antagonism was spent, Miss Holland and Ricardo became quite good friends, his derision giving way to admiration as she proved the horsewoman she was.

During these days Alexandra saw next to nothing of Jason. He spent most of the day out of the house, and after supper in the evening, he retired to his study to continue working. He worked hard, she acknowledged that, as hard as any of the men he employed, and involved himself in every aspect of the running of the *estancia*. Because he was an engineer, he had been able to put his technical skills to good use, and Ricardo had told them how he had installed the plumbing system at the house himself. He had also dug new wells to replace the dried-up waterholes used by the cattle, and consequently a long dry spell no longer meant animals dying of thirst, and enabled them to increase their numbers.

The *estancia* itself was huge. Alexandra believed Ricardo when he said it took several days to ride around the outer boundaries of the property, and how, at the yearly round-up, the men were forced to sleep rough during the long trail. She thought she would like to sleep rough, under the stars, making supper over the campfire. It was a romantic notion, and she paid little heed to Ricardo's jeers about snakes and lizards and poisonous spiders.

It was during one of their morning rides that she saw the black stallion again. They had taken the trail into the mountains, and came upon a herd of horses grazing together in one of the grassy gorges that fed the river. Their advent caused some nervousness among the animals, and Alexandra was so entranced by the sight of so many horses together that she didn't at first see the glossy black ears flattened in warning of their approach. By the time she did see him, the herd was already moving, the thunder of their hooves vibrating within the walls of the canyon.

'*Qué diablo!*' grunted Ricardo impatiently, as they disappeared from view. 'He is an arrogant devil, that one! He has the pride of Lucifer himself.'

'Are they wild?' asked Alexandra, still bemused by what she had seen, but Ricardo shook his head.

'There are no wild horses in Santa Vittoria,' he said. 'They are all descendants from a shipment of horses from Paraguay, left to run free on the *pampas*. The herd you have just seen belongs to the *patrón*, and like the cattle, they are rounded up every year and the surplus sold.'

'And—and the stallion?'

Ricardo laughed. 'That black bastard? He is a selfish beast, that one. He keeps all the mares for himself.'

'Jason said the Indians regard him as—sacred.'

'Some do. Some don't. The truth is, they are a—how do you say?—superstitious people. Because no one has been able to stay on his back long enough to break him to the saddle, he has become a *legendario, no?*'

'A legend?' Alexandra translated, smiling. 'But a nice legend, isn't it?'

'Except when we have to round up the mares,' amended Ricardo dryly. 'He knows every ravine and gully in these mountains, every pass, every canyon. It is the work of the devil to find them.'

Alexandra nodded, pushing back the brim of her hat, the sun warm on her thinly-clad shoulders. Already its rays had added a creamier texture to her skin, and this morning, to her horror, she had found freckles on her nose. As if remembering this, she pulled the brim forward again to shadow her face, and followed Miss Holland's broad back as they turned for home.

That evening over supper Alexandra spoke again of the black stallion, and was surprised when Jason raised dark eyebrows at Ricardo and said sharply: 'I thought you promised me you wouldn't ride into the mountains.'

There was anger as well as curtness in his tones, and Alexandra was surprised when Ricardo made a kind of half hearted apology. 'We did not go far, *patrón*,' he protested. 'We were never in any danger.'

'Danger?' Miss Holland, who invariably joined them for the evening meal now, looked astonished. 'We—that is, Alexandra and I—are both competent riders, Mr Tarrant. I don't think you need to worry about us.'

'Ricardo knows my orders, ma'am,' retorted Jason politely. 'For the present, I would prefer you to stay nearer the homestead.'

Miss Holland sniffed her disapproval, and attacked the beef and vegetables on her plate with more aggression than enthusiasm. Alexandra was puzzled too, half wishing she hadn't brought up their sighting of the black horse, but unlike her companion she said nothing, aware of Estelita's mocking amusement at the little affray. However, when Jason left the table some minutes later, she made a hasty excuse and followed him, surprised to find him on the point of going out the main door. She had thought he was on his way to his study, and she hesitated a moment before speaking his name. He turned abruptly, his expression thoughtful, and her mouth went dry as the words she had meant to use deserted her.

'Yes?' he said, and she thought she detected a certain wariness about his response.

'I—where are you going?' she asked, although she had not meant to ask that at all, and his mouth twisted.

'Would you believe—for a walk?' he enquired sardonically, and she took an involuntary step forward.

'May I come with you?'

Jason sighed. 'Don't you usually play chess with Miss Holland in the evenings?'

Alexandra didn't realise he had noticed. 'I do—sometimes,' she conceded, 'but Ricardo plays, too, and he gives her a much better game than I do.'

Jason looked down at his booted feet for a moment, and then lifted his eyes to her face again. 'All right,' he said, although his voice was clipped. 'But don't you need a coat?'

Alexandra was wearing an ankle-length gown of flowered chiffon, that was caught at the waist with a sash of the same material. She supposed it wasn't entirely suitable to the occasion, but she enjoyed changing into something feminine after wearing trousers for most of the day.

'I'm not cold,' she said now, and after a moment's silent appraisal he shrugged and said: 'As you like.'

He himself was dressed in the moleskin pants and silk shirt he invariably wore in the evenings, the collar unfastened to reveal the brown column of his throat. Sometimes, sitting opposite him at the table, Alexandra liked to remember what he had looked like without his shirt. He had such a nice body, she decided, wishing she understood this urge she felt to touch him all the time. He didn't invite it; he didn't even like it; but that didn't prevent her from feeling the temptation.

Outside, it was cooler than she had expected, but she wouldn't have dreamed of admitting it. It was such an unexpected treat, being alone with him like this, and she could not take the chance that if she asked him to wait while she collected a wrap, Miss Holland or Estelita might appear and decide to join them.

They crossed the courtyard at the front of the *hacienda*, and turned along the side of the house towards the paddocks. The fragrance of honeysuckle and night-scented stocks drifted to their nostrils, mingling with the earthier aromas of the animals, and the smell of roasting meat. From the bunkhouse they could hear the sound of someone playing a guitar, and more shrilly a mouth organ added its poignant harmony. The breeze that chased the clouds across the moon's curved face blew Alexandra's hair into her eyes, and she was tucking it back behind her ears when Jason turned to look at her.

'Well?' he said, and there was a trace of irony in his tones. 'I guess you have something to say to me, right?'

They had reached the poled rail of the paddock, and he turned to rest his back against the fencing, regarding her with a shadowed expression. The coolness of the breeze didn't seem to bother him, she noticed enviously, shivering a little, and deciding it was too chilly to linger, she said:

'I wanted to know why you told Ricardo not to take us into the mountains.'

Jason nodded. 'I guessed as much. Isn't it enough to know that I'd rather you remained in the valley?'

'It's not because you don't think we're capable of riding those narrow passes, is it?' she asked. 'It's something else. Is it to do with that black stallion?'

'Hell, no!' His denial was half amused, and she moved to the rail, resting her fingers over the poled surface, trying to read his expression. 'I just don't think it's a good idea, that's all. The mountains can be treacherous. When the mist comes down——'

'I'm sure Ricardo knows when the weather is likely to be dangerous,' asserted Alexandra flatly. 'Jason . . .' She turned to him appealingly, unable to resist the temptation to touch his sleeve. 'Can't you tell me the truth? I'm not a child, even though you like to treat me as one.'

Jason sighed. 'Perhaps I find it easier that way,' he remarked obscurely, and then, at her wide-eyed enquiry, he added: 'I've never had a daughter before. I'm not really equipped to deal with one.'

Alexandra pursed her lips. 'I'm not your daughter,' she declared impatiently. Then, tracing the line of the scar that was darkly visible beneath the fine silk of his shirt, she murmured: 'I see this is healing. You don't need a bandage on it any more.'

'No.' Jason was abrupt, his fingers as usual going to remove hers from their probing. 'Don't do that. I thought you came out here to find out why I wouldn't let you ride into the mountains?'

'You said you'd told me,' she reminded him softly, her fingers curving round his as he made to remove them. 'Mmm, your hands have callouses. Are they painful?'

'They're a man's hands,' he retorted. 'Working hands. Not the hands of an academic, like your father.'

'But you're that, too,' she protested, looking up at him. 'Ricardo told us. You were an engineer. He said you installed the water pipes at the house yourself.'

'Ricardo talks too much,' he stated harshly, but when her free hand came to join the other, he covered them both with his hard fingers. He stood for a long moment, looking down at their clasped hands, and then he smoothed his fingers over her knuckles. 'No one could accuse these hands of being hard, could they?' he murmured wryly. 'They're soft, as a woman's hands should be. Soft, and . . .' he raised them to his lips, '. . . sweet-smelling.'

Her heart was pounding heavily in her ears, the blood surging thickly through her veins as he spoke. The touch of those mocking lips against her skin was like a lick of flame to senses already scorched by his nearness. A feverish excitement gripped her, and although she knew she was courting danger, she did not retreat as she had done before. The feelings he was arousing inside her had to have some meaning, and in spite of her panic, she was eager to learn the truth about herself.

In the moonlight, the expression in those dark eyes was masked as he looked down at her, but presently irritation caused him to tighten his lips. 'What do you think you're doing, Alexandra?' he demanded, still gripping her fingers so tightly, she thought they might snap. 'Coming out here in that thin dress, when I can feel from your hands that you're shivering? Why did you really come? Why do you persist in running after me? Demanding attention! Encouraging me to kiss your fingers like the knight in shining armour you think I am! I'm not your *parfait* knight, Alexandra, I'm me! Just a man. Human, with all a man's weaknesses and imperfections.'

Alexandra's lips trembled. 'I know that,' she said. 'Why are you getting angry? Can't I show friendship towards you? Are you so immune from emotion that my feelings embarrass you?'

'Your feelings!' he echoed grimly. 'What feelings? What possible emotion can I arouse in your breast?'

'Affection,' she exclaimed at once. 'I'm very fond of you. You—you've been very kind to me.'

'Have I?' His tone was ironic, but she ignored it.

'Yes,' she insisted. 'And—I appreciate it.'

'Oh, I see.' His lips thinned. 'And this—this charade is in the nature of showing your appreciation, is it? There's a name for what you're doing, Alexandra, but it isn't *affection*!'

Alexandra tore her hands out of his grasp and faced him defiantly, hiding the pain he was unknowingly inflicting.

'You won't try to understand, will you?' she cried. 'All my life I've been surrounded by people who didn't try to understand how I felt, but when I met you, I stupidly imagined you might be different. But you're not. You're not! You're just as cold and unfeeling as the rest of them!'

Trembling uncontrollably now, she turned her back on him, gripping the rail with desperate fingers, needing its support as she fought back the tears that threatened to humiliate her completely. He was a brute and a bully, tying her immature overtures into knots and tearing them apart again, without either patience or sensitivity.

Wrapped up in her own misery as she was, she had not considered how Jason himself might be affected by her outburst, but even as she took little gasping breaths, trying to control her emotions, his hands closed on her arms just below her shoulders. His touch was sure and restrained, although his fingers bit into her flesh with careless strength.

'What do you know about me?' he demanded in low furious tones. 'What do you know about feelings—and emotions?' He uttered an ugly oath, compelling her backwards as he spoke, causing her to stumble against the hard, unyielding length of his body. 'You talk about friendship and affection, but what you really want is experience! Yes, *experience*!' This as she fought impotently to free herself. His arms slid around her, compressing her arms against her sides, hauling her close to the taut muscles of his lower chest and thighs. 'I knew I shouldn't have brought you here. I knew you were ripe for the kind of relationship you'd get from a boy of your own age. But you were so adamant it was what you wanted, so sure you wouldn't get bored with the limitations of our life out here——'

'I'm *not* bored!'

She almost shouted the words in her frustration, bringing up her hands to grip his arms and force him to release her. She had forgotten the vulnerable laceration in his flesh, but his uncontrollable reaction reminded her, and her anger fled in the face of his pain. Closing her eyes, she rested her head back against his chest, knowing an almost overwhelming desire to remain there, and the errant breeze whipped her hair into his face.

'Alexandra . . .' He spoke raggedly, then with a groan he bent his head and she felt the probing caress of his lips against her neck.

Almost immediately, she started to struggle, but he was stronger than she was, and in spite of his injury he overcame her futile efforts easily. Besides, as his mouth sought the hollow behind her ear, and moved exploringly along the curve of her cheek, her breathing began to quicken and other emotions weakened her desire to escape. Almost instinctively, she knew what her struggles were doing to him, and the thrusting masculinity of his body filled her with a strange and heady power. In spite of all his protests, she was capable of arousing him, and what was more, she was doing it against his will.

As he sensed her weakening, Jason's arms relaxed, and her breath caught in her throat as his hands moved upward, over her ribcage, to the pointed fullness of her small breasts. Again that sense of panic rose inside her. He ought not to be touching her there, she thought dry-mouthed, even while warring sensations welcomed his caress and caused her breasts to swell beneath his questing fingers.

'Don't hate me, Alexandra,' he breathed as her clenched fists brushed his thighs, but then he twisted her round to face him and his mouth on hers destroyed every shred of opposition she might have raised against him.

His mouth was firm and possessive, coaxing her lips to part and share their moist secret. Never having tasted a man's kiss before, Alexandra found herself responding blindly, unaware that her eagerness not to appear naïve made her response that much more provocative. Almost involuntarily, her hands unclenched and sought the silk-covered expanse of his chest, sliding over the fine material to touch his neck. As her arms lifted, the sleeves of her dress fell back so that skin encountered skin at her first tentative embrace. His mouth continued to explore hers, probing ever more deeply with each succeeding caress until her fingers closed on his nape, threading through the strong virile length of his hair and making their own experimental exploration.

His mouth hardened into passion and she felt as if she was drowning in sensual feeling, incoherent with emotion, scarcely conscious of the precipice she was walking. She wanted him to go on and on, uncaring of the strain she was putting on him, only wanting him to go on holding her and kissing her—letting her learn the throbbing contours of his body.

Jason finally summoned the strength to propel her away from him, but she uttered small sounds of protest, and he had to shake her half angrily to bring her to her senses. Forcing her back against the bar behind her, he kept her determinedly at arms' length, though there was compassion as well as impatience in his voice as he said:

'Well? Are you satisfied now?'

Alexandra licked her dry lips. 'Wh-why do you ask that?'

'It was what you wanted, wasn't it?' he demanded. 'Proof that you're growing into a desirable female? That even I am not totally immune to that fact, no matter how reckless proving it might be!'

She moved her slim shoulders, realising suddenly how cold the wind had become, although she had not felt it until that moment. 'We—we're just a man and—and a woman,' she declared. 'What we just shared was the natural——'

'No!' he interrupted her curtly. 'What we just shared was not natural at all. And we're not a man and a woman. I'm a man—but you're just a provocative child who enjoys teasing!'

Alexandra gasped. 'I was not teasing!'

'What would you call it, then?'

'I've just told you.' She wrenched her arms free of him, facing him defensively. 'You're not going to pretend you didn't—didn't *want* to touch me?'

Jason stared at her for a moment, then a look of wry self-derision crossed his face and he nodded. 'Oh, I wanted to touch you, all right,' he agreed harshly. 'I wanted to do a lot more than that!'

'Did you?' Her defiance melted before the uncertainty she saw in his face. 'Did you, Jason?' Her lips parted. 'Tell me . . .'

'No!' As if regretting his momentary candour, Jason's expression hardened. 'My God, you'd like that, wouldn't you? A man of my age—and a girl obsessed with curiosity about the opposite sex!'

'That's not true!' Alexandra was hurt. 'You know it's not. I—I'm not interested in Pepe—or Ricardo, or any of the men, for that matter.'

'So what are you suggesting?' His eyes narrowed. 'That you are—interested in me?'

Her cheeks flushed. 'Is that so surprising?'

'God!'

'Why should you say that?' She sniffed. 'You must know how I feel about——'

He swore angrily. 'Alexandra, I'm old enough to be your father!'

'You're not!'

'I'm thirty-six. Easily old enough, believe me!'

Her lips trembled. 'I don't care how old you are.'

'No?' His mouth tightened. 'I do. And whatever fantasy you're living out so far as you and I are concerned, forget it!' He raked his knuckles down his face in sudden frustration. 'Alexandra, stop fooling yourself. What you're looking for is experience. Just that—experience. And I happened to be around to experiment on——'

'No——'

'Yes. God, I should have had more sense, I know that. But I guess I was—well, flattered that you should seek my company.'

'I don't believe that!'

'Alexandra, I don't get involved with teenagers——'

'I'm not asking you to get involved!'

'—and I make no commitments——'

'I'm not expecting you to.'

'Then what are you saying?'

Alexandra tried to remain calm. 'I—why can't we talk about it? You wanted to—to kiss me. I wanted it, too. What's wrong with that?'

'Alexandra!' With a groan of impatience, he imprisoned her within the span of his arms, resting one hand on the bole of the fence at either side of her. Then he exclaimed: 'Stop pretending, can't you? You're no sophisticate, and we both know it. I doubt if anyone's ever touched you before, have they? I shouldn't have touched you, and we both know that, too.' He paused, and she forced her gaze not to waver before the disturbing penetration of his. 'So—don't go reading anything into it that wasn't there.'

Her lips trembled. 'Thank you,' she said inexplicably, and now his eyes narrowed.

'For what?' he demanded harshly, and she lifted her chin.

'For making your position so clear,' she replied stiffly, and his knuckles showed white through his skin where his hands gripped the rail.

'You don't make it easy for me, do you?' he grated, but Alexandra only bent her head.

'Why should I make it easy for you to avoid me?' she asked, a trifle wistfully, and almost against his will, his hands left the fence to grip her waist, jerking her roughly towards him.

This time his mouth was hard and seeking, his hands intimate on her buttocks, holding her deliberately against him and letting her feel every throbbing muscle between his thighs. But if he had expected her to fight him, he was mistaken. She was still aroused and eager for his caresses, her arms around his waist sliding beneath the silk material of his shirt to probe the smooth skin of his back. Her mouth was sweet and softly parted, a cushion to the bruising pressure of his. She no longer wondered why the sheik's fair captive had succumbed to her lover's embrace. In Jason's arms, she was learning the meaning of her own destiny, the demands of her own body that instinct alone told her only Jason could assuage.

Yet, even while she luxuriated in the urgency of his ardour, she knew that Jason himself would not forgive her for what she was doing. By deliberately arousing his passion, she was slamming doors on the kind of relationship they might have had, and while she wanted him to hold her and kiss her, she didn't want him to do it against his will. That wasn't the way. Her instincts told her that, too. And for that reason, and that reason alone, she tore herself away from him to stand trembling and breathless before him.

But it was already too late; she saw that from his face. The mocking expression she had come to know so well was twisting his lips, and derision coloured his tones as he said: 'Game over? I thought so. You haven't the guts to see it through, have you? At the first sign of danger, you run for cover!'

'That's not why I——'

Alexandra broke off abruptly when she saw the cold scepticism in his face. What was the point of arguing with him? He would never believe her. And why should he?—when she hardly understood what was happening herself.

Instead, she half turned away from him—away from the sensual temptation of his lean body, that was still arousing the most disturbing sensations inside her, away from the bitter scorn in his expression, away from the agonising knowledge that her life would never be the same again. She stared blindly down at the toes of her shoes just visible below the hem of her gown, and realised she was shivering quite openly now, though she hardly felt the cold. But, as if suddenly realising this fact himself, Jason seemed to pull himself together. Thrusting his shirt back into his pants, he gripped her arm without emotion and urged her roughly towards the house.

Shaking away the sense of unreality that was enveloping her, Alexandra made one last attempt to appeal to him. 'Will—will you tell Estelita about—about this?' she demanded as he strode bleakly at her side, and then winced at the crushing contempt he turned on her.

'Oh, yes,' he answered cuttingly. 'Of course, I'll tell everyone. How shall I put it? That our youngest house guest has ideas above her—er—abilities? That my—*ward*—has an intense curiosity about matters of a wholly immoral nature? Yes. That should arouse a suitable cry of outrage among the more religious members of my household!'

'You wouldn't!' Alexandra halted, staring at him in horror, and as if relenting, his hard features took on a mocking expression.

'No,' he agreed, after a heart-stopping moment. 'No, I wouldn't.' He made a sound of impatience. 'I'm not proud of what I just did. So why should I advertise the fact?'

'Jason . . .'

'Inside!' he ordered, not prepared to discuss the matter any further, and with a heavy sigh, she preceded him into the house.

CHAPTER SIX

ALEXANDRA spent the next few days in bed.

The morning following that traumatic encounter with Jason, she awakened with a streaming head and violent pains in her stomach. Miss Holland who came to find out why she had not joined them for breakfast immediately diagnosed gastric 'flu, and insisted she would have Mr Tarrant send for a doctor.

'Oh, please, that's not necessary,' Alexandra protested weakly, trying to get up on her pillows, but Miss Holland was adamant, pressing her back with firm fingers.

'One can't be too careful in a foreign country,' she insisted. 'We can't be absolutely sure it's a form of influenza. It could be food poisoning—or pneumonia!'

Alexandra expelled her breath on a sigh. 'It's a cold, that's all, Miss Holland,' she choked, as a bout of coughing gripped her. 'Just get me some aspirin and a hot drink, and I'll stay in bed for the rest of the day. I'll be fine tomorrow . . .'

But Miss Holland was not to be thwarted, and when she returned some fifteen minutes later, Estelita was with her.

The housekeeper viewed the patient with less sympathy. Alexandra had not forgotten the look Estelita had bestowed on her the night before when she and Jason came into the house together. The housekeeper had been in the hall when they entered the *hacienda*, and Alexandra had not been able to hide the guilty flush that stained her cheeks at the woman's speculative appraisal. She had almost felt that Estelita knew exactly what had been going on, and blamed her for it, and her fingers had probed nervously at the neckline of her gown, as if she expected to find the marks of Jason's fingers there for all to see. But there was nothing to betray her, she had reassured herself, even while that malevolent black stare had cooled her already chilled blood.

This morning Estelita's expression was less easy to read. There was speculation, certainly, but it was combined with a contemptuous amusement that made Alexandra wonder exactly what Jason had said to her. Indeed, she thought bitterly, if she had had anything to eat or drink after returning to the house, she might have been inclined to suspect that Estelita was responsible for her present condition, but after a brief word with Miss Holland, playing chess with Ricardo in the *salón*, she had retired to her room, exhausted both mentally and physically.

'Mr Tarrant had already left for the stockyards,' Miss Holland was saying now, by way of an explanation. 'So I asked Señora Vargas to come and give us her opinion.'

Alexandra made no answer, but Estelita allowed a faint smile to curve her thin lips. 'Miss Holland tells me you have pains—here!' she remarked, patting her own stomach. 'You have been sick?'

'No.' Alexandra shook her head, and Miss Holland took up the tale again.

'I think she should see a doctor,' she declared. 'It could be food poisoning, and that can be a serious illness.'

'I have a cold!' exclaimed Alexandra futilely, as Estelita began to protest with characteristic vehemence that her food could not have poisoned anybody, and Miss Holland retaliated by stating that in her opinion any highly-spiced food was hard to digest.

It was a heated exchange which might have continued indefinitely if Alexandra had not found it necessary to go at once to the bathroom, and by the time she returned, weak and trembling from an attack of vomiting, only Miss Holland remained.

'I've told Señora Vargas that I intend to get a doctor,' she declared firmly, tucking the sheet around Alexandra's shaking body, and the girl was too weak to argue any further.

In the event, it was Jason who brought the doctor to San Gabriel. With her own brand of determination Miss Holland had ridden out to the stockyards and found her employer for herself, and although she accepted Ricardo's escort back to the *hacienda*, she had a distinct air of triumph on her return.

Alexandra didn't much care what happened. She was unable to swallow anything but the very smallest measure of warm lemonade, and lay feeling as if she would never lift her head again. Even the thin beef broth which Miss Holland braved Estelita's wrath to produce refused to remain on her stomach, and the muscles of her abdomen ached from constant retching. She felt wretched, and she was sure she looked wretched, and she told herself she was glad that Jason made no attempt to come and see her.

The doctor was a dapper little man in his late forties, who had his practice in Puerto Novo. He arrived in the late afternoon, and although Alexandra was sure he meant well, his probing fingers were like sharp needles against her sensitive flesh.

After satisfying himself that there was no sign of swelling or inflammation, he diagnosed a severe chill and a mild attack of gastritis, aggravated by the cold germs. He left a bottle of antibiotics, and instructions that Alexandra should remain in bed for the rest of the week.

'You see . . .' Alexandra protested weakly, as Miss Holland came to tuck her up again after the doctor had departed. 'Just a cold. Nothing to get uptight about. And now Jason's got to drive to Puerto Novo and back again in the dark!'

'Mr Tarrant's not coming back,' retorted Miss Holland, briskly, straightening from her task. 'At least, not tonight, at any rate. He said he had some business to attend to in Puerto Novo anyway, so he's going to spend the night there, transact his business, and return tomorrow afternoon.'

'Oh!'

Predictably, this news was the last straw. Alexandra turned her face into the pillow and allowed the hot tears that had threatened all day to come, and blessed the fact that Miss Holland put her weakness down to physical causes.

By the end of the week Alexandra was up and about again. She was young and resilient, and the germ she had contracted was not strong enough to keep her confined to her bed for long. Even so, she accepted Miss Holland's direction not to stray beyond the immediate environs of the *hacienda*, and watched with some envy when her companion and the boisterous foreman of the *estancia* went riding together.

Encountering Jason at supper the first evening she was able to come downstairs for the meal was a nerve-racking experience. She had not seen him to speak to since the fateful evening at the paddocks, and she took her seat at the table with some misgivings. She wished she were more capable of hiding her feelings, particularly as Jason behaved little differently from usual. Apart from a polite enquiry at the start of the meal as to the state of her health, he made no effort to speak to her directly, and Alexandra realised, with a hollow emptiness in her stomach, that so far as he was concerned, the situation had not changed. His attitude was a deliberate demonstration of that fact; but that didn't prevent her from spending the meal casting covert glances in his direction, aware that her feelings towards him could not be so easily dismissed.

With time on her hands, Alexandra spent more energy in exploring the building. Whenever she knew Jason was out of the house, she ventured into his study where she had discovered a veritable library of books, many of them in English, and spent hours turning over the dusty tomes. She guessed some were books Jason had had when he was a student, but as well as theses on mechanical engineering and structural technology, there were also the novels of Dickens and Scott, alongside the more contemporary works of Scott Fitzgerald and Hemingway. She even found a copy of James Joyce's *Ulysses*, and spent a fascinating afternoon absorbed in its pages.

But the book that provided her with the most entertainment was a written course in speaking Spanish, and she set herself the task of learning another language. Her knowledge of French came in useful in the identification of words, and a natural aptitude for accent made even her first stumbling attempts sound plausible. She guessed Jason had used the book himself when he first came to South America, but she also realised that it was living in a Spanish-speaking country and hearing the language spoken every day that had given him the mastery he now possessed. Even so, it encouraged her to keep her ears ever alert for words she could recognise, and she was amazed at how swiftly she progressed.

One afternoon Estelita came upon her reciting a passage aloud from the book. She had heard the unusual sound of Alexandra's voice from beyond the door of Jason's study, and she burst into the room with scarcely concealed anger.

'*Qué hace usted aquí?*' she demanded, using her own tongue in her fury, and Alexandra astounded her by replying in kind.

'*Leo*,' she said proudly. '*Deseaba usted algo?*—is there something you wanted?'

Estelita schooled her features. 'Why are you using Jason's study?' she persisted, this time in English. 'Do you have his permission to read in here?'

Alexandra closed the book and rose abruptly to her feet. 'Do I need his permission?' she asked evenly. 'He's not here. I don't think he would object.' She gestured towards the books. 'I only read. I don't pry into his private affairs.'

Estelita's wide nostrils flared. 'What are you implying, *señorita?*'

'Nothing.' Alexandra was surprised at how quickly the other woman sprang to the defensive. 'I only meant——'

'I know what you meant, *señorita*,' retorted Estelita

angrily. 'You are quick with the—the smart answer, no? Is this what you say to Jason? Is this how you hope to twist him round your little finger, when I am not here to defend myself?'

'Estelita——'

'No!' The housekeeper interrupted her, her eyes flicking scornfully over the Spanish textbook Alexandra was trying rather unsuccessfully to hide. 'So—you are learning our language, too? Perhaps you hope to persuade *el padrono* to let you stay here for ever, *no*?' Her laughter was harsh. 'You are a fool! Make no mistake, as soon as you are old enough, he will send you back. Where you belong!'

The housekeeper's departure left a lingering taste of bitterness in the air, and Alexandra found she no longer had the stomach for study. Instead, she replaced the book in its place, and left the room, admitting as she did so that Estelita had won that particular battle.

The weather, which had been particularly warm and sunny, broke the following day. Alexandra, who had been looking forward to accompanying Miss Holland and Ricardo on their morning ride, awoke to find her windows streaming with water, the curtains damp where the rain had seeped beneath the balcony doors.

Padding to the windows, she stared out bleakly on a hazy world, a grey colourless mist that blanketed the hills all around in a miserable curtain of moisture. She hardly recognised the sodden vines that clung tenaciously to the balcony rails, and she shivered in the draught that sifted through the cracks in the woodwork of her window.

Later, dressed in warm grey harem pants and a tie-waisted sweater, whose high, cuffed collar framed her face in amethyst-shaded lambswool, she went down to breakfast feeling particularly dejected. The day stretched ahead of her dull and unexciting, with the added deprivation of the privacy of Jason's study to complete her disenchantment.

The sight of Jason himself, still seated at the kitchen table drinking a mug of coffee, was a disturbing diversion, and more surprising yet was the litter of dirty dishes that adorned the table, and the fact that Estelita did not appear to be in evidence.

Jason glanced up at her appearance and then, as if compelled to do so, he rose to his feet, lean and powerful in leather jerkin and pants, long black boots completing his attire.

'You're up early,' he commented, with a polite inclination of his head. 'Do you want some coffee?'

'I can get it.' Alexandra hesitated, glancing round to find the pot still bubbling on the stove. Then, casually: 'Where's Estelita?'

Jason leant against the table, one foot raised to rest upon his chair, his expression brooding. 'Didn't she tell you?' And as Alexandra showed her bewilderment, he added: 'She's not here. Pepe's driven her to Valvedra. Their mother's ill.'

'Their mother?' Alexandra had not realised Estelita's mother was still alive, and she almost scalded herself with the coffee pot as she turned to stare at him.

'That's right.' Jason expelled his breath heavily. 'A message came yesterday, via the doctor in Puerto Novo. Señora Gomez has been ill for some time, apparently, but now she's been taken into hospital and she's asking for both her children.'

'I see.' Alexandra took a sip of the coffee, grimaced at its bitterness without either milk or sugar, and then said carefully: 'She never mentioned anything to me.'

'No.' Jason's foot dropped to the floor and he straightened. 'She didn't want to go, but I persuaded her she should.'

'You did?' Alexandra felt singularly stupid, but for the moment she couldn't think of anything else to say. Even so, it did cross her mind that this might have had some bearing on the way Estelita had spoken to her the previous day.

'Yes.' Now Jason moved round the table to light a cheroot with a taper from the fire. 'Naturally, she was concerned about her work here.' He inhaled deeply on the thin cigar. 'Estelita's a very conscientious housekeeper.'

'I'm sure she is.' Alexandra put down her coffee to add milk to its murky depths. 'So . . .' She tried to keep the note of exhilaration out of her voice. 'How long will she be away?'

Jason shrugged. 'Who can tell? Two or three days, a week? Who knows? It depends, I suppose, on her mother's progress.'

'Yes. Yes—naturally I hope she progresses well,' murmured Alexandra at once, but she saw the look of scepticism in his face.

'Do you?' he demanded, and she turned to shift the dirty dishes from the table to the sink in an effort to avoid a direct reply.

There was a curious satisfaction in the menial task, and as she worked Alexandra's mind was active. If Estelita was away, there was nobody to cook the food or look after the house. And without Pepe, too, she and Miss Holland would have the house to themselves while Jason and Ricardo were working.

With the dishes in the sink, Alexandra turned on the taps, then stepped back in surprise when Jason came across to turn them off again. Looking down into her indignant face, he said dryly: 'I'm sure you're dying to prove to me that you're every bit as efficient as Estelita, but that won't be necessary. Chan is going to cook our meals along with the others, and Andrés' wife and daughters are only too eager to come and look after us.'

Alexandra's lips pursed mutinously. 'You enjoyed telling me that, didn't you?' she exclaimed. 'You knew I'd think I could make myself useful for once, but you had to go and spoil it, hadn't you?'

Jason gave her a scornful look. 'Playing house may appeal to you at the moment,' he said, 'but I don't know how long Estelita will be away, and I can't afford to turn down Andrés' offer, when in a couple of days I may have to ask his assistance again.'

Alexandra squared her shoulders. 'Who do you think looked after my father for the six months before he died?' she demanded. 'We couldn't afford servants. I even looked after the garden!'

'Very commendable,' remarked Jason brusquely, 'but that cottage in Ealing can hardly be compared with here, can it?' He tossed the end of his cheroot into the blaze on the hearth. 'Besides, I have Miss Holland to consider.'

'She doesn't like Estelita any more than I do,' retorted Alexandra recklessly, throwing all caution to the winds. 'I should think she'd be glad to help me——'

'No, Alexandra.'

'What do you mean—no? This is supposed to be my home, too.'

'No.'

'Why not?'

Jason shook his head. 'I don't intend to argue with you.'

Alexandra moved her shoulders in a defeated gesture. 'I bet *she* made you promise not to let me do anything!' she declared childishly. She looked up at him. 'What kind of hold does she have over you, anyway? Why does she always behave as if she has some divine right to be here?' She paused. 'Miss—Miss Holland thinks she's your mistress. Is she?'

Jason stared down at her for a long moment, and then the coldness in his eyes gave way to wry admiration. 'Do you realise what you're asking?' he demanded roughly. 'If any man had said that . . .'

Alexandra's face suffused with colour, and unable to sustain the penetration of his gaze, she dropped her lids to stare in acute embarrassment down at her toes. With the words uttered, she was wondering how she had dared to ask such a thing herself, and she wished the floor would open up and swallow her.

It didn't, and when Jason broke the ominous silence between them, there was a controlled tautness to his tones. 'Don't imagine what happened between us gives you any right to know where and with whom I spend my nights,' he told her grimly. 'If I have slept in Estelita's bed, that's only of concern to her—and me. Do I make myself clear?'

Alexandra's nod was jerky. 'Perfectly.'

'Good.' He moved away from her. 'So—what do you intend to do with yourself today?'

'Oh, honestly . . .' She couldn't prevent the tremor that invaded her voice as she turned on him. 'You sound exactly like Miss Holland! For God's sake, why do you persist in behaving as if I was twelve years old?'

Jason's mouth turned down. 'I think we've already had this conversation, haven't we?' he reminded her. Then he turned to the window, staring out broodingly at the pouring rain. 'Damned weather! I wanted to—well, I had things to do.'

He broke off at that point, and Alexandra, waiting for him to continue, realised that yet again she was being discriminated against. But Jason was already reaching for the thick plastic raincape that hung behind the door, and the matching leggings that went with it.

'Are—are you going out?' she asked unnecessarily, and he gave her an impatient stare.

'Does it look like it?'

'Yes.'

'Then I must be, mustn't I?'

'Are you going riding? Can I come with you?'

'In this weather? I think not.'

Alexandra hunched her shoulders. 'I can get wrapped up.'

'Look . . .' Jason was terse. 'You're just recovering from a chill. I'd be worse than mad to take you riding in conditions like these.'

'You won't let me do anything else!' she retorted sulkily, and he heaved a sigh.

'You make it very hard, Alexandra!'

'I'm sorry.'

'Oh, *God*!' He straightened after pulling on the leggings and stared resignedly at her. 'All right, all right,' he said at last. 'You can take charge of the house while Estelita's away. Does that satis——'

But he didn't finish what he had begun to say. Alexandra launched herself upon him, hugging him impulsively and bestowing an eager kiss upon his parted lips.

Maybe because he was more concerned with keeping his balance than controlling his response, Jason didn't immediately draw back from her warm mouth, and what began as a brief caress lengthened into an urgent assault on his senses. The hands that had moved to hold her back from him were suddenly gripping her closer, sliding beneath her sweater to find the soft skin of her midriff.

He tore himself away from her only as the back door burst open to admit Ricardo, but the look that accompanied his withdrawal was grim and frustrated. Avoiding his censure, Alexandra pulled her sweater down over her hips and faced the foreman's speculative gaze with all the composure she could muster.

Ricardo was followed into the room by two bedraggled girls, each holding a shawl over her head for protection, their full skirts dampened by the dash from the Range-Rover to the house. Their presence prevented him from making any comment about the scene he had interrupted, but his dark eyes were full of roguish conjecture. Alexandra guessed he would say something when he had the opportunity, but she prayed he would not chide Jason about her youth. What did it matter how old she was? When Jason held her in his arms, when he pressed her close against his lean hard body, she felt as old as Eve—and as eager to taste the forbidden fruit.

'This is Luisa and Elena Alberoni,' Ricardo was saying now, by way of an introduction for Alexandra's benefit, and she managed a faint smile in their direction. They were very alike, small and plump and dark, with their father's teak-coloured features, but the furtive glances they cast towards her spoke of shyness, not hostility. They looked at Jason shyly, too, but Alexandra recognised admiration as well as timidity in their dark eyes when they rested on the Englishman.

Then Ricardo turned to his employer, who was pulling on the heavy cape he had taken down earlier. 'I told Lucia I'd fetch her if she was needed,' he explained, flicking a look at Alexandra, and although Jason faced him calmly enough, she sensed the challenge in Ricardo's words.

'My—er—Señorita Durham will tell you what she wants you to do,' Jason said now, turning to the two girls, who had taken off their shawls and were presently smoothing their curly dark hair. 'You understand a little English, don't you?'

'*Hablo un poco español*,' murmured Alexandra cautiously. 'I speak a little Spanish, too, Jason,' she added, and this time his stare held only interrogation.

'You—speak—Spanish?' he echoed. Then: 'Who taught you?'

'I taught myself,' she answered defensively, and he shook his head as if he hardly believed her.

'Well . . .' He turned to the Alberoni girls. 'You may be able to work something out.' Then, as if compelled by a force stronger than himself, he looked back at Alexandra. 'Have you been reading my books?'

She nodded. 'Some of them.'

'So it was you.' He made an impatient gesture. Then: 'You think you can cope?'

'I can try,' she responded, holding his troubled gaze, and saw with trembling delight the kindling of reluctant admiration in his eyes.

'Right,' he said.

'Right,' she answered softly.

But as if he suddenly realised their exchange was being closely monitored by three independent pairs of eyes, Jason walked abruptly towards the door. 'Okay,' he said shortly. 'Coming, Ricardo?' and the burly foreman paused only long enough to bestow a wicked wink in Alexandra's direction before accompanying him outside.

With the departure of the two men, the girls broke into excited whispers, and it took all Alexandra's composure to remain where she was until they chose to look in her direction again.

'*Está bien*, shall we begin?' she suggested. 'Now, you are Luisa—and you are Elena, *si*?'

'*Si*.' The elder of the two girls, Luisa, spoke. 'And you are Señorita Derem?'

'Dur-ham, actually,' amended Alexandra, with a smile. 'But you can call me Alex, yes?'

'A-lex,' said the younger girl, who Alexandra guessed was about her own age. '*Si*, Alex.'

With the matter of identification behind her, Alexandra faced her two employees with some misgivings. Pressing her palms to cheeks grown warm as much from embarrassment as from the heat from the fire, she realised she hadn't the faintest idea about what wanted doing and what didn't. In truth, she wasn't altogether sure where Estelita kept her cooking utensils or cleaning equipment, and she would have welcomed a day on her own to familiarise herself with such things. However, if she could keep the girls busy for the morning, she could spend the afternoon finding out where everything was.

Luisa and Elena were washing the dirty breakfast dishes when Miss Holland appeared. That lady came into the room like a breath of English air in the overheated kitchen, and her first action was to throw wide the window and let some of the stale air out. That it also allowed the chilly gusts of wind to reverse the drawing power of the chimney was soon apparent, and closing the window again, Alexandra said:

'Estelita's gone away for a few days, so I'm in charge.' She raised her eyebrows. 'Can I get you some breakfast?'

Miss Holland regarded the two girls who were eyeing her with scarcely-concealed nervousness, and then said briskly: 'I'm quite capable of preparing my own breakfast, Alexandra.' She collected a cup from the dresser and approached the coffee pot. 'Where has Señora Vargas gone?'

'To Valvedra, actually,' said Alexandra, pushing up her sleeves and then pulling them down again, as nervous in her own way as the other girls. 'I—er—I persuaded Jason that I was—quite capable of running the *hacienda* in her absence.'

'I see.' Miss Holland looked up from her coffee, which she obviously found more palatable than Alexandra had done. 'And can you?' she asked.

Her question took Alexandra by surprise, but she had to admit, with characteristic candour, that she wasn't absolutely certain. 'It's finding things,' she offered, moving her shoulders in a gesture of uncertainty. 'Estelita would never show me where anything was kept, and when—when these girls finish the washing up, I don't know what I'm going to give them to do.'

'They can make the beds,' declared Miss Holland practically. 'They must know how to do that. And while they do, we'll examine the contents of those cupboards over there.'

Adjoining the kitchen, Alexandra discovered an enormous storeroom, and it was here Estelita kept most of the things they needed. Sacks of rice and grain, cardboard boxes full of tinned food, freezers crammed with meat and vegetables; Alexandra was amazed at the variety of food there was, and she determined that while Estelita was away they would have a more exciting diet than the staple one of stews and casseroles the housekeeper invariably produced. She would speak to Chan, tell him that she intended to cook their meals, and let Jason discover the difference for himself. She pictured them together eating candlelit dinners which she had prepared. It was a tantalising prospect and one which carried her through the exhausting day that followed.

It turned out that Estelita was not as efficient as she would have people believe. For one thing, she was not methodical, and Miss Holland, garbed in one of the housekeeper's aprons, expressed her disgust at the way many items of kitchen equipment had been allowed to tarnish. Discovering some polish, she and the Alberoni girls spent the remainder of the morning cleaning pans and cooking utensils, transforming blackened exteriors to gleaming copper and chrome.

Alexandra, cleaning out cupboards that did not look as if they had been touched for years, soon had to go and change her sweater for a cotton vest, and her face was smudged and streaked with sweat by the time Chan appeared with their lunch.

'Oh, Chan,' Alexandra exclaimed, as the cook set the dish of chili on the table, 'I wanted to speak to you. I believe Mr Tarrant asked you to prepare all our meals. Well——' she cast a defensive look in Miss Holland's direction, 'I—er—I shall be making our meals in future, so there's—er—no need for you to take the trouble . . .'

'It's no trouble,' Chan assured her doubtfully. 'You mean, you don't want supper this evening?'

'No.' Alexandra assumed a confident smile. 'I'm—er—I'm going to give Mr Tarrant some English cooking for a change. You don't mind, do you?'

Chan's smile was wry. 'It's your decision, *señorita*. I wish you luck.'

'Thank you.'

Alexandra closed the door behind him and surveyed her audience with a certain amount of defensive bravado, before she set about serving the undoubtedly expertly-cooked chili.

The rain stopped in the early afternoon, though it was still very humid, and Miss Holland supervised Luisa and Elena as they shook out rugs from the downstairs rooms, and dusted and polished the furniture. Gathering great bunches of poppies and verbena to fill the vases in the hall, Alexandra really felt as if she was making some progress, though by the time it came to start preparing the evening meal, she realised she was aching with tiredness. Perhaps she should have had Chan prepare the meal just for this one night, she thought with hindsight, but it was too late now, and Miss Holland had retired to take a bath after Andrés had arrived to take his daughters home.

She had decided to make a traditional English supper of roast beef and Yorkshire pudding, followed by baked apples and cream, but her misgivings about the meal were magnified by having to use the wood-burning stove. It was difficult deciding exactly how hot the oven was, the thermostat reading fluctuating rather erratically, but Estelita had managed and so would she.

Choosing a joint of meat was also a problem, and she wished Miss Holland was around to help her. But beef was beef, she thought, impatient with her own uncertainty, and the piece she chose looked succulent enough.

With the delicious smell of roasting meat pervading the atmosphere, she relaxed. Everything was under control. The meat was cooking; the batter for the Yorkshire puddings was made, and she had prepared the vegetables ready for boiling. There was nothing left for her to do but lay the table in the dining room, and go and change before the final preparations needed to be completed.

Miss Holland was still in the bathroom, so Alexandra went into her room and sank down wearily on to the side of her bed. Lord, she was tired! she thought exhaustedly. Even at the convent she had never worked as hard as she had worked today, and her weakness was such that she was forced to acknowledge the truth of Jason's words when he had said she was still recovering from her illness.

Flopping back against the coverlet, she allowed the softness of the mattress to mould itself to her aching bones, luxuriating in its yielding comfort. Was it really only eleven hours since she had woken in this bed? she wondered disbelievingly. It seemed much longer than that. Indeed, so much had happened since she got up that morning, it seemed more like days than hours since she had lifted her head from the pillows.

What a day! She stretched her arms lazily above her head. Starting so disastrously with the rain, and then transformed miraculously by Jason's presence. Remembering Jason, she allowed her tongue to emerge and moisten her upper lip. *Jason*, she breathed softly. Those moments in the kitchen had sustained her throughout the day. The searching pressure of his mouth, the hard muscularity of his body . . . No matter that he grew impatient with her. He couldn't deny that he enjoyed touching her, and sooner or later he would have to admit it.

A smile lifted the corners of her lips as her eyes closed, and almost before she was aware of it, sleep overtook her.

CHAPTER SEVEN

SHE awakened to a darkened room and the awareness of her near-naked body beneath the sheet. A tentative exploration essayed the knowledge that she was naked, apart from the bikini panties she wore, and her brows drew together in a concentrated effort to remember where she was and why she should be sleeping in her underwear.

The sudden crash of thunder that followed the ragged trail of lightning across the ceiling brought her upright with a start, and she stared bewilderedly towards the uncurtained windows. The storm must have awakened her, she realised uneasily, drawing the sheet about her as the cool air chilled her warm flesh. The rain was lashing against the balcony and running in rivulets down the windows, and the thunder continued to rumble round the valley, trapped by the impenetrable range of mountains.

Blinking, Alex pushed back the tangled weight of her hair and tried to think. What time was it? What time had the storm started? What time had she come to bed? And why hadn't she put on her nightgown as usual? Then she remembered . . .

Dry-mouthed, she recalled the events of the previous day—her argument with Jason and his subsequent relenting, the energy she had expended cleaning out the cupboards, and her plans for the evening that was to follow. Her *supper*!

Uncaring of the cold now, she thrust the sheet aside and put her feet to the floor. The rug was soft beneath her bare toes, and she paused a moment to wonder who had undressed her and put her beneath the covers. She guessed it must have been Miss Holland, although she was surprised she had not attempted to put on her nightgown.

Still, she had obviously not wanted to disturb her, and a sound of pure frustration escaped her. If only she had! Surely she had known how eager Alexandra was to prepare her first meal at the *hacienda*, and now that small triumph had been denied her.

Groping about in the darkness, she found her cotton dressing gown and pushed her arms into the sleeves. Then, wrapping its folds about her, she reached for the lamp. The switch clicked uselessly, and with a sigh she guessed that the storm had also fused the generating system. Making her way to the window, she peered at her wristwatch. It appeared to be after midnight, which would account for the hollow emptiness inside her, and she hunched her shoulders in despair. The evening was over. Everyone would be in bed by now. And she had not shared any of it!

Feeling ridiculously near to tears, she opened her door and peered out. Another flash of lightning illuminated the passage outside, but there was no sound other than the thunder. As she suspected, the household had retired, and only the lingering scent of her roast drifted irresistibly to her nostrils. It reminded her again that she was hungry, and with a dejected shrug she went silently along the passage to the landing.

The storm was almost directly overhead now, but she was not alarmed. Storms had never frightened her, and she was glad of the frequent discharges of electricity to light her way. Nevertheless, the resounding rumble of the thunder seemed to accentuate the isolation of their situation, and it was this that prickled goose-bumps all over her flesh as she entered the kitchen. For the first time she was glad of the log fire and the warming glow that emanated from it, and she held her hands towards the embers before helping herself to some milk from the refrigerator.

There was no sign of the joint she had roasted, she observed as she drank the milk, and another wave of resentment swept over her. Miss Holland must have made the Yorkshire puddings and served the meal herself. Had she mentioned the fact that it was she, Alexandra, who had prepared everything, who had put the joint in to roast and beaten up the batter? She sniffed. Probably the men had been so eager to eat the food they hadn't questioned its origins.

The unmistakable sound of footsteps in the yard outside dispelled all her misgivings about supper and sent a wave of apprehension tingling along her veins. Thank goodness she hadn't switched on the light, she thought weakly, wondering if it could possibly be one of the men coming home after a night on the town. Surely they didn't get prowlers out here! Not so far from civilisation.

But that was just the point, she fretted anxiously. They were so far from civilisation that laws virtually had no meaning. What kind of rough justice could anyone enforce, unless with the barrel of a gun?

The footsteps seemed to be approaching the house, and in an agony of uncertainty she wondered if Jason had remembered to lock and bar the door. Was that normally Estelita's duty? Might he have forgotten it in her absence?

Almost petrified with fright, she fastened her eyes on the shadowy handle, just visible in the light from the fire. She was holding her empty glass as if it was some kind of projectile she might hurl at a possible intruder, and when the handle was depressed and the door opened inward, she nearly let it go. But even in the half-light, Jason's lean frame was unmistakable, and with a strangled cry of relief she dropped the glass to splinter noisily on to the stone floor.

'God! Alexandra!'

Jason closed the door and leaned back against it weakly as she moved into the light, and it was arguable which of them had got the worse shock.

'What the hell are you doing down here?' he demanded, recovering more quickly than she had done. 'Creeping about in the dark! Couldn't you put a light on?'

Alexandra licked her dry lips. 'The lights don't work,'

she exclaimed defensively, and then gulped as Jason stretched out his hand and flicked the switch. Immediately the kitchen was flooded with light, and she was uncomfortably aware of the tumbled state she was in.

'They didn't,' he agreed, turning to lock the door before removing his soaking cape. 'But I've just been to fix them.'

'At—at this time of night?' she asked, striving for composure, and he nodded.

'We have freezers, as I believe you've discovered,' he observed. 'We can't afford to allow them to defrost.'

'No,' Alexandra nodded. 'I should have realised.'

'Why should you?' Jason had hung the cape aside now and was reaching for a towel to dry his hair. 'You're not used to our ways yet. Did the storm wake you?'

'I—I think so.' Alexandra looked doubtfully at the broken glass. 'I—I'm sorry about this. But you—you startled me.'

'You did a pretty good job of that yourself,' he remarked dryly, after towelling his head thoroughly. 'Why did you come down? Were you hungry—or frightened?'

Alexandra hesitated. 'A little of both, I suppose,' she murmured evasively, aware that her anxiety was giving way to a tingling kind of excitement. She and Jason were the only people awake in the whole house, and if he thought she was frightened . . .

'We do have pretty terrifying storms here,' Jason was saying now as he removed the thick sweater he had worn over his shirt to go outside. 'And this is a——'

The epithet he used was Spanish, but Alexandra guessed it was not a complimentary one. He grinned, and she realised it was one of the few occasions when he was not on the defensive with her. Why? she wondered. Because he felt he could handle the situation? Or because he thought she was unlikely to behave recklessly if she was frightened? The latter seemed the most likely explanation, and she speculated what he might do if he could read her thoughts at that moment.

'Had—had you gone to bed?' she asked now, bending to pick up the larger pieces of glass, and he nodded.

'I was reading,' he explained. 'It's happened before, and I was half expecting it.'

Alexandra placed the broken glass into the waste bin. Then she ventured quietly: 'I—er—I was sorry I missed supper. Did Miss Holland look after you?'

There was silence for a few moments before Jason finally said: 'Yes, I guess you could say that.'

Alexandra quelled the urge to reveal her indignation, and murmured instead: 'I feel such a fool, after—after I prepared everything.'

A curious look crossed Jason's face for a moment, then he turned away to throw a couple of logs onto the glowing embers. 'Yes, well—you were tired,' he said at last. 'We decided not to disturb you.'

'Who decided?'

Alexandra couldn't prevent her resentment from showing, and Jason glanced round at her. 'I did, actually,' he admitted. 'You were flaked out. You shouldn't have tried to do so much.'

'But this place was filthy!' she protested. 'I was only doing what should have been done months ago!'

'Maybe so.' His tone was annoyingly brusque. 'But it could have been done in easier stages.'

Alexandra pursed her lips. 'Of course, I should have known. You would say that.' Her determination to remain calm was fast disintegrating. 'You don't care that the cupboards were crawling with cobwebs or that the pans you ate out of had never seen a scrubber!'

A trace of amusement touched Jason's mouth at this point which infuriated her even more. 'I eat from plates and dishes,' he corrected her wryly, 'not pans. But do I take it you're the scrubber they've now seen?'

'Why, you—you——'

She glared at him furiously, and he relented, laughing at

her outraged face. 'I'm sorry,' he apologised. 'And naturally I do appreciate what you've done. But you shouldn't have exhausted yourself to the extent that you couldn't keep awake.'

Alexandra sniffed. 'Miss Holland should have wakened me. I wanted to serve your supper. I wanted you to enjoy a proper English meal.'

Jason shrugged, avoiding her eyes, sweeping the remains of broken glass into the hearth with his boot. 'Forget it,' he said. 'It's time we were both in bed. It's going to be a long day tomorrow.'

Alexandra was obliged to precede him up the stairs, but she dragged her feet. It was always the same. He could always better her when it came to an argument. It was only when she was physically close to him that she could weaken his resistance.

At her bedroom door, he went ahead and switched on the bedside lamp for her, standing aside as she came into the room.

'All right now?' he asked, and only then did she sense his sudden reserve.

Then, as if to deny the truth of his query, a particularly loud crack of thunder chose that moment to break over their heads, and in spite of her indifference to the storm, Alexandra started violently.

Afterwards, she wondered if her involuntary reaction had been wholly unintentional, or whether some sixth sense had known that Jason would not be immune to her fears. Whatever, the shocked pallor of her cheeks was enough to halt him in the doorway, and with a muttered curse he came back to her, throwing a reassuring arm across her shoulders.

'It's all right,' he exclaimed half impatiently, as she turned her face into the hollow below his arm. 'You're quite safe here. It sounds far worse than what it is, believe me!'

Alexandra's brain raced wildly. 'I—I hate storms,' she

lied, aware of the thudding beat of his heart beneath her cheek. 'I always have done. Ever—ever since I was a little girl.'

'You're not so big now,' muttered Jason, his breath fanning her temple. 'Shall I wake Miss Holland?'

'No!' Her response was immediate, and she lifted her head to gaze appealingly at him. 'No, don't do that. I mean—well, I'd feel such a fool ...'

'Will you be all right on your own, then?' he asked, and she sought desperately for some means to detain him.

'Couldn't—couldn't you stay—just for a while? Until—until the storm's over?'

'Me?' Jason would have drawn away, but she caught the hand that rested on her shoulder and clung to it. 'Alexandra, the storm could go on all night!'

'Oh, please ...'

She put such entreaty into her voice that unwillingly, he was moved, and half closing his eyes, he said: 'I can't stay here, but if you're really afraid to be alone, you'd better come along to my room.'

'To your room!'

Her voice rose an octave as she repeated his words, and she cleared her throat to disguise her sudden apprehension.

'Why not?' he countered now. 'One bedroom is much like another, and I do not intend outraging Miss Holland's sensibilities by spending the night in yours.'

Alexandra hesitated. She wasn't afraid, exactly, she told herself. It was just that she had never been in a man's company at this time of night before, and while her bedroom seemed safe and secure, his was alien territory. Then she chided herself. This was what she had wanted, wasn't it? By staying here, she would be admitting to a childish impulse to keep Miss Holland within calling distance.

'All right,' she agreed at last, and with a curt inclination of his head, Jason gestured her towards the door.

He switched out the lamp and closed her door before following her along the passage to his room. Then, as she hung back, he opened his door and urged her inside.

The thunder rumbled ominously around the house as she seated herself awkwardly in the armchair beside his bed. Jason closed the door, and avoiding his gaze, she turned her attention to the tumbled sheets. The book he had been reading was turned face-downwards on the coverlet, and from its jacket she could see it was a contemporary novel by a well-known author. But she could not summon the courage to pick it up and found her eyes focussing on a pair of cream silk pyjama trousers that were thrown carelessly across his pillow. Almost instinctively, her hands moved to touch the fine material, smoothing it between her fingertips and gaining a certain sensuous satisfaction from the texture.

'What are you doing?'

Jason's voice from just above her alerted her to the fact that he had come to stand in front of her. He stood looking down at her, feet slightly parted, big and powerful, and devastatingly sexual—and she wanted him to touch her so badly she had a physical ache inside her.

Lifting the yielding fabric of the garment, she cradled it against her cheek and only Jason's jerking it out of her grasp prevented her from turning her lips against the soft threads. Balling the pyjamas with impatient fingers, Jason hurled them across the room, then said angrily: 'So that's why you came, is it? My God, what did they teach you in that convent of yours?'

Alexandra's face burned, but she remained where she was, even while every nerve in her body cried out for her to get to her feet. 'I—I don't know what you mean,' she protested huskily, but she could see that he didn't believe her.

'Your father would be proud to see you now, wouldn't he?' Jason continued relentlessly. 'Insinuating yourself into a man's bedroom, pretending you were afraid of the storm——'

'I said I didn't like thunder; I don't!'

'Is that your excuse for promiscuity?'

That brought her to her feet, quivering with indignation, the force of the sense of injustice she was feeling overcoming her fear of his anger: 'I'm not promiscuous!' she declared fiercely. 'Just—just because I turn to you, because —as you pointed out—I have no father, you behave as if I was some kind of—of *groupie*!'

'Oh, come on ...' He turned away, raking agitated fingers through his hair. 'You didn't come in here looking for a father figure. We both know the little games you like to play. Only it's late and I'm tired, and not altogether in control of my actions, do I make myself clear? You may find the lateness of the hour romantic, but I find it only irritating, and if you're not scared of the storm, I suggest you go back to your own room before you run into something you can't handle.'

Alexandra's throat was dry. 'You mean—you mean you'd like me to stay here?'

'God Almighty!' His ejaculation was harsh and angry. 'How you do like to talk about these things!' He turned to glare at her. 'All right, I'll lay it on the line. Right now, I'd like to sleep with you, yes. But if—Estelita was here, she would do just as well!'

'*Oh!*'

Alexandra's hand went to her mouth, in horror at the obscenity of his words. He had been cruel before, but never so brutal, and she felt as if she had received a violent slap in the face.

'So,' he continued ruthlessly, 'do we understand one another now?' and as she nodded she felt the prickling heat of tears running down her cheeks and invading the parted contours of her mouth.

'Oh, God!' As if realising he had gone too far, Jason stepped into her path as she would have rushed to the door, gripping her shoulders with biting fingers and shaking her ever so gently. 'Alexandra!' he exclaimed frustratedly. 'I'm sorry ...'

Alexandra tried to pull away from him. 'Let me go,' she cried, in a muffled voice. 'You don't have to feel sorry for me!'

'Sorry for you!' Jason continued to hold her despite her struggles. 'Hell, I think it's me I feel sorry for most!' and with a defeated sound he hauled her towards him.

With his face buried in the scented hollow of her neck, it was incredibly difficult for Alexandra to remain unmoved. She felt his lips probing the sensitive nerves at her nape, and her hands crushed between them were all too conscious of the contracting muscles of his flat stomach. But what seduced her most was the warm scent of his body, the clean male smell of him that made her want to feel him so much closer than the barrier of his clothes would permit. His mouth trailed fire along her jawline, and then found hers. one finger parting her lips and invading the moistness within.

That was when she lost all control of her actions. Winding her arms around his neck, she strained closer to him and felt the unmistakable response of his body. Her breasts surged against his chest, and without releasing her mouth, Jason unbuttoned his shirt and pushed her wrapper off her shoulders. It parted easily, and with a groan of satisfaction, he swung her off her feet and carried her to the bed.

Somehow, he had shed his clothes and the length of his body was firm and smooth along the length of hers. His lips were probing her nipples now, stroking and nuzzling their pointed fullness, driving her to dizzying heights of desire as he continued to caress her. His mouth frequently returned to the urgency of hers, and her hands were gripping the hair at his nape, holding him closer, when there was a sudden knocking at the door.

It was only then that Alexandra realised Jason had left the lamp on, painting their bodies in its golden glow of warmth and intimate isolation. But they were isolated no longer. Someone was knocking at the door, demanding admittance, and even as Alexandra shook her head appealingly, Miss Holland's voice called:

'Mr Tarrant! Mr Tarrant! Are you there? Can I speak to you for a moment?'

Jason went rigid, and his lids closed over the torment in his eyes. 'No,' he muttered, 'not now . . .' and Alexandra twisted her arms around his neck.

'Don't answer,' she whispered achingly. 'She'll go away.'

'And if she doesn't?' he demanded thickly. 'No, damn her, I've got to answer!'

Rolling away from her, he groped impatiently for the pyjama trousers he had thrown aside earlier, sliding his legs into their silken casing. Then, as he pulled on a towelling bathrobe, he looked down at Alexandra, still lying as he had left her.

'Get under the covers,' he directed huskily. 'I won't be long.'

Obediently, Alexandra scrambled into the bed, and with a tense expression Jason went to the door. Miss Holland was waiting outside, an anxious figure in her blue woollen dressing gown and hairnet, her face creamed for the night.

'Oh, Mr Tarrant,' she exclaimed, as he stepped outside, half closing the door behind him. 'I'm so worried. Alexandra's not in her room.'

Alexandra, lying listening, could well imagine Jason's reactions to this statement, but his voice was composed as he said: 'She's not?' in quiet tones.

'No.' Miss Holland continued: 'I was awakened—I don't know why. I thought it might have been the storm, or perhaps a sound from Alexandra's room. I was concerned about her. After all, she's had nothing to eat since lunchtime. So I got out of bed and went to investigate. But she's not there. Her bed's empty.'

There was silence for a moment, and then Jason said: 'Perhaps she's gone downstairs to get something to eat,' but Miss Holland didn't think this was likely.

'There are no lights on,' she offered doubtfully, but Jason

seemed determined to make her believe that this was the most likely explanation.

'She probably turned them out after her,' he said shortly. 'After all, she wouldn't want to disturb anybody, would she?'

'You may be right . . .' Miss Holland was wavering now. 'Do you think I should go and see?'

Jason hesitated. Then he said: 'Maybe that would be the best thing. I wouldn't want to—well, alarm her. I'll put on some clothes while you're gone, and if she's not there, I'll go look for her.'

'But where else could she be?' fussed Miss Holland, still obviously most distressed, and Jason soothed her with reassurances that her charge must be somewhere in the house.

'She'd hardly go out on a night like this, would she?' he reasoned, and the woman was forced to concede that her anxieties were probably groundless.

But after Miss Holland had gone on her way, Jason came back into the bedroom with less composure. 'Come on,' he said, as Alexandra stared wordlessly at him. 'Out! I want you safely back in your own room before Miss Holland returns.'

'*Jason!*'

He turned away from the appeal in her wide violet eyes. 'I mean it, Alexandra. I was a fool to let you stay here. Now, hurry!'

'But, Jason——'

'Oh, God!'

He turned back then, tossing the covers aside and lifting her bodily out of the bed. But the feel of her yielding body against his was almost his undoing, and for a moment his mouth sought for hers, hard and passionate, and unutterably desperate.

'You have to go,' he groaned, even while his hands lingered on the creamy roundness of her shoulders, and she leant towards him to touch his throat with her lips.

'I love you,' she whispered, her breath mingling with the tortured expellation of his, and he had to tear himself away from the invitation in her eyes.

'Go to bed, Alexandra,' he muttered raggedly, and with a little choking sob, she left him.

Miss Holland came knocking at her door a few minutes later, raising her eyebrows in surprise when Alexandra answered, wrapped in her dressing gown.

'You were in the bathroom all the time,' she accused softly. 'Oh, my dear! I was so worried.'

'There was no need,' replied Alexandra tautly, and the other woman shook her head.

'Didn't you hear me talking to Mr Tarrant? I'm afraid I disturbed him unnecessarily.'

'Yes,' Alexandra nodded, 'he told me.'

'Oh, dear!' Miss Holland looked, if anything, even more concerned. 'He found you, of course. He seemed rather—annoyed about the whole affair. But if only I'd known . . .'

'Can we talk about this in the morning?' asked Alexandra, interrupting her. 'I—well, I am rather tired, Miss Holland . . .'

'Oh—oh, of course.' Miss Holland was apologetic, which made Alexandra feel even worse. 'Goodnight, my dear. Sleep well.'

'Thank you.'

Alexandra closed the door and leant against it for several minutes before moving to the bed. Then when she did seek the comfort of the mattress, it was only to sit staring blindly into the darkness. Jason wouldn't come now, she knew it, and she also knew that by blurting out her feelings for him she had humiliated herself completely.

CHAPTER EIGHT

THE next morning Alexandra slept in, and it was after nine o'clock before she dragged herself downstairs to find Miss Holland just taking a tray of bread rolls out of the oven. The Alberoni girls were there, too, peeling vegetables at the sink, and Alexandra felt an intruder in the kitchen.

It was a beautiful morning outside. The storm had left a certain lushness in the air, and the pasture sloping down to the river looked rich and succulent. The sun was already high, and a smell of damp warmth invaded the open door. The chickens were scratching noisily about the yard, and somewhere a blackbird was singing its heart out. It was the kind of day when it was good to be alive, but Alexandra only felt the crushing weight of depression.

She hovered awkwardly beside the scrubbed table, and Miss Holland set a mug of coffee and a plate containing a hot roll and some butter in front of her.

'Help yourself,' she offered briskly. Then: 'Luisa, when you've finished those beans, you can go and ask Chan where Mr Tarrant keeps his wine.'

Alexandra subsided into the chair beside the table, but although she sipped desultorily at the coffee, she made no attempt to touch the food. Miss Holland looked so at home in the kitchen, so calm and efficient, while she was struggling to remember the enthusiasm she had had the previous day.

With Luisa gone across the yard to speak to the Chinese cook and Elena outside, emptying the peelings, Miss Holland turned her attention to the girl hunched so dejectedly over the table.

'If I didn't know better, I'd say that Mr Tarrant had found the time to tell you what a disaster supper was last evening,' she remarked candidly, and Alexandra was shocked into attentiveness.

'My supper!' she gasped. 'What was wrong with it?'

Miss Holland uttered a mirthless laugh. 'What was right with it, you mean?' She shook her head. 'My dear child, you don't roast shoulder of beef, at least, not unless you have several hours to spare.'

Alexandra stared at her, her own miseries forgotten in defence of her cooking. 'Are you saying the meat was tough?'

'A little,' commented Miss Holland dryly.

'It's that oven!' declared Alexandra at once. 'It wasn't hot enough.'

'On the contrary, if anything it was too hot.'

Alexandra pursed her lips. 'And the Yorkshire puddings?'

'They were all right, I suppose. A bit lumpy, but that couldn't be helped.'

Alexandra's breathing came in shallow gulps. 'What—what did—what did they say?'

'Who? Mr Tarrant and Señor Goya?' Miss Holland shrugged. 'They were sympathetic, I think.'

'Sympathetic!' Alexandra almost choked with frustration. 'I don't want their sympathy!'

Miss Holland shrugged again. 'I thought I ought to warn you,' she declared evenly. 'I would have woken you last evening, but Mr Tarrant said it was kinder to let you sleep.'

Alexandra's bubble of indignation burst. 'You mean—you mean Jason—stopped you from waking me?'

'That's right. He went upstairs, and when he came down again he said you'd fallen asleep.'

'Did he?' With tremulous awareness, Alexandra recalled her eventual wakening during the storm. Tentative fingers strayed over her breast, its pointed tip probing her palm through the thin material of her cotton shirt, reminding her of her nakedness. Her mouth was dry as she added: 'Did he say anything else?'

'Not then, no.' Miss Holland poured herself a cup of

coffee, before continuing: 'What happened? Did you intend to have a nap or what?'

'No.' Alexandra shook her head vigorously. 'I just—closed my eyes. That's all I remember.'

'And then I suppose you got undressed before you went to the bathroom?'

'What?' Alexandra felt her cheeks turning pink. 'Oh—oh, yes, that's right. I—I must have disturbed you.'

'Yes.' Miss Holland sipped her coffee, viewing the girl over the rim of the cup. 'What did Mr Tarrant say when he discovered where you were?'

'N-nothing much.' Alexandra made an offhand gesture. 'Only—only that you were looking for me.'

'I see.' Miss Holland nodded slowly. Then, as if dismissing the topic, she turned back to the stove. 'Well, I suggest you go and get some air now. You're looking rather peaky. I'd join you myself, only I want to make a pie for supper. Does steak and kidney appeal to you?'

Alexandra sighed. 'I can't just go and—and leave you to it!' she protested.

'You can and you will,' insisted Miss Holland firmly. 'You've already had one dose of illness. Don't invite another. You worked hard yesterday. Today you can get some sun on those pale features.'

Ricardo came upon her as she was helping old Jave to sweep out the stables. It was cool and musty in the stables, the smell of the horses a balm to her troubled spirit. She enjoyed the exertion, too, and the comradeship she shared with the elderly Indian who understood her stumbling attempts at Spanish.

When Ricardo's huge shadow darkened the doorway, she thought for one heart-stopping moment that it was Jason come to find her. Then the foreman's hearty laugh rang out, and he exclaimed reprovingly: 'What's this? I thought the old one told me you were taking a rest, *niña*!'

Alexandra straightened, her back aching a little from the

stooped position she had been adopting. But she managed a faint smile of greeting, and said lightly: 'I wanted to go riding, but you weren't around to take me.'

'Ah-ha!' Ricardo tapped the side of his nose significantly and grinned. 'But I am here now, *no*? And I have brought someone to meet you. My son—Manuel.'

'Your son?' Alexandra followed him out into the bright sunlight of the yard. She had heard Ricardo speak of his son before. She knew he worked for Jason, too, but like the other men, he seldom ventured up to the house.

She would never have recognised the young man leaning against the bole of the gnarled old eucalyptus tree outside as Ricardo's son. He was of a much slighter build than his father, and his features were pale, not swarthy. His eyes were shy, not bold like Ricardo's, and his hair was as smooth and straight as his father's was unruly. Only his clothes matched those of the other men—shirt, waistcoat and pants, with leather chaps to protect his legs.

He straightened at their approach, and although his smile was gentle and unassuming, Alexandra was immediately conscious of the state of her hands and of the fact that her face was probably streaked with dirt, too.

'My son,' said Ricardo again, rather unnecessarily. 'Manuel, this is Señorita Durham.'

'I know.' Manuel spoke as good English as his father, if not better, and his voice was quieter, more cultivated.

'Manuel has been working at the *estancia* since he finished college three months ago,' stated Ricardo proudly. 'But it is only a temporary arrangement. He is going to be an engineer—like the *patrón*!'

'What my father really means is that at present I am unemployed,' put in Manuel, with a grimace. 'There are not as many vacancies for engineers as there are for *gauchos*.'

Alexandra found herself smiling at him. He really was a handsome young man, she thought approvingly, glad that there was at least someone else besides Jason who could disconcert Ricardo.

'And do you like being a *gaucho*?' she asked easily, and Manuel nodded.

'In summer, the work is good,' he conceded. 'Much better than some stuffy office. But come winter——'

'Come winter, you will be working in Brazil,' declared Ricardo uncompromisingly. 'You know Fredriksons have offered you a job!'

Manuel shrugged. 'I do not know that I want to go and work in Brazil,' he retorted, winking at Alexandra. 'And in any case, my plans can be of no interest to Señorita Durham.'

'Oh, they are——' Alexandra was beginning, when Ricardo interrupted her.

'It is true,' he agreed ruefully. '*Señorita*, Manuel is here to take my place for a few days, no? The *patrón* has need of me, and it was his suggestion that Manuel might be a suitable replacement. If you have no objection, *por supuesto*.'

Jason's suggestion! Alexandra felt the hot colour invading her cheeks even while a feeling of deflation filled her. Jason's suggestion that this handsome young man should take his father's place and keep her company. Should *waste* his time escorting her! And why? Because he had no time for her? Because he wanted to keep her off his back?

On the point of telling Ricardo that she needed no one to accompany her, resentment gripped her. Why should she satisfy Jason's ego to that extent? If he thought she could find a replacement for him as easily as for Ricardo, he might lose a little of that arrogance he possessed in such abundance. And Manuel was a very handsome young man ... Handsome, *and intelligent*, she amended bitterly, and nearer her own age, if she was not mistaken.

Now she rubbed her dirty hands over the seat of her pants, and said tautly: 'That was—very kind of him—of all of you. Particularly as I'm sure Manuel has more important things to do than provide me with an escort.'

'You have to be joking!' declared that young man, with gratifying eagerness. 'I shall be happy to be at your service, *señorita*,' and his father added his assurances.

'Manuel will take good care of you,' he promised, glancing up towards the sun, climbing to its zenith. 'And don't forget to wear your hat, *no?*'

It was good to feel the chestnut's flanks beneath her once more. Leaving the *hacienda* behind, Alexandra gave the mare her head, lying low over her neck as they galloped recklessly across the turf. Manuel was hard put to keep pace with her on his sturdy animal, which was built more for stamina than for speed, and eventually Alexandra relaxed and waited for him to catch up.

'Sorry about that,' she apologised ruefully. 'But it's ages since I came out here.'

'You've been ill. My father told me,' commented Manuel, reining in his palomino beside her. 'I hope you are fully recovered now.'

'Oh, yes.' Alexandra gave a wry laugh. 'It was only a chill.'

'But serious enough to get the doctor from Puerto Novo.'

'Oh . . .' Alexandra kicked her heels into the mare's sides and the horses ambled on together. 'That was Miss Holland's idea. You haven't met Miss Holland, have you? She's my—er—companion.'

'I have seen her,' nodded Manuel humorously. 'We see her riding about the *estancia*. She wears a round hat and trousers—like this!'

He pulled the leather chaps out from his legs in imitation of Miss Holland's jodhpurs, and Alexandra smiled. 'That's right,' she assented laughingly. 'Actually, they are what people wear to go riding in England. Only hers are rather—old-fashioned.'

'Hmm.'

Manuel showed his agreement, and they rode on for some way in silence. They followed the track Alexandra had learned with Ricardo, curving along the river for some distance, and then climbing steadily into the foothills. The scent of pine and juniper was strong after the rain, and the heat of the sun sent little swirls of mist rising from the undergrowth. Alexandra was glad of the coolness provided by the brim of her hat, but her hand went often to push the weight of her hair back from her brow.

If she turned sideways in the saddle, she could see the roof of the *hacienda* below them in the valley, the river swollen by the storm surging greedily downstream. She could see the rainswept branches of the acacia behind the storeroom, and the strewn petals of the blossoms that had been devastated during the night.

Turning back to Manuel, she said suddenly: 'Do you think we might see the black stallion today? He's a beautiful beast, isn't he? So strong and powerful! I've seen him a couple of times already, but what I'd really like to do is get close to him.'

'Would not we all?' Manuel replied dryly. Then, quellingly: 'I do not think it is likely, *señorita*. It is safer if we do not ride into the gullies until the prowler has been caught. My father said——'

But Alexandra had stopped listening to him. 'What prowler?' she demanded tensely, and she could tell immediately from Manuel's expression that he knew he had said the wrong thing.

'It is not important,' he protested, turning aside to point to a flock of geese rising from the reeds beside the river. 'See the colours of their tail feathers, *señorita*. Are not they beautiful, too? I had a friend, at the university, he used to paint the birds——'

'Manuel!' She leant across to grip the horn of his saddle, staring impatiently into his face. 'I'm not interested in birds, and nor are you. I want to know what you meant by a prowler! Do you mean there is someone—some man——'

'Man? No!' Manuel shook his head, looking down at her

fingers restlessly massaging the iron hook that he used when he was roping cattle. 'No human prowler this, *señorita*. Not at San Gabriel.'

'Then what?' Alexandra stared at him, but already an idea was occurring to her. 'An animal of some sort?' she questioned. 'A—a cat? A big cat?' Watching his expressive features as she spoke, she felt sure she was on to the right track. 'A lion?' she asked, with deepening apprehension. 'That's it, isn't it? A mountain lion?'

Manuel's shoulders sagged. 'A jaguar, most likely,' he agreed heavily, 'and my father will have my hide for telling you.'

'So that was why Jason——' Alexandra broke off abruptly as she felt the first twinges of real fear. Turning wide eyes in Manuel's direction, she exclaimed: 'But I thought wildcats kept to their own territory. Surely they don't venture down into the valley!'

'Not normally,' Manuel conceded. Then, as if deciding that as she already knew the worst there was no harm in talking about it, he sighed and went on: 'Cats are predators, but as you say, they don't usually prey near men. However, there are exceptions to every rule, and when an animal is old . . . or sick . . .'

Alexandra licked her dry lips. 'You mean—this animal is one of those things?'

Manuel hesitated. 'I believe so,' he admitted at last, but she sensed he was still holding something back.

'Have—have you seen it?' she asked, involuntarily tightening her hand on the mare's reins, but Manuel shook his head.

'Not me, no.'

'But your father? Or Jason?'

'They may have done,' he conceded, but she was not satisfied.

'Manuel!' she cried frustratedly. 'If you know something else, tell me! I—I *have* to know.'

Pictures of Jason riding alone into the mountains in search of some dangerous wild animal were flooding her brain. And even while she accepted that he would not take unnecessary risks, that he would be armed, she knew now that that was what he had intended to do the previous day had the weather not prevented him.

Manuel shifted uncomfortably in his saddle as she continued to gaze at him and finally he said: '*Está bien*, she is wounded! Carlos, one of *el patrón's* men fired on her three weeks ago.'

'You're sure?'

'*Estoy seguro*,' declared Manuel, speaking Spanish in his agitation. '*El patrón* himself has seen her. Unfortunately, he did not have his rifle with him at the time.'

'Oh, *lord*!' Imagining the worst that could have happened, Alexandra moved her head in a helpless gesture. 'And—and this creature has come down into the valley?'

'After dark, yes,' said Manuel reluctantly.

'Has it killed?'

Manuel uttered a harsh sound. 'Do cats not always kill? *Si, señorita*, she has killed. Sheep—cattle—and two nights ago, a horse.'

'How awful!' Alexandra looked round at the low range of hills ahead of them with new eyes. 'And—and it's hiding somewhere in there?'

'Somewhere,' agreed Manuel flatly. 'And now, come! I think we should be turning back, *no*?'

Alexandra's lips twisted. 'Are you frightened?' she taunted, and then felt remorse as the young man showed his indignation.

'No!' he declared fiercely. 'But my father——'

'I know, I know.' Alexandra pulled an appealing face at him. 'Your father told you not to take me into the mountains. Come on, then. I'll race you back to the river.'

'Take care!' he cried anxiously, as she swung the mare's head round and dug her heels into its flanks. But Alexandra only grinned at him, finding release from her own anxieties as the breeze's errant fingers tore the sombrero from her head.

She had almost reached the river when she saw him. Closer now than ever before, the stallion stood proudly on a ridge just across the swiftly-flowing current. He seemed to be staring straight at her, although she guessed his attention was more for the mare than for its rider, but she reined in wonderingly, her lips parting at his unconscious symmetry.

Manuel thundering up behind her was caught off balance, and his mount reared protestingly as he hung on the bit. The sudden commotion startled the stallion, and with an arrogant flick of its tail, it turned and plunged away across the *pampa*.

Alexandra was unreasonably irritated by what she considered Manuel's carelessness, and his casual comment that the stallion was a nervous brute caught her on the raw.

'You should be so nervous!' she retorted, tossing her head. 'He's beautiful! The most beautiful animal I've ever seen.'

Manuel shrugged, and infuriated by his indifference, Alexandra urged the mare forward, plunging down the slope towards the river with more enthusiasm than common sense. She guessed what was about to happen almost before disaster overtook her, but that didn't prevent the mare from putting its head down so that Alexandra went hurtling head over heels into a bank of lush grass.

She wasn't really hurt, only stunned, the breath knocked out of her, but Manuel scrambling down the slope after her wore an expression of such anxiety that she was tempted to pretend she had been knocked out. However, her innate sense of fair play would not allow her to tease him in that way, particularly when she had been to blame, and his hoarse; 'Alexandra?' as he hovered over her, brought a smile of reassurance to her lips.

'I'm all right,' she said softly, and he wrenched off his hat to twist it tortuously between his fingers.

'A *Dios gracias*,' he muttered, his face as pale as hers had become, and she rolled on to her knees to stretch a hand towards him apologetically.

'You called me Alexandra,' she said, squeezing his forearm which was agreeably muscular. 'I wish you would use my name. *Señorita* is so—formal!'

Manuel closed his eyes for a moment, and then opened them again to wipe the sweat from his brow with the brim of his hat. 'I was so worried!' he confessed. 'You are sure you are not hurt?'

Alexandra withdrew her hand to spread her arms expressively. 'Do I look hurt?' she demanded, and his handsome features suffused with colour.

'No,' he conceded softly. 'You look—*muy hermosa*.'

Alexandra's lips parted. 'I know what that means.'

'Do you?' He got to his feet, holding out a hand to assist her, and as she put her hand into his she said: 'You're very gallant, particularly after what happened.'

Manuel grinned. 'A beautiful girl always deserves gallantry.' Then he added: 'The mare has gone. I think we should make haste to the stables before Jave thinks I have lost you.'

Getting to her feet, Alexandra winced a little as the sudden action reminded her she had hit her head as well as other parts of her body. She allowed Manuel to help her up the slope to where the patient palomino waited, and then said:

'I can't take your horse! That wouldn't be fair!'

'I did not intend that you should,' retorted Manuel dryly. 'Piso can carry both of us, if you permit?'

Alexandra hesitated only a moment before swinging herself up on to the palomino's back. Why not? she thought recklessly. If Jason didn't like it, he had only himself to blame. She comfortably forgot that if she hadn't lost her temper and been thrown, the situation would not have occurred.

Miss Holland was waiting by the boundary fence when they rode back to the *hacienda*. Her anxious face was evidence of the agonising few minutes she had spent, but relief quickly gave way to disapproval when she realised Alexandra was all right. She looked askance at the way her charge had been returned to her, secure within Manuel's controlling arms, and hurried the girl down from the horse as soon as they reached her.

'It was my fault,' declared Alexandra at once, as Miss Holland began to remonstrate with her escort, and smiling up at Manuel, added quickly: 'It was all my fault. I was careless—showing off! I'm sorry the mare came back alone to worry you.'

Miss Holland pursed her lips. 'Being sorry is hardly compensation for my feelings when I saw that chestnut mare!' she exclaimed. 'Dear heaven, what have you been doing? There's grass all over your hair.'

Alexandra grimaced, pulling green strands out of the silky curtain about her shoulders. 'Manuel tumbled me in the hay,' she offered wickedly, but Manuel's mortified expression more than convinced Miss Holland that she was not telling the truth.

'You can tell me what happened later,' she told the girl shortly. 'Now I suggest you go and wash for lunch, and thank your lucky stars Mr Tarrant wasn't around when your mount came back!'

Alexandra's brief moment of exhilaration fled. 'I doubt if he would have noticed,' she stated tautly, before glancing up at Manuel again. 'Will I see you tomorrow?' she asked, horrifying Miss Holland still further by her presumption, and Manuel made a helpless gesture.

'If you wish . . .' he began, and Alexandra nodded.

'I wish,' she said, and sauntered away towards the house before Miss Holland could attempt to alter the arrangement.

CHAPTER NINE

'THERE was absolutely no need to behave so recklessly,' declared Miss Holland later that day, as she and Alexandra ate lunch together. 'You could have been killed! Don't you know you could have broken your neck!'

Alexandra pushed the delicious Spanish omelette round her plate, and chewed absently on a lettuce leaf. 'I didn't fall deliberately,' she protested, unable to deny the anxiety of not knowing where Jason was or what he was doing. 'It was just an accident, that's all. It won't happen again.'

'I'm sure it won't,' Miss Holland affirmed grimly. 'In future, I shall go with you, and I shall ensure you don't do anything foolish.'

Alexandra was too distraite to argue with her. Instead, she pushed her plate aside and said: 'What range does a rifle have?'

'A rifle!'

Miss Holland was clearly taken aback, and Alexandra pressed the advantage. 'A rifle, yes,' she said. 'I want to know how near a man has to be to a lion to be sure of killing it.'

Miss Holland stared at her bewilderedly. 'Really, Alexandra, you are the most perplexing child!'

'I'm not a child!'

'All right—girl, then.' The older woman sighed. 'What has the range of a rifle to do with our conversation?'

'Jason carries a rifle,' replied Alexandra idly. 'I'm—interested, that's all.'

'Well, I'm afraid that's a question you'll have to ask him,' said Miss Holland, getting up to clear the plates. 'I know nothing about firearms. Horrible things!'

'Didn't Lord Carleon ever go shooting?'

Miss Holland frowned, obviously puzzled at this turn of the conversation. 'Well—yes,' she admitted at last. 'But that was different. He used a shotgun, not a rifle.'

Alexandra traced the grain in the wooden surface of the table with a fingernail. 'Shotguns aren't like rifles, I agree. With a rifle, you must be accurate. Shotguns spray pellets in all directions.'

'Well, I wouldn't say that,' retorted Miss Holland indignantly. 'Besides, they're two entirely different weapons.' She shook her head impatiently. 'That young man—Manuel—hasn't been filling your head with ideas of a hunting expedition, has he? Because I warn you——'

'No!' Alexandra hunched her shoulders. 'It's *el patrón* who's gone hunting!'

'*El patrón?* You mean—Mr Tarrant?'

'That's right.' Alexandra looked challengingly up at her. 'Didn't you know?'

Miss Holland made a confused gesture. 'Know? What could I know? Alexandra, what are you talking about?'

Alexandra looked down again. 'Perhaps I oughtn't to tell you,' she murmured infuriatingly. 'After all, I wasn't supposed to know myself.'

'Alexandra!'

'Oh, all right ...' The brief stimulation she had derived from teasing the other woman quickly dissipated as the seriousness of Jason's mission swept over her again in chilling perspective. 'Some mountain lion's been raiding the *estancia*,' she admitted, the tremor in her voice belying her offhanded tones. 'Manuel told me.'

Miss Holland's reactions were less emotional than Alexandra's had been, but her lips were perceptibly tighter as she said: 'I gather he didn't have Mr Tarrant's permission to do so. He should have had more sense.'

'Why?' Alexandra was indignant. 'Why shouldn't we be told? We're not children!'

'No. But probably Mr Tarrant didn't want to alarm you

unnecessarily. I shall speak to Ricardo about that young man——'

'No! No, don't.' Alexandra sprang to her feet. 'He didn't mean to tell me. It—it was just something he said. It slipped out.'

'Nevertheless, he should be taught to guard his tongue.'

Alexandra sighed. 'Oh, honestly . . .' She moved restlessly towards the windows. 'What does it matter? It's Jason who's out there looking for the creature, not us. We're safe enough, aren't we?'

Miss Holland shrugged and moved to lift the coffee pot from the stove. 'I don't think you have any need to worry about Mr Tarrant, if that's what you're implying.'

'Don't you?' Alexandra's throat was dry.

'No.' Miss Holland was brusque. 'Now, I suggest you come and finish your lunch. As I've sent Luisa and Elena home, I shall want your help with the washing up.'

Alexandra was in her room when Jason and Ricardo returned. She heard their voices in the hall, and her heart beat a little faster with the relief of knowing that they were unharmed. She wondered if they had caught the prowler, and then realised that unless she betrayed Manuel she couldn't ask them.

However, with the burden of Jason's safety removed, there were other emotions to be dealt with. The prospect of facing him after what had happened between them the night before was no mean feat, and remembering her wanton behaviour she felt an overwhelming surge of humiliation. It was no use telling herself that he had been as much to blame. She had gone to his room, and had encouraged him to treat her like a tramp, and she could thank her stars that Miss Holland's intervention had saved her from herself.

How did one face a man after such an experience? she fretted. Her resourceful novel told of the cool-eyed captive spurning the advances of the passionate sheik, but not of his spurning her! Her breath caught in her throat. Was she so easy to ignore? Hadn't the love-making they had shared meant anything to him? And was Manuel really intended to be his replacement?

Smoothing velvet lounging pants over her hips, she jerked a pleated chiffon smock over her head and surveyed her appearance without appreciation. Was she too slim? she speculated critically. Were her breasts too small? And her hair, presently curling in moist tendrils about her temples, would it look better short? Manuel had not found her unattractive. On the contrary, she had recognised the expression in his eyes very well. Perhaps if she thought about him this evening, she could keep Jason's insensitivity at bay, and prove that her words spoken in the heat of the moment had meant nothing more to her than they had to him.

Downstairs, she found Miss Holland setting her delicious steak and kidney pie on the dining room table. Another cord to flay herself with, she thought bitterly, recalling her disastrous efforts of the previous evening. Jason and Ricardo had gone to change, Miss Holland told her, and Alexandra was more than eager to help with the vegetables, dreading that moment when Jason would appear.

She heard his voice first. He and Ricardo came into the dining room as she was laying serving spoons beside the tureens containing beans and carrots, peas and sweet potatoes.

'*Hola, señorita!*' exclaimed Ricardo at once, as she straightened to face them. 'You are looking flushed this evening, eh, *patrón*?'

It couldn't have been worse. Alexandra couldn't meet Jason's dark eyes, and it was left to him to say evenly: 'You're embarrassing her, Ricardo. I'm sure it's just the heat from the kitchen that has brought the colour to her cheeks.'

'Perhaps.' Ricardo was unrepentant. 'Or perhaps it is the

memory of the ride she took with my son this morning,' he teased. 'Manuel also was red-faced when I asked him about it.'

'Oh, yes ...'

Jason sounded uninterested, and inclining his head thoughtfully, he turned away to take his seat at the head of the table. Only then did Alexandra chance a look at him.

In dark corded pants and a bronze-coloured silk shirt, he was disturbingly masculine, and she found it impossible to dissociate her thoughts from the disruptive memories the sight of him evoked. The thinness of his shirt barely disguised the shadow of the hair that she knew covered his chest in a fine cloud, and arrowed down his stomach to his navel; and the darkness of his wrists, projecting from his cuffs, drew her eyes to the long brown hands that had so urgently taught her the meaning of sensuality.

Miss Holland, coming into the room at that moment, provided a welcome distraction. She spoke to Jason, asking if he had any objection to her choice of a red burgundy to drink with the meal, and while they discussed the merits of various red and white wines, Alexandra slipped into her own seat beside Ricardo.

The food became the talking point, much to Alexandra's relief, although she waited apprehensively for Ricardo to make some joking comment about her disastrous efforts of the previous day. But whether or not Jason had warned him not to say anything, she didn't know. She only knew that for some reason the subject was taboo, and in that respect at least she was allowed to relax.

Once she encountered Jason's eyes upon her. It was towards the end of the meal, and he held her gaze for a matter of some five or ten seconds before averting his eyes. Yet for all that, she was left feeling unpleasantly disturbed by his appraisal, and she was glad when she could make the excuse of helping Miss Holland to clear the table. There had been contempt as well as anger in that stare, and she guessed he despised her now for what he considered her promiscuity. As she loaded dishes into the sink, she wondered if he expected her to behave that way with Manuel. It was a bitter indictment, and she half wished she were the kind of person able to indulge in those kind of relationships. It would be a rough sort of revenge if she could make Jason jealous that way, for while he might abhor her behaviour, he could never deny the purely physical needs she aroused in him.

The next morning Manuel appeared as she was helping Miss Holland collect eggs from the hen-house. It was an undemanding occupation, and she was thinking how hot it was again and how nice it would be to plunge into the cool waters of the river, when he sauntered into the yard.

'*Buenos días, señoritas!*' he greeted them gallantly, sweeping off his hat in a theatrical gesture. 'It is a beautiful morning, is it not?'

Miss Holland glanced reprovingly at Alexandra, and then said shortly: 'Did you want something, *señor*?'

'Of course he did.' Alexandra stepped between them. 'You know I asked Manuel to take me riding again today.'

Miss Holland snorted. 'To fall off again, I suppose,' she exclaimed caustically, but Alexandra ignored her, demanding eagerly:

'What happened yesterday, Manuel? Did Jason find the lion? I wanted to ask last night, but I couldn't.'

She had forgotten to explain to Manuel that Miss Holland was in her confidence, but his eloquent expression was indication enough. 'Oh, it's all right,' she added apologetically, as he started making frantic gestures, 'Miss Holland knows. But I haven't told anyone else. Honestly!'

Manuel was still very doubtful, but the desire to tell what he knew overcame his scruples. 'They never even saw her,' he said. 'She is a wily old beast, and the rain had obscured her tracks. Maybe today . . .' He shrugged expressively.

In spite of the awful hollowness in the pit of her stomach that his words had evoked, Alexandra had to behave naturally. Besides, she was suddenly eager to get away from the house and its associations, and with a forced smile, she said: 'Let's go, shall we? I'll get my hat.'

'Alexandra!' Miss Holland's voice arrested her, and she glanced back reluctantly. 'Alexandra, where do you think you're going?'

'Riding. Where else?' Alexandra was offhand, but the older woman was not reassured.

'You wouldn't attempt to go looking for that—creature yourself, would you, Alexandra?' she exclaimed, unable to hide the note of anxiety in her voice, but this time it was Manuel who answered for her.

'We have more sense than that, *señora*,' he asserted quietly. 'Besides, if the *patrón* cannot find the old one, we assuredly will not.'

'We won't be long,' Alexandra promised. 'I'll be back to help you with lunch.' Then, her conscience pricking her, she added: 'Why don't you come with us?'

Miss Holland's homely features broke into a wry smile at this. 'Wouldn't you be disappointed if I said yes?' she countered teasingly. But she shook her head as Alexandra started to protest. 'No, my dear, not this morning. I'm a little tired. I think I'll get my book and sit here for a while, in the sun.'

Because it was so hot, Alexandra unfastened the neck of her shirt and rolled the sleeves above her elbows as the horses followed the track along the riverbank. Her thin jeans were clinging to her slender legs, but without them her skin would have suffered, and the brim of her hat was pulled low to protect her face. With the bees humming in the long grass, and the birds swooping and diving over the water, a reluctant feeling of well-being gripped her, and she determinedly put all thoughts of death and disaster out of her mind.

But Manuel, riding ahead of her, saw her thoughtful expression and misread it: 'You do not have to worry about the *patrón*,' he declared, and she looked at him in surprise.

'I know that is why you are so interested in the capture of the prowler,' he continued, as she made an offhand gesture. 'But Señor Tarrant has been in much tighter corners, believe me.'

'What do you mean?'

Alexandra spurred her mount until she was riding along beside him and Manuel explained: 'Did you not know he was once a soldier?' And as she shook her head, he went on: 'He was a—how do you say it?—a mercenary, yes? A soldier who fights for any country who can pay him.'

'I know what a mercenary is,' exclaimed Alexandra shortly. 'I didn't know that. When was this?'

'Oh, some years ago, I think.'

'Before he met my father?'

'Excuse me, I do not know of your father,' said Manuel doubtfully. 'But this was some—fifteen years ago, I think.'

'But he must only have been twenty or twenty-one at that time!' she protested.

'So? A man is a man. Whether he is twenty-one or fifty-one, he can still fight.'

Alexandra urged the chestnut ahead, digesting this without enjoyment. Her father had had no love of mercenaries, seeing them as heartless fortune-hunters, merciless killers, without even the saving grace of patriotism to excuse their bloodlust. Of course, her father had been an idealist, and any kind of violence was anathema to him. But nevertheless she felt there was some truth in what he said.

'So ...' Manuel came alongside her again. 'Does that relieve your mind?'

'Not really.' Alexandra moved her shoulders doubtfully, but not wanting to discuss her feelings with him, she changed the subject. 'Tell me, when will you decide whether or not you're going to take that job in Brazil?'

They rode every day that week, sometimes with Miss Holland, sometimes not, and Alexandra began to look forward to their outings. Manuel was a much more entertaining companion than his father had been, but perhaps that was because he was younger—and he flattered her. She knew he did, and while she accepted that his compliments were outrageous, it was good to feel that at least *he* found her attractive. Her relationship with Jason remained as ambiguous as ever. Because of his apparent indifference to her association with Manuel, he never referred to it, and those infrequent occasions when weakness made her try to heal the gulf between them brought a curt response. Yet, in spite of his attitude towards her, and the distasteful knowledge that he had made the money to buy San Gabriel out of other men's suffering, she was still as infatuated with him as ever. It was useless trying to pretend otherwise. Manuel was only a stopgap, someone to divert her thoughts from the blacker moods that came to claim her, but she had no desire for him to make love to her. They were good friends, and she was grateful for his friendship, but only Jason could 'set her aflame', a phrase she no longer had any difficulty in understanding. She dreaded Estelita's reappearance with all the agony jealousy could evoke; but so far there had been no word as to when she would return.

The mountain lion was still eluding capture, which curtailed the scope of their expeditions, and in spite of what Manuel had told her, Alexandra still fretted about Jason's safety. A diet of fictional adventures had alerted her to the dangers of an unexpected encounter, and she was always relieved when she heard him come home in the evening.

One morning, Manuel didn't arrive at his usual time. Alexandra, hot from helping Miss Holland clear out the *salón*, had been down to the river to dip her hands in the cooling water, and Chan's appearance on her return warned her that something was wrong.

'Manuel will not be coming today, *señorita*,' he told her apologetically. 'His father—he has need of him. They are fencing the western boundary, and he asks that you will excuse him.'

Alexandra let her shoulders sag. 'I see.'

'I am sorry, *señorita*.' And he obviously was, his olive-skinned face mirroring his regret. 'But you understand, his work must come first.'

'Of course.' Alexandra tried not to let the cook see how disappointed she really was. 'I'll see him tomorrow.'

At this, Chan looked discomfited, however. 'Maybe not,' he volunteered awkwardly. 'The *patrón*—he said it might take—several days.'

'The *patrón* did?' Alexandra's lips tightened. She might have known Jason had had some hand in this. What was wrong? Did he think she and Manuel were getting too close? Did he think it was time to call a halt to their relationship? Was he afraid she might corrupt one of his *innocent gauchos*?

She was so hurt and angry, she had to turn her face away from Chan so that he should not see the tears of frustration in her eyes. Fencing the western boundary! she thought bitterly. As if he hadn't enough men to handle that sort of work!

Watching Chan hurrying back to the bunkhouse, Alexandra felt a surge of indignation. So her outings were over for the time being, were they? When would they be started again? she wondered. When Jason considered that a suitable time had elapsed? Or when they killed the mountain lion and Ricardo could be recruited again?

It was so unfair, she thought moodily, scuffing her toe against a pebble. She and Manuel hadn't done anything wrong. They hadn't ridden into the mountains, or behaved irresponsibly. At least, Manuel hadn't, she conceded, remembering that first occasion when she had tumbled off the horse's back. Still, even Miss Holland had been favourably impressed by Manuel's politeness, and his courtesy to her as the older woman, and there was no reason why Jason should have taken it into his head to spoil their friendship.

Glancing back towards the house, Alexandra felt unsettled and restless. The idea of spending the morning sunning herself on the verandah had no appeal, and she looked longingly towards the stables. Jave had already saddled the mare in readiness for her departure, and now she would have to go and tell him she was not riding after all. Or would she?

Pushing her hands into the pockets of her jeans, she pulled a mutinous face. Why should she miss the outing just because Manuel wasn't here to accompany her? She knew the trails they followed as well as he did, and so long as she didn't stray off the beaten track . . .

She took a couple of steps towards the house to tell Miss Holland she was leaving, and then hesitated. She guessed without a shadow of a doubt, that the older woman would forbid her to go out alone, and unless she disobeyed her, all ideas of independence would be shattered. And why should she tell her, after all? She was behaving like the child she was constantly accused of being. Miss Holland didn't expect her back until eleven. There was no reason why she should even discover that Manuel had not gone with her.

Only Jave put up some opposition to her intention of riding off alone. '*A donde va usted?*' he exclaimed anxiously, looking round for the young man who usually accompanied her. '*Donde está* Manuel?'

'It's all right, Jave,' exclaimed Alexandra, speaking in his language with careful precision. 'I—er—I'm meeting him by the river.'

'*Qué?*' Jave was not entirely convinced, but when he let go of the bridle, Alexandra didn't wait to enter into any argument. With a wave of her hand she cantered out of the yard, leaving the old man to stare after her with evident misgivings.

The river had subsided considerably from the flood there had been after the storm. Now it was possible to cross at a shallower point Manuel had shown her, her feet splashing in the cool water as the mare waded almost shoulder-deep. On the far bank, there were clumps of poppies and dog daisies, and some of the sweet-smelling verbena that Miss Holland put to good use in the house. The grass was deeper here, and the few cattle that grazed nearby paid little attention to her. Urging the chestnut up the gentle incline towards the few stunted bushes that bordered the trail worn by generations of hooves, Alexandra decided she quite liked the feeling that being alone gave her. She even permitted a few strains of a favourite tune to pass her lips, and a gurgle of excitement welled up inside her.

The trail wound between outcrops of granite and the skeletal ribs of trees that struggled to survive in the rocky subsoil. Far away to her right, the ridges of the higher plateau beckoned, but she had more sense than to give in to any adventurous impulses. The last thing she wanted was for Jason to discover what she had been doing. It would give her such a feeling of superiority, knowing she had outwitted him at last.

Then her shoulders sagged. That wasn't strictly true. She didn't really want to outwit him at all. Yet she knew she was not likely to claim his attention any other way. Only by defeating him at his own game was she likely to sustain any feeling of self-respect.

When she estimated she had come far enough, she climbed down from the mare's back, and tethering her to some bushes, she seated herself on a smooth stone from where she was able to view the whole length of the valley spread out below her. It was incredibly beautiful, and incredibly peaceful, and Alexandra felt a pang when she considered that in a few short months this would no longer be her home. Since Estelita's departure, she had deliberately avoided thoughts of that kind, but it was impossible not to believe that the Spanish woman had been right. And if Jason ever learned that she had been deceiving him all along . . .

Determinedly, she turned her thoughts to less disruptive matters. The previous evening Jason and Ricardo had been talking about the yearly round-up of the mares and their foals, and she had listened intently, wishing she might join them on the trail. But there would be no question of that, she knew. Jason would never trust her—*or himself*, she conceded dourly, realising that the intimacies of such a trip were such as he would want to avoid at all costs.

Depressed, she turned her head, and as she did so, she caught her breath. Standing on the track behind her, not ten yards away, was the black stallion. Her absorption in her thoughts had been such that she had not heard the drumming of his hooves, but now he had halted, nervously alert, aware of an intruder in his domain.

'Oh, you beauty!' breathed Alexandra huskily, rising slowly to her feet, and as she did so, the horse shifted sideways, its ears flattening against its head. 'Steady!' she whispered, half to herself as her fingers left the supporting warmth of the rock. 'I won't hurt you.'

The chestnut had lifted her head, and the stallion snorted, an arrogant sound, that echoed around the rocky slopes. Alexandra guessed it was the mare's scent he had followed, and she smiled as she considered what his thoughts must be at that moment. The mare made a protesting sound then, but as if sensing that here was one conquest he was not about to make, he turned, and with a whinny of annoyance, disappeared as abruptly as on those other occasions when she had seen him.

Hardly aware that she had been holding her breath, Alexandra allowed it to escape in a disappointed sigh. Just for a moment he had seemed to be responding to her tentative overtures, but then, with characteristic capriciousness, he had shown her exactly what he thought of her puny efforts.

Flopping back on to her rock, she plucked irritably at a blade of grass, catching it between her teeth, and chewing hard. Ricardo had said the horse was proud, and he was right. What were his exact words? *As proud as Lucifer!* She grimaced. Who could say for certain that Lucifer was proud? There wasn't much pride in being thrown out of heaven, was there? A fallen angel! She half smiled, as her irritation dispersed. That was what she would call him:

Fallen Angel. It was a title that fitted someone else she could mention . . .

The clatter of the mare's hooves on the stony track broke into her reverie. Jumping up in dismay, she saw that somehow the animal had broken loose from the bushes, and was presently making off along the track that the stallion had taken.

'Hey! You!' she yelled angrily, but the mare was far too intent on following the stallion's scent to pay any serious attention to her. 'Come back!' she commanded, but there was a futility to the words she uttered, and all of a sudden the idea of being alone had lost its charm.

It was miles back to the *hacienda*, and the thought of walking all that way filled her with alarm. Her shoes were strong and serviceable, but they were not boots, and Manuel had warned her often enough of the snakes that could still be found in the valley. Besides, the idea of crossing the river and getting soaked to the skin did not appeal to her, particularly as she could imagine Miss Holland's reactions if she came back dripping with water.

Even so, the idea of going after the mare was also a doubtful one. She had not forgotten the reason why Jason had forbidden them to ride into the canyons, and she would be courting disaster if she went on foot.

The sun, which until a few minutes ago had been deliciously warm on her shoulders, was suddenly uncomfortably hot, and not quite sure what she ought to do, she walked tentatively up to the point where she had seen the stallion. The clouds of dust still hanging in the air indicated clearly which way the mare had gone, and with a feeling of apprehension, Alexandra started after her. There was always the possibility that she might be waiting just around the bend in the trail, and remembering the lushness of some of the gullies, Alexandra quickened her step.

There was a grassy canyon, just beyond the ridge, and Alexandra thought she would never cease to marvel at the wonders of nature. Within this wall of rock and sandy topsoil was a green oasis, where a tumbling waterfall pointed the way to a sun-dappled pool. *A pool . . .*

Alexandra's tongue appeared momentarily to moisten her upper lip. How she longed to dip her face into its dark depths, and relieve the dryness of her throat with its pristine coolness. In her delight at finding the pool, she almost forgot her anxiety over losing the mare, but even though she looked all round there was no sign of her.

Time ceased to be of importance. She was going to be late anyway, so why worry over the few extra minutes it would take to scramble down the side of the ravine? If the mare was thwarted in her search for a mate, she might come back, and besides she was so thirsty . . .

The sides of the ravine were steeper than she had thought, and without the mare's sure-footed steps to guide her she slipped and slid most of the way on the seat of her pants. But at last she was standing beside the pool, stretching her hands into the falls, and it was only as she saw the scarlet stains colouring the water that she realised her palms were torn and bleeding. Pulling them back, she stared at them in dismay. They were a mass of cuts and abrasions, and they stung unbearably when the numbing influence of the water was withdrawn.

Turning her head, she gazed up the slope that she had just descended. With the first real twinges of panic, she wondered however she was going to climb back again. The sight of her hands had knocked her sick, and to imagine groping and grasping for holds on that scratchy face would be a daunting prospect at any time.

Ordering herself to remain calm, she made a careful survey of her position. She was standing just below the head of the ravine, where the pool formed a natural basin to catch the falls. Beyond, the waters spilled into a pebbly gully and ran away down the ravine, no doubt reaching the river in due course. *The river . . .*

Her heart quickened its beat. Of course, that was the answer. Sooner or later, the stream must reach the river, and water did not flow uphill. The distances involved no longer mattered. Just so long as she didn't have to use her hands to save herself.

If only she had brought some food with her, she thought unhappily. A bar of chocolate, or some fruit. Anything to ease the nauseous emptiness inside her, which was made more acute by her anxiety over the amount of blood she was losing. One of the cuts was quite deep, and although she bound it with her handkerchief, it still persisted in seeping through.

It was a little after noon when she reached the end of the ravine. The sun shimmering overhead had made mirages of the solid wall of rock that confronted her, and the pass she had expected to find was merely a dark chasm into which the bubbling waters of the stream disappeared.

She stared aghast at that narrow cleft, slippery with moss and overhung with creepers, realising that even if she could squeeze herself inside, she would be blind to the dangers within. She had no way of knowing what passage the stream would take through the rock. No surety of being able to make her way back again should the cleft become too narrow for her. This was a box canyon, a perfect spot for an ambush, and exactly the kind of place Jason had warned them to avoid.

She was tempted then to sit down and weep. It had taken over an hour to get this far and now to find it had all been wasted effort was almost too much. She looked down at her hands. They were trembling, but that was hardly surprising considering her whole body was quivering with exhaustion. Her handkerchief was soaked with blood, and on impulse she bent down and rinsed it in the sparkling water, wincing as she squeezed it out. At least, the cut looked clean, she thought ruefully, realising the amount of blood she had lost had disinfected the flesh, but it was still oozing, and she wished she had something dry to wind around it.

Hunched beside the stream, she felt the unfamiliar pangs of self-pity engulfing her. What if she couldn't make it back to the trail? she fretted. How would anyone know where to look for her? She scarcely noticed her acceptance of the fact that someone would have to come looking for her, and even the thought that it might be Jason no longer had any fears for her. But this area was honeycombed with canyons, Ricardo had told her that, and if they couldn't find the mountain lion, why should they have any more success with her?

A cold chill descended on her at this realisation. For the past hour or so, she had been so intent on discovering the way out of the ravine, she had almost forgotten why Jason had forbidden them to ride in the mountains. Now she glanced round apprehensively, half afraid she had inadvertently found the jaguar's lair.

But she was alone. Behind her the slopes of the ravine mocked the descent she had just made, its rugged contours shifting and shimmering in the noonday heat. She couldn't even see the waterfall from here, and her legs ached at the prospect of the walk ahead of her. It was no use delaying any longer, she realised. She was getting weaker all the time she was without food and although her hands had stopped bleeding, somehow she had to get out of this canyon before the sun set.

Stumbling and sometimes falling, she began the gentle ascent to the head of the ravine, stopping every now and then to rinse her handkerchief in the stream. She made slow progress, and all that kept her going was the knowledge that Miss Holland would be desperately worried about her. Jason might not yet know of her disappearance, and she guessed Miss Holland might mount a search party without telling him. She had not betrayed her before when she fell from her horse, and she knew as well as anyone that Alexandra would want to avoid his censure. She made a silent promise that if she came out of this alive, she would never disobey Miss Holland again.

Once, as she knelt beside the stream, she saw flecks of blood staining the grass. It was upsetting to think that she had made those stains on her way down the ravine, wasting all that energy in a futile quest. It was strange, too, that in spite of the blood she had lost, her pulse was still pounding through her temples, throbbing in her ears . . .

A sudden scattering of stones behind her brought her abruptly to her feet. One pebble bounced across the turf to land almost at her feet, and with a gasp of horror, she closed her eyes. In those petrifying seconds, she was convinced the mountain lion had found her, and although she opened her mouth to scream, no cry emerged.

'Alexandra!'

Even the sound of her own name was an unreal intrusion into her terror, and not until it was repeated, with an added imprecation to God to be given strength, did she open her eyes to see Jason striding across the grass towards her.

She thought at first she was hallucinating, but somehow the drawn pallor of his features convinced her that this was Jason as she had never seen him before. He was hatless, his hair rough and uncombed, his shirt open down his chest to the low belt of his Levis. He was advancing down the slope towards her, and looking beyond him, she saw his horse and that of Ricardo waiting at the head of the ravine with the burly foreman. That was what she had heard, she realised, the pounding she had thought was in her head . . .

'Jason!'

Now in no doubt as to his reality, she extended her hands towards him, stumbling forward eagerly, and as he swept her into his arms, she heard his agonised: 'God, I could kill you!'

CHAPTER TEN

WITH her tearful face pressed to the moist skin of his chest, she could think of nothing but the heaven of being in his arms again. It was so long since he had held her, so many days and nights when she had thought he hated her, but now she was where she wanted to be, where she belonged. It didn't matter that the urgent way he was holding her was more in anger than any other emotion. He had been concerned about her, his trembling flesh told her that, and the sweating heat of his body spoke of the anguish he had suffered. With his hand at her nape, his fingers moving almost involuntarily among the damp curls, he was making a supreme effort to control himself, but the fierce throbbing of his heart would not subside so obediently.

Alexandra, for her part, clung to his strength with an urgency born of the torments she had experienced, uncaring of the pain to her torn and bleeding hands. Her whole body surrendered to the closeness of his embrace, and she had no thought for anyone but herself and Jason. She loved him, she *needed* him, and she didn't care if he knew it.

As if sensing her feelings, Jason would have pulled back then, but as he drew away from her, saying harshly: 'How much of this do you think I can take?' he saw the blood that stained his chest and smeared the clinging fabric of her shirt. His features contorting, he grasped her wrists, turning up the palms for him to see, and then caught his breath on a tortured groan.

'Oh, God!' he muttered, in a strange voice. 'So that's where it came from!' He bent his head to press his lips to her disfigured palms, his tongue gentle against the mutilated flesh. 'We—that is, Ricardo and I—found some blood on the rocks, up there.' He glanced impatiently up the ravine. 'We thought—God! we didn't know what to think.' He shook his head in painful remembrance. 'Alexandra, Alexandra, what am I going to do with you?'

Her eyes clung to the beloved contours of his face. 'Wh-what do you want to do with me?' she whispered, and his eyes closed over the torment that was mirrored there.

'Don't ask,' he muttered huskily, but when he opened his eyes again, the uncertainty in her face tore away his last vestiges of control. 'Oh, Alexandra . . .' The words were wrung from him, and this time when he jerked her close, his mouth sought hers.

There was no thought of restraint. The agonies they had both gone through had sharpened their senses, and they kissed with a desperate passion. Repressions and inhibitions were swept away by the urgency of a hunger long denied, and the swelling hardness of Jason's body left her in no doubt as to the effect she was having on him.

'When you didn't come back——' he got out thickly, his hand sliding into the neckline of her shirt to probe the rounded fullness of her breast. 'Have you any idea how I felt?'

'I'm sorry, I'm sorry,' she breathed, his caresses almost stopping the breath in her throat. 'I didn't want to worry anyone, but the mare ran away, and I didn't know what to do . . .'

'*You* didn't know what to do!' he said dementedly, cradling her hands against him. 'God, I nearly went out of my mind!'

Alexandra looked up at him eagerly, lips parting in unconscious appeal. 'I—I thought you'd be so angry——'

'*Angry!*' He made a sound of frustration. 'Angry doesn't describe my feelings at that moment. I just wished I had you in my hands——'

'Like this?'

'No, not like this,' he groaned, his half-closed lids shadowing the desire that burned in his eyes. 'I wanted to shake you—or strangle you! Anything to prevent you from —destroying me!'

She gulped. 'What do you mean?'

'Oh, Alexandra!' Shielding her with his body, he turned to glance up to where Ricardo was watching, waiting ... 'I've tried to ignore you, but I can't. I've tried to make you hate me, but it doesn't seem to have worked very well, does it?'

'I love you, Jason.'

'You think you do,' he retorted quellingly. With a determined effort, he pulled her shirt over her shoulders and fastened the buttons. 'You're too young to know what you want, Alexandra——'

'I'm almost eighteen.'

'Almost eighteen,' he echoed grimly. 'Alexandra, eighteen is no age at all. You've done nothing yet, you've seen nothing of life. Living in a convent all those years! It wouldn't be—fair for me to do what—what my instincts tell me to do.'

'Which is?' she exclaimed breathlessly, but he shook his head.

'That night,' he murmured, smoothing her hair back from her damp forehead with slightly unsteady hands, 'that night you came to my room, I would have made love to you, you know that, don't you?' She nodded, and he went on: 'I couldn't have stopped myself. I knew what I was doing was wrong, but you were there, in my bed, and I wanted you ...'

'Then take me!' she pleaded urgently, but he shook his head as he continued:

'Miss Holland breaking it up like that was a blessed reprieve——'

'For you!'

'No, for you,' he contradicted her gently. 'If—if we had slept together, I don't think I would have the strength to let you go——'

'To let me go!' she echoed painfully, and his hands descended on her shoulders as she took an involuntary step back from him.

'Listen to me!' he urged tensely, and she was compelled to do so, albeit reluctantly. 'As I said before, you're too young! Me, I'm almost twenty years older. I've been around. I've seen something of the world—of life. I've even been married, although that was over long ago.'

That was a shock, and her lips trembled as she enquired tautly: 'Was that before or after you were a mercenary?' and his mouth turned down at the corners.

'Who told you that, I wonder?' he demanded. 'I can guess, of course. It was Manuel, wasn't it? Idealistic Manuel, with his youth, and his good looks, and his charm—and his irritatingly candid admiration for you!'

His words were harshly spoken and suddenly Alexandra thought she understood. 'You were jealous,' she said, only half believing it even then. 'Jason, you were jealous of Manuel!'

His grim features revealed a faint trace of self-derision. 'Yes,' he agreed, but there was no joy in the admission. 'Crazy, isn't it? A man of my age jealous of a girl scarcely out of the schoolroom!'

'Oh, Jason!' With a sob, she wound her arms around his neck again, laughing and crying together as relief bubbled up inside her. 'You don't have to be jealous of anyone, don't you know that? I don't care about Manuel. I love *you*! Only you.' She shook her head helplessly. 'Hold me,' she pleaded. 'Just hold me. I can't bear it when you turn me away.'

His arms came round her unwillingly at first, but the feel of her slim body straining against his was more than he could withstand. He could hear Ricardo shifting his feet impatiently on the ridge behind them, his spurs jingling audibly in the echoing reaches of the canyon; but the need to feel that warm mouth beneath his again overcame his scruples, and he knew that without Ricardo's presence he would have lost his head completely. As it was, the urgent demands of his own body drove him to part from her, the ache in his loins too painful to sustain.

'What am I going to do?' he groaned, dragging himself away to stare down at her with smouldering eyes. 'I can't let you stay here, feeling as I do. It would only be a matter of time before I——' He broke off abruptly, raking restless fingers through his hair, but his meaning was clear. 'There is only one solution, and I guess I've known it all along. I've got to send you back to England.'

'*No*——'

'Yes.' His firm submission overrode her horrified denial. 'It's all I can do—for my own sanity!'

She stared at him in hurt incredulity, and he shook her with gentle insistence. 'Don't look like that. It's not the end of the world. I'm not abrogating my responsibilities—I just think it would be the best thing—for both of us. A breathing spell, if you like. It needn't last for ever.'

'What do you mean?' Alexandra sniffed. 'You know that once I'm eighteen, your responsibility for me is at an end.'

'You think so?' His eyes darkened with emotion. 'You really think that your having a birthday is going to make that much difference to our relationship?'

'I—well, you can't go on supporting me after—after I'm of age.'

'Why not?'

'Because—oh, because you can't.' Alexandra bent her head, realising suddenly how fragile their relationship was. 'You know I'll have to get a job——'

'A job!' He made an impatient sound. 'You really think that your being eighteen cuts the ties between us? Dear God, have I said that? Have I given that impression?' He cast a resigned look in the foreman's direction. 'We can't talk here any longer. I've already condemned myself in Ricardo's eyes by touching you at all, and——'

'Condemned yourself?' Alexandra lifted her head to see the wry self-mockery that twisted his features.

'Yes.' He sighed. 'Ricardo's a religious man, although you may not have guessed it from the way he behaves sometimes. But he considers I'm too old for you, too, and he thought he'd found the perfect solution . . .'

Alexandra's tongue appeared. 'Then it was *his* idea . . .'

'. . . to substitute Manuel, yes.' Jason gripped her wrists as she would have moved closer to him. 'It was a good idea. Unfortunately, I couldn't take it.' His eyes dropped possessively down the length of her body. 'Maybe he'd have more sympathy if he knew what you do to me.'

'Oh, Jason!'

'Stay away from me, Alexandra,' he groaned, raising her palms to his lips once more. 'Don't make me despise myself any more than I do already.'

With an arm around her waist, Jason helped her up the rough incline to where Ricardo was waiting. His boots were firm on the shifting scree, and he dragged them up with clumps of turf until they were standing on the sandy track at the top of the ravine. Looking back, Alexandra shivered, but then Ricardo claimed her attention.

'What happened?' he demanded, and there was disapproval in every line of his bulky body.

Jason sighed again, taking hold of his horse's bridle. 'The mare made off,' he answered, and Alexandra realised her explanation had been far too brief for the length of time Jason had spent with her.

'I—I saw the stallion,' she offered, glancing awkwardly at her guardian. 'I'd dismounted for a rest and I guess I didn't tether the mare very securely.'

'Hah!' Ricardo snorted. 'If Manuel had been with you——'

'But he wasn't,' said Jason, and there was a hard quality in his voice that brooked no argument. Then he turned to Alexandra and indicated his mount. 'Come on. We'd better get back before Miss Holland has hysterics.'

'You did not seem so concerned for her welfare some minutes ago,' observed Ricardo caustically, and when Jason ignored him, he went on: 'What were you doing in the ravine, *señorita*? When we found the blood, we thought we had found——'

He broke off abruptly at that point, but Alexandra, now astride Jason's horse, turned to look at him. 'What did you think you'd found, Ricardo? The wounded mountain lion? Oh, yes——' this as Jason sucked in his breath in angry disbelief, 'I know about the prowler.'

'Then in God's name why did you go into the ravine?' snapped Jason, suddenly angry, swinging himself up behind her so that his hard thighs dug into her back. 'Who told you? Manuel, again? He should learn to keep his mouth shut.'

Even Ricardo looked sheepish at this, and Alexandra hastened on: 'It wasn't truly his fault. It just—slipped out.'

'Really?' Jason did not sound convinced, but he dug in his knees to urge the horse forward and Alexandra gave herself up to the pleasures evoked by the movement of his body behind her. They rode ahead of Ricardo out of the ravine, and as they did so, she saw the trail the mare must have taken snaking away around its rim.

Resting her head back against Jason's shoulder, she murmured softly: 'You're not really angry with me, are you? I didn't mean to worry anyone. I just wanted to—to——'

'—thwart me,' he finished huskily, his hand sliding over her midriff to the swelling mound of her breast. 'I'm not a fool, Alexandra.'

Her breath caught in her throat at his caresses, but she had to go on. 'I thought you despised me. I thought you stopped Manuel riding with me because you thought he might be—corrupted by my company.'

'Oh, God!' He bent his head to inhale the fragrance of her hair, and she felt his lips against her nape. 'If you only knew how I felt when you and Ricardo discussed those trips in the evening . . .'

Alexandra relaxed against him. 'Then you're not going to

send me away?' she breathed, but immediately, he stiffened.

'Six months,' he said, and her stomach contracted. 'Six months is a reasonable period. It will give you time to get things into perspective.'

'It will give you time, you mean!' she blurted hotly, and his fingers bruised the soft skin of her breast.

'No,' he contradicted savagely. 'I know what I want. But I respect your father's memory too much to abuse the trust he placed in me.'

Alexandra's hands clenched painfully. Now she should tell him the truth. Now she should reveal exactly how little trust her father had placed in him. But she couldn't. She couldn't!

'Miss Holland shall go with you,' he was continuing relentlessly. 'It will be winter here soon, but it's spring in England. Go to England, Alexandra. Have the summer to think it over. Come back to me at the end of the year, if you still want to.'

'If I still want to . . .' she whispered tearfully. 'Oh, Jason, you can't do this!'

'I assure you, I can,' he affirmed, and there was an implacability about him that separated them even as they rode together.

As if sensing it was now acceptable for him to ride with them, Ricardo came alongside at that moment, saying crisply: 'What a welcome home Estelita has had, *no*? Still, it is as well she is there to comfort the old one.'

With Jason's hand shifting to grip the pommel, he did not feel the retching upheaval of Alexandra's stomach, and she strove desperately for control. Until then it had not occurred to her to wonder how Jason had discovered she was missing, but with Ricardo's words she had her answer. When he left that morning, it had not been to go out with the men as she had imagined. He must have driven to Valvedra to fetch Estelita.

As if annoyed with the foreman for blurting it out like that, Jason explained quietly: 'Estelita's mother is making good progress. She sent a message yesterday, via the doctor at Puerto Novo, that she was ready to come home.'

To come home! The words tore into Alexandra's already shattered defences, ripping her to shreds with their intimate intonation. Home! Estelita's home. But not hers. *Never hers!* He was sending her away, just as Estelita came back, and the implications were impossible to avoid. She was almost glad when she saw the *hacienda* ahead of them, and when Miss Holland ran to meet them she wrenched herself away from Jason and down from his horse's back, to throw herself into the older woman's arms.

There were reproaches, of course, and recriminations, but the injuries to her hands were such that not even Miss Holland could remain immune from their vulnerability. Instead, she whisked Alexandra upstairs with the minimum of preliminaries, leaving Jason and Ricardo to explain what had happened.

But in the bathroom, with the door locked securely behind them, she gave vent to her feelings.

'You could have died!' she exclaimed, fussing over the cuts and scratches on her palms. 'You knew how I would feel if I discovered where you had gone, but you didn't care.'

'I did care,' protested Alexandra tremulously. 'Only—only——'

'Only you had to show Mr Tarrant how independent you were!' finished Miss Holland tersely. 'Oh, Alexandra! You should have heard the language he used to me when he discovered you were missing!'

Despite her misery, Alexandra couldn't help the sudden sense of excitement at Miss Holland's words. 'Why?' she cried. 'What did he say? Was that after he brought Estelita back?'

'He didn't bring Señora Vargas back,' retorted Miss Holland, dabbing at her hands tenderly with a swab of cotton wool, but Alexandra hardly felt the pain.

'He didn't?' she probed. 'Then who——'

'Señor Goya,' replied the older woman, concentrating on

her task. 'Mr Tarrant came home to take you riding. When he discovered you had gone, he was frantic. That was when Señora Vargas walked in.'

'Jason was going to take me riding,' echoed Alexandra faintly, closing her eyes against the images that evoked. 'Oh, Miss Holland! If only I'd known. If only I'd known!'

'Yes, well——' Miss Holland pursed her lips as she pulled another swab of cotton wool from the roll. 'You should know by now that Mr Tarrant goes to a lot of trouble on your account. It can't be easy for him. I know that.'

Alexandra licked her lips before taking her courage into her hands, and murmuring: 'What would you say if I told you—I was in love with him?'

There was silence for a few moments as Miss Holland sought for a tube of antiseptic ointment. Then, unwinding a sterilised bandage, she said: 'I would say that I guessed something was going on.' Her grey eyes were shrewd. 'Have you slept with him?'

Alexandra was flabbergasted. She had never expected the older woman to be so forthright. 'I—no. No, I haven't,' she admitted. 'He—thinks I'm too young.'

'He could be right,' remarked Miss Holland dryly, and then as Alexandra started to protest, she added: 'So? What does he intend to do about it?'

Alexandra hunched her shoulders. 'He wants me to go back to England—for six months.'

'Six months?' Miss Holland raised her eyebrows. 'An excellent suggestion, I should think.'

'An excellent suggestion?' cried Alexandra painfully. 'It's a terrible suggestion. He doesn't think I'll come back, that's what it is. He thinks that once I get to London I'll forget all about him.'

'You might,' said Miss Holland practically, applying the ointment to the bandage before winding it about her palm. But as the girl stared at her with tears in her eyes, she added: 'Then again, you might not. I take it he feels the same way?'

Alexandra hung her head. 'I—don't know.'

'Oh, come on. You must.'

'No.' She sniffed. 'He—he wants me, I know that. I think he needs me. But—love . . .' She shrugged helplessly. 'He's never said he loved me.'

Miss Holland nodded. 'I see.' She smoothed the bandage with expert care. 'But you must remember, Alexandra, it's harder for a man like him to admit to such a thing. I mean, he's not a boy. I hope you realise that.'

Alexandra's lips quivered. 'You sound so—experienced. Yet you've never married.'

'No.' Miss Holland applied herself to her task for a few taut minutes. Then she looked up. 'What would you say if I told you that the reason I never married was because the man I loved already had a wife?'

Alexandra gasped. 'Is that true?'

'As a matter of fact, yes.' Miss Holland reached for a second bandage. 'Like Mr Tarrant, he was a lot older than I was, but I wouldn't have had it any other way.'

'Did he love you?'

Miss Holland's smile was rueful. 'He said he did. And I think perhaps it was true, in a way. But he loved his reputation more.'

'Lord Carleon?' exclaimed Alexandra disbelievingly, and the faint colour that ran up Miss Holland's face was enough. 'Oh, Miss Holland! I'm so sorry.'

'Don't be.' Her companion was philosophical. 'It was all over years ago. Charles is almost eighty now, much too old to entertain those kind of fancies.'

'And did you—did you——'

Alexandra found she couldn't voice the words, but Miss Holland answered anyway. 'Did we have an affair?' she asked, and smiled. 'I suppose really I shouldn't tell you, should I?' She paused, and then seeing the girl's anxious face, she relented. 'We had a relationship,' she conceded. 'I'm not saying it was anything like the relationship you are having with Mr Tarrant. I didn't go around in skin-tight trousers or a shirt that exposed every curve of my bosom, but I did allow him to kiss me, and once we even went swimming together.'

'Would you—would you have married him if you could?'

'If he'd asked me,' agreed Miss Holland, with a sigh.

'Jason was married. He told me. But that was over a long time ago, too.'

Miss Holland completed her task and surveyed her handiwork critically. 'There, that should do,' she said, and Alexandra looked down at her bandaged hands.

'I look like a mummy,' she protested, depression at the remembrance of Estelita waiting downstairs overtaking her again. Then: 'What should I do?'

'What can you do?' retorted Miss Holland crisply. 'Do as he says. Go to England. Spend the summer there. If you love him, you'll come back, and if he loves you, he'll be waiting for you.'

'But what if he's not?'

Miss Holland shrugged. 'Isn't it better to know?' she asked, and Alexandra had to concede that she was probably right.

Alexandra didn't want any lunch, and spent the afternoon lying on her bed. She felt sick and disorientated, and even the news that Jason had gone to fetch the doctor from Puerto Novo to see her could not arouse her from her apathy.

Miss Holland brought the doctor up in the late afternoon. He smiled when he saw his patient and said half impatiently: 'If you do not care for yourself, *señorita*, perhaps you should care for the people who care for you. Señor Tarrant is most anxious about you. Did you lose a lot of blood?'

Alexandra twisted restively on the bed. 'Not a lot, no,' she replied, resenting his reproving tones. 'There was really no need for you to come, *señor*. Miss Holland has dealt with my injuries quite satisfactorily.'

The smile he cast in Miss Holland's direction was the

tolerant one exchanged between adults when a child is being unnecessarily fractious. 'Fortunately, Miss Holland understands the dangers of wounds of this kind,' he remarked. 'Tetanus is still an extremely dangerous disease, *señorita*. You would do well to remember that.'

The injection that followed was not pleasant, and Alexandra was left feeling helplessly near to tears. What was Jason doing now? she wondered. Would she see him again today? Or was she doomed to suffer Estelita's supercilious contempt while he drove the doctor back to Puerto Novo?

She was loath to go down for supper, but a determination to show the housekeeper she was not completely helpless made her bath and change into black culottes and a loose-fitting smock of black lace. She had never worn the outfit before, always secretly considering it too old for her, but tonight she felt she needed some defence.

However, when she came down the stairs, she found Jason standing in the hall. He was staring out into the blackness beyond the door, hands folded behind his back, and with a fast-beating heart she went to slide her bandaged palm into his.

Immediately he swung round, staring down at her intently, encasing her hands within the cool strength of his. 'Well?' he said, and there was more than anxiety about her health in his query. 'How do you feel?'

'Sore,' she answered at once, looking down at their hands entwined together. 'How about you?'

He didn't answer that, but asked instead: 'Was Miss Holland very angry?'

'She was more concerned with what you had said to her,' replied Alexandra unsteadily. 'I—I—you didn't tell me that Estelita was coming back today.'

'I was going to tell you this morning,' he answered. 'Did Miss Holland not tell you that I came back to take you riding myself?'

'Yes.' She darted a look up at him. 'I'm sorry, Jason. Oh, I always seem to be saying that to you.'

'Don't you?' he agreed. Then: 'Your hands—they're going to be all right?'

'Of course. They're not seriously injured,' she exclaimed, half impatiently. 'Jason—about going to England?'

'Yes.'

He released her hands then, thrusting his into his pockets, exposing the bulging muscles of his thighs. For a moment she gave herself the pleasure of just looking at him, and then his darkening expression forced her to go on.

'If—if that's what you really want me to do,' she got out jerkily, 'I—I'll do it.'

'I see.' There was a pregnant silence, and then he added curtly: 'Do I have Miss Holland to thank for this?'

It was almost as if he was disappointed with her submission. Alexandra stared up at him bewilderedly, trying to read the dark nuances of his expression, and then a voice she knew she would never be able to forget said silkily:

'Ah, the *señorita* is feeling better, no? How good it is to see you recovered, Miss Durham. I should not have liked you to miss supper on my first night home.'

They ate one of Estelita's meals—a stew of meat and vegetables, flavoured in the way she liked it. No mention was made of the scouring and cleaning which had gone on in her absence, and with a pang Alexandra realised that in the space of a day things had returned to normal. Except that Pepe was not with them. He had remained behind in Valvedra, with his mother, and would not be returning.

After Miss Holland's cooking, Estelita's left much to be desired, and Alexandra pretended it was this which closed her throat and left her feeling sick and miserable. But the truth was that the thought of leaving Jason was like a cancer inside her, eating away her emotions and leaving her weak and vulnerable. How could she contemplate six whole months without seeing him, without speaking to him, without being near him? It was an agonising prospect, and one which drove her constantly to seek his face, to imprint every angle of his features on her subconscious mind, so that when she looked away she could still see him.

Jason looked at her, too. She was not unaware of that, and when their eyes met, her stomach twisted with a feeling, half pain, half ecstasy. Then Estelita spoke, and when he turned to look at her Alexandra could have scratched her eyes out. Would Estelita still be here if she came back at the end of the year? she wondered despairingly. And if she was, what then?

When supper was over, Ricardo asked if he could speak to his employer, and with some reluctance Jason went with the foreman, leaving Alexandra alone with Estelita. Miss Holland had already gone into the *salón* to set out the chess pieces for later, and Alexandra was pushing back her chair, preparatory to leaving the table, when Estelita pulled a letter out of her blouse and threw it across to her.

'Here,' she said. 'I collected Jason's mail before leaving Valvedra. I thought this one might be of some interest to you.'

'To me?' Alexandra turned the parchment envelope over in her fingers. 'Why should it—*oh*!'

She broke off abruptly as she recognised the small neat handwriting, but its precise quality was unmistakable, as was the plain convent envelope.

'I see you know where this letter comes from,' observed Estelita slyly. 'Perhaps you wonder why the convent at Sainte Sœur should be writing to your guardian, *no*?'

Alexandra frowned. 'How do you know where it's from?' she exclaimed. 'The letter's addressed to Jason, and it's sealed. You—you opened it!'

'You should be thankful that I did, *señorita*,' retorted Estelita coldly. 'For I know what is inside it, and I am sure Jason would be very interested to hear that your father wanted you to return to the convent when he died.'

Alexandra blanched. 'What do you mean?'

'I mean, *señorita*, that the good sisters at the convent know nothing of any plans to put you in Jason's care.'

Forcing herself to remain calm, Alexandra defended herself. 'Why should they?' she countered. 'They were not involved——'

'Oh, but they were, *señorita*.' Estelita's face had taken on the grotesque quality of a mask. 'You see, your father telephoned the good sisters only two days—*two days*—before he died, telling them of his wishes, advising them that his solicitors would be in touch with them.'

Alexandra was trembling now, but she dared not let Estelita see how shocked she was. 'I don't believe you,' she said jerkily. 'Why should I believe you?'

'Why should I lie?' retorted Estelita contemptuously. 'Open the letter for yourself. See what is written in it.'

Alexandra shook her head, turning the envelope over in her fingers. 'It's addressed to Jason.'

'Yes, it is,' Estelita nodded. 'And can you imagine what his reactions will be when he reads it? When he learns that *you* tricked him. Oh, yes, *señorita*, I have had time to work it all out. *You* wrote the letter to the solicitors which purported to have come from your father. *You* made Jason your guardian. Why, I wonder? You had never met him. Were you so desperate for a man, *señorita*?'

Alexandra's chair thudded on to the floor behind her as she sprang to her feet. 'Don't you dare say such a thing to me!' she declared tremulously. 'You wouldn't understand. You wouldn't understand in a million years!'

Estelita sneered, 'You think Jason will?'

Alexandra trembled. 'I don't know ...' She said the words almost inaudibly, as much to herself as anyone else.

'Then I will tell you, *he won't*!' declared Estelita coldly. 'No man likes to be made a fool of, particularly by a slip of a girl young enough to be his daughter!'

Alexandra put a hand to her head. It was swimming, and she wondered if the antibiotic the doctor had given her was responsible for her dizziness. Or perhaps it was because she had had nothing to eat all day. Whatever, she felt sick and confused, and Estelita was only voicing what she had feared all along.

'Why—why did you show me this letter?' Alexandra asked now, supporting herself against the table. 'Why haven't you given it to Jason?'

Estelita rose now. 'I had my reasons.' She placed the palms of her hands squarely on the table. 'I want you to leave here, *señorita*. And I do not care what methods I have to use to achieve that objective.'

'I don't—understand——'

'I will explain.' Estelita was very much the mistress of the situation at that moment. 'As I have said, Jason would not like to think you had made a fool of him. Can you imagine how he would feel if the men—the *gauchos*—learned that you had tricked your way into his house? He would be—how do you say?—a laughing stock, *no*? Do you think he would like that?'

'No!'

'No. So I think to myself, there is no reason why he should see the letter, why *anyone* should see the letter, but our two selves. If you agree to leave without fuss, I will destroy it, and you can explain the situation to the nuns after you have returned to England.'

'You mean—you're blackmailing me?' Alexandra had to get this straight. 'If—if I don't agree to leave, you'll make this letter public?' She caught her breath on a sob. 'Aren't you afraid of what Jason will say when he learns you've been reading his mail?'

Estelita shrugged. 'So—he is angry! So what? He needs me here. He is not likely to dismiss me because of a little thing like that, is he?'

Alexandra pressed her lips together to hide their trembling. 'What—what if Jason won't let me go?'

Estelita's mouth thinned to an ugly red line. 'I saw the blood on his clothes today, *señorita*. I know what you have been trying to do while I have been away. But I also know what you said to him in the hall before supper, and I do not think he will stand in your way.'

Alexandra pressed a hand to her stomach. 'You think you

have all the answers, don't you? But—but what will you do if I come back?'

'My—*husband* and I will always welcome guests into our home,' retorted Estelita mockingly, and Alexandra gasped. 'Oh, yes, he will marry me, *señorita*,' she added. 'Even if I have to become pregnant to force his hand.' Her lips curved sensuously. 'He is so careless about these things, you know. He relies on me entirely. You understand?'

Alexandra understood. She understood only too well, and the knowledge almost robbed her of the strength to leave the room. But somehow she had to get away—away from Estelita, away from San Gabriel, and most important of all, away from Jason . . .

CHAPTER ELEVEN

The furnished house Miss Holland had leased was in a fashionably attractive square in Belgravia. Tall and narrow, its Georgian façade stretching skywards, it was more grand than anything Alexandra had expected, but her companion had told her that Jason had insisted on their being comfortable. Area steps to the side of the door led down to a basement flat occupied by the housekeeper and her husband, and Mrs Beesley, as the housekeeper was called, kept everywhere in spotless order. The house was really too big for two women living alone, but Miss Holland said that flats were soulless places, and she at least appreciated its luxury.

Alexandra showed little interest in her surroundings. She had shown little interest in anything since their departure from South America, and spent most of that first week with her face buried in a book. There was a comprehensive library at the house in Mountsey Square, and in those early days she spent most of her time there, despite Miss Holland's admonitions to get out into the watery spring sunlight.

Since that terrible scene with Estelita, she had had plenty of time to think, and her thoughts were not pleasant. Too often she was brought back to the conclusion that Jason's prime objective in persuading her to leave was because of the housekeeper. He had been attracted to her, it was true, and during Estelita's absence his natural appetites had not been appeased. That was why he had turned to her, why she had found it easier to arouse him. But once he knew Estelita was coming back, he had realised he could not satisfy two women without one of them becoming jealous. That was when he had decided that Alexandra must leave. All that talk about his not being able to keep her feeling as he did, his protestations of wanting only the best for her, and the need for her to get things into perspective, had all been a blind, a clever ruse to persuade her to do what he wanted. He had known that once he got her out of the valley, she would not return uninvited, and in the meantime, Estelita had her own plans for the master of San Gabriel.

Things had moved quickly once Alexandra had agreed to go. She was never quite sure who arranged that they should leave at the end of that week, but Jason seemed curiously indifferent to the whole situation. It was Estelita who relayed that a flight had been booked for them on the Friday morning, and it was arranged that Ricardo should drive them to Valvedra.

On Thursday evening, Jason asked Miss Holland if he could have a few words with her in his study once supper was over. Alexandra, who had half hoped he would include her in the invitation, was left to face the unpalatable realisation that so far as Jason was concerned she was still a child, and as such, not worthy of inclusion in their discussions. She guessed he was giving Miss Holland instructions for their journey, and that lady's later revelations that they were to spend the first few days at an hotel while she looked for a suitable house to lease confirmed this assumption. Alexandra went to bed without seeing Jason again, and the first painful seeds of distrust were sown.

Although she hardly slept that night, first light found her down at the stables, saying goodbye to Jave. She bestowed a tearful kiss on his gnarled cheek before bidding farewell to Placida, the little mare who had so patiently borne her first stumbling efforts. She couldn't say goodbye to the chestnut mare. She had not returned, and she hoped with all her heart she would not fall victim to the jaguar, who still ran free somewhere in the mountains.

Her farewell to Jason was a stilted affair. He appeared as she was having breakfast, and seemed irritated to find her already at the table. Perhaps he had hoped she would break down, she thought maliciously, cloaking her vulnerability in a shell of indifference. Well, she wouldn't. She would not give him that satisfaction.

Instead, after Ricardo had loaded their cases into the Range-Rover and Miss Holland had said her goodbyes, Alexandra held out her hand for Jason to shake, and saw the kindling anger in his eyes. It was as if they were strangers, she thought, unfriendly strangers, wary of further contact.

But short of causing a scene, there was little he could do, she realised that. She realised, too, that he had probably expected to kiss her goodbye. He had enjoyed kissing her—he had made no secret of that fact. And she was glad of the little victory her coldness afforded. But once aboard the Boeing that lifted off the airport at Valvedra, she locked herself in the toilet and gave in to the weakness of tears.

To begin with, she had cried a lot, usually into the secrecy of her own pillow, and her face grew pale and drawn. But gradually her vulnerability gave way to a certain hardness, a cynical contempt for her own immaturity, that gave her the strength to go on. Jason had been an experience, she told herself coldly. Her *first* experience—and the one and only time she would give her heart to anyone.

This decided, she gave herself up to a determined effort to enjoy life again, but by the end of her first month at Mountsey Square, she knew she was bored. Miss Holland's outings to museums and theatres bored her, as too did the prospect of spending the rest of her life searching for artificial pleasures. She had never been used to needing entertainment on the grand scale. At the convent, she had had to amuse herself, and her thoughts had never been a trouble to her as they were now. It was frightening to realise that what she was really trying to do was fill her days so that she would have no time to think, and that was no life at all.

But she hated London, with its close, narrow streets and

noisy traffic. It gave her a feeling of claustrophobia, and she yearned for the open spaces of the *pampa*, and the feel of the mare's strong muscles between her thighs. It took her some time to realise it, but gradually it came to her that what was really happening was that like the recurrence of some awful disease, she was having a second attack of homesickness for San Gabriel, and Jason. It was useless telling herself she hated him. The longer they were apart, the harder it became to put him out of her mind. And no matter how he had treated her, she would never forget him.

That was when she decided she would have to get a job. But what? A discussion with Miss Holland was not satisfactory, since that lady proffered the belief that Alexandra should give herself more time before rushing into anything so binding as a career. Wait until the end of the summer, she said, knowing nothing of that terrible scene Alexandra had shared with Estelita. What had happened to her determination to return to South America? Was she already regretting that decision, or had she some other plan in mind?

Alexandra put her off with vague excuses that she was not happy doing nothing, that she would prefer to be occupied, and hoped that sooner or later it would filter through to the older woman that all was not as straightforward as it had at first seemed. It was too soon to talk about her future, she averred, realising as she did so that Miss Holland would probably think she had changed her mind, and put it down to her extreme youth.

The six-months lease on the house had been paid by Jason, but Alexandra decided that as soon as she had regular employment, she would suggest to Miss Holland that they moved into a flat of her choosing. She realised that Jason was paying Miss Holland's salary, and she couldn't be absolutely sure what that lady would do once Alexandra broke free of her guardian, and for the present she had to accept his largesse. But she still had the nest-egg provided by the sale of her father's house, and surely that would provide enough funds to furnish a small apartment when the need arose.

She said none of this to Miss Holland, however. The older woman was enjoying a well-earned rest, revisiting all her old haunts and meeting up with old friends. After her strenuous stint at the *hacienda*, she deserved a break, and there was no point in worrying her unnecessarily.

During those early weeks Alexandra had visited her father's solicitors and cleared up the matter of her father's letter. She crossed her fingers as she maintained that he must have forgotten having written to Jason, and as she was obviously fit and well cared for, the elderly solicitor was more than willing to let the matter drop. He would write to the convent, he promised, and she left his office feeling an overwhelming sense of relief.

It wasn't easy finding a job, however, without either references or qualifications. Office jobs all needed good passes in English and an ability for typewriting which Alexandra did not possess, and the more menial type of post paid such low wages. She realised if she wanted to earn a salary suitable to maintain a reasonable standard of living, she would have to go back to school and take examinations, and while she was willing to do this, there were no courses starting again until September.

In consequence, she eventually accepted a job as a waitress in a coffee bar in Chelsea. It wasn't a very fashionable coffee bar, and it was owned by a rather sleazy-looking Greek called Stefanos, but at least it meant she had somewhere to go through the long daylight hours.

Miss Holland was horrified. She had never dreamt Alexandra would go through with actually taking such a job, and her disapproval was more than eloquent.

'How do you think I feel, knowing you're working in that dreadful place?' she protested. 'What will Mr Tarrant think when he finds out I'm living here in the lap of luxury, while you're spending every day in that unhealthy atmosphere?'

'I really don't care what Mr Tarrant thinks,' Alexandra retorted tautly, adding cream to the coffee Mrs Beesley had served after dinner that evening. 'As—as a matter of fact, I'd rather you didn't tell him.'

She knew Miss Holland was obliged to write a weekly report to her employer, and she had often wondered what she found to write about, but in this instance she would rather her affairs remained private.

'I don't understand you,' exclaimed Miss Holland now, shaking her head. 'Less than two months ago, you told me you loved him, and now, here you are, taking a job you know he wouldn't approve of, and asking me not to tell him!'

Alexandra heaved a sigh. 'Yes, well—I've been meaning to tell you about that,' she mumbled unwillingly. 'I—Jason and I—we're washed up—finished. You know—it's all over.'

'All over?'

Miss Holland stared at her disbelievingly, and Alexandra closed her eyes against the astonishment in her expression. 'Yes,' she insisted, pressing a hand to her churning stomach. 'I've wanted to tell you for some time, but—well, you know how it is.'

'No, I don't know how it is,' retorted Miss Holland impatiently. 'Alexandra, are you telling me you've changed your mind?'

'And if I was?'

'I wouldn't believe you.' Miss Holland's fists clenched. 'Good heavens, girl, you're eaten up with love for that man, even I can see that! I just don't understand what you're trying to do.'

Alexandra rested her elbows on the table and rested her chin on her knuckles. 'You don't have to understand,' she said unevenly. 'It's over, I tell you. He doesn't want me. He never did. I was just a—a diversion while Estelita was away.'

'You don't believe that!'

'I do. I do.' Alexandra sniffed, feeling the smarting sting

of tears behind her eyes. 'If you only understood ...'

'Understood? What's to understand?'

'About—about Estelita ...'

'What about her?'

'She—Jason's going to marry her.'

'I doubt that, very much.' Miss Holland looked disbelieving. 'If he had been going to marry Estelita, he'd have done so before now.'

'Well, she wants to marry him.'

'Might I remind you, I wanted to marry Lord Carleon? Much good it did me.'

'But if—if you'd been pregnant ...'

'Estelita's not pregnant!'

'No, but she might be.' Alexandra caught her lower lip between her teeth. 'If she—let it happen ...'

'You're implying that Mr Tarrant would be responsible?'

'Yes.'

Miss Holland snorted. 'I never heard anything so fanciful! Do you honestly believe that a man like Mr Tarrant, with his experience of the world and its vagaries, wouldn't take damn good care something like that didn't happen unless he intended it to do so?'

Alexandra stared at her, her lips trembling. 'You accept then that they do sleep together?'

'I don't accept any such thing. I'm not saying that they might not have, in the past. She's obviously willing, and Mr Tarrant is very much a man, after all.'

'Oh, Miss Holland ...' Tears oozed down Alexandra's cheeks. 'If only you were right!'

'Well, at least give me the benefit of the doubt.' Miss Holland leant across to pat her arm. 'My dear, surely you're not going to let a woman like Estelita keep you from finding out the truth for yourself?'

'How?'

'Go back at the end of the summer. See—Jason.' It was the first time Miss Holland had used his given name. 'Do that, if you do nothing else.'

Alexandra rubbed her palms across her cheeks, noticing as she did so how the scars were fading. They were pale, of course, and still very painful if she used them unwarily, but no longer raw and vulnerable. If only the same could be said for her!

'You don't know everything,' she admitted at last, when Miss Holland continued to look at her with expectancy. 'I lied to Jason. All the time I was at San Gabriel, I was living a lie.'

Miss Holland frowned. 'Go on.'

Alexandra hunched her shoulders. 'Well ...' she began reluctantly, 'my father didn't write that letter asking Jason to be my guardian, I did.'

'You?'

'Yes.' Painfully, Alexandra explained the situation, making no excuses for her behaviour. 'I didn't want to go back to Sainte Sœur. I just wanted to be free,' she finished lamely, and Miss Holland felt a surge of sympathy for this girl who had known no other life but that of the convent.

'Why didn't you tell Jason?' she asked now, squeezing Alexandra's arm. 'I'm sure he'd have understood. I'm sure he *will* understand.'

'No.' Alexandra shook her head. 'There was a letter, you see. Estelita brought it that day she came back from Valvedra. It was from the convent. They—they must have contacted Daddy's solicitors, and learned that he was dead and that I was living in Santa Vittoria. At any rate, they had written to Jason, telling him that my father had telephoned *them*, asking them to look after me when—when he died.'

'Who told you this?'

'Can't you guess? Estelita. She had opened the letter, you see. She showed it to me, but not to Jason.'

'Where is the letter now?'

'Estelita destroyed it, I suppose. I don't know. I never saw it again after that night she came back to San Gabriel.'

'I see.' Miss Holland was thoughtful.

'Do you?' asked Alexandra now, shifting on her chair. 'Can you see how Jason would react if he learned the truth? He—he never wanted to take me to San Gabriel, you know that. If he found out I'd deliberately deceived him . . .'

'Nevertheless, I think you should tell him,' declared Miss Holland at last. 'If, as it appears, you do not intend to return to San Gabriel, what have you to lose?'

'No.' Alexandra shook her head. 'No, I couldn't do that.'

'Why?'

'Estelita threatened to make the letter public knowledge if I didn't leave the *hacienda*. She said Jason would hate being made to look a fool.'

'What a nasty piece of work she is!' exclaimed Miss Holland impatiently. 'I can't imagine why Jason ever made her his housekeeper.'

'She was a widow, and she needed the work,' replied Alexandra practically. 'Besides, not everyone would want to live so far from the city.'

Miss Holland nodded. 'That's true, of course. And I suppose she does care for him in her own way. Even so, I think he deserves to know the truth. Perhaps I should——'

'No. Oh, no.' Alexandra shook her head again. 'Don't do anything. This is between me—and Jason. Whatever happens, I have to handle this myself.'

It was approximately two weeks later that Alexandra had an unexpected visitor to the coffee bar. She was clearing tables when a voice behind her said: '*Buenos dias, señorita. Cómo está usted?*'

She swung round eagerly, half believing it might be Jason, to gaze in amazement at Manuel Goya. 'Manuel!' she exclaimed bewilderedly. 'Heavens, what are you doing here?' Her eyes darkened. 'Do you have bad news? Is anything wrong? Is Jason well?'

'No, no, and yes,' he responded, his eyes twinkling with wry amusement. 'That answers your questions, *si*? As to why I am here, I came to see you, of course.'

'No, but . . .' Alexandra glanced round nervously. 'How did you find me? What are you doing in London?'

Manuel smiled. 'We cannot talk here, in the middle of a coffee house. Can you have lunch with me?'

Alexandra hesitated. 'Lunchtime is our busiest time,' she confessed. 'I could have dinner with you this evening.'

'Unfortunately, that is not possible,' said Manuel sadly. 'I am passing through London on my way to Rome. I have to leave on this evening's flight.' He sighed. 'I did not realise you had a job. Jason did not tell me.'

'Jason doesn't know,' said Alexandra unhappily. 'Oh, Manuel! If only I'd known you were coming!'

'*Si.*' He looked disappointed, too. Then his expression lightened a little. 'I know,' he said. 'I will have lunch here, at the coffee bar, *no*? Then, in between times, we can talk.'

It wasn't very satisfactory, but it was the best they could do. Alexandra was kept busy from twelve o'clock onwards, but in between serving hamburgers and toasted teacakes, she managed to snatch a few words here and there.

It appeared that Manuel had taken his father's advice at last, and was working for the Fredrikson organisation. Because the firm had offices in Rome, Manuel was being sent there for three months to learn European methods of engineering, and it had been his father's suggestion that he stop off in London to see Alexandra. Knowing Ricardo's pride in his son, Alexandra guessed the older man had wanted her to see how successful Manuel had become, and maybe he hoped that their friendship would develop now that there were fewer miles between them. It was sad, she thought, that Manuel had not been the one to capture her heart. He would have been so much easier to love.

Once in London, Manuel had gone straight to their address in Mountsey Square, and from Miss Holland he had learned where she was working. Like her, he was distressed that Alexandra should not have asked Jason's advice before starting on such a career, but he gave an unwilling promise not to interfere.

Talking about Jason was less easy, Alexandra found. It was difficult to ask the questions she wanted to ask without giving away her feelings, but it seemed that the situation at San Gabriel was much as usual. At least he was not married, she thought with relief, although she acknowledged bitterly that such things took time. Nevertheless, so long as he remained unmarried, she could entertain thoughts of going back there, even if the chances of her doing so were slim indeed. Jason had never written to her. So far as she knew, he had never even sent a message to her. And he must know that she could never return without his invitation.

Manuel left to catch his plane, and Alexandra watched him go with a terrible sense of isolation. For a time, she had felt close to Jason again, and hearing Manuel talk about the *estancia* and its problems had brought it all into painful focus. But now he had gone, and she was left with the unpalatable knowledge of her own duplicity. If only she had told Jason right at the beginning! she thought despairingly. If only she had confessed to her ploy before the letter arrived, condemning any hope of his forgiveness.

June was a hot month in London, and working in the sweaty atmosphere of the coffee bar, Alexandra was sapped of all strength by the time she got home. She didn't even have the energy to go seeking a flat, and the realisation that in less than three months the rent on the house would fall due again filled her with anxiety. She could pay it, she supposed, using the money her father had left her, but it would take a sizeable slice out of the funds she had hoped to use to furnish her own apartment. Besides, there was Mrs Beesley's wages to consider, too. She was part of the deal, without the added burden of what they would eat. That was a detail Jason had not neglected in his arrangements with Miss Holland, and knowing the price of food, Alexandra dreaded the thought of how much money he had already spent on them.

So many problems, she reflected wearily, in her lower spirits. And all of them seemingly insoluble. Perhaps she should have stayed at the convent. Life there had been uneventful, it was true, but at least she had not had this burden of guilt to bear. Perhaps she ought to write and ask the nuns if they would take her back. Sanctuary sounded very sweet to someone robbed of all self-respect.

Because she started work at eight-thirty, Alexandra was always up first in the mornings. Mrs Beesley would prepare her coffee and toast, and then disappear downstairs to attend to her husband's breakfast. Mr Beesley worked as commissionaire to a block of offices, and Alexandra sometimes saw him when she was leaving, erect and military-smart in his uniform. He would raise a hand in greeting, and she would wish him 'Good morning', and then they would go on their way, she to walk to the coffee bar, and he to catch the tube to the Barbican.

One morning towards the end of June, Alexandra slept in, and it was gone eight-thirty when she came down the steps of the house. Seeing the man coming up the area steps, she thought Mr Beesley must have slept in, too, and she had opened her mouth to commiserate with him before she realised that the thick dark hair and sun-bronzed skin were not those of the housekeeper's husband. Besides, the expensive suede suit was not the sort of thing a man in his sixties would wear, and the broad shoulders and lean, muscular body moved with the lithe grace of a much younger man.

Although she needed no second look to recognise who it was, Alexandra could not drag her eyes away from him, and it was only as she felt the metal of the handrail digging into her still-tender palms that she realised she had paused in mid-flight.

Jason climbed the area steps and halted on the path below her, tall and disturbingly familiar. She realised she knew every detail of his face, from the lines that bracketed his mouth to the thickness of his lashes, and his nearness was almost her undoing. She wished he would speak. She wished he would say something—anything—to explain what he was doing there, and whether he was alone. He seemed tired, she fretted anxiously, and perhaps he had lost a little weight, but he was still the only man who could send the blood thundering through her veins, and turn her bones to water.

'So you are up,' he commented at last, hardly the words she had expected him to use, and she nodded jerkily, saying:

'Actually, I'm late. I'm usually out of the house before this. Unfortunately, I slept in.'

She didn't add that the reason she had overslept was because she had cried herself to sleep the night before, but Jason's shrewd gaze lingered on the dark rings around her eyes, and the slight puffiness that betrayed her distress.

'Oh, yes ...' Jason put his foot on the first step and came a little nearer. 'Your famous job at the coffee bar. I hadn't forgotten about that.'

Alexandra gasped. 'How did you know I had a job? Oh, I see ...' Her mouth took on a mutinous curve. 'Miss Holland told you. She promised——'

'Miss Holland didn't tell me a thing,' contradicted Jason flatly, taking another step until there was only the space of one slab of concrete between them. 'Although I would have expected her to, knowing I trusted her.'

Alexandra stepped to one side. 'Well, if that's why you've come——'

'It's not,' he retorted, sidestepping himself to block her path. 'Shall we go inside?'

Alexandra drew a deep breath. 'I—I can't. I've just told you, I'm late. Mr Stefanos doesn't approve of unpunctuality. I'm sorry if you've chosen the wrong time to catch me——'

'I didn't choose the time,' he told her, deliberately taking the final step that brought his body into touching distance of hers, or would have done if she had not hung back. 'I came straight here from the airport.' He glanced at his watch. 'I arrived from Rio a little over an hour ago.'

Alexandra's mouth was dry. She didn't know why he had come, or how he had found out about her job. Unless it was from Manuel. But he had promised not to interfere . . .

'Jason, please——'

'No. You please—me!' he declared harshly, and reached for her handbag. 'I assume you do have keys in here, do you?'

'Don't! I mean—you have no right . . .'

'Don't I?' His tone was grim. 'I think your landlord would disagree with you there,' he retorted, and finding her key, he inserted it in the lock.

'Oh, you—you——' Alexandra could think of no adjective suitable to her opinion of him in that moment, stripping away as he was her last vestiges of self-respect, but Jason wasn't even listening to her. Instead, he caught her wrist in a vice-like grip when she would have escaped him, and practically dragged her into the hall behind him.

'If you think because you pay the lease——' she began tremulously, as the door slammed shut behind them, but Jason pulled her after him, across the hall and into the sunlit elegance of the drawing room. Only then did he release her, but he made sure she was in the centre of the room, while he positioned himself behind the closed door.

'Now,' he said, folding his arms, 'before we discuss the matter of your resignation, suppose you tell me how you perpetrated this little fraud?' And from his pocket he drew the small white envelope with Reverend Mother's handwriting upon it.

Alexandra's legs were like jellies as she stared at that small square of parchment. He had found out, then, she thought dully. Even though she had left San Gabriel, even though she had cut herself off from everything she held most dear, Estelita had still found it necessary to betray her.

'That—that's a letter from Sainte Sœur,' she murmured, playing for time. 'I—I recognise the handwriting.'

'Do you?' He inclined his head. 'I believe you also know what the letter contains.'

'I—well, I know of it,' she faltered. Then, as if appealing to him at this late date would do no good, she added: 'I—I'm not ashamed of what I did. It—it was worth it, even if—even if you do despise me now. I—I would do it again . . .'

'Would you?' He raised dark eyebrows.

'Yes. And—and Estelita promised me you would never see that letter.'

'Let's leave Estelita for the time being, shall we?' Jason's mouth tightened. 'I'd like to know how you managed to get your father to write that letter.'

'Oh.' Alexandra was disconcerted. 'Well, I—I wrote all his letters for him, you see. He—he didn't have a steady hand, and he only signed them.'

'Ah,' Jason nodded. 'Now I begin to understand.'

'I—I wanted to tell you,' she said wretchedly, needing to say something. 'But you already resented the responsibility . . .'

'Did I do that?'

'You know you did.' She sighed. 'If only I'd been a boy!'

'Indeed.' Jason inclined his head, and she could not see his expression.

Alexandra felt even worse. 'Why did you come here?' she appealed. 'If—if it's the money . . .'

'What money?' Jason looked at her, but she could not meet his gaze.

'Supporting me and—and Miss Holland,' she ventured, and grew hot all over when he left the door to walk slowly across to her.

'Of course,' he said, halting before her. 'What else could it be?'

Her eyes darted nervously toward his face, but his expression was as enigmatic as ever, and she licked at her dry lips. 'Who—who told you I was working?' she asked. 'If it wasn't Miss Holland, it must have been Manuel. Did—did you send him here to—to spy on me?'

'You think I'd do a thing like that?' he probed, a trace of amusement tugging at the corners of his mouth, and it came to her in a flash that he was playing with her now, like a cat plays with a mouse. Whatever reason had brought him to London, Estelita must have had something to do with it, and she must be very sure of him if she dared to send him here alone.

'How—how is Estelita?' she asked, not really caring, but wanting to wipe that mocking smile from his face, and his eyes narrowed.

'I expect she's very well,' he replied at last. 'I don't know. I haven't seen her for over a week.'

Alexandra stared at him then, but it was useless trying to read his expression, and with a little cry she turned her back on him, trying desperately not to jump to conclusions. But when his hands descended on her shoulders, she didn't resist him, and the feel of his long length behind her was at once an agony and a delight.

'Alexandra,' he murmured, and there was no mistaking the emotion now that thickened his tones. 'Oh, Alexandra, why did you let me send you away? Have you any idea what it's been like without you? And when Ricardo told me you had got a job——'

'Ricardo!'

'Yes, Ricardo. Your Miss Holland was very shrewd. She didn't write me that you imagined I didn't know about that letter from Sainte Sœur, or that you had decided not to come back to San Gabriel. She wrote to Ricardo, knowing full well it was he as much as anybody who had prevented me from riding roughshod over any qualms I might have had about your youth and marrying you!'

'Jason?' She twisted round in his arms then to stare at him disbelievingly. 'I—is that true?'

'Would I lie to you?' he demanded, unable to resist the urge to touch her temples with his lips.

'But—you said we needed time . . .'

'I said *you* needed time,' he muttered, unfastening the

buttons of her blouse with fingers that shook a little. 'But, by God!' he bent his head to her breast, 'I think I've given you enough, don't you?'

For several minutes, Alexandra could not reply. With Jason covering her face with kisses and seeking the moist sweetness of her mouth, she could think of little but him, and the hardness of his body that even the suede suit could not disguise. Somehow his waistcoat was unbuttoned, and the silkiness of his shirt was a sensuous abrasion to her breasts, while his hands threaded themselves through her hair and caressed the sensitive skin of her neck and shoulders. They were hungry for each other, and only the awareness that Miss Holland might hear them and come to investigate made Alexandra eventually draw back.

His eyes glazed with emotion, Jason was loath to let her go, pulling her down on to the couch beside him, imprisoning her yielding body beneath his.

'Miss Holland ...' murmured Alexandra, only half protesting now, and Jason rubbed his tongue across the tip of her nose.

'I have words to say to Miss Holland later,' he said. 'Somehow I don't think she'll be too surprised to see me.'

Alexandra blinked, trying hard to think coherently. 'You—did you say—I *imagined* you didn't know about the letter from the convent?' she breathed, and with a sigh, he rolled to one side of her and took meticulous care over fastening the buttons of her blouse.

'All right,' he agreed. 'We'll talk. But afterwards ...'

His eyes left her in no doubt as to his meaning. Unguarded, they were warm and intimate, and her heart leapt in her throat at the realisation that she had aroused those emotions in him.

'First of all,' he said, unfastening his tie and pulling it off with evident relief, 'let me tell you about Estelita.'

'What did you mean when you said you hadn't seen her for a week? You said you only arrived from Rio an hour ago.'

'I did.' He stroked her mouth with a teasing finger. 'Be patient, and I'll explain.' She nodded and he went on: 'To begin with, we'll deal with the letter, shall we? I gather Estelita pretended I knew nothing about it.'

'That's right. She did.' Alexandra's eyes were wide.

'Well, that was—how do they put it?—a bloody lie!' His lips twitched at her shocked expression. 'My darling, Ricardo collected my mail that day, not Estelita. She doesn't have that kind of authority. My God, knowing her as I do, I would never trust her with my private affairs.'

He paused, and Alexandra recalled again how infuriated the housekeeper had been when she had found her in Jason's study.

'Anyway, to continue ... Ricardo collected the mail, as I say, and naturally he gave the letter to me. If you remember, I had to drive to Puerto Novo to fetch the doctor, and consequently it was almost supper time before I got around to reading it.'

Alexandra pressed her lips together. 'Were you very angry?'

Jason half smiled. 'Do you remember coming downstairs and finding me in the hall? I'd just read the letter then, and my thoughts were full of it. Then you said you were leaving, and I guess my feelings showed.'

Alexandra recalled the occasion very well. 'I thought you acted strangely,' she murmured reflectively. 'As if—as if you had expected me to act—differently.'

Jason sighed, tracing the line of her jaw with his lips. 'I did.' He touched the corner of her mouth. 'After reading that letter, I would have cut out my tongue before I sent you away!'

'Jason!'

Her lips parted, and for a long moment there was silence in the room. Then he stirred himself sufficiently to say: 'Can you not understand? I realised how desperate you must have been to write that letter, and when you said you were leaving ... I was shattered.'

'If only you'd told me!'

'If only,' he agreed softly. 'I did try. The morning you were leaving, I came to your room before you were up. I knocked long enough. You must have heard me. But you didn't answer.'

Alexandra propped herself up on one elbow to stare down at him. 'But the morning I was leaving I was up early, terribly early. I was down at the stables at first light.'

Jason closed his eyes. 'So that was why——'

'I thought you seemed angry when you came in to breakfast and found me already there.'

'I was.' Jason's fingers curved round her nape. 'I was sure then you must have heard me. And then when you shook hands ...' He squeezed her neck cruelly for a moment. 'Dear God, you've given me some bad moments!' He pulled her down to him for a moment and punished her very satisfactorily, and then he added huskily: 'If I had known what Estelita had done, I'd have killed her.'

'You never found out?'

'How could I? She wasn't likely to tell me, and you had forced Miss Holland's hand.'

Alexandra hesitated. 'She—she said she was going to get you to marry her. She said—even if she had to get pregnant——'

'Oh, God!' Jason buried his face in her hair. 'To get pregnant you have to do more than cook a man's meals or do his laundry,' he averred roughly. 'And that's all Estelita has been doing for me.'

Alexandra's lips trembled. 'She said——'

'I don't care what she said. I'm not saying I haven't entertained ideas of going to bed with her. I have. But like I said to you on one famous occasion, I never make those kind of commitments. To be crude, it's far too easy to drive into Puerto Novo or Valvedra, if I have to.'

Alexandra's cheeks burned. 'Did you—did you after—after——'

'After the night of the storm?' he enquired dryly. 'My

dear child, I have no intention of satisfying you on that score. But if you remember, I had other things to worry about.'

'The mountain lion!' she exclaimed. 'Have you caught her?'

Jason nodded. 'Ricardo shot her the week after you left. It was an unfortunate affair. One of the men had injured her on a hunting trip. They'd gone out after geese, and Carlos was never a marksman. Of course, she had to poach to survive. She must have been in great pain.'

'Poor thing!' Alexandra was moved, although she could still remember her terror in the canyon.

'Yes,' Jason nodded. 'Anyway, returning to Estelita, Ricardo had this letter from Miss Holland some time before he told me. He knew Manuel was going to Rome, so he had him stop off and see what was happening for himself. When Manuel confirmed the gist of what Miss Holland had said, Ricardo decided that much against his better judgment I would have to be told.'

He shook his head. 'I won't bore you with the details of what he and I said to one another, or indeed the scene I had with Estelita. Sufficient to say, she packed her bags at once, and Ricardo drove her back to Valvedra.'

'Oh, Jason!' Alexandra couldn't help feeling a twinge of pity for the Spanish woman.

'She'll make out,' Jason replied laconically. 'She has her brother to care for, and her mother will be coming out of hospital soon.' He pulled a wry face. 'She could never get it into her head that I had no intention of marrying again.'

Alexandra's lips parted at this and he bent to cover them with his own. 'Don't jump to conclusions,' he said. 'I said I *had* no intention of marrying again. Unfortunately, that was before I met you.'

Alexandra linked her arms around his neck. 'And when did you decide to come back to England?'

'Immediately. But it wasn't that easy. I have an *estancia* to run, and it's nearing lambing time.' He sighed. 'You see the trouble you put me to! Like a fool, I jump on the first plane, take a taxi to Mountsey Square, dump my luggage with Mrs Beesley—and then face a fiery virago!'

Alexandra's eyes appealed for his understanding. 'I thought—oh, I don't know what I thought. And I was late.'

'You're even later now,' remarked Jason smugly. 'You'll probably lose your job. That will save you the necessity of resigning.'

'You're very sure of me.'

He grimaced. 'Am I? You wouldn't turn me down now, would you?'

For a moment he had a vulnerability that was disturbingly attractive, and she pressed herself closer to him. 'What do you think?' she breathed, and his mouth sought the eagerness of hers.

'Well . . .' he said at last, and she could feel the tremor that went through him as he strove for control, 'Ricardo can only cope for a few days. Is that enough?'

'Enough?'

'To pack?' he demanded. 'I want to marry you. But not here. In Puerto Novo, in the church there. Just as soon as I can get a licence.'

'Oh, but . . .' Alexandra hesitated. 'How long will that take?'

Jason relaxed. 'Not long. Until then, you'll have to be content with being my mistress.'

There was another satisfying silence, and then Alexandra whispered huskily: 'That day—that day in the canyon, you said you couldn't betray the trust my father had given you, but—but you suspected he hadn't written to you. Why didn't you challenge me?'

'Because I wanted *you* to tell *me*,' retorted Jason quietly. 'Besides, I still feel I owe your father so much.'

'That's not why——'

'Why I'm marrying you?' he teased. 'Oh, Alexandra, you know so little about men! Do you honestly think I'd tie myself to any woman out of a debt to her father?'

Alexandra stroked his cheek. 'I'll make you a good wife,' she averred. 'I know I'm not much good as a cook, but I'm quite efficient at cleaning. And I'm willing to learn.'

'I know you are,' he assured her. 'But for the time being, Miss Holland's going to come back with us to help you.'

'Miss Holland?'

'Of course. You didn't think I could abandon her, did you?'

'But how do you—what if she——'

'I phoned,' he admitted half sheepishly. 'But don't blame her for keeping it to herself. I told her what I'd do if she let me down a second time.'

Alexandra couldn't find it in her heart to be anything but grateful to the older woman. 'But she's not a housekeeper,' she protested, and Jason smiled.

'With luck, her task will be shortlived,' he agreed. 'But for the present, she'll take the burden of responsibility from your shoulders. Then, later, when our sons are born . . .'

Alexandra's cheeks burned. 'Our sons!'

'And daughters, too, I hope,' he teased. 'Oh, not immediately—I want you all to myself for the present. But Luisa and Elena are willing to resume their duties, and you'll learn to organise them. And besides, we'll need a good nanny eventually.'

Alexandra could hardly take it in. 'What about Ricardo?' she ventured. 'Will he accept me?'

'Ricardo has resigned himself to the inevitable,' Jason responded gently. 'You must forgive his familiarity. We've known each other a lot of years.'

'He said he knew my father,' said Alexandra reminiscently, and Jason nodded.

'He did. Like me, he worked in Mexico, too, and when I discovered how good he was with horses, I offered him the chance to work for me when I got San Gabriel. I sank every penny I had in the *estancia*, and I have your father to thank for that.'

'You mean—you paid for the *estancia* with the money you earned with my father?'

'Yes,' Jason nodded again.

'Oh!' Alexandra licked her lips, and when he looked puzzled, she confessed: 'I thought—when you were a mercenary—I'm sorry, I didn't realise . . .'

Jason understood. 'That money was lost in a speculative venture in the States,' he agreed. 'There wasn't a lot of it. The job sickened me after the first few months.'

Alexandra was glad. 'So you and Ricardo went to Santa Vittoria.'

'Yes. Ricardo—and Manuel. He was just a boy then.'

'He still is,' said Alexandra at once. 'How could you think I . . .'

'A man in love thinks crazy things,' retorted Jason passionately. 'God, the torment you've put me through!'

'Miss Holland told me you—you put me to bed the night of the storm,' murmured Alexandra inconsequently, seeing the beads of sweat start on his forehead.

'I did.' He closed his eyes in remembered agony. 'That was when I deluded myself I could handle the situation.'

'So that was why you were so—so casual in the kitchen afterwards.'

'Casual? Was I?' He grinned. 'You saw how casual I was a few minutes later.'

Alexandra wriggled closer to him. 'I can't wait to go back to San Gabriel. I've hated London. I've hated being apart from you. When can we leave?'

'Soon,' he promised huskily. 'But don't worry, I'll never leave you again.'

Alexandra sighed. 'You know what I want to do,' she murmured dreamily. 'Go with you on the trail—next time you round up the horses.'

'When the snow has gone?' he asked lazily, and laughed at her astonished face. 'Oh, yes, we get a little snow. Not a lot, but some. Why? What are you planning to do? Look for the chestnut mare? There's no need. I got her back, safe and sound.'

'You did?'

He nodded, a wry smile crossing his face. 'Actually, perhaps safe and sound was the wrong description. She's in foal. I'll let you choose the name when her time is due, shall I?'

'The black stallion!' exclaimed Alexandra ruefully. 'My downfall and my salvation!'

'No—mine,' Jason corrected her softly, and when Miss Holland came to find out if everything was well, she tiptoed away again, unseen.

FOLLOW THY DESIRE

On the day of her wedding, Helen realised that she could not go through with it—not now that she had met Barry's half-brother Morgan. So instead she accepted Morgan's invitation to go back with him to Africa to look after his young daughter. But Morgan had not mentioned marriage, and in fact had made it clear that the job was all he was offering her. Was Helen making a complete fool of herself—or worse?

FOLLOW THY DESIRE

BY

ANNE MATHER

MILLS & BOON LIMITED
15–16 BROOK'S MEWS
LONDON W1A 1DR

First published 1978
This edition 1983

ISBN 0 263 74487 6

09/1183/

Set in 10 on 10½ pt Intertype Lectura

Made and printed in Great Britain by
Cox & Wyman Ltd, Reading

CHAPTER ONE

It was just a week to the wedding. Sitting before the mirror of her dressing table, putting the finishing touches to her make-up, Helen couldn't quite believe it. Wide-eyed, she stroked mascara on to her lashes, her brows ascending in a gesture of incredulity. Six months ago, when Barry had first put his ring on her finger, the fifteenth of October had seemed a very long way away. But gradually, through those warm lazy days of summer, the time had slipped away, and now it loomed ahead with nothing between but a last-minute fitting for her bridal gown, and the usual round of gatherings arranged to meet the members of Barry's family with whom she had yet to become acquainted. Barry had still to meet her aunt from Coventry who was coming north for the wedding, and her cousins Alison and Linda, who were to be bridesmaids, and there was his uncle and aunt from Basingstoke, and his stepbrother, Morgan, from East Africa, all of whom Helen had never met.

She had heard of Morgan, of course. Barry's father had died when he was quite young and his mother had married again, to a widower who already had a teenage son. Barry had been too young to have much in common with his older stepbrother, and university followed by several years training at a London teaching hospital had not helped to seal the gap. By the time Barry was old enough to go to university, Morgan had married and left the country, and was presently living in Osweba, one of the emergent African states. Barry didn't talk much about him, but his stepfather did, more in fact as time went by, and Helen guessed the old man regretted that his only son should have chosen to live so far away from his family. Yet his marriage to Barry's mother had produced a daughter, and Barry and Susan were as close as any brother and sister. She was also to be one of Helen's bridesmaids, although Helen herself found the younger girl rather silly and spoilt.

Rising from the padded bench that faced the mirror, Helen considered her reflection with critical eyes. Shoulder-length hair, the colour of maple syrup, framed a face which what it lacked in beauty more than made up for in warmth and vivacity. Wide brown eyes, unusual with her colour of hair, high cheekbones, and a full-lipped generous mouth, she attracted attention wherever she went, and while she wasn't conceited, she was aware that men found her attractive. She was quite tall and slim, although not excessively so, and her work in therapy had taught her the art of listening to what people were saying and giving them her full attention, which was in itself an attractive trait. So many girls were too busy or too full of their own importance to pay attention to what other people were saying, particularly older people, but Helen always showed interest and maybe that was why Barry's father had confided his anxiety about his son to her.

Wrapping the long cream velvet skirt about her waist, she recalled what he had told her the previous week. Mr Fox had written to Morgan, inviting him and his wife and daughter to the wedding, telling him that they were welcome to stay with the family. Morgan's reply had been less than reassuring. He would be coming to England for the wedding, he said, but his marriage had broken up and his daughter, fifteen-year-old Andrea, preferred to stay at their home in Nrubi and therefore would not be accompanying him.

Now, as Helen tied the cords of the cream figured jerkin that matched her evening skirt, she felt a pang of sympathy for the man who had always treated Barry like his own son. Still, Morgan had arrived home early this morning, and when Barry telephoned her later, inviting her round for dinner that evening, he had not sounded too concerned about his stepfather.

'I can't promise you the fatted calf,' he had teased his fiancée, 'but Mum and Mrs Parsons have been in the kitchen since nine o'clock, and I'm pretty sure it will be something special.'

Helen had laughed and said she was looking forward to meeting his brother, but she couldn't help wishing Morgan Fox had not brought his troubles to blight this week which should have been such a happy one for all of them.

Her bedroom door opened as she was adding a touch of perfume to her wrists, and her younger sister, Jennifer, stood regarding her admiringly. Jennifer was just fourteen, but she was tall, as tall as Helen, in fact, and although Susan Fox was three years older they were much of a size. Jennifer was the fourth bridesmaid, and as it was her first opportunity to attend at a wedding, she was more excited about the ceremony than Helen herself.

'Barry's here,' she said now, hands tucked into the waistband of the jeans she invariably wore. 'Are you ready?'

Helen nodded. 'I think so. Do I look all right?'

Jennifer pulled a critical face. 'I guess so. That's new, isn't it? Honestly, you've got more clothes than anyone I know!'

Helen gave her an old-fashioned look. 'When you start earning some money,' she replied, 'you'll be able to buy your own clothes, too. And besides, this is part of my trousseau.'

'So why are you wearing it tonight?'

Helen sighed. 'I don't see what it has to do with you, but as I'm meeting Barry's brother for the first time, I wanted to look—decent.'

Jennifer grimaced. 'Decent!' she echoed. 'You always look decent, and you know it. What is it with this brother of Barry's? Why should you want to impress him?'

'It's not a question of impressing him,' exclaimed Helen tersely. 'Anyway, you should mind your own business.'

'Why? He's nobody. He's old, isn't he? Barry's twenty-four, and he said he was at least twelve years older than him.'

Helen raised her eyebrows. 'Oh? So you've been talking to Barry about him, too, have you?'

Jennifer coloured then. 'I only asked. I was curious, that's all. Barry said I could go round and meet him tomorrow, if I liked.'

'That won't be necessary.' Helen was beginning to feel impatient now. 'Mum and Dad are inviting him to dinner on Tuesday. You can meet him then.'

'Barry says he has a daughter about the same age as me, but she's not coming to the wedding. He said that he and his wife have split up.'

'Barry seems to have said an awful lot,' declared Helen, picking up her fur jacket and slinging it about her shoulders, not quite knowing why that knowledge irritated her so, and Jennifer made another face before flouncing off downstairs ahead of her.

Barry was waiting with her parents in the lounge. He was a tall, good-looking young man, with dark curly hair and blue eyes. After passing his exams he had got a good job in the Borough Surveyor's department, and he and Helen were to live in a furnished flat in York until they could afford to buy a house of their own. Helen was to go on working for the time being, and as she was only twenty-one, there would be plenty of time for having children later. She had known Barry for years, they had attended the same grammar school, but it was not until about a year ago that she had actually consented to go out with him.

Now he came to greet her warmly, bending his head to bestow an affectionate kiss on her lips. 'You look great!' he murmured, and then moved aside to allow her parents to look at her.

'Are you sure that skirt won't get marked?' asked Mrs Raynor anxiously. 'It would be a shame if you spoiled it before you went away.'

Their honeymoon was booked in Majorca, and they all hoped the weather would be warmer there than it was in England at present.

'It is washable,' said Helen tolerantly, and her father from his stance before the hearth added: 'Take no notice of her, love. You look beautiful, doesn't she, Barry? All in cream like that. Could be a wedding gown!'

'Oh, don't say that!' exclaimed Mrs Raynor, shaking her head. 'Don't you know it's unlucky for the groom to see the bride in her wedding dress before they're in church!'

'But she's not wearing her wedding dress, is she?' demanded her husband irritably. 'I only said——'

'I know what you said,' Mrs Raynor interrupted him, and sensing an argument, Helen took Barry's arm and drew him towards the door.

'Come on,' she said. 'Let's leave them to it. I'm hungry if you're not.'

Outside, Barry's sleek Triumph sat smugly on the drive of the Raynors' semi. He helped Helen into the front seat, and then walked round the bonnet to climb in beside her, flashing her another smiling look of possession as he stretched for the ignition.

'Dinner's not until eight,' he said, reversing carefully into the road. 'Morgan's slept most of the day, so Mum's put the meal back an hour.'

Helen nodded. 'I expect he was very tired. It's a long journey.'

'Yes.' Barry frowned. 'I'm surprised he came, actually, as Andrea wasn't coming and Pamela's left him.'

'Well, I'm not.' Helen's brows drew together. 'Mr Fox is his father, after all. And he hasn't seen him for—what? Five years?'

'Four,' said Barry shortly. 'But I don't see the connection. We've seen next to nothing of him ever since he qualified.'

'Yes, but you're getting married now,' said Helen gently. 'Naturally he would want to attend your wedding.'

'Would he?' Barry didn't sound convinced, and Helen wondered if he wasn't feeling just the tiniest bit resentful of the fuss his parents were making of the prodigal.

Deciding a change of subject was needed, she put her hand on his arm and said softly: 'I wonder what we'll be doing this time next week?' and was rewarded by a return of Barry's good humour.

'Well, not spending the evening having dinner with my parents,' he declared huskily, and she bent her head to rest it against his shoulder.

'I can't help wishing it was this time next week,' she murmured, but not quite for the reasons he imagined. 'I shall be glad when all the fuss is over. I wish we'd planned to have a quiet wedding, with just the two families, instead of this enormous affair at St Giles, and a hundred guests at the reception.'

'You'll enjoy it,' exclaimed Barry, covering her hand with his own. 'You'll see. Besides, after the way Morgan went off and got married in a register office, Mum wanted me to have a proper wedding. We couldn't disappoint everyone.'

'No, I suppose not.' Helen allowed a faint sigh to escape her, and then Barry was turning between the gates of Banklands, the Foxes' detached house on the outskirts of town.

Mr Fox was in the textile trade, and while some years ago his firm had suffered a recession, in recent months things had begun to improve. The introduction of chemicals into the wool fibre to enable it to be machine-washed without shrinking had rallied an already increasing demand for woollen products, and Helen knew Barry expected a generous donation towards the deposit on their house when they decided to buy. This mercenary streak in her fiancé was the only fault she abhorred, but she was sure that once they were married he would stop depending on his stepfather for every large outlay he had to make.

Banklands was a nice house, Helen thought. Built of Yorkshire stone, with square walls and a solid appearance, it had become almost a second home to her in recent months, and Mrs Fox already treated her like a second daughter.

It was Barry's mother who met them when they entered the panelled hall of the house, looking much younger than her forty-seven years in a simple, but expensively-styled, gown of apricot silk. She exchanged a warm smile with her son, offered her perfumed cheek to his fiancée, and then said: 'Oh, good. I'm glad you're here. The dinner's going to be ready a full fifteen minutes before we expected, so if you'd like to go and have a drink I'll tell Mrs Parsons we'll be ready at a quarter to.'

Helen removed her jacket and left it on the padded chair at the foot of the stairs, and then walked at Barry's side across the carpeted floor and into the Foxes' drawing room.

This was the largest room in the house, with the high corniced ceiling of a bygone age. Mr Fox had employed a firm of interior decorators to do the house through just over a year ago, and now the tall walls were hung with gold-figured silk which exactly matched the tapestry work on the olive green sofas that faced one another across the width of the hearth. The thick carpet underfoot was green and gold, too, while the furniture was soft colours, teak and walnut, with an ebony baby grand piano to grace the window embrasure.

Mr Fox was standing on the hearth as they entered, talking to a man who was stretched lazily on one of the sofas, his head resting against the upholstery, his legs extended across the hearth. The man got to his feet politely as Helen and Barry entered the drawing room, and like his father he smiled as they approached.

But there the resemblance ended. Morgan Fox was an inch or two taller than both his father and Barry, and infinitely leaner. His skin, startlingly brown against that of the other men, was stretched tautly across his features, accentuating the hollows in his cheeks and drawing attention to the curious yellowish cast of his eyes. But it was his hair that attracted Helen's interest—so pale as to appear silver in some lights and such an unusual contrast with such dark skin. His clothes, too, did not fit as snugly as Barry's, as if he had lost weight recently; yet there was about him an aura of sensuality that required no further propagation. Altogether a disturbing man, Helen thought, shocked by her instantaneous recognition of this.

If she was disturbed by her reactions to Barry's stepbrother, Morgan at least did not return her feelings. His polite smile of greeting did not reach those peculiar eyes, and almost immediately he turned to Barry, asking him what they would both like to drink.

'I can manage, thanks,' retorted Barry offhandedly, and asking Helen if she would like the usual, he went towards the bar which, when closed, was completely concealed behind a row of bookshelves. Presently, however, it stood open, displaying its mirror-lined interior, glittering with an array of bottles and glasses. Judging by the two empty glasses resting on the mantelshelf, Helen guessed that Morgan and his father had been imbibing already, which might account for that air of brooding detachment about him.

To cover the slight moment of embarrassment Barry's behaviour might have caused, Helen exchanged a look of apology with Mr Fox and then smiled at Morgan. 'Did you have a good journey?' she enquired, hoping she sounded more casual than she felt, and was relieved when his father remarked:

'I was just saying to Morgan how far away Africa always seems, and yet one can fly there in a matter of hours.'

'Yes,' Helen nodded. 'The world's getting smaller all the time.' Then, realising her words were trite, she flushed as Morgan Fox's eyes rested fleetingly upon her.

'Have you travelled much—Helen?' he asked in the space that followed, and she quickly made a negative gesture.

'Oh, no, not really. Not any distance, anyway. Just to Spain—and to France. For holidays, you know. I went to France with the school, actually. Barry went too, as it happened, but he was older than I was and I didn't know him very well in those days.'

She was chattering, and realising she was, she shut up, offering a look of apology to Barry as he came to rejoin them. He handed Helen a Martini and soda and then, raising his glass to her, took a mouthful of his own gin and tonic.

'Is it cold out?' asked Mr Fox, indicating that Helen should take a seat, and she sank down on to one of the low sofas as Barry said: 'Not as cold as it was earlier. The wind's dropped.'

'I expect it still feels pretty cold to you, Morgan, doesn't it?' his father commented wryly, and his son moved his shoulders in a dismissing gesture.

'The nights can be damn cold where we live,' he replied evenly, turning to lift his glass from the shelf. 'Can I get you another drink, Dad? Or is that your limit?'

Mr Fox agreed to have another Scotch, and he accompanied his son to the bar as Barry dropped down on to the sofa beside Helen. 'Drink all right?' he murmured, the coolness he had exhibited towards his stepfather and Morgan evaporating as he looked at her, and she nodded.

'How—er—how long is Morgan staying?' she asked in a low voice, hoping to take the tension out of the situation, but Barry's lips tightened as she mentioned his stepbrother's name.

'I don't know. Ten days—a fortnight, maybe. He'll be gone by the time we get back from our honeymoon, thank God!'

'Why?' Helen stared at him aghast, and his pale cheeks darkened with sudden colour.

'Oh, I don't know. He just rubs me up the wrong way, I suppose. Coming back here. Acting like he owned the place. Offering *me* a drink!'

Helen smoothed the pad of her thumb round the rim of her glass. 'Well, this is his home, too,' she observed reasonably, and her fiancé gave her an impatient look.

'It's not his home. His home is in Nrubi, wherever that might be. It's a pity he didn't stay there.'

Helen sighed, and then Susan Fox erupted into the room with her transistor, slim and attractive in purple pants and an embroidered smock. 'Hi, Helen,' she greeted her brother's fiancée lightly over the din of the pop programme being broadcast, and then went to join her father and Morgan by the bar. 'Can I have a Martini?' they heard her asking, before Morgan said something in response that made them all laugh.

Beside Helen, Barry stiffened, and she felt a reluctant sense of sympathy for him. He was jealous, she realised regretfully. For so long he had commanded Mr Fox's undivided attention that he had come to regard it as his right. Morgan's blood relationship to his stepfather was a thorn in his side, but it was only a temporary thing. Why couldn't he see that? wondered Helen uneasily, herself aware that Morgan Fox was not a man one could ignore.

She was seated beside Morgan at dinner. In the spacious dining room they were seated at the square mahogany table which Mrs Parsons had decorated with slender silver rose holders, and the candles in the silver candelabrum gave off a delicate perfume as they ate. There was minestrone and roast beef, accompanied by real Yorkshire pudding, and a steamed pudding to follow.

'Real north country fare,' said Mr Fox with satisfaction, as Mrs Parsons brought in the apple dumpling, and Morgan gave him a wry smile.

'You're making me wish I'd never left home,' he remarked, wiping his mouth with his napkin, and Mrs Fox regarded him reprovingly.

'You look as though you could do with some home cooking,' she commented with characteristic candour. 'Look at your father and Barry. They must be at least half a stone heavier than you!'

Morgan accepted his generous portion of apple dumpling without comment, but glancing sideways at him, Helen caught the mocking gleam in his eye.

'Do I look so undernourished?' he asked in an undertone, and she had to school her features to prevent herself from giggling.

'Not to me,' she answered in a low voice, and this time he looked directly at her.

It was a devastating experience. This close she could see the silvery tips of his lashes, short thick lashes that just missed being feminine. But there was nothing feminine about his face, with its gaunt cheekbones and deeply set eyes. It was aggressively masculine, and possessed that doubtful distinction—sexuality. Returning his gaze was like looking into a deep pool, that invited as well as repelled.

The sure awareness that Barry was watching them brought her eyes back sharply to her plate, but when she ventured to lift her lids her fiancé was still looking at her. She arched her brows in silent, if not very convincing, interrogation, but Barry just continued looking at her, his eyes cold and lacking in sympathy.

The remainder of the meal passed, for Helen, in discomfited silence, and she was glad when Mrs Fox suggested they had coffee in the drawing room and she could escape from Barry's inimical stare.

Susan joined her as they crossed the hall, whispering

insinuatively: 'Just six more days, Helen! Just imagine—a week tonight you'll be in Alcudia.'

'Yes.' Helen sounded distracted and Susan gave her a second look.

'What's wrong? Getting cold feet?'

'No——'

Helen was impatient, but Susan overrode her denial, insisting: 'I know. It's Morgan, isn't it? I saw the way you were looking at him at dinner. Are you thinking he's more of a man than Barry will ever be?'

'Susan!'

Helen was angry now, but Susan was unrepentant. 'You can't fool me,' she insisted. 'I can see how attractive he is. I could even be attracted to him myself.'

'*Susan!*'

'Oh, don't worry, I'm not quite that stupid. But if I was only his stepsister . . .'

Mrs Fox's hand on Helen's arm made her start violently, and the older woman looked at her strangely as she said: 'Pour the coffee, will you, Helen? I want to help Mrs Parsons clear the table and then she can load the machine while I relax.'

'Yes, Mrs Fox.' Helen swallowed her embarrassment, and seated herself beside the low table where Mrs Parsons had already placed the tray, just as Barry and his stepfather came into the room. Barry came straight across to her, seating himself beside her, and she gave him rather a nervous look before asking Mr Fox how he would like his coffee.

'Oh, black, please,' declared the older man, slipping his arm about his daughter's waist as she came to stand beside him. Then he bestowed a teasing look upon her. 'I suppose you'll be next,' he remarked, squeezing her affectionately. 'I wonder who the lucky man will be?'

'Don't you mean the *unlucky* man?' remarked Barry sarcastically, and Susan pulled a face at him.

'Well, when I do choose to get married, it won't be to some stuffy civil servant!' she retorted. 'Why—why, Morgan's got more guts in his little finger than you've got in your whole body!'

Her words were intended to be jibing. Barry and Susan often indulged in this harmless kind of baiting, and neither of them took it seriously. But tonight Helen sensed an underlying note of bitterness, and she guessed Susan's admiration for her half-brother had added fuel to Barry's already smouldering resentment. It was perhaps fortunate that Morgan was not around to hear his stepbrother's savage indictment of doctors who allowed this country to pay for their training and then took themselves off to some more lucrative practice overseas.

'I hardly think Osweba qualifies in that category,' Mr Fox interposed quietly, at this unwarranted criticism of his son, and Helen hastily handed Barry his coffee before he could say anything more.

It was with mixed feelings that she saw Morgan coming into the room just then, but as Helen's hands were occupied with her own coffee, Susan took the opportunity to pour Morgan's coffee herself.

Barry replaced his empty cup on the tray with a decisive clatter, and then said shortly: 'Well?'

Helen, who had been expecting this, made no attempt to evade the question. 'If you mean what I think you mean, then aren't you being a little small-minded?'

'Is it small-minded to object if my fiancée makes eyes at my stepbrother?' he snapped, and Helen gasped.

'I—I didn't!'

'What would you call it, then?'

'I—we—we spoke half a dozen words together, that's all.'

'I'm not objecting to what you *said*!'

'Oh, Barry . . .' Helen replaced her own cup now, glancing about them uncomfortably. But fortunately no one seemed to be paying any attention to them and she turned reproachful eyes upon him. 'Can't I even look at another man? Heavens, he's your own brother!'

'Stepbrother,' Barry corrected briefly. Then he scuffed his toe against the leg of the coffee table. 'Oh, what the hell! There's nothing I can do about it.'

Helen sighed. 'There's nothing to do!' she said imploringly, fiddling with the coffee pot. 'Would you like another cup?'

'No, thanks.'

Barry shook his head, but Helen was relieved when his mother came to join them and conversation became general. Naturally the wedding came under discussion, and those final arrangements that were still left to make. Talking about the white Mercedes he had hired for the occasion, Barry came out of his black mood, and Helen relaxed as her fiancé extolled the virtues of foreign cars. It was a favourite topic with him, and she allowed her head to rest against the back of the sofa and her thoughts to drift.

Almost compulsively, her gaze moved round the circle to rest on Morgan Fox's unusually light hair. It was thick and straight, with a side parting that left several heavy strands to fall across his forehead. From time to time he pushed them back, his long brown fingers combing through his hair and occasionally resting in a curiously weary gesture at the back of his neck. His hair was shorter than Barry's, barely brushing his collar at the back, and he didn't wear the long sideburns Barry effected and which gave her fiancé's face a rather artistic appearance. She thought he looked rather tired, and this knowledge brought a wave of unwilling anxiety sweeping over her. Yet what did it matter to her if Barry's stepbrother needed some sleep? Why should she be concerned? Anyone who had just flown five thousand miles would be tired, particularly bearing in mind the time change.

Realising she was staring at him again, she quickly looked away, relieved to see that no one else had observed her betraying appraisal. But even though she concentrated on the delicate pattern of the coffee cups, she could still see his face and the sensual fullness of his bottom lip.

He moved, giving her a reason to look his way, and her eyes ran over the long muscular legs outlined beneath the dark blue lounge suit he was wearing. She wondered if he was more at home in shorts or safari suits, and guessed he found an excess of clothing uncomfortable after so long in the tropics. This time his eyes flickered over hers, but their appraisal was cool and detached, and she pretended there was a speck of dust on her skirt in an effort to avoid detection of her interest.

The conversation had shifted to Morgan now and Helen listened as he answered his father's questions about the politics of Osweba. Then, inevitably, his daughter was brought into the conversation and it was with obvious reluctance he produced his wallet and the photograph of the bespectacled teenager everyone called Andy.

Barry barely glanced at his niece, but Helen studied the portrait with avid curiosity, trying to gauge something of the girl's personality from that small likeness.

'She doesn't look much like you,' remarked Susan, with her usual lack of tact, but Morgan merely smiled.

'Oh, she is, I assure you,' he said, pushing the picture back into his wallet. 'There are more ways than one of resembling someone.'

'Do you mean she's brainy?' demanded Susan, rolling her eyes in mock derision, but her mother reproved her, saying:

'I expect Morgan means that she likes the same things he does,' which aroused a contemptuous snort from Barry.

'What are we supposed to infer from that?' he enquired unpleasantly. 'When she can't even be bothered to turn up for the wedding?'

'Barry!' Mr Fox halted the conversation there, and Helen felt as embarrassed as if she had been a party to her fiancé's outburst. 'I think we're all suffering from a bout of pre-wedding nerves, and as I'm sure Morgan will be glad to get to bed, I suggest you take Helen home now, hmm?'

Barry looked as if he would have liked to have said more, but his mother's disapproval, added to that of his stepfather, kept him silent. Morgan said nothing and it was left to Susan to break the ominous silence that had fallen.

'Can I come round tomorrow and try on those sandals you said I could borrow?' she asked lightly, as if nothing untoward had occurred, and Helen rose to her feet, nodding her relief.

'Of course,' she said, as Morgan and his father rose, too. 'It's Sunday, so come whenever you like.'

'All right.' Susan grinned cheekily up at her older brother. 'You can take me, if you like. You'd like to meet Helen's parents, wouldn't you?'

Barry's face was reddening again, and Helen urged him towards the door. But outside, with her goodnights said and the irritation of Morgan's polite farewell colouring her tones, she exclaimed:

'What on earth did you think you were doing? Speaking to your stepbrother like that! Embarrassing everybody!'

'Embarrassing you, you mean, don't you?' retorted Barry moodily, leaving her to close the passenger side door herself and striding angrily around the bonnet. 'I don't know what's got into you!'

'What's got into me?' she echoed, as he pulled away. 'Don't be ridiculous! You've been spoiling for an argument ever since we got into the car to come here.'

'Oh, have I?'

'Yes, you have. And it's purely jealousy, that's all. You're jealous because your stepfather is making a fuss of his own son. His *own* son! Don't you think you owe it to him to be polite, whatever your private feelings might be?'

Barry did not answer and they covered the rest of the distance between Banklands and her parents' house in silence. But after he had brought the car to a halt and Helen made to get out, Barry's hand on her arm stopped her, and in the light from the street lamps she saw his scowl of contrition.

'I'm sorry,' he muttered grudgingly, and she knew it was up to her to make the next move.

'So am I,' she murmured, and his lips brushed lightly across her cheek and found hers.

For several minutes there again was silence in the car, but this time of a much more satisfying sort. Nevertheless, when Barry's hand probed beneath the fastening of her jacket, she gently pushed him away and thrust open the car door.

'We've waited this long,' she reminded him lightly, and he bowed his head in reluctant assent.

'Okay,' he said, leaning across to close the door again.

'I'll see you tomorrow night? You haven't forgotten we're going to Peter and Liz's, have you?'

'Tomorrow evening?' She shook her head. 'Of course not. What time will you pick me up? About seven?'

'About then,' he agreed, and with a smile he left her, the Triumph reversing away noisily into the quiet road.

If Helen's parents had expected a long discussion about Morgan Fox's arrival, they were disappointed. After the briefest of explanations about the dinner party and why she should be home by half past ten, which was early for her, Helen excused herself and went to bed, glad that Jennifer was not around to add her voice to the proceedings.

But in her room she found that sleep was very far from her thoughts. For the first time, she really began to contemplate the implications of the step she was taking, and to wonder whether Barry would have recovered his good humour so willingly if they had already been man and wife. She had never really considered that Barry might be a jealous person. In truth, she had never ever given him cause to display such feelings, content as always just to be with him, to know herself cared for and protected, the envy of many of her friends. Barry was everything any girl could ever wish for—tall and dark and handsome, with a good job with good prospects, and no financial problems. He had always treated her with gentleness, respecting her rather old-fashioned notions of chastity, realising that if he tried to force her to do something she would regret, he would lose her loyalty and trust.

This evening he had displayed an entirely unknown facet of his character, and why? Because she had shown a quite natural interest in his stepbrother. What had she done, after all? Spoken to Morgan at dinner, and shared a perfectly innocent joke with him. It was ludicrous for Barry to get angry over something so innocent. Good heavens, if she had been found in Morgan's arms he could not have reacted more positively, short of actual physical combat, and the injustice of his behaviour brought a wave of resentment sweeping over her.

Untying the waistband of her skirt, she tore it off impatiently, tossing it carelessly on to the bed. She should have said more, she fumed, unlacing her jerkin. So why hadn't she? The answer was as unpalatable as the question, and she pulled her silk wrapper over her shoulders with fingers that were not quite steady. The truth was that deep inside her she knew Barry had had some justification for his suspicions. Not that he could have known that, of course. Her feelings had been well hidden. But she couldn't deny that Morgan Fox disturbed her in a way that she had never experienced before, and that knowledge had left her feeling raw and exposed. She remembered once, some years ago, a girl she used to go to school with had asked her whether she had ever lost control with a boy. Helen had regarded the girl rather pityingly and replied that she didn't believe in all that nonsense; that people said things like that to excuse their own inadequacies. The girl had retorted tartly that if that was what she thought, she must be either stupid or frigid, and Helen had never forgiven her for throwing her remarks back in her face. Tonight, however, she felt strangely vulnerable to that memory, as if she stood on the brink of some certain revelation that would put paid once and for all to her sane and ordered existence.

CHAPTER TWO

HELEN was in the garden, helping her father to clear away all the leaves and broken twigs left by the winds of the past week when Jennifer came charging out to tell them that Susan had arrived accompanied by her stepbrother.

'Barry?' exclaimed Helen, looking up, and then coloured as Morgan Fox came round the corner of the house.

'No. Me,' he announced wryly, as Helen's father walked to meet him. 'How do you do? You must be Mr Raynor.'

'That's right.' Helen's father shook hands, removing his gardening glove to do so. 'Nice to meet you. How are you finding England after all this time? Cold, I expect.'

Morgan's mouth lifted slightly. 'Cold, indeed,' he agreed, as Mr Raynor passed him, indicating that he should follow him into the house, and then he looked back at Helen: 'Good morning. Are we interrupting anything?'

'Oh, no. No.' Helen shook her head quickly, noticing how much better his cream denim pants fitted him, the thigh-length sheepskin jacket accentuating the width of his shoulders. 'We—er—we were just tidying up the garden. It's been quite windy this last week and everywhere is covered with leaves.'

'Hmm, autumn,' drawled Morgan, making no effort to follow her father through the conservatory and into the warm kitchen. 'I've almost forgotten what it's like to smell woodsmoke on frosty air.'

Helen shifted awkwardly, conscious that her brown chunky sweater had holes at the elbows, and that her jeans after several washings clung to her like a second skin. 'I expect you'd miss the heat, though, wouldn't you?' she ventured, licking her lips. 'I mean—you must regard Africa as your home.'

His lips twisted then, and his eyes when he looked at her were cold and calculating. 'Oh, yes,' he agreed flatly. 'There's no chance of me coming back to live in England, if that's what you're afraid of.'

'I—I'm not afraid!' Helen was indignant. 'I only meant——'

'I know what you meant. I've had it from Barry since I got here. I forfeited my right to live at Banklands when I married Pam and went to live in Osweba!'

'Did he say that?' Helen was aghast.

'In so many words.' Morgan sighed, and then made a dismissing gesture. 'Oh, forget it. I have. As it happens, I have no desire to come back to England. My—work is in Nrubi. But there's still Andrea . . .'

'Your daughter.'

'Yes.' He glanced towards the house. 'We'd better be going in or your parents are going to suspect we're conducting some illicit liaison.'

'I don't think so,' said Helen quietly, and then on impulse

she added: 'Why did you mention your daughter? Does she want to come to England? I thought—when she didn't come with you ...'

'I know. And you're right. She didn't want to come, but not because she's indifferent. She—well, she's very shy.'

'But we—the Foxes, that is—they're her family!'

'I know that.' Morgan's eyes had lost their calculating gleam, but they were still cool as he changed the subject, saying: 'I've asked Barry what you would like for a wedding present, and he says I should ask you. What about it? Have you any ideas?'

Helen scuffed her booted toe in the soil at the edge of the path. 'Oh, I—anything you like.'

She couldn't look at him for a few moments, but when she lifted her head his eyes were upon her. Immediately, she felt that unfamiliar weakness inside her, that sense of wanting and need that had nothing to do with the emotion she felt towards her fiancé. She knew an almost overwhelming desire to touch him, to make him as aware of her as she was of him, and as if the thought was father to the deed, she felt her muddy boot slide across the concrete, forcing her to grasp his arm to save herself. She felt the taut muscles beneath her fingers, palpable through the rough skin of his jacket, the heat of his body, as just for an instant she was close against him. And then he had stepped back from her, a muscle jerking betrayingly in his cheek.

'I'm sorry,' she said, her face flaming brilliantly. 'I—I lost my balance.'

His eyes revealed none of his feelings, but he made a polite gesture towards the house and she was forced to go ahead of him. They walked through the glass-roofed conservatory where her father nurtured his collection of semi-tropical plants, and then in through the kitchen, scented with the smell of roasting meat.

Mrs Raynor was in the kitchen, and Helen introduced Morgan awkwardly, glad to go on into the living room where Jennifer was showing Susan her collection of pop pictures. Mr Raynor was there, too, lighting his pipe, and he smiled when his daughter came into the room, asking her whether her mother had got the kettle on.

Morgan came to join them and Helen thankfully took Susan upstairs to show her the sandals she wanted to borrow. But Susan had not been unaware of how long Helen had spent in the garden with her brother, and she was more interested in that than anything else.

'What were you talking about?' she asked, flopping down carelessly on to Helen's bed and flicking over the pages of a magazine she found on the bedside table. 'You looked awfully embarrassed when you came in. What was he saying to you?'

Helen's embarrassment was rekindled. 'We were talking about autumn, if you must know,' she declared impatiently. 'Look, do you want to try these sandals on or don't you?'

Susan's expression was resigned, but she obediently pulled off her boot and slipped one of the gold-strapped sandals on to her foot.

'Hmm, nice,' she agreed critically, turning her foot from side to side. 'How lucky we both take the same size.' Then she tossed it off again, and reaching for her boot returned to the attack. 'I should be careful if I were you anyway,' she said seriously. 'Barry was really mad last night, wasn't he? Jealous as hell!'

'I'm sure your mother wouldn't approve of you using that kind of language!' retorted Helen severely, hiding her unwilling anxiety in irritation, but Susan was not subdued.

'You talk like an old maid sometimes, do you know that?' she demanded. 'Just because I'm trying to give you a piece of advice, you act like I was a schoolgirl trying to advise the teacher. Well, let me tell you, Helen, I know more about men than you do. You might be older than I am, but emotionally speaking, you're not even in the running!'

Helen thrust the sandals into their box and held them out to the younger girl. 'Here,' she said. 'Take them. And stop trying to tell me how to run my life.'

Susan took the box and stood up. 'All right,' she said, moving her shoulders indifferently. 'But don't say I didn't warn you.'

'Warn me?' Helen couldn't let that go, although she knew she would regret it later. 'Warn me about what?'

'Why, about getting involved with Morgan, of course.'

'Getting involved with Morgan?' echoed Helen in disbelieving tones. 'I'm not getting involved with anyone—except Barry.'

'But don't pretend you wouldn't like to,' put in Susan infuriatingly. 'You're attracted to Morgan, aren't you? But you're wasting your time. He's married already.'

'I think you'd better go,' said Helen, controlling her temper with difficulty. 'And please don't repeat what you've said to me to anyone. To *anyone*, do you hear?'

'Don't worry,' Susan sniffed. 'I won't tell Barry, if that's what you're afraid of.'

'I'm not afraid of anything,' retorted Helen coldly, and led the way downstairs again herself.

Morgan and her parents were drinking coffee in the living room. Jennifer had returned to the study where she was doing her homework, and thankfully Susan went to find her, leaving Helen to face the others on her own. But at least she did not have the ignominy of feeling Susan's eyes upon her at every turn, and she poured herself some coffee and seated herself almost unnoticed in the corner.

Morgan was talking about Africa, telling Mr Raynor about the tropical diseases he had to contend with in the course of his work and the advances which had been made in vaccination and inoculation. It was fascinating listening to him describing conditions in an African village, the contrasts between the youths who went to the city to get educated and their parents and grandparents who still lived by the tribal customs which had existed for hundreds of years. He talked of the hostility which still existed in some areas between the so-called white man's medicine and the medicine men of the tribe, who used ritual magic and herbal remedies to effect their cures.

'But do they get results?' asked Mr Raynor smiling, as

he tapped his pipe against his palm, and Morgan gave a rueful grin.

'Sometimes,' he conceded honestly. 'I suppose faith has a lot to do with it, but occasionally some miraculous recovery comes to light. No one knows why. There are times when I'd say that by forcing a sick patient to drink some obnoxious mixture or applying a poultice made out of chicken feathers and God knows what else to an open wound would be fatal; but then I visit the village again and I find this chap going hunting with his brothers and I realise modern medicine has taken another backward step.'

'It must be quite frustrating,' said Mrs Raynor sympathetically, but Morgan shook his head.

'Not frustrating, no. I'm always glad when a patient gets well, by whatever means. I think perplexed is a better word. I'd like to learn more about these primitive medicines, study them in depth.' He paused, and Helen saw a strange expression cross his face. 'But that's not very likely, I'm afraid.'

'No,' Mr Raynor nodded. 'I imagine these witch doctors guard their secrets closely.'

'Yes,' Morgan agreed, but Helen had the distinct impression that that was not what he meant at all.

Soon afterwards, he said he would have to be leaving, and Mrs Raynor took the opportunity to invite him for dinner on Tuesday evening.

'Could we make that Wednesday or Thursday?' he asked apologetically. 'I—er—I have an appointment in London on Tuesday, and I don't suppose I'll be back much before ten.'

'Of course.' Mrs Raynor was eager to oblige. 'Thursday, then. If that's all right with you, Helen?'

Helen nodded. 'Any night suits me,' she shrugged, realising as she did so that she sounded offhand. But Susan's words still lingered, and she half wished she didn't have to see Morgan again until the day of the wedding.

Helen left her job at the hospital on Tuesday evening. She would be returning after her honeymoon, but it was good to feel herself free for almost three weeks. Not that she didn't enjoy her work. She did. It gave her great satisfaction to know that she was helping someone recover the use of their limbs, particularly if the patient was a child or an elderly person who had given up hope of ever being able to walk again. But the quality of her work was demanding and this week before the wedding was demanding enough in itself.

Nevertheless, the following morning found her at a loose end, with her parents and Barry at work, and Jennifer in school. During the afternoon she planned to go to the flat she and Barry were going to lease and take along some of the household things they had collected over recent weeks, but the morning was fine and sunny and she didn't much feel like applying herself to housework. Instead she took herself off into town, and in the paperback book department of W H Smith she encountered the one person she least wanted to meet.

'Morgan!' she said, rather dismayed, after practically walking into him round the end of one of the fixtures. 'Fancy meeting you here.'

'It's my usual port of call on visits to England,' he replied evenly, pushing a textbook on neural surgery back into the rack. 'I always take a pile of books back with me.'

'Yes,' Helen nodded, folding her fingers firmly round the strap of her handbag. 'Did you—er—did you have a good day in London?'

Morgan regarded her with a faintly mocking expression. 'Do you really want to know? I got the impression you didn't particularly want to meet me just now.'

'Oh, no.' Helen reddened. 'It was just—I was surprised to see you, that's all.'

Morgan inclined his head, and she moved jerkily away from him. Dear God, she thought sickly, what was wrong with her? Why couldn't she stand near him without becoming overpoweringly conscious of his hard masculinity? Why did the very sight of him in his worn leather jacket and black suede pants affect her with something very like a physical shock when Barry never ever had this reaction on her?

'Helen.'

He was speaking to her, and she swung round nervously, her fingers probing the buttons of her own suede coat. 'Yes?'

'Can I buy you a cup of coffee?'

'What? Coffee?' She moved her shoulders offhandedly. 'I—why, yes, I—suppose so.'

'Good.' He gestured towards the exit. 'Shall we go? I can call back here later.'

'All right.'

Outside, he turned towards the market place and she fell into step beside him, wondering rather anxiously what Barry would say when he found out that she had been having coffee with his stepbrother while he was at work. And then, she decided, she didn't care. She wasn't doing any harm, and besides, if she was honest she would admit that she had wanted to accept Morgan's invitation. But why that should be so after the way she had felt when she encountered him, she did not care to analyse.

They sat at a table in the window of a small café that overlooked the Shambles, and after the waitress had taken their order Helen was glad of the activity outside to distract Morgan's attention. But presently, after the coffee was served, he looked her way, and she put her hands down on to her lap to hide their damp unsteadiness.

'I'm sorry,' he said at last, and her eyes flickered bewilderedly up to his.

'Sorry?'

'Yes.' He tipped the front legs of his chair back and regarded her through narrowed lids. 'I shouldn't have invited you to join me. But I selfishly felt like some company.'

Helen didn't know how to reply. 'I—it was very kind of you invite me——'

'No, it wasn't.' He shook his head. 'I didn't do it out of politeness anyway.'

Helen licked her dry lips. 'Wh—why did you do it, then?'

Morgan's chair dropped back on to all four legs with a protesting creak. 'Because I find I like talking to you,' he said, and the ready colour that never seemed far away in his presence poured back into her face.

'I—I shouldn't have thought that was something to apologise about,' she murmured awkwardly at last, but when she ventured a look at his face she saw the wry cynicism in his expression.

'Something makes me think Barry wouldn't agree with you,' he remarked dryly. 'He made his feelings very clear the other evening.'

'Oh, Barry says a lot of things he doesn't really mean,' exclaimed Helen, moving her shoulders protestingly. 'He's very glad you've come home.'

'Is he?' Morgan sounded unconvinced. Then as once before, he changed the subject, saying abruptly: 'My father tells me you're a physiotherapist. Do you like working with old people?'

Glad of the respite from personal matters, Helen said: 'Not all my patients are old. There's a fair percentage of children, too, and in any case, I like the work.'

'Very commendable,' he remarked, raising his coffee cup to her. 'Have you ever thought of working outside the hospital system? In schools for handicapped children, for example?'

'I'd like to,' she answered frankly, 'but I still have my training to complete.'

'You didn't go to university.'

It was a statement and she shook her head. 'No. You did, though, didn't you? What made you decide to be a doctor?'

Morgan shrugged. 'I don't know. An interest in humanity, I guess, combined with a lucky ability to remember anatomical terms.'

Helen smiled, relaxing somewhat. 'I don't believe that. Your father said you got a double first.'

'My father talks too much,' he retorted without rancour, and Helen sipped her coffee, thinking affectionately of the man who had made her feel so welcome in his home.

'I suppose he told you about my marriage breaking up,' Morgan said suddenly, and Helen's new-found relaxation fled.

'I beg your pardon?'

'There's no need to look so flabbergasted—it's no secret. Pam and I separated two years ago. We were totally incompatible.'

Helen cleared her throat. 'He—I believe he did say something about it. Does—I mean—your daughter lives with you, doesn't she?'

'Yes.' Morgan finished his coffee and pushed the cup aside. 'Pam never wanted children. I don't think she'd have married me at all if Andrea hadn't already been on the way.'

'Oh!'

Helen's embarrassment was plain, and Morgan's lips curved teasingly. 'Oh?' he echoed. 'Is that all you can say? *Oh?* That doesn't shock you, surely. Not these days when every girl you meet accepts going to bed as part of the deal.'

'I don't!' declared Helen hotly, deriving a certain amount of courage from the strength of her convictions. 'And I don't believe *all* girls do either. That—that's just a rumour put around by those who do to excuse themselves!'

'Oh, yes?' His eyes were lazily mocking. 'Do I take it then that you and Barry—don't?'

'You can take it whatever way you like!' she retorted shortly. 'And now, if you've finished your coffee, I've got some shopping to do.'

The baiting light went out of Morgan's eyes, and without another word he thrust back his chair and got to his feet. But when she went to pass him, his hand caught her wrist, his fingers closing over it tightly.

'Wait,' he said, his warm breath fanning her forehead. 'Don't go rushing off like this. Perhaps we could have lunch together. Allow me to make amends for embarrassing you. Will you?'

Helen's breathing felt constricted. Because of the narrowness between the tables, her body was close to Morgan's, the muscles of his legs hard against hers through her skirt and the suede pants he was wearing.

'I—I don't know,' she got out jerkily, and because they were beginning to attract attention, he let her go and she made her way outside with air-gulping relief.

But in the narrow street outside, the question had to be answered, and although she knew she ought to refuse him she found herself agreeing to meet him in a couple of hours outside a pub they both knew.

For the rest of the morning she tried to justify her actions, but without much success, and by the time she had dumped her shopping in the boot of her Mini, parked on the outskirts of town, and walked the quarter mile or so to the Bartlemy, she was as taut as a violin string.

It didn't help when Morgan kept her waiting almost ten minutes only to find that the restaurant was closed and the bar already full to overflowing with people wanting snacks.

'I'm sorry,' said Morgan as they came out into the wintry afternoon again. 'I got held up at the bank.'

'The restaurant would still have been closed,' replied Helen tartly, and then, realising she was being shrewish, she added: 'It wasn't your fault.'

'I suppose we could go somewhere else,' he suggested thoughtfully, hands thrust into the pockets of his coat. 'Or should we just—forget it?'

Helen's heart gave a curious lurch at his words. 'Oh, no,' she found herself saying desperately. 'We can go somewhere else. We could even buy some food and have a picnic by the river ...' But as if to destroy even this nebulous suggestion, a few spots of rain blew into their faces.

Morgan turned his face up towards the lowering skies. 'No picnic,' he said ruefully, looking down at her again. 'Perhaps we'd better try somewhere else.'

Most of the popular eating places were crowded, and Helen didn't much fancy sharing a table with a crowd of students. Morgan was beginning to look weary of the whole idea, and almost without considering the ethics of the situation, she said: 'Let's buy some food and take it to the flat. I was going there anyway this afternoon.' And as her face betrayed the sudden guilt that swept over her, she added defensively: 'You'd like to see where Barry and I are going to live, wouldn't you?'

Morgan hesitated, a frown creasing his brow. 'That's not really the point, is it?' he asked. 'What is Barry going to say when he finds out?'

'Barry's not my keeper,' she retorted indignantly. 'But if you don't want to go——'

'It's not that,' he muttered, and then, as if a pain had suddenly made itself unbearable, he nodded, raking back his hair with an impatient hand. 'Why not?' he agreed shortly. 'How do we get there?'

Helen almost lost her nerve, but she managed to say quite coherently: 'My car—is parked on that lot near the river. We can go in that.'

'Where is the flat?'

'Gainsborough Crescent.'

'Gainsborough Crescent.' She could see him trying to place the vaguely familiar name. 'Yes.' He nodded. 'I know it. But my car—or rather my stepmother's—is nearer. We can buy what we need on the way there.'

'All right.' Helen had no objections. No one in Gainsborough Crescent would recognise Mrs Fox's yellow Volkswagen, whereas her blue Mini might incite attention.

Morgan bought some eggs and cheese and butter, and some rolls still warm from the oven. He also added a bottle of wine to the steadily increasing load in Helen's basket, and then they made their way to where he had left the car.

'You drive,' he said, after unloading their possessions into the back, and with a puzzled shrug of acceptance, Helen climbed behind the wheel. Morgan got in beside her, supporting his head with evident relief against the padded rest, and she gave him an anxious look before starting the engine.

'Are you all right?'

'Mmm,' he nodded. 'Just a slight headache, that's all. I've got something I can take for it when we get to the flat.'

Helen didn't waste any more time. The Volkswagen was easy to handle, and she swung out of the parking area and into the stream of traffic with the expertise born of experience. She had been driving since she was seventeen, and even Barry had had to concede that she was good.

It only took a matter of five minutes or so to reach Gainsborough Crescent, and she parked the car at the kerb before reaching into the back for her basket.

Morgan's hand closed on her arm, however, preventing her from reaching it. 'I'll get it,' he said, thrusting open his door and getting out, and reluctantly she went ahead into the building.

Gainsborough Crescent was a terrace of tall Victorian houses, most of which had been converted into flats now. Families were no longer so large as to require half a dozen bedrooms, and the rooms on the attic floor were snapped up by students wanting an economical bed-sitter.

The flat Helen and Barry were to occupy was on the first floor. It was small—just a bedroom, a living room, a tiny kitchenette and a bathroom, but at least it was all their own. The furnishings were the prime drawback. Nearly all the furniture had done service for more years than Helen would have liked to have guessed, and she hoped it wouldn't be too long before they could buy and furnish a house of their own.

Leading the way into the living room, she realised that this was the first time she had ever actually invited anyone there. Her mother had seen the flat, of course, but Barry's parents were waiting until they returned from their honeymoon and they could have a proper flat-warming.

Morgan closed the door behind him, glancing about him appraisingly as Helen bent to light the gas fire. The room was chilly, but the fire created a warm glow, casting enveloping shadows over the worn patches on the hide-covered couch.

Morgan walked straight through to the kitchenette, and when she followed him she found him taking two tablets with a mouthful of water direct from the tap.

'Hey,' she exclaimed, 'we have some glasses!' But he shook his head and straightened, saying:

'It's okay, they've gone. Now—do you have a frying pan?'

They ate in the kitchenette, seated on stools beside the

breakfast bar. Morgan had grated the cheese while Helen beat up the eggs, and then while she made light, fluffy omelettes, he opened the wine. His headache seemed to have disappeared as suddenly as it had come and she was relieved, aware that ridiculous as it might seem she had been concerned about him.

Although the wine was unchilled, it had never tasted so good and they drank the bottle between them. Helen felt quite reckless, drinking so much in the middle of the day, and she hoped that by evening the feeling of lightheadedness would have evaporated.

Morgan insisted on washing the dishes afterwards, and Helen commented on his efficiency. 'A man can learn to do a lot of things if he has to,' he replied, with a wry smile, and she knew he was referring to the break-up of his marriage.

'I suppose—Andrea helps,' she commented, picking up a tea-towel to polish their glasses. 'I mean—she's fifteen, isn't she? Almost grown up.'

'Almost,' he agreed, a frown drawing his brows together. 'Yes, she does what she can. But she was ill some time ago, and she's never really properly recovered, I'm afraid.'

Helen stared at his profile, wondering if she dared ask what was wrong with her, and then chided herself for her inquisitiveness. It was nothing to do with her, after all, and yet everything about this man troubled and intrigued her, and it was impossible for her to remain unmoved by his statement.

'Ill?' she said now, concentrating on the glass. 'How—ill?'

'She contracted pneumonia,' said Morgan flatly, and her murmur of dismay was barely stifled before he added: 'You wouldn't expect that in Africa, I suppose, would you? But in certain circumstances, it's quite possible. It's left her weak and—apathetic. What she needs now is care and encouragement, but God help me, I don't have the time to give it to her.'

Helen finished drying the glass and set it down with exaggerated precision. Then, as he had finished washing the dishes and was drying his hands, she ventured: 'Are—aren't there any centres where she could go? You know—to be with young people of her own age?'

'Not in Nrubi, no.'

'There are in Engl——'

'I know that!' He spoke harshly, and then, as if regretting his outburst, he muttered: 'I'm sorry, but that's one of the reasons why I came here. I thought, if I could persuade Susan to come back with me, to stay a few weeks—two, three months maybe—she might be able to help Andrea, give her back her confidence, show her that there are other people who care about her just as much as I do.'

'And?'

The word came automatically from Helen's lips, and Morgan looked at her as he rolled down the sleeves of his cream silk shirt. 'No,' he said dispassionately. 'It wouldn't work. I can't take Susan back there, even if she wanted to go, which I doubt. She and Andrea would have nothing in common. I doubt if she'd even get close to her. Andrea's too—sensitive. Susan would scare her, and besides, she's far too much of a liability. I have enough responsibilities as it is.'

'I see.'

'The pity of it is, I know that if I could get her to come to England, let her get to know my father, she'd be all right when——'

He broke off abruptly at that point and strode through to the living room, and after a moment's hesitation Helen followed him. He was standing before the fire, staring down into the flames, and she watched him for a few moments before saying awkwardly: 'Are you cold? Shall I turn the fire up?'

He turned then and she saw the look of strain he had worn a few minutes before had been erased. In its place was the polite mask of detachment he had worn when she first met him, and she felt curiously disappointed. Not that she wanted him to confide in her, she told herself impatiently, but the silent protestation did not quite ring true.

'I'm not cold,' he said now, with a slight smile. 'Are you ready to leave?'

'To leave?' Helen glanced behind her. 'I—well, I had intended to do some housework this afternoon. To leave—to leave the flat ready for when we get back from—from Majorca.'

'From your honeymoon,' agreed Morgan dryly. 'I see.' He paused. 'But how will you get back to town?'

'I can catch a bus,' declared Helen shortly, realising she sounded offhanded and despising herself for it. But she had hoped he would offer to wait for her, which in itself was a stupid thing to expect.

'All right.'

Morgan reached for his coat from the back of the couch where he had thrown it before having lunch, and Helen stood by tensely while he pulled it on. Then, checking the knot of his tie, he walked towards the door.

'Thanks for lunch,' he said, and she forced a faint smile.

'Thank *you*,' she countered, wrapping her arms protectively about herself, and he made a dismissing movement of his shoulders.

'Do I tell Barry I've been here or not?'

Helen shrugged. 'Please yourself.' She pressed her lips together for a moment to prevent them from trembling. 'I don't suppose it matters.'

Morgan stared at her for a long disturbing moment, and then with an exclamation, he wrenched open the door. 'I'll keep it to myself,' he declared harshly, and the door slammed heavily behind him.

Helen's hands went towards the panels after he had gone, fingers spreading against the dark wood as if to repel the feelings that swelled inside her. Then, withdrawing her hands again, she pressed them tightly together, forefingers resting against her parted lips. It took several minutes to get herself in control again, before she turned to face the room behind her with the tight ball of suppressed emotion in her throat almost choking her.

She was getting married on Saturday, she kept telling herself over and over again. This was to be her new home.

In less than three days, she would be Mrs Carson, Mrs *Barry* Carson, and here she was, allowing herself to indulge in futile fantasies about his own stepbrother. A married man, moreover, who had never at any time given her reason to suppose that he found her attractive, too. All he had said was that he liked talking to her—*talking to her*, nothing else. But nothing could alter the fact that she was attracted to him, which seemed totally disloyal to the man who was to be her husband.

Yet as the immediacy of the situation passed, and practical issues reasserted themselves, she began to put things into perspective. What was happening to her was not so unusual, after all, she told herself reassuringly. It was natural that in these final few days before the wedding she should have second thoughts about giving up her freedom. It was probably quite common for girls to imagine themselves attracted to some other man, particularly if the other man was hard and tanned, and disturbingly alien to her way of life. Why, even Susan had said what an attractive man he was, and she was his sister. Even so, it took her a long time to summon any enthusiasm to do the dusting and vacuuming she had planned, and when she left the flat it was with a feeling of escape ...

CHAPTER THREE

By Thursday evening Helen was congratulating herself on her common sense. What had happened the previous afternoon had been the culmination of a build-up of tension, a natural escape valve which had opened and allowed all the pent-up emotions she was feeling to break loose. Now she was herself again, her emotions were no longer in any danger of exploding, and she could face the future with increased confidence.

She dressed for her parents' dinner party with extra care. She wanted to look good, for Barry's sake, she thought affectionately, sliding half a dozen gold bangles on to her wrist. She had chosen to wear silk harem trousers in a particularly attractive bronze shade, teaming them with a buttoned shirt that almost exactly matched her hair. The colours gave her an all-over golden look, and the unbuttoned neckline of the shirt exposed a smooth length of creamy throat and the faintest shadow between her breasts. Round her neck was suspended a gold amulet which her father had brought back from North Africa after the war. It was Egyptian in origin, and the light caught the lettering that circled its coinlike design.

Jennifer pulled a face when Helen joined her parents downstairs, but her whistle of derision merely hid a mild sisterly jealousy. Mr Raynor smiled his approval, and her mother contented herself with saying: 'You do look nice, dear, but don't you think you ought to wear a sweater? It's an awfully cold evening.'

'Not in here, it isn't,' interposed her husband mildly. 'Stop fussing. She looks beautiful. I'm proud of her.'

'Thanks, Dad.' Helen flashed him a smile as the sound of a car turning into their drive came to her ears, and with a twinge of trepidation she realised their guests had arrived.

Jennifer went to open the door, wearing a long dress for once in deference to the occasion. Helen could hear her calling a welcome to Mr and Mrs Fox, and as her parents moved out into the hall to greet their visitors, she dutifully followed after. There was nothing to be alarmed about, she told herself severely. Barry was here now, and he would see that she had no time to worry about anyone else.

But when the Foxes came into the hall, Barry was not with them, and seeing Helen's anxious face, Mrs Fox exclaimed immediately:

'Now don't get upset, Helen. Barry's not coming. He's been off colour all day, a head cold, I think, and I've insisted that he stays home tonight to make sure he's fully recovered for Saturday.'

'That's right.' Mr Fox added his reassurance to his wife's. 'Morgan's had a look at him and he says it's nothing serious.'

'I—I see.' Suddenly the evening loomed ahead fraught with uncertainty. 'Well, if you're sure ...'

'He'll ring you tomorrow,' said Mrs Fox comfortingly, patting her arm, and as she did so, Morgan came in through the open door.

Tonight he was wearing a dark grey lounge suit, that looked almost black in the subdued lighting of the hall, but it was evidently new and fitted much better than his other suit had done. It threw his light hair into stark relief, complementing the darkness of his tan.

'I locked the car,' he said to his father, tossing the keys in his hand, and then turned to Helen's parents, greeting them with ease and friendliness. To Helen he addressed the politest of smiles, complimenting her on her appearance with characteristic detachment.

Mr Raynor closed the front door, and Mrs Raynor led the way into the sitting room. While their parents exchanged small talk about the weather and helped themselves to a drink, Jennifer took the opportunity to ask Morgan when he was going back to Osweba.

'In about ten days, I guess,' he replied good-humouredly. 'I promised Andrea I'd be back before her birthday, and that's in just under a month's time.'

'How old is she?'

Jennifer was not troubled with shyness, and he smiled. 'Fifteen,' he answered. 'Fifteen years old.'

'So she's fourteen now. Like me.'

'I suppose so.'

'I'll be fifteen in April. Where does Andrea go to school?'

'She doesn't,' replied Morgan ruefully, and Mrs Raynor turned to reprove her younger daughter for asking so many questions.

'Things are done differently in Africa,' she said, giving Jennifer a quelling look, and Jennifer muttered that she wished she lived in Africa if that was the case.

'You'd find life very boring, I'm afraid,' said Morgan, accepting a Scotch and soda from Mr Raynor. 'No clubs or discothèques, very little television and practically no cinemas.'

'What do you do, then?' asked Jennifer, aghast, and Helen nuged her in the ribs and told her to mind her own business.

'I don't mind telling her,' said Morgan, his eyes meeting Helen's with faint mockery. 'We swim, and play tennis. And we read a lot. And occasionally we go into Charlottesville and have dinner at the Yachting Club.'

'Do you have a yacht?' exclaimed Jennifer, in awe, but Morgan shook his head.

'No. But I have use of one when I need it. I have a very good friend in the government who lends me his from time to time.'

Helen looked down into the Martini her father had handed her. It didn't sound a boring life to her. On the contrary, she thought how satisfying it must be, living quite a simple life, using his skills as a doctor to treat people of a different creed and culture. She wondered why he wanted to bring Andrea back to England. She would miss the kind of life she was used to, and no doubt she would miss her father, unless he planned to come back to England to live, too. Her heart missed a beat. What would she do if Morgan came to live in York again? If he moved into Banklands with his father and stepmother now that Barry was getting married and moving away? There was no reason why he shouldn't, if that was what he wanted, but the prospect of finding him there when she visited her in-laws filled her with a ridiculous sense of dread.

She helped her mother to serve dinner. Mrs Raynor had no daily help, only old Mrs Latimer who came in two mornings a week to do the rough work, and as she was in her seventies now, more often than not Helen found herself cleaning up after her. But Mrs Raynor wouldn't hear of asking her to leave, and besides, she enjoyed the gossip the old cleaner usually had to impart. Mrs Raynor herself worked three days a week as a dental receptionist, more to get her out of the house than any need for the extra money, but on her days off she and Mrs Latimer put the world to rights over pots of tea in the kitchen.

The meal was delicious, as usual—soup and fish, and a

sweetly basted duckling in orange sauce. No one could find much room for the raspberry meringue that followed, but Morgan gallantly had a second helping, earning Mrs Raynor's undying gratitude.

Afterwards, they all adjourned to the sitting room again. Helen, strung up and nervous, perched uneasily on the arm of her mother's chair until Mr Raynor, noticing her restlessness, said:

'Take Morgan into the study, Helen. I'm sure he's not interested in all this woman's talk. Show him that book I bought in Harrogate last week. All about his part of the world, it is. It's a collector's piece. I'm sure it would interest you, Morgan.'

Morgan, who had been seated on the couch between his stepmother and Jennifer, rose to his feet politely. 'If Helen has no objection,' he essayed smoothly, and after a moment's hesitation, she got off the chair arm and walked towards the door.

'Can I come?'

Jennifer's treble was overridden by her father's denial, and while her sister grimaced her disappointment, Helen led the way along the hall to her father's study. Perhaps she should have invited Jennifer to join them, she thought, as Morgan leant past her to open the study door. She wasn't at all sure her nerves were proof against being alone with him again.

The book her father had bought was lying on his desk and while Morgan closed the door, she went towards it determinedly, pointing at its worn leather binding. 'It's a guide to Southern Africa,' she declared jerkily, 'published before the First World War. My father collects books, as you can see.' She gestured towards the book-lined walls. 'And this book interested him because just recently he was reading Burton's book about his pilgrimage to Mecca.'

Morgan seated himself on a corner of the desk, leaning over the book to turn the pages. 'Your father's interested in Africa?' he queried, and Helen moved round the desk as she nodded.

'He—he was there during the Second World War. North

Africa, at least. They say it's the most exciting continent, don't they? That it gets into your blood? Maybe that's why my father finds it so fascinating.'

'He'd like to go back there?' Morgan asked, straightening and folding his arms, and she shifted uneasily beneath his gaze, fiddling with the amulet that hung around her neck.

'I—I think so. Not that he's ever tried. He and Mum—well, they usually spend their holidays in Spain, but perhaps after Jennifer grows up they'll have the chance to be more—adventurous.'

'Adventurous?' echoed Morgan wryly. 'Is that how you see it?'

He slid off the desk then and to her horror came towards her. Her mouth went suddenly dry and her tongue clove to her palate, but she could not move. Every intimate thought she had ever had about him rushed through her mind in a chaotic stream, and weakness brought a betraying tremble to her knees. What was he going to do? she wondered desperately. Had he guessed why she was so nervous in his company? Had he sensed the paralysing awareness she felt in his presence that made a mockery of her feelings for Barry?

When he stopped before her, she almost swayed against him, but his hand reached out and lifted the gold amulet on its chain, and when he moved closer it was to read the inscription.

'Do you know what this says?' he asked, and the normality of his tone was like a cooling draught against her forehead.

'I—what—oh, no! No.' She shook her head, and as she did so, the chain moved sinuously against her neck. 'It—it's in Arabic, isn't it?'

'Yes.' Morgan's brows had drawn together in a frown as he observed her agitation, but with a tightening of his lips, he read: *'Follow thy desire while thou yet livest!'* He dropped the amulet again. 'Such things were engraved on the walls of temples and tombs. Rather too late for their inhabitants, but not a bad maxim for the mourners at the funeral feast.'

Helen's tongue appeared to moisten her upper lip. 'Is—is it a maxim you follow, too?' she asked unsteadily, aware that for some reason he was angry with her, but unprepared for the violence her words evoked.

'No,' he said harshly. 'No one can. Not unless one is totally without conscience.' His tawny eyes raked her upturned face with grim bitterness. 'Are you totally without conscience, Helen? Is that why you're looking at me like that? What do you want me to do, I wonder? Does a last-ditch affair appeal to you, before the bonds of matrimony tie you down? If so, you're wasting your time here. Find somebody else to satisfy your desires, because I happen to have a conscience, and whatever Barry thinks of me, I respect him!'

For a minute, Helen was too stunned to answer him, but then a kind of guilty indignation came to her rescue. 'How—how dare you?' she gasped, choking on the words. 'I didn't invite you here, and I certainly didn't want to spend any time alone with you! You've mistaken a natural effort on my part to act in a polite and friendly fashion towards my fiancé's brother for something quite ludicrous, and embarrassed us both. You're despicable! I think you'd better leave. You can make whatever excuses you like to my parents, I don't care, but I hope I never have to speak to you again!'

She whirled on her heel to make her grand exit, but almost against his will, his arm came out barring her way, and when she turned in the other direction he stepped into her path. There was a look of torment in his face, his mouth twisting with self-derision, and then he reached for her, his hands curving around her nape, compelling her firmly towards him.

'God, *Helen* ...' he muttered with a groan, and all her talk of despising him went for nothing beneath the demanding possession of his mouth.

Her head swam with the first touch of his lips. It was all one with the caressing compulsion of his hands on her neck, his thumbs probing the hollows behind her ears, his fingertips exploring the source of her spinal cord. Her hands were crushed between them and when she moved her fingers they encountered an unbuttoned opening in his shirt and curled inside. His skin was warm and roughened with hair, and when she separated more of the buttons from their holes she felt the responsive constriction of his muscles.

His mouth left hers to seek the hollow of her neck, and his hands slid down her spine to her hips, drawing her close against the hardening muscles of his thighs. She had never been so close to a man's body before, but instead of wanting to pull away, she pressed herself to him, arching her body and creating an intimacy between them that destroyed any hope of dismissing this embrace as the casual result of enforced proximity. They were both fully aware of what they were doing, and his tortured breathing was the only sound she could hear.

It was his hands on her upper arms that finally separated them, forcing her back from him while he still had the strength to do so. Her eyes, seeking his face, could see the actual physical control he was exerting and the strain it was putting upon him.

'You're crazy, do you know that?' he demanded, pushing back his hair with an unsteady hand, but when she made a sound of protest and swayed towards him again, he turned his back on her and put the expanse of her father's desk between them. 'Stop it, Helen!' he ordered tautly. 'We can't do this. My God, anybody could have come in and found us!' He broke off, shaking his head disbelievingly. Then he went on: 'That sister of yours, for example. How do you think she would have felt if she had come in? How would she have reacted finding her sister in another man's arms only two days before the wedding!'

Helen drew a deep breath and endeavoured to recover her composure, but it wasn't easy. He was right, she told herself dully, so why didn't she feel ashamed? Why wasn't she tearing her hair out, or dressing herself in the mental equivalent of sackcloth and ashes? Why hadn't she been the one to draw back, instead of him?

She trembled. She had always controlled the situation with Barry. She had never let his lovemaking get beyond certain limits. But Morgan wasn't Barry, and that was the trouble. With Morgan, she didn't want to draw back, she wanted to go on and on, giving herself to him, caring little for things like modesty or self-respect, only wanting to please him as he was pleasing her ...

Shades of that school friend's advice, she thought sickly. So much for her bland statements about inadequacy. What price virginity now? She pressed her palms down on to the cool surface of the desk. She was crazy. It was true. Because even now, with half the width of the room between them, she felt nothing but regret that he hadn't gone further ...

'Helen ...' He was looking at her as he fastened the buttons of his shirt she had opened. 'Helen!' He sighed. 'Oh, what's the use of denying it? I was as much to blame as you were, but hell, you invited it!'

She moved her shoulders in a little helpless gesture. 'I know.'

'What do you mean—you *know*?' He expelled his breath noisily. 'Helen, what can I say? What can I do to show you that I mean it when I say I'm sorry? God help me, I'm sorry.'

She wiped her damp palms down the seams of her silk pants. 'I—don't want you to be sorry,' she said carefully, aware of his harsh incredulity. 'That—that's what I mean.'

His eyes were narrowed until they were almost slits beneath his lowering brows. 'What did you say?'

'You heard me,' she insisted, her fingers opening and closing against her thighs. 'Why do you sound so surprised? Do you think I go in for this sort of thing? Do you think I'd let any man hold me as you have just held me? Do you imagine I've let Barry get that close to me?'

'And haven't you?'

'*No!*' Her lips trembled with indignation. 'I—I told you once before that—that I——'

'—that you don't sleep around, I remember.' Morgan's

response was curt. 'All right, all right. So what am I to gather from that? That I broke some of the rules?'

'*Rules?*'

Helen's voice broke on the word and now she turned her back on him, snatching a tissue out of the box on her father's desk and dabbing furiously at her eyes. She mustn't cry, she told herself desperately, not now, not when, as he said, their parents or Jennifer could come in at any moment.

'Helen ...' He said her name close by her ear and she realised with a start that he had come to stand right behind her. 'Helen,' he said again, and there was the same note of anguish in his voice that she had heard before. 'Don't make me hate myself any more than I do already.'

Her breathing was coming in short, uneven gasps, but she tipped her head back to rest against his chest, and with a groan of defeat his arms slid round her waist, propelling her back against him. Her body moulded itself to his almost as if it had been designed for just that purpose, and he buried his face in the curtain of silky hair that curled into her nape. His hands moved carelessly upward, over her ribcage to the buttoned neckline of her shirt, sliding inside almost possessively to close over the ripe fullness of her breasts. They surged against his fingers and she felt the unsteady draught of his breath against her neck as his tongue stroked the erratic pulse that fluttered below her jawline. His own heart was pounding behind her and the throbbing demands of his body were no longer in any doubt.

He was twisting her round in his arms to seek the parted sweetness of her lips with his mouth when they heard voices coming along the passage. Almost immediately she was free to do what she could to restore her clothes to order, while Morgan placed himself protectively in front of her, tightening his tie with something less than detachment.

Mrs Raynor came into the room first, followed by Mr and Mrs Fox, with Mr Raynor bringing up the rear. Fortunately, Jennifer was not with them to comment on Helen's hectically flushed cheeks, or to ask why her mouth was bare of all lipstick, but Mrs Raynor looked at her daughter rather doubtfully, before asking what Morgan had thought of the book.

Morgan, at least, appeared unperturbed. 'I found it very interesting,' he replied, and only Helen knew that his smile was a trifle forced. 'Er—Helen tells me you're interested in the dark continent, Mr Raynor.'

Helen's father had been looking thoughtfully at his daughter, too, but now he transferred his attention to the younger man. 'What? Oh, yes—Africa,' he nodded. 'I was in Egypt during the war.'

'So Helen told me.'

'Have you and Helen been having a nice chat, darling?' Mrs Fox queried, seemingly less suspicious of what had been going on than Helen's parents had been. 'I've just been suggesting to your father that perhaps we ought to be going. After all, Barry is on his own at home, and it would be unkind to be late.'

Helen had stood through all this with a feeling of numbed unreality. The curious looks her mother had been giving her, Morgan's polite responses, Mrs Fox's coy reference to Barry's isolation—none of it seemed real somehow. It was as if she was standing outside herself observing what was going on, but not taking any actual part in the proceedings. She looked at Morgan, but he was not looking at her, indeed, he seemed to be avoiding looking at her, and a sense of panic swelled inside her. Was he not going to say anything, then? Had what had happened between them meant so little to him that he was prepared to go away from here in the sure knowledge that in two days' time she was going to marry his stepbrother? It couldn't be true, and yet what else was she to think?

Mrs Fox turned to her then, bringing her down to earth with a distinct thud. 'I'll give Barry your love, shall I?' she asked, touching Helen's hand playfully, and cravenly, Helen could only nod her head. 'I expect you'll see him tomorrow,' his mother added. 'I doubt if he'll be prepared to wait until the ceremony to see you again.'

Gradually they all moved out into the hall, Morgan following the two couples, but just for a second Helen grasped his hand and held him back.

'Take me with you!' she whispered imploringly. 'Please—take me with you?'

'Take you where?' he demanded in a low harsh voice. 'Back to Banklands? Can't you wait until tomorrow to see your fiancé?'

The look of pain that crossed her face at his deliberately cruel words effected a miraculous change in his expression, and his fingers closed tightly over hers for a moment. 'Where can I take you?' he demanded, in an entirely different voice, and she breathed:

'To Osweba—to Nrubi!'

He stared at her grimly for a moment, then he shook his head. 'I can't do that.'

'Why can't you?' she appealed, but he turned away releasing her fingers.

'Marry my stepbrother,' he advised her roughly. 'I have nothing to offer you.'

Helen did not appear to wave goodbye to their guests, and when Mrs Raynor came to find her some minutes later, she was still standing blindly in the study. Her mother entered the room reluctantly, not entirely convinced that she ought to interfere, but sufficiently concerned to know she would have to get to the bottom of the matter.

'Helen,' she ventured softly. 'Helen, what are you doing?'

Like a statue that is suddenly brought to life, Helen lifted her shoulders in a curiously tentative gesture, then, as if gaining confidence from that small activity, she shook her arms and faced her mother courageously.

'I'm not doing anything,' she said, but her voice belied the carelessness of her words. 'Have they gone?'

'Of course.' Mrs Raynor came further into the room. 'But I expect they're wondering, as I am, why you didn't bother to go and see them off.'

'Oh ...' Helen spread her hands with assumed indifference. 'I didn't think it was—necessary.'

'No?' Her mother sounded sceptical. 'You're not usually so casual. Is something wrong?'

'Wrong?' There was a squeaky note in Helen's voice

which she quickly disguised with a cough. 'I—what makes you think that anything's wrong?'

'You tell me,' retorted her mother tersely, and Helen gave a short mirthless laugh.

'What could be wrong? All the arrangements for the wedding are made, the reception's booked, my dress is in the wardrobe upstairs, and Barry already has the tickets for our flight from Luton. What could be wrong?'

Mrs Raynor looked at her worriedly, shaking her head, 'I don't know. I don't know what it is. But something's happened, I know that. I know you, Helen, and I can sense that everything's not as it should be.' She paused. 'Did Barry's brother say something? I thought you looked a little flushed when we came in here, but at first I put it down to the heat. It's very warm in here.'

Helen had hardly noticed, but now she shook her head, saying tautly: 'You're imagining things, Mum. I—Morgan said nothing. Nothing at all.'

Mrs Raynor frowned. 'He didn't do anything else, did he?'

'Anything else?' Helen turned her back on her, moving towards the desk, and closing the book Morgan had been looking at earlier. 'What on earth do you mean?'

'You know what I mean,' declared her mother shortly, coming round and forcing Helen to look into her face. 'Helen! Did Morgan Fox touch you?'

'Touch me?'

'Stop repeating everything I say! I'm asking you a straight question. Did Morgan Fox lay his hands on you?'

'Ellen!' Mr Raynor's voice interrupted them. 'Ellen, for heaven's sake, what's going on? Why are you catechising the girl? What's she done?'

'That's what I'm trying to find out,' exclaimed his wife, her face pale and anxious. 'Didn't you think something was wrong when you came in here before? Didn't you think Helen looked upset?'

Mr Raynor shrugged. 'I thought she looked hot, that's all.' His eyes shifted to his daughter's. 'Is something wrong, sweetheart?'

Her father's gentle enquiry was almost her undoing, but

Helen managed to blink back the tears that trembled at the back of her eyes and shake her head vigorously.

'There you are, then,' said her father, addressing his wife. 'If Helen says there's nothing wrong, then that's good enough for me. What could be wrong anyway? Heavens, she was all right before the Foxes arrived!'

'That's just my point,' declared Mrs Raynor irritably. 'She was all right before—*Morgan* Fox arrived.'

'Morgan?' Mr Raynor shook his head. 'What has Morgan to do with anything?'

'Don't you understand?' Helen's mother heaved a sigh. 'Helen and Morgan were in here together when we came in.'

'I know that. I sent them in here.'

'I know you did, but what happened in here, that's what I want to know.'

'What happened?' Her husband stared at her impatiently. 'What could happen, Ellen? Good lord, Helen's going to marry Barry on Saturday. Don't you trust her?'

'Of course I trust Helen. But Morgan Fox is a totally different proposition.'

'But Morgan is already married!' exclaimed Mr Raynor, exasperatedly. 'Helen! For goodness' sake, tell your mother what you and Morgan were talking about before—*Helen*!'

But Helen had left them, running desperately along the hall and up the stairs to her room.

CHAPTER FOUR

The Lady of the Camellias, thought Helen bitterly, surveying herself before the long mirror of her wardrobe. Not that the flowers she was carrying were actually camellias, but burgeoning white roses, their stems hidden beneath the binding of white ribbon that circled her bouquet. But they might more suitably have been those blossoms, always associated with grief and tragedy, for not even Marguerite Gauthier, the heroine of Dumas' famous novel, could have felt more wretched than Helen did at present.

Time was slipping away, and in less than an hour she was due at the church to make her vows to Barry, to promise to love him and cherish him, and obey him. Yet how could she do that when she no longer knew whether what she felt for him was love or simply associated feelings compounded of liking and affection?

During the past thirty-six hours, since she had been with Morgan in the study, she had tried to tell her mother how she was feeling, but it was as if, after that confrontation when Morgan and his parents had departed, Mrs Raynor had decided to let well alone. Maybe her father had advised her not to press Helen too hard. Whatever it was, her mother had evaded discussions of a personal nature, using the last-minute arrangements for the wedding as an excuse to keep out of her daughter's way.

It was possible that she suspected Helen was having doubts and didn't want to recognise them. After all, this wedding had already cost more than they could afford, and Helen cringed from the possibility of calling it off. How could she? Even knowing how she felt, how could she throw her parents' generosity back in their faces? Whatever happened now, the reception would have to be paid for, her dress and the dresses of the bridesmaids had already been paid for. To back out now would be a betrayal of everything they had ever done for her, and *why*? Because a man she had known less than a week had entered her life and turned it upside down. He didn't want her: he had said so. He found her physically attractive, but then so had a lot of men before him. If only he had not been the one who had made her feel like a woman, who had taken all her preconceived ideas of love and marriage and stamped them into the ground. Until his advent, she had been happy with Barry, content to accept his lovemaking without expecting any miraculous response from her. But all that was changed now. Now she knew what it should be like—what it *could* be like—and she knew she would never be satisfied with anything less.

Yet here she was, only an hour before the wedding,

dressed in her lace wedding gown, still allowing circumstances to dictate her life. Downstairs, her aunt and cousins were chattering away to her mother, as the girls put the last-minute touches to their bridesmaids' dresses, and in her bedroom adjoining, Helen could hear Jennifer humming as she, too, prepared for the big day. Susan would be arriving any minute, already attired in the rose-pink polyester Helen had chosen for her attendants' dresses, and in the hall, laid out on the table, were their bouquets of pink and white carnations.

It was like a snowball gathering momentum as it rolled, she thought fatalistically. From the minute Barry had placed his ring on her finger, the train of events had been set in motion which would end abruptly at the altar at eleven o'clock. No, not end, she corrected herself despairingly. After the service was over, there would be a new beginning, that was all, the beginning of her life as Mrs Barry Carson.

A wave of sudden panic swept over her. She *couldn't* go through with it. It was no use telling herself that without Barry she had no future. Better a life of loneliness and isolation than a life governed by the dictates of a man she didn't love.

Moisture trickled down her spine as she contemplated going downstairs and announcing that the wedding was off. She couldn't begin to imagine what her mother would say, what her father would say! Would they think she was capricious and selfish, considering her own feelings above everybody else's? Would they plead with her not to disgrace them in the the face of so many friends and relations? Would they even begin to understand why she had hesitated so long?

She paced restlessly across the carpet. Outside, a faint glimmer of sunlight was breaking through lowering clouds, highlighting the hoar-frost that still sparkled on the grass of the lawn. It was going to be a fine day after all, and she shivered as she imagined all the people gathering at the church. What would they think if she didn't turn up? Traditionally, it was the groom who abandoned his bride, seldom the other way about.

She turned back into the room. If it had to be done, it was better done at once. Before Barry and his best man left Banklands. For the first time, she contemplated his reactions. She could imagine his anger, and with good reason. She was letting him down, and she deserved his censure and contempt. And yet wasn't it better to let him down now than at some nebulous future date? Sooner or later he would begin to suspect she didn't care about him as she should, and there was always the possibility of Morgan coming back into her life. If he brought his daughter to England as he said he intended to . . .

Morgan!

She pressed her hands to her stomach as a wave of misery swept over her. What were his thoughts this morning? How did he feel about the wedding? Or was it of supreme indifference to him as he had maintained? Didn't he feel even a trace of envy that she was presumably marrying his stepbrother instead of him? But of course not. He was already married. Why did she keep forgetting that?

With an intense feeling of sickness invading her stomach, she put down her bouquet on the bed and stretched her hand round to unzip her wedding gown. It dropped in folds of lace at her feet, and she stepped out of it carefully, aware that her knees were shaking. Trembling fingers peeled off the sheer tights she wore underneath, and replaced them with the trousers of her lovat green tweed suit, the suit she had laid out in readiness for her departure for Majorca later in the day. There was a scarlet shirt to wear with it, and she buttoned this quickly across her pointed breasts, tucking it into the waistband of the pants. The jacket was jerkin-length, and fitted snugly about her waist, and as a final rejection of her bridal status, she replaced her sandals with suede boots.

She was studying her reflection with anxious eyes when the door behind her suddenly opened. Helen had been unaware of anyone's approach, and she swung round guiltily to find Susan Fox standing in the doorway, staring at her.

'Well, well,' she observed, coming into the room and walking round her critically. 'That's a novel wedding gown,

I must say. Do you think pink silk really goes with dark green tweed?'

Helen was in no mood for facetiousness. 'What are you doing here, Susan?' she exclaimed through tense lips, realising the girl was not yet attired in her bridesmaids' dress. 'I—I don't have time to chatter now. I'm busy.'

'So it appears.' Susan made no move to leave her. Instead she bent and lifted the lace bridal gown from where it still lay on the carpet. 'I must say, you're very casual with something that cost over seventy pounds.'

'Susan, will you go?' Helen didn't mince her words. 'Please. I—I have things to do.'

'What things?' Susan frowned. 'That's your going away outfit, isn't it? Oh——' Her lips formed themselves into an astounded circle. 'You're not planning to elope, are you? How romantic! All the guests waiting at the church and the happy couple speeding on their way to Gretna——'

'Susan, I am not planning to elope! I'm not planning anything. I—I just want to be left alone.'

'It's a bit late to feel like that, isn't it?' Susan consulted her watch. 'In exactly forty-five minutes' time, you'll be walking down the aisle at St Giles, with dozens of people just waiting to catch a glimpse of you.'

'I know that, Susan.' Helen heaved a sigh. 'But—well, I have some things to do first.'

'What things?'

Helen shook her head, and as on another occasion, Susan leapt to the right conclusion. 'You're thinking of backing out, aren't you?' she exclaimed incredulously. 'My God! You really have got cold feet, haven't you!'

'I don't know what you mean.'

Helen turned abruptly away, but not before Susan had seen the betraying anguish in her face. 'Oh, Helen!' she breathed, in a low tone. 'Helen, for heaven's sake! You can't back out now.'

Helen slanted a look over her shoulder. 'Why can't I?' she countered tremulously, and Susan spread her hands.

'Because—because you can't. Glory, Barry would have a fit! You should have heard him yesterday when he couldn't get in touch with you. He rang here half a dozen times, but you were always unavailable.'

'I—I was out most of the day. I had my hair done ...'

'Some hair appointment that lasted eight hours!' remarked Susan acidly, but then she too sighed. 'Helen, why didn't you tell him yesterday? Why didn't you confide your anxieties in him? Surely he's the person to turn to—the person most involved, besides yourself, of course.'

'I did ring him yesterday evening,' Helen defended herself, and Susan regarded her disbelievingly.

'You knew Barry had arranged to go out with his friends last night,' she said. 'It was seven o'clock when you rang. You must have known he would be out by then.'

The accusation was justified, Helen knew. She had put off ringing until it was too late, but she hadn't known how to tell him.

'By the time he came home, he was in no condition to ring you back,' continued Susan reminiscently. 'Morgan had to practically carry him out of the car.'

Helen licked her lips. 'Morgan—went with them?' she asked, and Susan nodded.

'Sort of. He went along to drive them all home afterwards. Somebody had to stay sober.'

'I see.'

Helen bent her head and with a sound of exasperation, Susan pressed her hands together. 'You'd better get changed. You're leaving for the church in half an hour's time.'

Helen felt cold, but suddenly resolute. 'I'm not going to church,' she said quietly. 'The wedding's off.'

'*Off!*'

Susan stared at her aghast as Helen picked up her handbag and left the room. She made no attempt to follow her as she went determinedly down the stairs, and only as Helen reached the living room door did her steps falter for a moment. Then, not waiting to hear what was going on inside, she opened the door and went into the room.

Her entry caused no small ripple of consernation. Her cousins, Alison and Linda, were there, prettily attired in their bridesmaids' dresses while her mother and Aunt Mary were pinning pink carnations to the lapels of their wedding suits. They all stared in surprise at Helen in her tweed pants suit, and Mrs Raynor made a gesture of impatience.

'Helen! Aren't you dressed yet? You went upstairs over an hour ago. We have to leave in——'

'I'm not leaving, Mum. Not for the church, anyway. That's what I've come down to tell you. I'm not going to marry Barry. I've—changed my mind.'

Mrs Raynor uttered a sound of stunned disbelief and collapsed into the chair behind her. Aunt Mary hurriedly instructed one of the girls to get Aunt Ellen a glass of brandy and then herself turned on Helen.

'Have you taken leave of your senses, girl?' she demanded, no trace of sympathy colouring her tones. She gave a short mirthless laugh, 'You must be out of your mind, coming down here only minutes before you're due to leave for the church and upsetting your mother like this. For goodness' sake, this is no time to have second thoughts. Go and get dressed at once, and stop giving your mother a heart attack!'

'I'm sorry, Aunt Mary.' Helen was adamant. 'I can't do that. I'm not going to marry Barry.'

'Helen ...'

Her mother's frail cry was almost her undoing, but she had to stand firm. 'It's no good, Mum,' she cried, shaking her head. 'I tried to tell you yesterday, but I was too much of a coward to get the words out. I'm sorry—you don't know how sorry I am. But I can't marry someone I don't love, not even for you and Daddy.'

Mrs Raynor sipped the brandy Alison had given her. 'But you were so happy ...' she exclaimed. 'You and Barry. You were so much in love ...'

'I thought I loved him,' said Helen, nodding. 'But now I know I never did.'

'How do you know that?' asked Aunt Mary irritably. 'What's happened to make you change your mind?'

'It's that stepbrother of his, isn't it?' cried Mrs Raynor, revealing she was not as prostrate as she appeared. 'I knew it was the other night, but your father persuaded me to leave well alone.'

'What stepbrother?' Aunt Mary looked puzzled, and her sister explained:

'Barry's stepbrother, Morgan Fox. You remember—I told you that Mr Fox had been married before. Morgan's the son of his first marriage, just as Barry was the son of his mother's late husband.'

'Ah . . .' Aunt Mary nodded, and Helen's mother went on:

'He's a doctor. Lives in Africa somewhere.'

'Osweba,' said Helen automatically, then coloured as they both looked at her.

'It is Morgan Fox at the bottom of this, isn't it?' demanded her mother bitterly, but Helen hastened to deny it.

'Morgan's married, you know that!' she protested, but Aunt Mary only snorted.

'Since when has a set of marriage lines prevented two people from getting into bed together?' she snapped, and Mrs Raynor began to dab her eyes with her handkerchief.

'Oh, Helen,' she exclaimed. 'How could you? How could you?'

'How could I what?' Helen was indignant. 'I've done nothing. I'm certainly not having an affair with Morgan Fox, if that's what you think.'

'Then what are you doing?' cried her mother, as Mr Raynor appeared in the doorway.

'Now what is it?' he asked, looking round the group with unconcealed impatience. 'I can hear your voices in the kitchen. What's going on? Helen, why aren't you dressed?'

'She's not getting married, that's why,' declared his wife, and burst into tears.

'Not getting married?' Mr Raynor looked blank, and with reluctance, Helen explained. 'But, Helen . . .' Her father obviously found it difficult to put his feelings into words. 'Helen, you can't do this!'

'Oh, Dad, please! I am doing it. Can't you try to understand? I know it's mean and selfish, I know I'm letting you both down, but would you rather I married Barry only to end up in the divorce court?'

'But how do you know you don't love him?' protested her father, and Mrs Raynor sniffed:

'Because she thinks she's in love with somebody else.'

'Somebody else?' Her father was obviously confused. 'Who?'

'Ellen thinks it's Barry's stepbrother,' declared Aunt Mary, reprovingly, 'Whoever he might be. Do you know him?'

'You mean—Morgan? But he's married——'

Mr Raynor looked staggered, and something inside Helen snapped. 'Yes,' she said then, uncaring what they thought of her, only intent on clearing Morgan's name. 'Morgan is the reason why I've changed my mind. But not because he's asked me to marry him. As you keep pointing out, he is already married. But since I've got to know him, I've realised that—that what I felt for Barry was only—only affection. Not love!'

'Love!' sneered Aunt Mary, and her mother shook her her head in despair.

'Barry's a fine young man,' she exclaimed. 'He's got a good job and he thinks the world of you! How can you throw him over because you're infatuated with a man who doesn't even care about you?'

Helen could feel tears pricking her own eyes now. 'Do you think I don't realise what I'm doing? Wouldn't it have been easier for me to marry Barry? I mean, I know Barry is all the things you say, and he'll make some girl a marvellous husband. But not me!'

'Well, I think you're overwrought,' said her father flatly. 'I think this whole thing has been too much for you. Planning the wedding, getting the flat—all the people you've invited. What you really need is a holiday, love, away from all this. When you get to Majorca——'

'When I get to—*Dad*! I'm not going to Majorca! Can't you accept that? I'm *not* going! I've thought about it and I've decided—you can have the money I've saved towards the house Barry and I were going to buy. That should pay for the reception. I realise I can't repay you for all the time and trouble I've caused, or the disappointment you must be feeling, but I can't go through with it feeling as I do, I just can't!'

'Helen!' Her father caught her arm. 'I won't let you do this. Do you understand? I won't let you make a fool of us like this. You're going to marry Barry if I have to carry you to the church bodily, do you hear?'

Helen gasped. 'You can't be serious!'

'Oh, can't I?' Mr Raynor looked grim. 'All girls go through this—this stage-fright. Even I had doubts on the morning I married your mother, and look how that's turned out. I'm not going to let you throw away your life for a whim. Because that's all it is, a whim!'

Helen pulled away from him. 'You can't make me marry anyone,' she cried, and hearing her words she thought how obscene they sounded in a house which only minutes before had been full of happiness and excitement. 'You can take me to the church, you can lead me down the aisle, but you can't make me say "I will".'

'Oh, Helen ...'

Her mother burst into further floods of tears, and Helen wished with all her heart that she could comfort her. But the only words Mrs Raynor wanted to hear she could not utter, and with a choking throat she ran out of the room.

Uncle Ben, her aunt's husband, stared in amazement at her as she ran through the kitchen where he was helping himself to a second glass of whisky. Outside, the yellow Volkswagen Susan had arrived in blocked the drive. On impulse, she ran to that and climbed behind the wheel. As usual Susan, with her natural disregard for property, had left the keys in the ignition, and the engine fired at once. Whether her parents had guessed what she planned to do, Helen didn't know, but in the rear-view mirror she saw Barry's sister run out as she accelerated swiftly down the road. At least she had believed her, thought Helen bitterly, noticing Susan was still wearing the jeans and sweater she had worn to come round in.

Perhaps she had been foolish to come to the flat, she thought some time later, when the hammering came at the door. It was the first place they would have thought of looking for her, and for a moment panic gripped her as she contemplated what Barry was going to say. Still, she had to face his wrath sooner or later, and getting up from where she had been huddled on her knees beside the gas fire, she went to the door.

But it was not Barry who was standing outside, hands pushed aggressively into the pockets of his overcoat. It was Morgan, and judging from his expression he was no less angry than his stepbrother would have been.

Helen didn't want to let him in. She was afraid of what he was going to say. But he pushed past her, and short of leaving the door ajar for any passing stranger to eavesdrop, she had no choice but to close it after him. He had stationed himself on the hearth, and when she turned to face him, his mouth was a thinly drawn line.

'Well?' he said, and there was savagery in the word. 'What the hell do you think you're playing at?'

Helen chose her words carefully. 'I'm not—playing at anything——'

'Damn you, you know what I mean. What game is this you're instigating? What do you hope to gain from making a fool of everybody, including yourself?'

Helen pressed her palms tightly together. 'I—don't hope to gain anything,' she replied, again using his words. 'I'm sorry, but——'

'You're *sorry*!' Morgan glared at her. 'Do you think *sorry* makes everything right? My God, you're a cool one! Jilting my stepbrother on his wedding day, and then turning round and saying you're sorry! Couldn't you at least have had the decency to tell him? Instead of skulking here like the bitch you are?'

His words tore into her heart like so many burning bullets, and it was all she could do to continue looking at him, to hide the pain he was deliberately inflicting.

'I—I told my parents——'

'And Susan—thank heavens!'

'Susan?'

'Yes, Susan. Who the hell do you think told Barry?'

'I thought—my father——'

'Your father did nothing except swallow enough whisky to sink a battleship. And your mother ...' He shook his head. 'She's taken to her bed, and refuses to see anyone.'

'Oh, *God*!'

'Yes—oh, God!' he mimicked her cruelly, 'Helen have you got no conscience?'

'Of course I've got a conscience,' she cried helplessly. 'But what would you have had me do? Marry your brother knowing I didn't care for him as I should?' She pulled a handkerchief out of the pocket of her pants and blew her nose. 'You don't understand ...'

'Oh, spare me the dramatics! And if you start to cry, so help me, I'll strangle you! You have nothing to cry about. You're the one who started all this. You've got what you wanted, so don't turn on the tears for my benefit.'

Helen caught her breath. 'You're—you're so cruel!' she choked. 'I didn't want to hurt anyone.'

'But you have,' he declared flatly. 'Like your father, Barry uses alcohol to assuage his feelings, but when he gets over his grief, you're going to feel the brunt of his anger and resentment.'

'Then that should please you,' she retorted, taking refuge in retaliation, but his next words disarmed her.

'Strangely enough it doesn't,' he muttered grimly. 'I've had the experience of a marriage that didn't work, and it can be hell! I've told Barry that, but something tells me he won't take my word for it.'

The reminder of his married state was like another knife turning in an already open wound. Helen's arms wrapped themselves almost convulsively about her slim body, and for the first time she looked beyond the immediate present to the hollow emptiness of the days ahead. She knew Morgan was right about one thing. Barry would be vindictive in his resentment, and there was every possibility that he might try to do her some bodily harm. She remembered his jealousy of Morgan, and knew if he ever heard the real reason behind her rejection of him, his temper could well get the better of him. She wasn't frightened of what he might do to her, rather apprehensive of the way he might choose to humiliate her.

'So ...' Morgan withdrew his hands from his pockets to hang loosely at his sides. 'Why did you do it?'

It was the question she had been dreading, and bending her head she made an offhand movement with her shoulders. 'I—I don't love him.'

'It's a bit late to decide that now, isn't it?' he snapped. 'As I hear it, you've been engaged for six months.'

'We have.' Helen moved her shoulders again. 'I—well, I suppose I'm entitled to change my mind.'

'Change your mind, be damned!' In an instant he had covered the space between them and grasped her by her shoulders. Shaking her until her head tumbled back on her neck like a broken stem, he raged: 'It was what happened the other night, wasn't it? The night I kissed you? You let a moment's promiscuity erase feelings that have tempered and matured over months of care and consideration! You've let the fire of passion blind you to the real and lasting emotion you share with Barry——'

'*No!*'

'How can you say that?'

'I know it!' she declared tremulously. 'I—Barry has never kissed me like you did!'

'Perhaps you should let him,' he retorted coldly, but she shook her head.

'I—I couldn't. Don't you see? I couldn't let him—touch me as you touched me.'

'Why not?'

'Because—because I couldn't.' She moistened her dry lips with her tongue. 'Morgan, I've never wanted any man to touch me before——'

He thrust her away from him so violently she almost fell and went to stand by the window, staring broodingly at the street outside. He had pushed his hands into his pockets, but she could see their balled outline through the material of his coat, and she knew he was by no means recovered from his burst of temper. Now and again a spasm crossed his face, as if of pain, and when he turned back to her he lifted a hand to his head and massaged his scalp as if it hurt him.

Speaking through his teeth, he said slowly: 'I told you the other night, Helen, there can never be anything between us. You're a beautiful girl, and I enjoyed—touching you. But that's all, do you understand me? That's all.'

It was like a blow to the solar plexis. It had the same breath-stopping impact. Helen weathered it bravely, and then said: 'It makes no differenece. I still can't marry your stepbrother.'

Morgan made a sound of frustration. 'But that's crazy! Helen, there might be a chance—just a chance—that Barry will come round and forgive you for today's fiasco. Just a chance, mind you. But if he did—if he could be persuaded——'

'No,' she said, clearly and succinctly. 'No, Morgan. I won't change my mind.'

'*God in Heaven!*'

He turned back to the window again, and Helen moved nervously across to the kitchenette. 'Do you—that is, would you like some coffee?'

'Coffee?'

'Yes, coffee. I—I have some dried milk, or at least, there's some here. I don't suppose technically it is mine any longer . . .'

'Helen!' His use of her name was agonised. 'Helen, don't do this. Please! Come with me to Banklands now. Tell Barry it was all a terrible mistake——'

'With sugar, or without?' she asked tautly, and his groan of impotence went unacknowledged as she filled the kettle.

There was something steadying about preparing coffee, Helen thought, concentrating on the task to the exclusion of everything else. Spooning the instant grains into the cups, waiting for the kettle to boil, she could pretend that everything was as it should be—that only hours before she had not abandoned her bridegroom and her family and run away, that the pile of presents laid out in the reception hall of the hotel were not waiting to be returned to their donors, that Morgan had not just delivered the most shattering rejection of her life. It was unbearable to imagine what life would be like after he returned to his home in Osweba. To consider the days and weeks, the months and probably years before she might lay eyes on him again was too tortuous to endure, and she had to steel herself not to rush into the living room and beg him to take her with him . . . in any capacity he cared to name.

The cups rattled irritatingly in their saucers as she carried the tray through to him. She set it down abruptly on the table by the window and pushed a cup and the sugar basin towards him.

'Help yourself!'

'I don't want any coffee!' Morgan expelled his breath on a sigh. 'I don't know how you can drink the stuff. In your place, I'd be feeling pretty damn sick!'

Helen, who had raised her cup to her lips, put it down again. 'I do feel pretty damn sick!' she retorted tremulously. 'But I have to go on, don't I? I have to survive. With or without your permission.'

'My permission!' Morgan shook his head bitterly. 'My God, if I'd known—if I'd suspected——'

'—what kissing me might bring about?' she finished flatly, and he nodded.

'Yes. Yes.' He raked back his hair with the gesture she was coming to know so well. 'Helen, you don't know how bad I feel about this.'

'There's no need——'

'There's every need, damn you! God, why did I do it? Why did I let you goad me into it?'

'G-goad you into it?' Helen stared at him disbelievingly. 'Is that how you see it? Is that the conclusion you've reached to satisfy your conscience?'

Morgan's fists clenched. 'I'll never do that,' he retorted. 'Satisfy my conscience, I mean. I'll never forgive myself for what I've done to Barry, or you too, for that matter.'

'I don't want your forgiveness!' she burst out raggedly, and the pulse at his temple jerked spasmodically.

'What do you want, then?' he demanded, and she took

a deep breath before giving in to the impulse to plead with him.

'I want to go back to Osweba with you. Take me with you! You said you wanted someone to help with Andrea. Let me do it. I'm used to dealing with children, and I'm sure I could help her——'

'*No!*'

'Why not?' She trembled. 'What's the matter? Don't you think I'm fit to have charge of your daughter?'

'That has nothing to do with it,' he muttered, pacing restlessly across the room.

'What has, then?' She paused. 'You needn't worry about—about you and me——'

'Needn't I?' His tone was sarcastic.

'No.' She moved her shoulders expressively. 'I—I should regard it as a job of work. I wouldn't get in your way——'

'You'd be living in my house.'

'I—I'll stay at a hotel, then.'

'In Nrubi?' He shook his head. 'I don't think so.'

Helen twisted her hands together. 'I—I'm not afraid of what—of what people might say. Living in your house, I mean.'

'Aren't you?'

'No, I—why, if I was to leave here with—with you, there'd be plenty of talk——'

'Don't I know it?'

'—so that—so that anything that happened in Nrubi——'

'And what about when you had to come back here?' he enquired coldly. 'What then?'

'I—I would face that when the time came.'

'No, Helen.'

'Why no?'

'Because—because——' Morgan sighed heavily. 'I explained to you. I want Andrea to come back here to live. The time between then and now would be—four, five months at the most. Could you come back and face your family and friends, not to mention my family, at the end of four months?'

'Yes,' she cried eagerly. 'Yes, if you'd let me.'

'Oh, Helen!'

He stared at her impatiently, but she sensed he was weakening and hurried on: 'I haven't—forgotten about your wife, you know. I realise she might object to me living in your house——'

'Pamela has nothing to do with this,' he stated grimly, and she realised, with angry self-depreciation, that she had overstepped the mark again.

'I'm sorry,' she muttered, bending her head, and he uttered a violent oath.

'You've no idea what it's like living in Africa,' he said. 'The heat—and the flies! The insects! Are you afraid of spiders, because I tell you, we get some enormous long-legged monsters, that can move faster than you can.'

Helen couldn't help the shiver of unpleasant anticipation that ran over her skin like the brush of a spider's web, but her voice was steady as she lifted her head and said: 'Does that mean you're going to take me?'

Morgan's lips tightened. 'No! That is—dear God, Helen, you don't know what you're asking. There's nothing for you in Osweba. Just the heat, as I've said, and a lack of proper sanitation—and the company of a girl who may not even like you!'

Helen shrugged. 'I'm prepared to take that chance.'

'Why?' Morgan's eyes narrowed. 'Because you think I might conceivably change my mind about you? Oh, Helen, I won't do that. I can't. And what's more, if—and it's a big *if*—if I were to be foolish enough to take you out there, you and I would have to have a new arrangement.'

'What do you mean?'

'I mean I'd be your employer and you'd be my employee. Just that. Nothing more. If you're hoping an African moon will alter anything, forget it. I've got no intention of ever touching you again, do you understand?'

His words were almost as painful as his denunciation had been earlier, but she hid her humiliation on a show of dignity. 'Have I asked you to?' she demanded indignantly, but he was not deceived.

'I just wanted you to know that you'd be wasting your time if you're planning to play the *femme fatale*!' he declared brutally. 'Do you still want to take the job?'

CHAPTER FIVE

THE flight from Nairobi up the coast to Charlottesville was not long, but it was very uncomfortable. After the pressurised cabin of the jetliner which had flown them across two continents to the Kenyan capital, the twelve-seatered transport of Osweba Domestic Airlines jarred and bucketed them about like a cork on a particularly choppy sea. Apart from themselves, there were only three other passengers, which added to the lightness of the craft and made it that much less stable. Helen, who had never suffered from airsickness in her life, began to feel distinctly queasy, and Morgan's look was wry as he assured her they would be landing in fifteen minutes.

Fifteen minutes to Charlottesville, thought Helen, and excited tremors added to her nervousness. Yet, for all that, she would not have wished herself anywhere else than with the man lounging moodily in the seat beside her, knowing there was no immediate chance of their separation. All the way from London, she had told herself that, over and over again, hardly able to believe that he actually agreed to take her with him.

Not that it had been easy—for either of them. The days following the expected day of the wedding were not ones she would want to live over again, and she had learned what it felt like to be a social leper.

Of course, everyone blamed Morgan as well, and she realised what she owed him for allowing them to think that. It would have been so much harder to bear it all alone, and while when they were alone he treated her with a kind of veiled contempt, in company he nevertheless stood as a shield between her and the world at large.

It was natural that Barry should despise both of them, but Mr Fox had shown an unusual amount of understanding. Perhaps that was only as it should be as Morgan was his own son, but whatever his motives Helen was grateful for one person who did not hate her.

Her own parents took it rather differently. With them, it was more a case of loss of face. She had humiliated them, and they could not forgive her for that. Even Jennifer, thwarted of her big day, was bitter and resentful, furious with her sister for spoiling everything. She had not liked going in to school and having to tell them that the wedding had not taken place. There were too many rumours going around about it being Barry who had jilted Helen, not the other way about, and while Helen welcomed them, Jennifer treated it all as a personal slight.

The real crunch had come, however, when Helen announced that she was going with Morgan when he returned to Africa. Until then, her mother had adopted an aggrieved air which Helen knew she would discard with time. The news that her elder daughter was planning to travel five thousand miles with a man everyone knew to have a broken marriage behind him threw Mrs Raynor into a horrified panic, and all manner of threats had been produced in an effort to persuade her not to go.

Helen had given in her notice at the hospital on the Monday following the fatal Saturday, gaining her immediate freedom as the weeks of her holiday provided the weeks of her notice, but it was not until the Wednesday of that week that she had summoned up the courage to tell her parents what she planned to do. By then, she had had the necessary medical examination and vaccinations against smallpox, cholera and yellow fever, and was feeling very much under par. Her mother's pained recriminations and her father's tight-lipped disapproval proved the last straw, and she had burst into tears and fled up the stairs to her room.

But, as if knowing with some sixth sense that something was wrong, Morgan had arrived that evening to speak to Mr and Mrs Raynor. In Helen's subdued presence he had explained why she was accompanying him to Osweba. He had assured her mother and father that his invitation had had nothing to do with Helen's decision to call off the wedding, and that it was only a temporary post until Andrea could be persuaded to come back to England with him.

'But why Helen?' Mrs Raynor had protested, still not convinced of his integrity. 'Why not some other girl? Susan, for instance.'

'I did think of Susan,' Morgan admitted, 'but could you see my sister living such a simple life?' He shook his head. 'No. Susan would never do it, and besides, surely it's better for Helen to get away right now, until all the gossip dies a natural death?'

'Well . . .' Mr Raynor was looking less tense now. 'If that's what she wants . . .'

'It is,' said Helen, speaking for the first time, and only she had seen the flicker of anger that lit the fires in Morgan's eyes at her words.

Her interview with Barry had been brief, but inevitable. She had expected him to appear on Sunday morning, black-browed and aggressive, but it was Thursday before he put in an appearance. Later, she guessed he had kept away in the faint hope of bringing her to her senses. Maybe he had practised a waiting game, knowing how it would play on her nerves. But Wednesday's announcement had filtered back to him, and he had known that his time was running out.

He came to her home in the early evening. As it happened, Mr and Mrs Raynor and their younger daughter were out, a parents' evening at the local grammar school which Jennifer attended, and Helen had been glad to have the house to herself. Her arm, punctured with hypodermic needles, was sore, and the headache that plagued her eyes was a hangover from the reaction. When the doorbell rang, she went to answer it on leaden feet, and stood back aghast when Barry barged in.

'I gather you didn't expect to see me,' he remarked, surveying her with cold eyes. 'My God, you look lousy! What's the matter with you? Can't you sleep or something?'

'I—I have a headache,' said Helen quietly. 'But I'm glad you've come, Barry. It gives me a chance to apolo——'

'Don't give me that!' he cut in on her rudely. 'You're not sorry, so why pretend you are?'

'Barry, I didn't want to hurt you——'

'Hurt me? That's a laugh! You jilt me almost at the church door and then tell me you didn't want to hurt me!'

'I know, I know.' Helen's head was pounding, and she was beginning to feel sick. 'There's no way I can make up to you for what I did. Saying sorry isn't enough, I know, but they're the only words I have.'

'Huh!' Barry glared at her. 'So sorry that you're clearing off to Osweba with that precious stepbrother of mine! I bet you felt really cut up when you agreed to go with him, didn't you? Was that before or after you took him to the flat?'

'Barry——'

'Shut up!' His lips curled. 'You make me sick, do you know that? All that talk about saving yourself for our wedding night! It was all moonshine, wasn't it? How long did you save yourself with Morgan? One hour? Two?'

Helen said nothing, just stared mutely at him knowing he was only trying to expunge all the bitterness he was feeling. But her silence seemed to irritate him more than her retaliation would have done, and he stepped nearer to her, thrusting his face close to hers.

'So innocent, weren't you?' he sneered unpleasantly. 'So pure and virginal! I should have destroyed that myth once and for all while I had the chance!'

Helen shook her head helplessly. 'I know you won't believe this, but—but I haven't—I have never—slept with —with anyone.'

'Like hell, you haven't!'

'I haven't!' She stared at him appealingly. 'Barry, can't you see? All I had was doubts, doubts about loving you. Would you rather I had married you feeling as I did? Not knowing whether or not we would end up in a divorce court in a couple of years' time? Why won't you think of that? I probably did you a favour!'

'Some favour,' muttered Barry sourly. 'I could have killed

you on Saturday, you know. I couldn't believe you'd do such a thing!'

Helen sighed. 'I'm sorry.'

'So you keep saying.' Barry's lips curled. 'I should have known. I saw the way you looked at him. Did you arrange to meet him that night, or the next morning?'

'We didn't arrange anything,' protested Helen desperately, pressing a hand to her churning stomach. 'Honestly, Barry, Morgan—well, he doesn't—he isn't interested in me in that way.'

'In what way, then?'

'In no way, except as—as a companion for—for Andrea.'

'And you're giving up a several thousand pounds a year job just to go out to Osweba to be a companion to a fifteen-year-old girl?' He stared at her scornfully. 'Oh, pull the other leg, please!'

'All right. All right.' Helen's control snapped. 'I'm not *just* going out to Osweba for that! I admit it. I am attracted to your brother—he knows that. But he's not attracted to me, more's the pity!'

'You *bitch*!'

Helen's fingers sought her cheek now as she remembered the blow he had struck her. She didn't remember much that happened after that. She must have passed out, because when she came round she was lying on the couch in the living room and there was a terrible argument going on over her head. She was too confused then to understand why Morgan should be there, but later she had learned from her mother that he had apparently arrived just as they returned from school, which was almost immediately after Barry had hit her. Barry had been on his knees beside her in the hall when they came in, but after a swift examination Morgan had brushed him aside and carried her into the living room.

She had felt so sick, she remembered with loathing, a feeling which still lurked persistently in the lower reaches of her stomach. But then she peered out of the window and realised that the sickness she was feeling now was caused by the pilot's erratic descent towards the runway at Charlottesville.

She turned to look at Morgan, and her heart quickened its beat as he returned her gaze. But his eyes were cool and calculating, and she was forced to look away from their contemptuous appraisal. He had slept most of the way to Nairobi, slumped in the comfortable seat beside her, awakening only when one of the pretty stewardesses came to offer him lunch or dinner, but she had still been conscious of him and of her own feelings towards him. Now, awake, he was no less disturbing and she wondered how long she would be able to sustain this detachment between them.

They had landed at Khartoum and Morgan had changed his clothes, discarding his dark suit for mud-coloured levis and a matching denim shirt, but Helen, still in her tweed pants and silk shirt, was already feeling the heat. Still, she thought, tonight they would have reached their destination, and she had plenty of lightweight pants and dresses in her suitcase.

The De Havilland was coming in low now and Helen forgot her discomfort in the thrill of seeing the shores of the Indian Ocean spread out below them. Inland from Nairobi, she had glimpsed the lakes of the Great Rift Valley, but nothing had prepared her for the beauty of the ocean. Fringed by the reef, which Morgan in one of his less taciturn moments had told her was more or less continuous along the whole length of the East African coast, it had a quality of unreality, its fine coral sand and waving palm trees looking like some latterday paradise.

The city of Charlottesville, capital of Osweba, curved in a horseshoe along the edge of the ocean. Tall, skyscraper blocks of offices and flats were superseding the shack-like dwellings that still sprawled in ungainly squalor around the outskirts of the city, and the thoroughfares were wide and tree-lined, with sun-splashed sidewalks thronged with people of all nationalities and colour.

Airport formalities were swiftly dealt with. Their entry into Africa having been monitored at Nairobi, the Osweban authorities conducted the most perfunctory of checks, and then they were free to collect their luggage and seek transport into the city. Following Morgan, Helen was bemused by the strangeness of her surroundings, and he had to wait impatiently for her to catch up with him and their black-skinned porter before summoning one of the bright orange cabs waiting outside.

The drive into Charlottesville took them along the coast highway, and Helen exclaimed with delight at the blue-green waters edged by their scarf of coral sand. It was hot in the car, and the sea breezes were very welcome, loosening her hair from its securing band and blowing it into Morgan's face. Conscious of this, she turned to find him wiping hairs out of his mouth, and she quickly restrained the errant strands.

'I'm sorry,' she said, and her faint smile was an appealing plea for understanding, but he accepted her apology without comment.

It was late afternoon when the tyres of the cab screeched to a halt before the impressive portals of the Charlottesville Yacht Club. Helen, who hadn't really considered that they might be spending the night in the city, stared apprehensively at the white-painted façade of the verandah where already several groups of people were gathered, drinking from long frosted glasses, decorated with slices of fruit. In her tweed pants and scarlet shirt, she was hardly attired for a tropical evening, and she wished Morgan had suggested she changed her clothes at Khartoum as he had done.

Through the palm trees that provided welcome oases of shade in the grounds of the club, she could see the shifting line of the ocean, but nearer at hand there were tennis courts and a swimming pool, as well as a play area for children. Obviously, it was a popular meeting place for the wealthier inhabitants of Charlottesville, although she saw that its patrons were a mixture of every race and creed.

Morgan and the cab driver had unloaded their cases, and Helen stood by awkwardly as her new employer paid the fare. Before the car could pull away, however, they were being hailed from the verandah, and Morgan turned with a smile to greet the dark-skinned man who came down the steps to meet them.

'Hey, man!' the newcomer exclaimed warmly. 'Why didn't you let us know you were coming back today? I'd have had Moses come out and meet you. No need for you to take a cab!'

'I don't mind riding in a cab, James,' protested Morgan goodhumouredly, accepting the man's hand and his arm about his shoulders with evident affection. 'I don't warrant a private car and chauffeur. I'm no force for power in the cabinet.'

'Nevertheless, you are a very dear friend,' the man assured him seriously, and Helen saw a curious look pass between them, before he added: 'Andrea will be so happy that you are back. She has missed you.' Then he turned bright, interested eyes in Helen's direction. 'I see you have brought a visitor ...'

'Yes.' Morgan's eyes flickered coolly over her. 'This is Miss Raynor, Helen Raynor. She's going to work with Andrea. Try and—persuade her to come out of her shell.'

'Not Susan, then.' Again that exchange of glances, and as Morgan shook his head, the man called James took Helen's hand in his huge black one. 'How do you do, Miss Raynor,' he asked, with a flash of white teeth. 'I hope you are going to enjoy your visit to my country.'

'Allow me to introduce James Oneba,' Morgan put in rather sardonically at this juncture. 'Mr Oneba is Minister of Cultural Studies in President Cehgwi's government—and a fine yachtsman.'

Helen was taken aback. Was this the friend in the government Morgan had spoken about to Jennifer? The one whose yacht he borrowed from time to time? Foolishly, she had expected the man to be white, but she managed not to let her surprise show in her face. In any case, James Oneba was one of the most striking-looking men she had ever seen, tall and broad and muscular, his light-weight lounge suit barely concealing the strength of his biceps and the powerful expanse of his shoulders.

Now she thanked him for his welcome, and assured him politely that she liked what she had seen so far.

'Good. Good.' James Oneba was pleased. 'We are just a small country, but we need to attract tourists like yourself, people who visit here and can take back useful impressions to friends and relations.'

'Something tells me Miss Raynor's friends and relations won't be visiting Osweba,' observed Morgan, his mouth twisting wryly, and then as his friend looked puzzled, he went on: 'I thought I'd find you here, James. How are things? How is Andrea?'

'She's fine, fine.' Oneba snapped his fingers to a dark-skinned boy, dressed in the safari uniform of the club, who hastened forward to gather their suitcases, and then led the way up the steps and into the clubhouse.

Following the two men, Helen wished she could change out of the clinging tweed suit. Even carrying the jacket over her arm made her skin prickle, and she wished Morgan would explain what their immediate plans were. Why had he asked James Oneba about his daughter? Where was she? Were they not returning to Nrubi tonight?

Several of the people on the verandah of the clubhouse spoke to Morgan in passing, women as well as men, and Helen felt herself the cynosure of all eyes. Obviously, these people were wondering who she was and what she was doing here and why she was with Morgan. She realised with a pang that perhaps some of them even knew his wife. No one had told her where Pamela Fox lived, whether indeed she still lived in Africa. It could be embarrassing if Mrs Fox lived in Charlottesville, or worse, Nrubi. Maybe that was the reason Morgan had been so loath to bring her.

James Oneba led the way through the entrance hall of the club, which was refreshingly air-conditioned, into a cool light bar at the back, overlooking the swimming pool. Here, in the pleasant draught of the air-conditioning, one could sit in low rattan loungers, comfortably cushioned, and enjoy the scenery without feeling the heat. The long bar served drinks of every kind, including English and American lagers, and there were dishes of nuts and olives, cheese straws and chipsticks, for anyone who couldn't wait for the adjoining restaurant to open.

Helen was ensconced in one of the striped loungers while Morgan and Oneba went to the bar. Left alone, she was more than ever conscious of inquisitive eyes upon her, and concentrated her attention on the kidney-shaped swimming pool beyond the meshed screen that kept the night insects at bay. The area surrounding the pool was mosaic-tiled, and there were more of the rattan chairs and glass-topped tables to take bottles or glasses. Patterned air-beds invited relaxation, but now it was early evening and the swift tropical twilight was rapidly giving way to total darkness. The floodlighting was switched on even as she watched, and the pool, lit from within, looked more inviting than ever.

Her eyes turned reluctantly to the bar, and she saw Morgan and his companion talking seriously together. What were they saying? she wondered nervously. Was Morgan explaining to his friend why she was here and why she had wanted to leave England?

A circle of sweat had appeared on the back of Morgan's shirt, and Helen put her hand inside the neckline of her own, wondering how she could prevent it sticking to her. Fortunately she was wearing a bra, which protected her modesty, but looking round at the other women in the room she realised she was probably unique in this respect.

Faint colour invaded her cheeks at this awareness. It was her first experience of the differences between England and Osweba, a kind of relaxing of moral codes of conduct that was in itself disturbing. Foolish really, to think this of such a simple thing, but their lack of self-consciousness was not assumed. What did she know of Africa, after all? Apart from what she had seen on newsreels and the like. Would she find her own values undermined in this alien society, where the heat came first in the order of things? What was it about the place that already she was aware of her own alienation when compared to the hot-blooded sensuality she could feel all about her? Was that what she had sensed in Morgan? Was that what had set him apart from his stepbrother?

But no. Watching him as he made his way towards her again, carrying a tall frosted glass containing something that looked like lime juice, she knew it was more than just his sensuality that had attracted her to him. She was aware of every small detail about him, from the thick smooth vitality of his light hair to the long-fingered capability of his hands. She knew the changing moods that lightened and darkened his expression, the harsh gashes that bracketed his mouth when he was angry, and the whimsical twist of his smile when he was not. She had felt the hard length of his body against hers, and known the demanding possession of his mouth, and in blacker moments had suffered the whiplash cruelty of his tongue. He could be hard and aggressive, gentle and considerate, mockingly sarcastic or devastatingly intense; in all his moods, he played on her emotions with the same ravaging impact.

Now he set the glass down in front of her and indicated that it was hers. 'Fruit punch,' he said, 'with just a trace of something more potent.'

Helen looked at the glass and then up into his face. 'Morgan, what is going on? How long are we staying here? When are we leaving for Nrubi?'

A flicker of impatience crossed his face. 'What's wrong? Don't you find this place appealing?'

Helen sighed. 'Of course. At least, I have no opinion about it, one way or the other, only——'

'Good. Then you won't be disappointed when I tell you we're spending the night with the Onebas,' he announced, glancing round to see the other man making his way towards them carrying two glasses. 'Here's James now. Put on your best smile. He thinks you're very attractive.'

Helen tightened her lips as James Oneba came to join them, but he and Morgan seated themselves relaxedly, apparently unaware of her discomfort.

'Morgan tells me you are training to become a physiotherapist,' Oneba ventured with obvious interest, and Helen was obliged to answer him.

'Yes,' she replied politely, picking up her glass to taste its contents experimentally, but Oneba went on: 'Is it not unusual to interrupt a course of that kind?' and she was forced to elucidate.

'I—it is—unusual, yes. But—circumstances made it desirable to take a break at this time, and as—as Doctor Fox required someone to help with his daughter . . .'

Her voice trailed away, and she concentrated all her attention on the liquid in her glass. What had Morgan told him? she wondered, for the second time, but Morgan's face when she glanced at him was enigmatic.

Oneba was nodding slowly. 'Morgan is fortunate indeed to have so charming an associate,' he remarked gallantly, and Helen's sigh of relief went unnoticed as he turned once more to his friend. 'Did you see Marsden?'

Morgan's pose of relaxation fled as he straightened in his seat. 'Yes,' he said flatly, his voice suddenly harsh and abrupt. Then: 'How has she been? Did the children make any difference?'

The change of topic was startling, even to Helen, and James Oneba's mouth turned down slightly at the corners. 'Very well,' he said, and Helen guessed he was answering some unspoken bone of contention between them before continuing: 'She has been much as usual. We have seen little of her. She has spent most of the time in her room.'

Morgan nodded, cradling his glass in his palms, legs apart, his forearms resting along his thighs. Judging by the brooding expression he was wearing, Helen guessed they had been talking about Andrea and feeling the need to take some part in this conversation, she asked:

'Has Andrea been staying with you, Mr Oneba?'

'James! Please, you must call me James.' James Oneba smiled, his white teeth flashing brilliantly. 'I am not like your so-respectful employer who insists on formality.' He glanced with a return of humour at Morgan. 'And yes, Andrea has been staying in my house since her father went away.'

That explained their overnight stay in Charlottesville at

least. Helen looked defiantly at Morgan and then, seeing that he had almost finished, gulped hurriedly at her drink.

The two men rose as she finished, and she put down her glass and joined them, allowing James Oneba the privilege of carrying her jacket for her. She followed him towards the door, with Morgan bringing up the rear, trying not to feel concerned about his eyes upon her back.

Outside, with the sun extinguished, the air was warm but no longer so exhausting, and while they waited for James's car to be brought round from the parking area, Helen looked excitedly towards the brightly-lit shops and thoroughfares that ran at right angles to the ocean. Traffic was quite considerable at that hour of the evening, but although the components of the scene were familiar, the whole was not. There was a curious vibrance in the atmosphere, a sense of awareness, of excitement almost, that Helen decided had something to do with her own feelings towards the country. It was impossible not to be aware of its potential dangers, and that in itself was something wholly elemental. Or maybe she was aware of the danger Morgan presented to her, and that was all bound up in her reactions to the situation.

Their luggage was loaded into the boot of James's sleek Mercedes, and then, with James himself driving and Morgan seated beside him, they turned into the stream of traffic heading towards the city centre. In the back of the car, Helen stared through the windows eagerly, trying to immerse herself in her surroundings to the exclusion of everything else. There was plenty to see, and the prospect ahead of her of meeting not only Morgan's daughter but also James Oneba's family was sufficient to dispel any lingering thoughts of Morgan himself. Nevertheless, his behaviour towards her was a continual abrasive to her emotions.

They left the busy heart of the city behind and climbed the quiet hills behind to the Oneba house. Floodlit, as were many of the houses in the area, it presented a white, columned portico, reminiscent of pictures of plantation houses Helen had seen. It sprawled over half an acre, and was surrounded by grounds covering three or four times that area. Helen could see a wealth of gorgeous trees and flowering shrubs, all moon-pale in the artificial lighting, and as they circled the gravelled forecourt, she heard the sound of water falling into a stone basin.

'Welcome to my home, Miss Raynor,' James Oneba announced with pride, as he swung open his door and turned at once to help her alight. 'Welcome to Zimbake!'

'Thank you.'

Helen got out rather bemusedly, looking about her uncertainly as several servants came hurrying out to greet their master, taking charge of the car and the luggage, and ushering their guests towards the entrance of the building. She was relieved to find Morgan beside her, urging her forward, although his low-voiced words did nothing to reassure her:

'Prepare yourself to greet *both* of James's wives with equal civility. A Muslim is entitled to take four wives, if he so wishes.' And at her look of dismay, he added mockingly: 'Who knows? Perhaps he is considering you as a possible third.'

There was no time to make any suitable retort or to reassure herself he was only teasing her, before they entered into an exquisitely-tiled hall, with a high arched ceiling from which was suspended a magnificent crystal chandelier. By its trembling prismatic light, Helen saw the tall pedestals with vases filled with exotic blossoms, the delicate statuary of an inner fountain, the fan-like widening of a shallow staircase that swept in a semi-circle to the balcony above. Veined marble and intricately-wrought iron, porcelain and alabaster; Helen had never seen such magnificence, and to imagine herself staying in such surroundings was yet another skein of unreality that wound itself about her.

Several children came rushing to greet their father as he strode ahead of his guests, and he swung the two smallest up into his arms, turning to face Helen with their arms about his neck.

'See,' he said, with unselfconscious candour. 'We have

visitors. Andrea's papa has brought a beautiful young lady to stay with them.' Then he smiled. 'Irena and Hugo,' he added, for Helen's benefit. 'Are they not alike?'

The two children were indeed twins, but while Helen was trying to think of some suitable thing to say, two women came hurrying down the stairs to join them, obviously alerted by the excited chatter of the children. They were totally unalike, in that the older of the two had skin as black as ebony, while the younger was strikingly pale. The girl, for Helen could see she was little more than seventeen or eighteen, was obviously of African origin, but her blood had been mixed with a gentler blend and only her hair retained its lustrous darkness.

At their approach, James put down the twins and they ran off to join their older brothers and sisters who clustered in a little group, watching the visitors with wide eyes. That their gaze lingered longest on Helen was probably due to the fact that they were already acquainted with Andrea's father, but nevertheless, after what Morgan had said, Helen felt discomfited by it.

Still, the appearance of their mother—*mothers?*—Helen's shoulders moved in silent uncertainty—provided a diversion, and James drew her forward to perform the introductions. It soon became apparent that the two women were more nervous than Helen of meeting a stranger, but they greeted her shyly as she shook hands with each of them in turn. Their names were Sarah and Mariana, Mariana being the younger of the two.

'And now we will show you to your room, Miss Raynor,' her host declared firmly. 'I am sure you would like to rest a while before we have supper, and Morgan, I know, is eager to go in search of his daughter.'

'A—a wash would be most welcome,' Helen confessed, glancing round awkwardly at Morgan, but he had gone to speak to the children and it was left to Mariana to lead the way upstairs.

Followed by a servant carrying her suitcases, Helen climbed the shallow staircase after the girl. From time to time, Mariana would turn and offer her a wide, encouraging smile, and although Helen's gaze was drawn more often to Morgan and his host, still talking together in the hall below, she appreciated the African girl's friendliness.

A galleried hallway opened off the balcony overlooking a floodlit inner courtyard where scarlet poinsettia and frangipani and exotic African lilies competed between paved walks and creeper-hung trellises. Doors opened off galleried walkways at each level, and across the courtyard Helen could see both the floor above and the floor below. Her fascination with her surroundings excused her lack of conversation and not until Mariana opened double doors into the room which was to be hers for the night did she allow the bemusement to escape her.

The room into which Mariana was leading the way was huge and magnificent. Walls hung with swathes of apricot silk, a ceiling arched in the Moorish fashion and exquisitely painted, furnishings of fine oak and cedar, with a tasselled silk bedspread and wild silk curtains that matched the jewel-coloured rugs strewn about the polished floor. Even the bed was huge, square and four-posted, with curtains caught up in cherubs' fingers.

'This is where I'm to sleep!'

Helen's words were almost a protest, and Mariana looked concerned. 'You do not like it?' she ventured doubtfully, but Helen quickly reassured her.

'I love it!' she exclaimed extravagantly, wanting to show her appreciation. 'I just meant—its seems so grand!'

Mariana smiled at this, not without some relief. 'It is a beautiful house,' she said, with obvious satisfaction. 'I am happy that you like it, too.'

The servant departed after leaving her suitcases on the stand at the end of the bed, and Helen chanced a question of her own: 'Have you lived here long, Mariana?'

The girl held up her head. In her long citron-coloured gown, she had a certain dignity that was suddenly evident. 'I have been the wife of James Oneba for almost two years,' she declared proudly. 'Already we have a son and soon, in five or six months, we will have another.'

Helen hoped the girl had not considered her question

too personal, but it was too late now to retract it, and smiling, she gestured towards her cases. 'I suppose I'd better unpack a nightgown . . .'

'If you will tell Lisa what you require, she will do it for you,' the other girl said at once, but in this Helen decided to demur.

'I can do it. Thank you,' she added, to soften the words.

'Very well.' Mariana moved towards the door. Then she stopped again. 'You will find the bathroom through that door,' she directed, and with a faint smile, left her.

The bathroom was as luxurious as the bedroom. Obviously, whatever the financial state of Osweba, its ministers lived in style and comfort, and the enormous bath was big enough to swim in. It was a temptation to fill it and do just that, but Helen didn't know how much time she had and contented herself with a shower instead. She ran the water slightly less than body heat and came out shivering slightly, glad of the enveloping folds of the honey-brown caftan she had chosen to wear for the evening.

It was good to feel cool again, and refreshed, the sweat of time and travel washed from her body. Beneath the ankle-length skirt of the caftan, her thighs brushed together softly, without the stickiness she had felt since their departure from the plane at Nairobi. Her hair, too, had been brushed until it shone and the lightest of make-up was all she applied. She took the longest time over her eyes, outlining them with a creamy-beige eyeshadow and darkening her lashes with mascara.

When she was satisfied with her appearance, she turned out the lamps and opened the bedroom door. A glance at her watch, synchronised to local time on the plane, told her it was a little after seven-thirty, and not quite knowing what to do or where to go, she moved along the gallery to the balcony overlooking the entrance hall.

All was quiet. Even the servants who had seemed so plentiful before had all disappeared, and she descended the staircase slowly allowing her hand to trail along the wrought iron balustrade. She guessed from the ambient atmosphere that the house was air-conditioned, and a faint humming sound seemed to confirm this.

Several doors opened from the hall and a triple-arched entry invited inspection of the lamplit living area beyond. Helen moved towards this seemingly appropriate place to wait for her host, or hostesses, but she saw as she passed between the moulded pillars that supported the arches that the room was already occupied. A girl was seated in a corner, almost invisible in the shadows where the lamplight did not reach. Only the light glinting in her spectacles attracted Helen's eyes, and for a moment she thought it must be another of James Oneba's daughters. But as she moved further into the room, Helen saw that the girl's hair was as pale as Morgan's and she had no doubts in identifying her as Andrea Fox.

'Hello,' she said, glad of the opportunity to speak to the girl without anyone else being present. 'You're Andrea, aren't you? I'm Helen. Did your father tell you about me?'

The girl, whose knees were already drawn up on to the chair, seemed to withdraw even further into the shadows. Eyes of an indeterminate shade stared briefly into Helen's through thick lenses before she cast them down, long lashes brushing the revealing hollows in her thin face.

Helen suppressed a sigh, and glanced about her. Like the rooms upstairs, this living area was opulent in its comfort, its armchairs and sofas richly upholstered in satin and damask, the enormous circular carpet covering most of the tiled spaces of the floor of obviously skilled workmanship. Helen guessed it had been designed in Bukhara or Tashkent, but the colours of sapphire blue, ruby red and lustrous turquoise were as jewel-bright as the day they were made.

Her eyes went back to Andrea, and she wondered how the girl felt about staying in such luxurious surroundings. Obviously, she preferred the people and places she knew to those she didn't, or she would have accompanied her father to England. Helen caught her lower lip between her teeth. Morgan must have spoken to her, must have told her he had brought someone back to befriend her. Had the girl no views on the matter? Or was Helen's presence here of complete indifference to her?

Deciding to try again, Helen said quietly: 'I expect you are looking forward to going home, are you, Andrea?'

The girl's lids lifted at this, and she stared at Helen with sudden hostility. Then she spoke, and her words were entirely unexpected.

'Why didn't you marry Uncle Barry?' she demanded tensely, knuckles clenched about her knees, and Helen realised that any hope she might have had that the past could be forgotten while she was here in Osweba was a futile one.

CHAPTER SIX

If Andrea expected an answer to her question, Helen could not give her one. Not then. Not when she was still shocked by the vehemence of the girl's tone. What had Morgan told his daughter that Andrea should feel so antagonistic towards her? Why had he mentioned her involvement with Barry at all?

She was still trying to regain her composure when Morgan himself came strolling into the room. Like her, he had changed, and his lean body responded well to the dark pants and shirt he was wearing. The darkness of his apparel accentuated the ash fairness of his hair, and Helen felt the impact of his personality like a physical force against her own vulnerability.

He looked from Helen to his daughter, and then back to Helen again. Andrea had made an instinctive move at his appearance, but she quickly squashed the urge to leave her chair and remained curled in the corner, watching them, like some avenging spirit.

'I see you've met,' remarked Morgan dryly, aware of the tension in the room. 'I hoped to get down in time to introduce you.'

Helen expelled her breath rather unsteadily, and then said: 'Yes. We've met,' in rather taut tones.

Morgan looked at his daughter thoughtfully. 'Why are you hiding away there? Is something wrong?'

Helen licked her lips. 'Andrea's just asked me why I didn't marry her uncle,' she declared stiffly. 'How did she know I was going to?'

'How did she know—*Helen*!' Morgan stared at her impatiently. 'How do you think she knew? My father wrote and told us so.'

His father!

Helen's shoulders sagged. How could she have been so stupid! Of course, his father had written to tell them about the wedding, and what more natural than that he should mention the name of his stepson's fiancée?

'I'm sorry . . .' Helen shook her head. 'I thought that you——'

'No, Helen.' His eyes were cold. 'No. I merely explained that you had wanted to get away from England at this time.'

Andrea had watched this interchange with guarded eyes, but now her father turned to her again and held out his hand. 'Come along, Andrea,' he commanded gently. 'There's no point in trying to evade the issue. Helen's here now, and she's staying.'

The girl uncoiled her length from the chair with obvious reluctance. She was taller than Helen had expected, as tall as she was, in fact, but so slender! The flaring white pants helped to disguise the narrowness of her hips, but nothing could hide the painful thinness of her arms protruding from the sleeves of her embroidered smock, the fragility of wrists that looked as if they could be snapped without effort. Her hair was only several shades darker than Morgan's own, and its length did nothing to soften the angular contours of her features, and her skin, unlike her father's, was pale and showed no propensity to tan. Her spectacles were the final straw, Helen felt, guessing that Andrea was not unaware of her appearance. Was this why she hadn't wanted to come to the wedding? Or was there more? Helen sensed it went deeper than that.

Morgan was watching her reactions to his daughter and

she met his gaze bravely. It was as if he was challenging her with the problems facing her, maybe even chiding her for imagining she could help the girl, feeling a stirring regret that he had given in to her demands to come with him.

There was a moment's awkward silence, and then Helen said carefully: 'How far is it to Nrubi, Andrea? I'm looking forward to seeing your home.'

Andrea looked at her father for guidance, and then, bending her head so that the words when they came were low and mumbled, she replied: 'Sixty-three miles.'

Again Morgan's eyes were challenging hers and Helen wondered for the first time whether she had been too ambitious in imagining she could help the girl. She was obviously selfconscious and painfully shy, but worse than that, she was antagonistic towards this intruder into her home. Why? Helen asked herself. Andrea knew nothing about her, other than what her father had told her. Unless she was jealous ...

Fortunately, James Oneba chose that moment to put in his appearance, resplendent this evening in ceremonial robes embroidered in shades of blue and red and gold. He looked like some latterday potentate with his wives and older children about him, but at least his colourful presence ensured there would be no awkward silences thoughout the rest of the evening.

The food was rich and exotic, but Helen had little appetite. She found Morgan's eyes upon her from time to time, but mostly she spoke to James Oneba, dismissing Morgan's earlier mockery about their host's propensity for acquiring wives. Sarah and Mariana spoke little in his presence, and only when spoken to, but Morgan at least attempted to keep them entertained. Andrea said nothing, picking at her food without interest, her head bent over her plate. An older son of the Onebas who had been introduced as Jonathan endeavoured to make her laugh, but although he coaxed a smile from her lips, she remained silent.

When the meal was over, James suggested that Helen might like to see his botanical garden, and although she looked back longingly at Morgan and the others taking coffee in the huge withdrawing room, she was obliged to go with him.

A long corridor gave on to the back of the house, and here a glass-covered orangery was filled with all kinds of plant-life. Ferns and orchids, herbs and spiky cactus; there were specimens there from every continent, and adjoining them was a small laboratory where James said he experimented with herbal remedies.

'A kind of twentieth-century witch doctoring, I suppose you might call it,' he laughed humorously. 'But no, I am not competing with our friend inside, merely experimenting like a small boy with a chemistry set.'

'It's very well equipped,' said Helen admiringly, stroking her nail along a row of burettes, and James turned to face her, folding his arms.

'And are you?' he enquired, so softly that at first she thought she had imagined the question. But the interrogative lift of those dark eyebrows was unmistakable, and she moved her shoulders in a gesture of uncertainty.

'I beg your pardon?'

'I said—are you well equipped also? To cope with whatever is to come?'

Helen realised he was refer ‹g to Andrea, and faint colour stained her cheeks. 'I hope so,' she said quickly. 'Er—what's this?'

'A retort—Helen!' He made an extravagent gesture. 'Helen, I want you to promise me—if there's anything I can do—at any time . . .'

Helen shifted uncomfortably. She didn't altogether understand what he was getting at, unless she suspected that Andrea might make life difficult for her, but all of a sudden what Morgan had said did not seem so fantastic after all. With a feeling of unease, she moved towards the door, and he was there before her, smiling and opening it for her, making a mockery of her ridiculous fears.

A maid awakened Helen next morning, drawing back the curtains from the long windows, letting in the filtered rays of the sun through the slatted blinds. The aroma of coffee alerted her to the awareness of the tray on the table beside her, and after thanking the girl as she smiled and made for the door, she asked what time it was.

'Nine o'clock, Miss Raynor,' the girl answered politely, and Helen was horrified to realise she had overslept.

The night before, Morgan had indicated that he intended to leave early in the morning, before the sun gained its noonday heat, and the unearthly hour of seven o'clock had been mentioned. Now it was long past that time, and Helen wondered in agony if he and Andrea were impatiently waiting for her to join them. But the maid had gone, departing in the wake of Helen's anxiety, and hardly glancing at the glass of freshly-squeezed orange juice, the warm rolls under their perspex cover, or the jug of strong black coffee, she got hastily out of bed.

She had slept surprisingly well in the circumstances, particularly as her final memory before submitting to oblivion had been of Morgan's face when she returned from the orangery with their host. His expression had displayed coldness and disapproval, and an underlying interrogation, and she wondered if he suspected that James had used their time alone together to his advantage. What else could account for that brooding enquiry, that brought a chilling glitter to his eyes and a certain harshness to his speech? James was his friend. Surely he could not conceive of him speaking in a derogatory fashion of either himself or his daughter?

Brushing aside the slats of the blind, she stole a moment's glimpse at the gardens of the house. As she had seen the night before, there was a profusion of exotic growth, their blossoms almost too rich and swollen to someone used to the gentler colours of a temperate climate. Beside the dripping petals of jacaranda and flame trees, the slender canes of papyrus grass seemed almost commonplace by comparison, but the birds that swooped across the lawns were almost as brilliantly coloured as the flowers.

The temptation was to linger, taking in all the sights

and sounds with bemused concentration, but the awareness of the passage of time sent her hurrying into the bathroom.

Regretting she had not used the bath the night before when she had had the chance, Helen quickly took a shower and dressed in pink cotton dungarees over a plain, short-sleeved denim shirt. Her hair needed little more than a swift brushing and she decided not to bother with make-up at all. Then she looked longingly at the breakfast tray. The orange juice was delicious and refreshing, and she poured herself some of the aromatic coffee as she bit into a flaky roll. She would have liked to have lingered over her breakfast, too, having several cups of the strong black beverage, but again time was against her.

It only took a minute to repack the few items she had taken from her suitcase the night before, and after locking it again, she left the room. Running down the stairs, she noticed the scents of the flowers pervading the atmosphere, and the more pungent aroma of beeswax polish. Already the servants had been about their duties and there were fresh flowers in the hall, replacing the orchids residing there the night before.

There seemed to be no one about in the house, although she could hear the sound of children's voices echoing from outside, and she was hesitating at the foot of the stairs, doubtful of what she ought to do, when Andrea appeared from the back of the house. Her eyes flickered when she saw the other girl, but she would have passed her without a word if Helen had not spoken:

'I'm sorry if I've kept you and your father waiting,' she apologised quickly. 'I'm afraid I overslept.'

Andrea halted with evident reluctance, one hand on the baluster at the foot of the stairs, indicating her intention to go up. In a sleeveless dress of printed cotton and white ankle socks and plimsolls, she looked younger than she had done the night before, and her hair plaited into a single braid added to the illusion.

'You haven't kept us waiting,' she muttered now, head bent as usual. 'Excuse me . . .'

Helen watched her as she ran lightly up the stairs, her face troubled. What had Andrea meant? Wasn't Morgan ready to leave after all? She shook her head perplexedly, and as she did so, Mariana came out of a room to the right of the stairs. She smiled when she saw Helen, and then, as her eyes followed the other girl's and she glimpsed Andrea's slight figure disappearing round the corner of the gallery, she made a sympathetic gesture.

'Poor Andrea,' she said. 'She so desperately wanted to go home today.'

Helen didn't attempt to hide her confusion. 'Are we not leaving for Nrubi after all?' she asked, blankly.

Mariana hesitated, frowning. Then she moved her lissom shoulders uncertainly. 'Perhaps later,' she conceded slowly. 'Do you drive, Miss Raynor?'

Helen sighed. Despite her request that Mariana should call her Helen, the African girl persisted in addressing her more formally, but right now she had more important matters on her mind.

'Yes, I drive,' she admitted quickly. 'Why?' A pause. 'Is —is Morgan ill?'

'Ill, no.' Mariana shook her head, twisting her hands together, seeking for words. 'From time to time, he has these —headaches, you understand? Unfortunately, he awakened with one this morning.'

'I see.' Helen felt a twinge of anxiety. She remembered another occasion when Morgan had had a headache, and she had taken him to the flat . . . Licking dry lips, she hastened: 'Where is he? May I see him?'

'I do not think that would be a good idea at this moment,' declared Mariana pleasantly, but firmly. 'He is still—in his room. James has been to see him, and he has taken some medication. I suggest you join the children and their nursemaid on the patio outside. I will ask one of the servants to fetch you some coffee.'

Helen's expellation of her breath was frustrated. If Morgan had migraine, and that was what it sounded like, they were hardly likely to leave for Nrubi today, and much though she appreciated the Onebas' kindness, she was eager to see Morgan's home.

Mariana smiled now, and after giving her directions to reach the patio, she went away to attend to her own duties. Helen moved unwillingly towards the sound of the children's voices, looking back longingly towards the stairs. No doubt that was where Andrea had been going, she thought. To see her father. She wanted to see Morgan, too. There was a ridiculous ache inside her at the thought of him being ill, and she wanted to assure herself that he was only suffering from a headache.

On impulse, she turned back, and after reassuring herself that Mariana had disappeared, she ran swiftly up the stairs. The long gallery curved away in either direction and the futility of her efforts hit her. How could she find Morgan when she had no idea which room he occupied? He could be anywhere, and the row of doors stretched away endlessly, each one as anonymous as the first.

She walked to the edge of the gallery and looked down. The architecture of the inner courtyard looked Moorish in the light of day, the arches of the lower gallery protecting its sanctuary. A pair of brightly-coloured birds squabbled in the leaves of the trellis and a lily pond glinted coolly in the heat of the sun.

A sound from along the gallery alerted her to someone's presence, and glancing round she saw Andrea again, just emerging from a room some doors along from that which Helen had occupied. Her room, or Morgan's? speculated Helen doubtfully, but before she could summon the words to enquire, Andrea was gone, hurrying in the opposite direction, obviously unwilling to enter into any further conversation.

With a sound of impatience, Helen walked hesitantly towards the door Andrea had just closed. It mightn't be either her room or Morgan's she thought irritably. It could even be a bathroom.

There was only one way to find out. Stepping to the door, she tapped lightly on the panels, and hearing no response, projected the door inward. The room beyond was still shuttered, but by the filtering light she could see an unmade bed, with the sheets tossed carelessly to one side. But the bed was empty, and she was just digesting this fact when a man came through the door at the left of the room, saying wearily: 'What do you want now, Andrea? Can't it wait——'

He broke off abruptly when he saw Helen and even in the half light she could see the sudden hardening of his features. He had obviously just finished shaving, and was wiping the remaining soap from his face with the towel about his neck. His only apparel was his cream Levis, hanging low on his hips. Despite her disconcertment, Helen saw that his body was indeed brown all over, the muscles moving smoothly beneath the texture of his skin.

She sensed his involuntary withdrawal, but the words of denuciation did not come. Instead it was she who hurried into speech, saying awkwardly: 'I'm sorry. I didn't mean to come barging in on you like this, but—but Mariana told me you—you weren't well . . .'

Morgan dropped the towel on to a chair and reached for the shirt lying waiting for him on the bed. 'How did you know where to find me?' he enquired harshly. 'Surely you didn't ask Mariana!'

'No, I—as a matter of fact, I saw Andrea——'

'And you asked her!'

He sounded furious, but she shook her head. 'No! I—I saw Andrea leaving this room.'

'So you waited until she'd gone, and then investigated for yourself,' he charged bitterly, and put like that it sounded damning.

'No,' she protested again. 'Andrea didn't speak to me. I—I was going to ask how—how you were.'

Morgan buttoned his shirt with brooding impatience. 'Well, as you can see, I'm perfectly all right now, so——'

'Morgan!' Her use of his name was a plea for understanding. 'I'm sorry if I've annoyed you by coming here but——'

'Annoyed me?' His tone was coldly incredulous. 'Why should it annoy me if you're seen coming to my bedroom? I expect James and his family consider it only natural that the girl I have employed to be a companion to Andrea should enter the room where I'm supposed to be in bed without anyone around to act as chaperon!'

'To act as chaperon!' Helen echoed disbelievingly. 'Why should I need a chaperon?'

'Because this is a Muslim household and certain moral codes are adhered to!' he retorted, pushing his shirt into his pants. 'And in any case, whether or not I have a headache should be of no concern to you.'

All this time, Helen had been standing half inside the room, holding on to the door handle as if for support. Now the brutality of his words caused an actual physical pain in her stomach, and with a sound of protest, she put herself outside the door and closed it before he could hurt her again. Yet her fingers still lingered on the handle, and when the door was wrenched inward seconds later, she jerked away in dismay, afraid of the wrath to come.

Morgan emerged, looked up and down the gallery, and then, with iron-hard fingers biting into her upper arm, propelled her inside his room again. Her breathing was so shallow, she felt almost faint, trembling with fear and anticipation, and when his free hand closed on her shoulder, her heart palpitated wildly. It was two weeks since that never-to-be-forgotten night in her father's study, but her flesh responded to the demands of his fingers with humiliating eagerness.

However, Morgan's intentions were not what she had foolishly imagined them to be. Instead of pulling her towards him when the door closed, he pressed her back against it, glaring at her in a way that offered only rejection, not desire, and made a mockery of her weakness.

'Listen to me,' he said, his tone controlled but savage. 'Obviously I didn't make the situation plain enough before we left England. I thought I had, but it seems not.' He paused, his cold eyes raking her without liking. 'I brought you out here for Andrea's benefit, do I make myself clear? Any fantasy you're entertaining concerning our relationship is purely that, do you understand me? *Fantasy!* Not fact. There is nothing between us. There can be nothing between us. And all this exaggerated concern about my health is nothing but a waste of energy. The sooner you accept that fact the easier it will be on all of us!'

Helen was trembling so badly, she thought if he had not been supporting her she might well have lost the use of her legs and collapsed in an ignominious heap at his feet. As it was, she managed to get some semblance of control into her voice as she replied, albeit unsteadily:

'You—you can't accept that—that I might feel concern for—for anyone in similar circumstances, can you?'

'Concern?' His eyes narrowed.

'Yes, concern.' Her voice gathered strength. 'After all, I've suffered from migraine occasionally myself. I—I know how —how unpleasant it can be.'

'Unpleasant?' he echoed, and a curious expression crossed his lean face. 'Yes, it is—unpleasant, isn't it?' he agreed. His fingers unclenched, allowing the blood to flow back into her arms again. 'So your concern was only—objective.'

Helen looked down at her feet, willing the hot colour to drain from her cheeks before replying. *Objective!* she thought hysterically. If only that were so!

Now, he straightened, looking down at her with that brooding concentrated regard she had felt before. Then he said quietly: 'It seems I—over-reacted. I apologise. Naturally, you were—concerned about your position here. Fortunately, that has been resolved now. We're leaving for Nrubi as soon as I'm dressed.'

Helen nodded, still not trusting herself to speak, half turning to reach for the door handle. But politeness forced Morgan to forestall her, and his arm went past her to perform the small duty. It was an involuntary thing, an action borne of years of such courtesies, but Helen's confusion set her in his path and his arm brushed sensuously across her breasts. She at once recoiled, but not before her startled gaze had encountered the smouldering passion of his, and as her lids lowered she sensed the revealing tautness of the muscles beneath his close-fitting clothes. His arm was withdrawn as swiftly as it had been projected and his balled fists thrust into the hip pockets of his denim pants, but the situation had subtly changed, and they both knew it.

'Morgan ...' she breathed, but this time there was no mistake. He jerked the door open, and stepping aside, said harshly: 'Wait for me downstairs!' and she had no alternative but to obey him.

CHAPTER SEVEN

Beyond the environs of Charlottesville, before the coastal plain gave way to the purple-shadowed valleys of the higher altitudes, stretched an area of open bushland, a semi-desert area, largely unsuitable for human habitation but entirely habitable for the herds of wildlife which had made this country a vast reserve. To Helen, unused to seeing giraffe and zebra outside of a zoo, it was a fascinating safari, and her interest in her surroundings succeeded, for a while at least, in banishing the confused anxiety of her feelings towards Morgan. She saw deer and wildebeest, and once she thought she saw the rump of a rhino as it ambled away into a stand of low scrublike trees that were indicative of the area. It gave her a slightly uneasy feeling knowing how vulnerable the station wagon might be if faced with a charging rhino, but she had also noticed the rifle slung carelessly into the back of the vehicle, and guessed that in these surroundings one had to be prepared for anything.

They had left the Oneba house soon after ten with Andrea occupying the front seat of the station wagon beside her father, and Helen uncomfortably ensconced in the rear with the suitcases. Not that the luggage was responsible for her discomfort. But the station wagon was not air-conditioned, and although the windows were open for most of the time, it was still enervatingly hot. She wondered how Morgan could drive in such conditions, particularly after his earlier indisposition, but apparently the medication he had taken had successfully discharged his headache and she wondered what it was to be so efficient. She had not known there was any successful cure for migraine, but perhaps as a doctor, Morgan experimented upon himself.

Since getting into the car, Andrea had become more animated than Helen had previously seen her, even smiling at her father now and then, and speaking to him in low tones of what she had been doing while he was away. That her conversation did not include the girl in the rear of the vehicle meant less than the relief Helen was feeling at knowing that Morgan's daughter could behave much like any other girl of her age and was not entirely uncommunicative.

The sun was directly overhead when they left the plain and began the rocky climb into the hills. Away from the heat and the choking dust, the air became infinitely fresher, and the windows could be lowered without suffering the irritating flies that invaded the vehicle and attacked every inch of exposed flesh. It was possible to breathe without tasting grit between one's teeth and without smelling the pervasive odour of the burnt landscape.

As the vegetation became thicker, so too did the villages. The station wagon passed through several settlements where some effort had been made to cultivate the soil, and although the living accommodations were primitive, the people looked reasonably healthy. However, the baneful influences of Helen's society, those of obesity combined with a lack of exercise, were not in evidence here, so perhaps they had problems of another kind. Certainly the sanitation left a lot to be desired, and Helen flinched from the sight of a grubby finger thrust playfully into a baby's mouth.

Perhaps taking pity on her, Morgan glanced round once and said: 'Not much further now. Only a matter of some eight miles. We should reach Nrubi by one o'clock.'

'One o'clock.' Helen digested this thankfully. 'Good.'

'I suppose you imagined the journey would take much less time,' he remarked, his eyes meeting hers through the reflection in the rear-view mirror, but Helen refused to appear completely ignorant.

'I guessed the roads would make the distance seem longer,' she countered. 'I didn't expect a three-lane motorway, if that's what you're implying.'

'Then you weren't disappointed,' he responded politely, and she realised with impatience that her words had sounded perter than she had intended.

Nrubi was in fact more than a village. Helen supposed one would describe it as a small town, although there were none of the facilities one might expect to find in a town of a similar size in England. But compared to the villages they had passed through, it was a veritable metropolis, with shops and stores and taverns, and houses of a much more habitable size. Its appearance was Moorish, Helen decided, with lots of white-painted buildings that repelled the glare of the sun. There were even several burnous-clad individuals lounging about in doorways, reminiscent of the tribesmen from the north, and what one could see of their dark faces revealed the aristocratic arrogance of the desert. The sun had bleached the pavements white, too, and the glare after the gentler colours of the countryside was blinding.

Morgan drove through the town, raising his hand now and then in acknowledgement of the greetings addressed to the station wagon. Obviously, everyone knew who he was, and even Andrea responded to their almost royal progression. Of course, thought Helen wryly, this was all the girl had known, this and Charlottesville, and the opulent surroundings of the Oneba household. She was wondering where Morgan's house could be, and whether Andrea would react differently to her now that she was back in her own domain, and while the outline of Nrubi was imprinted on her brain, her thoughts were far from its narrow steets.

There were few cars about. Most of the people they saw were cycling, or on foot, and occasionally they glimpsed a black figure mounted on a mule; but such vehicles as there were were old and dented, and in obvious need of repair. Yet there was an air of inconsequence about their very indifference which was curiously appealing to someone used to the unspoken rigours of a so-called civilised existence, and Helen felt her spirits lifting as she stared wide-eyed through the open windows.

Morgan's house stood on the outskirts of the town. There seemed an absence of any kind of fencing dividing one plot from another, but the house itself was built on three sides of a central courtyard which provided all the privacy she desired. Like the rest of the buildings she had seen, it was made of a kind of stucco, painted white, and sprawled without regard for the limitations of design. Several extensions appeared to have been added to the original building, and later she was to learn that this was where Morgan had his surgery and consulting rooms.

Morgan parked the station wagon in the shade of an umbrella-like acacia, and then thrust open his door and got out, stretching with evident relief. But no sooner had he done so than a boy came running from the house to greet him and behind the boy, in the shadowy porch of the building, a young African woman carrying a child hovered uncertainly.

'Oh, stuff!' exclaimed Andrea irritably, before climbing out herself, and Helen wondered at the event which had evoked such an unexpected response.

Realising no one was about to play doorman, she opened the rear door and was thrusting out her legs when the boy reached Morgan. She could see now that he was older than she had at first imagined, perhaps eighteen or nineteen, but there was no mistaking his obvious pleasure at their arrival.

'Massa sir,' he exclaimed eagerly, shaking Morgan's unresisting hand. 'Welcome home, Massa sir. Kori most concerned when Massa late in returning.'

'Hello, Kori,' responded Morgan amiably. 'Nice to know I've been missed by someone. Who's that you've got with you? Another of your relatives?'

Kori glanced round off-handedly at the woman with the baby, then turned back, shaking his head with apparent impatience. 'Her name is Mfani, Massa sir. Pay no attention to her. She can wait. Tell me about your trip. You have a good wedding?'

As he spoke the boy's eyes moved first to Andrea, then to Helen, widening as they took in her slender, curving figure, and silken fall of hair. Aware of his inquisitive interest, Helen doubted he was listening for Morgan's reply, but Andrea distracted him by saying coolly:

'There was no wedding, Kori. It was a wasted journey!' before stalking off into the house.

The silence that followed this statement was discomfiting. Helen exchanged a glance with Morgan, but his expression was enigmatic and she sensed his anger was directed more towards herself than towards his daughter. Luckily, Kori recovered quickly, and switching his attention back to the man said:

'You hungry, Massa sir? You like Kori make some steaks and salad?'

'The woman, Kori,' Morgan reminded him wearily. 'What is she doing here? Has she been waiting for me? How long?'

Kori cast a reluctant stare over his shoulder. 'You don't have to worry about Mfani, Massa sir. She Bosumi's woman. She can wait——'

'Kori!'

The boy heaved an exaggerated sigh. Then he shrugged his black shoulders, bare but for the straps of the white vest he wore over knee-length shorts. 'Two—mebbe three days,' he conceded at last. 'I told her I didn't know when you'd be back, but she wouldn't go.'

'And you didn't make any attempt to dislodge her, I suppose,' remarked Morgan, his face so grim that Helen wondered what was making him so angry. 'You let her stay. And I'd hazard took full advantage of your inflated status!'

Kori was looking increasingly anxious. 'What could I do?' he protested defensively. 'The baby's sick. I couldn't send her away.'

'So sick she can wait while you ask about the wedding,' pointed out Morgan shortly. 'Oh, get out of my way. Send the woman to the surgery. I'll see her there in five minutes.

As soon as I've had time to wash my hands.'

'Yes, sir, Massa sir.'

Kori made what looked suspiciously like a salute and would have moved away when Morgan added: 'By the way, this is Miss Raynor. She's going to be staying with us for a while. See that the bed is made up in the spare room, and the cases brought in, and you can make us all some steak and salad when you've installed the woman in the surgery.'

'Yes, sir.' Kori switched his attention to Helen again. 'Pleased to make your acquaintance, Miss Raynor,' he said, with the broad smile he had earlier bestowed upon his master. 'I hope you'll be happy here at Hawk's Drift.'

Hawk's Drift. Helen had not heard the words before, and she looked at Morgan for explanation. But he had merely nodded curtly to the woman who had emerged from the porch to stare admiringly at him, and was presently entering the shadowy interior of the house.

'Pleased to meet you, Kori,' said Helen in a rush, cringing at the hackneyed words of greeting, and then hastened after Morgan before he disappeared from sight. The African woman stared after her, too, and the baby, a puny-looking little thing, began to cry. But some unintelligible words from Kori attracted her attention, and Helen heard the shrill interchange that ensued as she followed Morgan into the house.

Her first impression was one of quietness and space. The airy entrance hall was wide and light, the walls painted a soft beige and hung with carvings and icons, and other examples of religious significance. Across the hall, open doors invited inspection of a cloistered verandah that circled the central courtyard of the house and to left and right ran shadowy passageways leading to the other apartments. It was all on one level, but the walls were enormously thick which accounted for the lack of noise, and the coolness. Beyond the courtyard she could see tangled vegetation, and through it the tantalising glimpse of water.

Morgan had halted in the hall and was waiting for her, his mouth drawn down at the corners. 'I'm sorry everything seems to be so disorganised,' he said tersely. 'I suggest you wait in the living room or on the verandah until Kori shows you to your room, and we'll eat as soon as I've dealt with the child.'

Helen moved her shoulders awkwardly. 'Oh—please, don't worry about me——'

'I'm not *worried* about you. I'm simply trying to be polite. Believe me, it's quite a strain at the moment.'

Helen straightened her back. 'Why? Because of what Andrea said?'

'Andrea?' He shook his head. 'I can deal with Andrea. Right now I have other things on my mind—not least what that damn-fool Kori has been doing with Bosumi's woman.'

'What he's been do——' Helen broke off, shaking her head. 'I'm afraid I don't understand.'

Morgan raked back his hair with a tired hand. 'You will. If Bosumi comes here looking for her!'

'You mean . . .'

'That's right.'

'But she's Bosumi's woman. Kori—said so.'

'I wouldn't trust that boy as far as I could throw him, and the last thing I need right now is a vendetta opening up on my doorstep.' He sighed, his gaze flickering over her broodingly. 'Go and find yourself a seat on the verandah. I have to see my patient.'

He strode away, and although Helen watched him, he didn't look back. On impulse, she didn't go immediately on to the verandah, but wandered instead in the opposite direction to that which Morgan had taken, and presently found herself on the threshold of a moderately streamlined kitchen. There were wall-cupboards and sink units, and a scrubbed wooden table, and perched on a stool by the sink, staring out over the luxuriant vegetation that grew almost to the windows of the house, was Andrea Fox.

If Helen had set herself the task of looking for the girl, she would in all probability never have found her, but there, unlooked-for, she was, and Helen decided it was time they had a real conversation.

Unfortunately, Andrea didn't seem to see it that way. As soon as she saw the other girl hovering in the doorway, she slid off the stool and would have walked straight past her if Helen's hand on her arm had not prevented her. For a moment they stared at one another, their eyes almost on a level, but then Andrea's lids dropped, revealing her veneer of maturity.

'I'd like to talk to you,' Helen said then quietly, but without releasing her arm. She was afraid if she did so Andrea would disappear again, and that kind of humiliation she could do without. 'I'd like to explain why I didn't marry your uncle.'

Andrea pushed her lips forward mutinously, but she didn't say anything. Helen could find it in her heart to feel sorry for her. Obviously she would like to say so much, but she simply didn't have the courage.

Now Helen chose her words carefully: 'When—when two people plan to marry they have to be absolutely certain that it's what they want—what they both want. It's no good getting married and then finding out afterwards they've made a terrible mistake.'

Too late, she realised that that was exactly what Andrea's parents had done, and the sudden shock of remembrance drew all strength from her fingers. Sensing the unexpected withdrawal, Andrea wrenched her arm away, and ran away along the corridor while Helen was still trying to gather her scattered composure. But as self-possession returned, anger was uppermost in her mind, anger with herself for her carelessness, and anger with Morgan and his wife for allowing their incompatibility to destroy their daughter's confidence.

Kori came to find her on the verandah some time later. He had supplied her with a jug of iced lime juice, for which she was very grateful, and she had been watching the antics of a weaver bird in the dipping branches of a gnarled old tree that grew within the shaded environs of the courtyard. She was speculating about the stretch of water, whose reed-bounded shores stretched invitingly beyond the bushy vegetation that surrounded the villa, when he announced that her room was prepared.

'You would like to wash before lunch?' he enquired, with

his ingratiating smile, but remembering what Morgan had said, Helen responded with only polite acquiescence.

To her surprise, Kori invited her to follow him along the verandah, and they entered the room which was to be hers from the courtyard. It was a decent-sized room, with a huge fan moving slowly at ceiling level. The walls were pastel-washed, but otherwise plain, and the bedspread was of some woven native design, fringed to touch the tiles of the floor. An old-fashioned wardrobe and dressing table, a cedarwood ottoman, and a circular rug beside the divan completed the furnishings, but it was obviously clean and pleasantly attractive.

'Thank you, Kori,' Helen said, standing in the middle of the room and looking round. 'This is very nice.'

Her suitcases had been placed side by side on the ottoman, and now Kori moved to run his fingers over the leather. 'You would like Kori to unpack your clothes?' he suggested insinuatively, but remembering the scraps of lingerie that represented her underwear, she hastily declined.

'I'll do it later,' she demurred. 'It will give me something to do.' She smiled to take the sharpness from the refusal. 'Er—where's the bathroom?'

Kori's dark face which had been registering disappointment brightened. 'I show you,' he declared, and she followed him out of the doors which led into the corridor of the house, and along again in the direction of the kitchen.

The bathroom was almost opposite the kitchen, which Helen herself noted for future reference. There apparently only was the one bathroom, and she guessed Kori, from his position in the kitchen, would note all comings and goings. No flitting around in her nightdress or underwear, she thought dryly, relieved to remember she had brought a dressing gown with her. Still, the bathroom was reasonably efficient, with hot and cold running water, which Kori took much pleasure in pointing out. That the bath had clawed feet meant less when compared to the ancient clankings of the boiler, and the heat emanating from that direction gave the room the atmosphere of a sauna bath.

There was an appetising smell coming from the kitchen, and leaving Helen to wash her face and hands, Kori excused himself to attend to the meal. When Helen emerged again, she could see steaks sizzling under the grill and Kori was doing his best to toss some salad in a wooden bowl. She was tempted to offer advice, but decided against it, and walked instead into the small dining room adjoining where someone had laid the circular table for three.

Sighing, Helen wondered if Andrea would join them for lunch, and then thrust that particular problem aside. There was time enough to make friends with Andrea. Right now, she needed time to think, to adjust to these new surroundings, and to get her feelings for Morgan under control.

She was sitting at the table, staring unseeingly at a print of the Drakensberg peaks when she heard the sound of raised voices coming from the kitchen. She couldn't understand what they were saying, but the tone was unmistakable, and recognising Morgan's voice above Kori's indignant squeal, she guessed he was getting the raw edge of his employer's tongue.

She shifted uncomfortably. Although she couldn't comprehend what was being said, she didn't like to be an unwilling eavesdropper, and she had risen to her feet when Morgan himself appeared in the doorway. His shirt sleeves were rolled back above his elbows, and around his arms and across his chest, the shirt clung to him in folds of dampness. His light hair, too, was artificially darkened by sweat, and tension had carved lines of weariness beside his nose and mouth.

'I'm sorry,' he said, switching to English automatically when he saw her. 'I'm afraid I shan't be joining you for lunch after all. But Kori will serve you, and I'll speak to Andrea and insist that she eats in here.'

Helen licked her dry lips. 'Oh, but——' She gestured towards his sweat-stained shirt. 'I can wait while you change——'

'I'm not about to change,' he interrupted her shortly. 'I'm taking the child and its mother down to the hospital in Charlottesville. I'll be back as soon as possible.'

He would have turned away then, but Helen's jerky words of protestation stopped him. 'But you can't!' she exclaimed. 'I mean—you—couldn't you get someone else to drive them down?'

'Who do you suggest?' he enquired coldly. 'Kori? I think not.'

'But you look so—so tired.' She coloured. 'I mean, you did have a headache this morning, didn't you?'

His nostrils flared for a moment, and then he nodded with a faint softening of his expression. 'All right,' he agreed shortly. 'I know you mean well. But right now I'm not in the mood to discuss my own shortcomings. Like I say, have lunch, take a rest. I should be back around eight o'clock.'

'Eight o'clock!' Helen's nails dug into her palms. 'I see.'

Morgan turned away, but again she stopped him:

'It—it's serious, then? The baby's illness, I mean.'

'You could say that,' he muttered harshly. Then he gave her a wry look. 'Don't ask—that's my advice to you. Just don't ask. And he strode away out of sight.'

It was easier said than done. Helen walked to the door of the dining room, but Morgan had already gone and a few minutes later she heard the sound of the station wagon's engine being started. It drew her to the windows, and she watched as Morgan reversed expertly on to the road, and drove away towards the village.

When the dust of his passing had settled, Helen turned back to find Kori just carrying a tray into the room. Expecting a hangdog expression, at least, she was surprised to find he looked as cheerful and unconcerned as ever, and his gesture towards the food invited appraisal.

Shaking away the feeling of unreality which had suddenly gripped her, Helen moved to the table and duly admired the succulent-looking steaks and the salad nestling on its bed of crushed ice.

'It looks very nice,' she said, because it was obviously expected of her, and wondered if it would taste as good as it looked.

'Please to sit down,' he insisted, drawing out a chair,

and obediently she took her seat. 'Now, you would like me to serve you?'

'No, no, that's all right. I can serve myself.' Helen didn't need his obsequious presence. 'Er—perhaps you'd tell Miss—Miss Andrea—that lunch is ready.'

'She knows,' declared Kori blandly. 'Massa sir, he told her, before he left for Charlottesville.'

His complacency infuriated her, and it was all she could do to prevent herself from ordering him out of the room. But instead she said, with what she hoped was cutting coolness: 'Doesn't that bother you at all? That your—employer has had to drive all the way back to Charlottesville half an hour after his arrival?'

Kori's dark eyes were wide and innocent. 'It nothing to do with Kori,' he denied. 'If stupid woman believe in tribal doctor's medicine, it nothing to do with Kori.'

Helen looked down at her plate. *Let it go*, her conscience was appealing. *Say no more. It's nothing to do with you!* But like Pandora she was unable to deny her curiosity.

'What—what was wrong with the baby?' she asked, lifting the serving fork in hands that were not quite steady, and sensed that Kori was speculating how much he ought to tell her.

'Baby sick,' he announced at last. 'Baby have pain—here.' He patted his own flat stomach.

'I see.' Helen rested the fork on her plate. 'Then let's hope the doctors at the hospital will be able to help.'

'Mmm.' Kori didn't sound too concerned. 'Boy weak,' he decided at last, and then shrugged, as if dismissing it from his mind. 'You like sauce? Mustard?'

'No.'

Helen felt impatient with him and impatient with herself for trying to probe. It didn't help when Andrea chose that moment to appear in the doorway, a bloodstained cloth in her hands.

'I've washed the floor of the surgery with disinfectant, Kori,' she told him. 'Will you dispose of this for me?'

'Sure thing, Miss Andrea.'

Kori took the cloth from her and Andrea ran her palms

down the skirt of her dress. Helen's appetite rapidly disappeared. The blood oozing from the steak was too reminiscent of what she had just witnessed, and she guessed, in spite of her efficiency, that Andrea had enjoyed shocking her like that.

Now the girl took her seat at the table and helped herself to a thick steak. She spooned salad on top of the hot meat and then shook mayonnaise on top. Helen looked at the steak on her own plate, and then reached for the jug of water. Kori had thoughtfully placed a muslin cloth over it, but the added warmth had melted the ice and it was unpleasantly warm. But at least it was easy to swallow, and dispersed the discomforting dryness in her throat. Helen knew Andrea was waiting for her to ask what the bloodstained cloth meant, but she held her tongue, and presently she managed to swallow a little of the tossed salad.

Kori brought in a bowl of fruit when he thought she had had time to finish her meal and looked with alarm at the untouched steak.

'Is not good?' he asked in surprise, but Helen shook her head.

'I wasn't hungry,' she managed to explain, and with a shrug he took the plate away.

Andrea had eaten a good meal, Helen saw. Obviously the less palatable aspects of her father's profession did not worry her, but Helen felt her callousness had been deliberately assumed. She doubted Andrea sat down to lunch every day without first washing her hands, and she guessed that if her father had been there it would have been a much different story.

Thinking of her father inevitably brought her own anxieties about him to the fore. She was concerned about the baby, of course, particularly as it seemed that the upset stomach was far from a simple one. But somehow she sensed that Morgan ought not to drive himself as hard as he did, and it was impossible to be wholly objective about it.

The coffee Kori served at the end of the meal was revitalising. In fact, the whole meal had been unexpectedly good and Helen wondered whether the boy's efficiency made up for the less acceptable aspects of his character. Whatever, he certainly knew how to cook and serve a meal, and judging from the appearance of the villa, he was also extremely good at housekeeping.

Andrea seemed disappointed that her ruse to arouse Helen's curiosity had not succeeded, and declining Helen's offer of coffee, rose to leave the room. That was when Helen's impatience overspilled.

'Where are you going?' she demanded, looking up at the girl. 'Don't you think your father would expect you to entertain your guest in his absence?'

It was not perhaps the best method of gaining Andrea's attention, but the idea of spending the next few hours alone was even less appealing than suffering Andrea's unwilling company.

The girl didn't immediately say anything, however. She hung her head and looked uncomfortable, but at least she didn't rush away. Gathering confidence, Helen added:

'I'm sorry if you considered my remarks earlier were in bad taste, but they were spoken in good faith, and I had no intention of upsetting you.'

The silence stretched, and clearing her throat, Helen went on: 'Your father thinks you spend too much time alone, do you know that? He thought perhaps you might welcome another female about the place, someone you could talk to. Oh, I know you don't know me yet, and naturally you're a little suspicious, but honestly, I just want us to be friends. And if you disappear every time I try to talk to you, it's going to be hopeless!'

She paused again and this time caught the fleeting glance Andrea threw in her direction. Their eyes met and held, and then the younger girl lifted her head, almost defensively.

'Why did you come here, Miss Raynor?' she asked, much to Helen's surprise. 'Did my father ask you to come?'

Helen wished she could have been forewarned of the question. It had such a double edge. On the one hand was the obvious danger of suggesting a relationship that, so far as Morgan was concerned anyway, simply did not exist, and on the other the pitfalls implicit in admitting she had begged to come. And she could hardly blurt out the truth, that Andrea's father was planning to send her back to England, with or without his involvement.

Groping desperately for a middle course, she said: 'You know the situation in England. Well, it seemed a good idea for me to get away for a while. Your father—was kind enough to offer me the—the hospitality of his home.'

'In return for what?'

Helen's lips parted. What a suspicious little mind Andrea had, she thought uneasily. Why did she think her father had brought another woman to Hawk's Drift? Did she imagine Helen to be his mistress? Had she hopes perhaps that one day her parents would be reunited and saw Helen's presence as a threat? Did that account for the tangible hostility?

Now, remembering the old adage about attacking being the best method of defence, she asked: 'Why do you think your father brought me here?'

For a moment, Andrea was silent. Then, hot colour burning in her pale cheeks, she said: 'He won't marry you, you know. He told me. He promised he would never marry anyone else!'

Helen felt as if someone had just punched her hard, in the area immediately below her ribcage. It wasn't that the girl's words were so unexpected. It was hearing them from her. Knowing that they had discussed her.

'I couldn't anyway, could I?' she managed to point out at last. 'I—your mother's still alive.'

'My mother!' Andrea said the words with cold bitterness. 'Oh, yes, she's still alive. But what does that matter? They're divorced!'

Divorced!

Helen tried not to look as astounded as she felt. Morgan was divorced! And he had never told her!

And yet, she argued, why should he? A man could be so sickened with one marriage that he would swear never to marry again. Obviously that was what Morgan had done, and what was more, meeting her had made no difference to his feelings.

That hurt, almost as much as Andrea's denunciation. Almost as much as knowing that whatever Morgan felt for her, he did not consider it important.

It was difficult to be calm and collected after that, but somehow she succeeded, saying quietly: 'Even so—we could be friends,' although even as she said the words she knew that the last thing she wanted right now was to make friends with Morgan's daughter.

Andrea considered this. Watching the play of emotions across her thin young face, Helen felt her compassion stirring. After all, she argued with herself, the girl was obviously insecure. It was natural that she should resent a stranger coming into her home to shred what little security she had.

Finally she said: 'I'm not a very interesting person. Why should you want to be friends with me?'

It was a cruel self-indictment for one so young, and Helen felt a ridiculous impulse to take her in her arms and reassure her like the child she was. But Andrea would not have welcomed such a display, and besides, Helen didn't know her well enough to be sure she was not playing some sophisticated game with her. She didn't think she was, but only time would tell.

'You underestimate yourself, Andrea,' she said now. 'I don't think you believe that about yourself, any more than I do. What you need is someone to talk to, that's all. Someone to discuss things with.'

'What sort of things?'

Andrea was still suspicious, and Helen sighed as she rose to her feet. 'Clothes,' she offered carefully. 'Hair styles, music, make-up.'

'Make-up?' echoed Andrea in surprise, and Helen knew she had scored one point at least.

'Why not?' she asked. 'You'll be fifteen soon, won't you? It's time you started to take an interest in your appearance.'

'My birthday's in two weeks,' admitted Andrea, without enthusiasm. 'But what can I do about my appearance? I'm too tall and too thin—and I wear glasses!'

Helen's fingers stroked tentatively along the seams of her pants. At last, she thought with satisfaction. At last she was beginning to make some progress. It wouldn't be easy. It was never easy to persuade someone that they could compete on equal terms with everyone else, particularly if they had got it into their heads that they couldn't.

She remembered a case they had had at the clinic. A girl, not much older than Andrea, injured in a car accident, and convinced she would never walk again. She had lost all interest in herself, convinced herself that no boy would ever look at a *cripple*. Her plight had aroused everyone's sympathy. Yet, with time and persuasion, she had been taught to use her legs again, and although she would never be able to run or play games, they had given her back mobility—and self-respect.

But Helen's moment of self-congratulation was short-lived. Andrea's face had crumpled as she waited for the other girl to reply, and in muffled tones she gasped: 'Is that why he's brought you here? To make me take an interest in myself? Is he so ashamed of me?' And while Helen strove to find the words to deny the accusation, she added dramatically: 'I wish I was dead!' before running in distress from the room.

CHAPTER EIGHT

THE station wagon pulled on to the drive leading to the villa at about a quarter to nine. Helen, who had been sitting in the living room for over an hour waiting for Morgan's return, felt her nerves stretch automatically. Her first impulse was to get to her feet, rush out into the hall to meet him, and blurt out the mess she had made of her first real exchange with Andrea; but the anxiety she had suffered waiting for his return was now uppermost in her mind, and she was afraid her relief at seeing him would undo the stringent controls she had determined to put on her emotions.

So she remained where she was, sitting in the lamplit room, counting again the squares of the tiles that stretched from her chair to the door. She already knew there were sixteen, she had already counted them a dozen times; but somehow she had to remain calm and composed.

It wasn't easy. She had just spent one of the most awful days of her life, and what she needed most was sympathy—sympathy for herself, and escape from the traumatic turmoil of her thoughts. She needed someone to pour her troubles out to, not least someone to reassure her that she had not been responsible for lacerating Andrea's self-confidence.

She had not laid eyes on the girl since that disastrous interchange after lunch, and again, while her instincts had been to go after her and try to reassure her, she had been afraid she might do more harm than good. Instead, she had spent the time flaying herself for her own crass clumsiness.

Kori had produced a meal around seven—a highly-spiced curry, the smell of which almost sickened her. But the hollow feeling inside her was not all nerves, and she had known that starving herself would only add to her physical discomfort. Forcing herself to swallow a few mouthfuls of the strongly-flavoured meat had not been easy, but she had managed it, and the small exchange with Kori over the collapsed soufflé that followed helped to delay the feeling of isolation that the onset of night was inevitably arousing.

That had been over an hour ago now, however, and the walls of the villa had begun to close around her, a sensation that was heightened by the repeated attacks of insects against the window panes and a weird howling sound which she couldn't identify. She had speculated on its being a lion or an elephant, but had decided it was more likely a hyena, which chilled her blood when she considered Morgan's plight should the station wagon break down miles from home. But, one way or another, he had returned, and hearing footsteps in the hall outside, Helen wondered if Andrea had chosen to go and greet her father.

With sharpened senses, however, she heard only masculine voices beyond the door, Kori's shrill and anxious, and Morgan's deep and inexpressibly weary. Unable to sit still any longer, she crossed the space between her chair and the door and swung it open.

The two men turned at her appearance. Morgan was leaning heavily on Kori's shoulder, she saw with dismay, his face white and strained, and it was obvious they were on their way to Morgan's room further along the corridor.

'What's happened?' The words spilled from her, and with an obvious effort Morgan pulled himself upright.

'Nothing's happened,' he stated flatly. 'My headache's returned, that's all. Driving back here almost blinded me, but don't worry, I'll be all right in the morning.'

Helen took a step towards them, her eyes darting to Kori and then back to Morgan again. 'Let me help you,' she said impulsively. 'There must be something I can do.' She paused. 'Have you had anything to eat? Would you like something? Maybe a drink?'

'I'm not hungry,' he retorted, swaying slightly, but Kori took up Helen's suggestion.

'Some soup,' he offered, his white teeth brilliant in his dark face. 'A cup of tea. You like Kori should make you some tea?'

'No——'

'Yes, Kori.' Helen's acceptance overruled him. 'I think Mr Fox would appreciate some tea,' she declared firmly. 'You go and make it. I'll escort your employer to his room.'

'You will not!' Morgan snapped the words. 'I tell you I——'

'Go along, Kori.' Using what little authority she had learned during her years at the hospital, Helen dismissed the boy, and with an admiring grin he went.

At once Morgan turned the force of his anger on her. 'If you think——'

But Helen was already passing him, glancing frowningly about her. 'Shall I help you to your room?' she asked, with cool efficiency, and she heard his angry intake of breath.

'For God's sake, Helen, get lost, will you?' he demanded

tiredly, and she was almost tempted to give in to him. 'All I need is my bed. Can't you get that through your head?'

Helen accompanied him to his room. Putting the memory of the morning's visit firmly out of her mind, she looked around her with guarded interest.

His room was plain, like hers, with a predominance of brown in the decorations—beige-brown walls, brown printed curtains, a brown and yellow spread across the bed. The bed was bigger than hers, wider and longer, and she guessed he had once shared it with Pamela, his ex-wife.

Now he sank down heavily on to the side of the bed and stared at her unsmilingly as she hesitated in the doorway. 'Well?' he said, and his voice was harsh. 'Are you going to undress me? Is that why you're here?'

Helen couldn't prevent the flush of colour that stained her cheeks. 'You know it's not,' she replied. Now it was her turn to be on the defensive. 'I just wanted to make sure you were all right. And—and I did want to talk to you, although I realise now is neither the time nor the place.'

'So you're leaving?'

'I—well——' Helen caught her lower lip between her teeth. 'The baby,' she said after a moment. 'How—how is he?'

Morgan bent down to unloosen the laces of his suede boots. 'What is it they say on these occasions?—as well as can be expected!'

'He—he's going to be all right?'

Morgan kicked off his boots and looked up. 'He may live,' he conceded coldly, getting to his feet, and she could see the lines of pain engraved across his face. 'Now, if you'll excuse me . . .'

'Is there nothing I can do?' She felt so helpless, but his face darkened with anger.

'For whom?' he demanded bitterly. 'The baby—or for me?'

'E-either one,' she breathed, and he uttered a violent oath as he turned his back on her and started to unbutton his shirt.

'Get out of here, Helen,' he muttered savagely. 'I'm too

weary to fence with you tonight.'

Helen hesitated a moment longer, then she took the steps that put her right behind him. 'Morgan . . .' she whispered tremulously. 'Don't shut me out, Morgan, *please*!'

He tipped his head to stare grimly at the ceiling and from her position Helen could see the heavy strands of hair that coiled into the nape of his neck. Below the width of his shoulders, his shirt clung damply, and her hands moved almost involuntarily to touch him. When he didn't immediately repulse her, her arms slid round his waist until her hands met at the buckle of his belt, bringing her face to the moistened hollow of his spine and her stomach to the taut muscles between his hips.

'Morgan . . .' she said again, more huskily this time, and the flatness of his stomach was tensed with sinew.

'What the hell do you think you're doing?' he groaned, his hands at his sides clenched and restive. 'I've told you, Helen, you're wasting your time with me. For God's sake, what do I have to do to convince you?'

Helen allowed her tongue to wet her lips before replying. Then, resting her chin against his back, she said softly: 'You can't deny I disturb you, Morgan.' Her hands strayed daringly below the heavy buckle. 'Shall I prove it?'

His hands moved convulsively to cover hers, pressing them hard against him for a moment. Then, with a muffled imprecation, he turned to face her, and the bare brown expanse of his chest and the bulging muscles of his thighs were so much more intimate than when he had his back to her.

'All right,' he muttered, his eyes moving hungrily over her face. 'All right. If that's what you want, why should I hold back? So long as you're prepared to accept the consequences.'

'What consequences?' Helen's lips trembled. 'What do you mean? Why are you talking like this? What did I do?'

'Goddamn you, you know what you're doing!' he swore angrily. 'God, I'm beginning to think that Barry is well rid of you!'

Helen's face blanched. 'That's a horrible thing to say!'

'Is it? Well, yes, I think perhaps it is. But damn it, Helen, this is madness, and you know it.'

She drew an unsteady breath. 'Is it madness to want to kiss me?'

'To *kiss* you!' His short laugh was anguished. 'You know I want to do more than that.'

'Do you, Morgan?' Her breathing felt constricted. 'Tell me.'

He held off for one moment, staring desperately towards the open door, as if willing Kori to return. But then the parted temptation of her lips got the better of him, and his hands at her nape brought her mouth unerringly towards his.

His lips trembled over the widening contours of hers and his hot breath in her mouth was suffocatingly intense. She felt his hands move from her neck, across her back to her hips, lingering senuously at the tops of her thighs. Then, keeping his mouth on hers, he pressed her backward on to his bed, and when she subsided against the soft coverlet, he allowed the whole weight of his body to descend on top of her.

'Mmm, that feels good,' he breathed, his mouth seeking the side of her throat with increasing urgency. 'You know what?' he added. 'I feel better already.'

'Do you?' She was almost incoherent with the eager urgency of her desire to please him. The thought of holding back from him as she had always done with Barry scarcely entered her head, and when his fingers probed the laced fastening of her shirt, she felt her breasts burgeoning against his hands.

But the laces proved difficult to unfasten with one hand and Morgan swore softly as they resisted all his efforts to loosen them. 'God, couldn't you wear buttons like everyone else?' he demanded, drawing her hand from his hair to the offending fastening.

Helen quickly untied the laces but a faint smile touched her lips as she felt his impatience. 'You'll get used to them,' she ventured daringly. 'What you need is practice.'

'What do you mean?'

There was the faintest of suspicions in his tone and she wondered if she dared tell him that she knew about his divorce. But she was afraid she might destroy whatever it was there was between them by precipitating a declaration, so she remained silent. She was sure she would be able to change his mind, and when he discovered that no other man had ever touched her . . .

She cupped his face in her hands and drew his mouth to hers once more, exulting in the feel of the hair-coarsened skin of his chest against the softness of her breasts.

'Helen . . .' he breathed, drawing back to coax the swollen peaks with his lips, and then suddenly a convulsive shudder shot through him. With a groan, he rolled off her and on to his back, and for a moment his body arched with pain. Then he lay still.

Immediately, she jack-knifed into a sitting position, leaning over him worriedly, noticing the greying pallor of his skin and the drawn tightness of his features.

'Morgan!' Her use of his name was agonised. 'Morgan, what's wrong?'

'Massa sir . . . ?'

Kori's imitation of her tone was at once a shock and a reassurance. Dragging the folds of her shirt about her, she wondered with fleeting distaste how long he had been a willing voyeur to their lovemaking, but close on this thought came the thankfulness of knowing there was someone else she could turn to. Morgan's eyes were closed and he was making no movement at all, and fumbling the laces into some semblance of a knot, she exclaimed:

'Kori did you see what happened? What can I do?'

The boy moved to the bed and looked down doubtfully at his master. 'You hit Massa sir?' he enquired curiously, and if she hadn't felt so worried she would have laughed at his expression.

'Hit him?' she echoed now. 'No. No, of course I didn't hit him!' She lifted a tentative hand and laid it against Morgan's forehead. It was damp with sweat, but not fevered, and she withdrew it again to stare helplessly at Kori. 'He—he sort of—collapsed.'

Kori assumed what she guessed he considered to be an intelligent frown. Cupping his chin in his hand, he moved his shoulders in a dismissing gesture. 'Massa overtired,' he announced at last. 'We leave him sleep. He all right in morning.'

Helen shook her head impatiently. 'We can't do that——'

'Why not?' It was Morgan who spoke, pushing himself up on to his elbows. 'Heavens alive, what is this? A wake? I'm all right. Like Kori says, Helen, I'm overtired. I think you'd better go and leave me to sleep it off.'

Helen stared at him. 'But, Morgan——'

'Go, Helen!' he ordered harshly, and reluctantly aware of Kori's interested appraisal, she slid off the bed and walked towards the door. She looked back once, but Morgan wasn't looking at her. He was giving Kori some keys, directing him to go to the surgery and get something for him, as remote from her as he ever had been.

In the morning it was difficult to remember the events of the night before without a sense of unreality. Had Morgan really intended to make love to her? Had his apparent collapse been real or just assumed? Had she any hope of breaching his defences a second time knowing that only his intense weariness had weakened his resistance to her?

She rose early, aroused by the sound of animals and voices. She had not slept well, only fitfully, but standing by the slatted blinds of the windows, she felt a little of her composure returning as she glimpsed the two small boys driving a herd of goats through the trees beyond the courtyard. It was such an ordinary sight that she was almost grateful to them for disturbing her, although consciousness brought the enormity of her problems into focus. And not least of these was Andrea.

The previous evening she had had no opportunity to speak to Morgan about his daughter, but this morning she would have to, and that prospect was not an appealing one. What would he say when he discovered her incompetence? It was always possible he might dismiss her, send her back to England, and get someone else. Her only hope was that

Nrubi's remoteness might deter any but the most undaunted female.

The air that flooded into the room when she opened the shutters was pleasantly cool, and she shivered in her thin nightshirt. A glance at her watch essayed the knowledge that it was barely seven o'clock, but unable to rest until she discovered how Morgan was feeling this morning, she slipped on her pink cotton wrapper and opened her bedroom door.

There was the reassuring smell of bacon from the kitchen, but she turned in the opposite direction, making her way to Morgan's room. The ethics of entering his room troubled her a little, particularly after what he had said at the Onebas', but before she could stretch out her hand to push open the door which was already ajar, Kori's ubiquitous voice observed:

'Massa not there, missy. He have breakfast half hour ago and he gone.'

'Gone!' Helen knew she sounded as dismayed as she felt. 'Gone? Where's he gone?'

Kori came a little nearer, wiping his black hands on the spotless white apron he was wearing. Combined with his bare chest and baggy shorts, it was quite an outfit.

'Dushombi, missy.' Then, seeing her lack of comprehension, enlarged: 'Dushombi village, missy. Old man sick. Boy came as soon as it daylight.'

'Oh.' Helen's spirits sank depressingly. 'Did—er—did he say when he'd be back?'

'No. But Dushombi not far. Only nine—ten miles, maybe.'

Helen nodded. That was a relief anyway. It sounded as if Morgan would be back before lunch. 'Is—is Miss Andrea up yet?'

'No'm.' Kori shook his head, and now, as his eyes moved with evident appraisal over her thinly-clad figure, she drew the wrapper closer about her. 'You like breakfast?'

Helen made a negative gesture. 'I'll get dressed,' she said. 'Maybe then . . .'

'You like bacon? Eggs?'

Realising she was hungry, Helen nodded. 'One egg,' she decreed. 'Poached, if possible. No bacon.'

Kori looked disappointed, but he went away, and breathing a sigh of relief, Helen went back into her room. Collecting her toilet bag, she made her way with some reluctance to the bathroom. But Kori was engrossed in his cooking, and she was able to slip inside and lock the door without observation.

Only then did she see the disgusting sight of the hand-basin. Enormous cockroaches were crawling loathsomely around the rim, and her gasp of horror was loud enough to attract the attention of the one person she had hoped to avoid. She heard his fingers beating a tattoo on the panels of the door, and his voice enquiring if anything was wrong.

Unable to deal with the creatures herself, Helen wrenched open the door. 'Yes,' she said, through taut lips. 'Look! What can I do about them?'

'Ah!' Kori's grin was smug. 'Missy not put plug in hole last night. This what happens.'

Helen swallowed, remembering she had removed the plug from the wash basin when she had sluiced her face earlier in the day, and the previous evening she had not thought of replacing it.

'But doesn't anyone else use this bathroom?' she exclaimed, and Kori shook his head.

'Massa sir, he use bathroom between his room and Miss Andrea's. I guess Miss Andrea use that, too.'

'I see.' Helen absorbed this with resignation. She ought to have guessed there would be more than one bathroom in a house of this size. 'Well, what can I do now?'

Kori looked at her thoughtfully. 'You want Kori should squash them?'

'Squash them?' The thought of so many crushed bodies spilling blood on to the wash-basin made her feel positively sick. 'I—well, if you must.'

'Leave it to Kori,' he said, and she did, going out into the kitchen, unable to remain with him while he wielded the heel of his sandal with such devastating detachment.

'All clear,' he announced, coming back into the room as he stepped back into his sandal. To her relief Helen saw he went at once to wash his hands. 'You remember now, hmm?'

'I'll remember,' she agreed tersely, and went unwillingly into the bathroom again.

Although the basin was spotlessly clean again, she chose to take a bath instead, welcoming the tepid water against her overheated body. But she ensured that the plug was replaced before leaving the room again, and this time Kori was waiting for her as she emerged.

'Breakfast ready,' he said, indicating the place set at the kitchen table behind him, but Helen declined to join him yet.

'I must get dressed,' she insisted firmly, and as she shed her wrapper and stepped into thin blue cotton pants, she hoped he was not going to be a problem, too.

She was halfway through the deliciously poached egg and lightly buttered toast, when through the open windows she saw several people coming towards the house. They were all from the village, she guessed, in various states of dress, from tightly-bound sari-like garments to little more than a loincloth, some of the children not wearing any clothes at all. They stared at her as she was staring at them, but when she turned to Kori to ask him to answer the door, she saw they were turning away along the side of the building.

'Patients,' said Kori, in answer to her unspoken question. 'To see Massa doctor. You understand?'

'Of course.' Helen chided herself for her stupidity. Of course Morgan would have a surgery, just like any other doctor. 'But he's not here.'

'They wait,' declared Kori indifferently, collecting her dirty plate. 'You like more coffee?'

'No, thanks.' Helen pushed her cup aside and rose to her feet. 'I—er—I think I'll go and get some air. That is permissible, isn't it?'

'Why not?'

Kori shrugged, and glad to escape his knowing eyes, she

walked quickly out of the kitchen, and across the living room to the doors leading on to the verandah.

She was too restless to sit still, and leaving the cloistered walkway, she crossed the courtyard to the tangled path which seemed to lead to the water's edge. But the possibility of meeting more insects like those she had seen in the bathroom, or alternatively some other wild creature of which she had no knowledge, deterred further exploration. Instead, she looked up at the wide arc of blue overhead and wondered at the complex series of events which had led her from the comparative safeness of her life in England to this hilly plateau in East Africa. And yet, in spite of all the difficulties she faced, she knew she would never regret her decision to accompany Morgan, whatever happened.

The sound of chattering voices drew her round the side of the house, but she stopped aghast at the sight of a dozen or more people squatting in the dust outside the fluted windows of what she guessed to be Morgan's surgery. Here were the women and children she had seen earlier together with several others, and they all stopped their chattering to stare at her open-mouthed.

Unused to attracting such obvious attention, Helen would have walked away again, but one of the younger women rose to her feet and approached her. Not quite sure what she ought to do, Helen submitted to the girl's admiring fingering of her hair. Obviously, she was intrigued that dark hair could be so straight, and she beckoned another of her friends to come and see.

The girl was quite beautiful, and although her striped skirt and a multitude of coloured necklaces were all she wore, she was quite without self-consciousness. On the contrary, she apparently found Helen's cotton sweat shirt with its campus motif rather amusing, and feeling embarrassment prickling over her body, Helen was inclined to think the same.

She was unutterably relieved when she heard the familiar sound of a car approaching, and presently the station wagon swung into the forecourt. The engine died, and Morgan levered himself from behind the wheel, lean and disturbingly attractive in the harsh glare of the sun.

His gaze flicked briefly over Helen registering her relief, and then moved on to the patients awaiting his return. His native greeting was incomprehensible to Helen, but then he strode towards her and her heart quickened its already hectic beat. However, his intention was merely to unlock the waiting room door, and he disappeared inside followed eagerly by the others.

Shoulders sagging, she was turning away when he emerged again, and called: 'Helen! Wait! You can help me.'

'Help you?' She trudged back doubtfully. 'Why? How are you this morning?'

A flicker of irritation crossed his face. 'I'm all right—I told you last night. It was exhaustion, nothing more. Now, do you want to help me, or don't you?'

'How?'

'You can change dressings, can't you? Take temperatures? Tie bandages?'

'Of course.'

'Of course,' he mimicked. 'So you can help me. Come on.'

As cool as that! Helen stared after his retreating back with vague resentment. Not a word about what had happened the night before, not a hint of emotion. Just brusqueness—and detachment!

Still, she consoled herself, at least it would help to fill in the time until she could talk to him about Andrea, and it might even make their relationship easier.

Two hours later her fingers ached from handling bottles of antiseptic and gripping the narrow base of the thermometer. She had thought, remembering pictures from newsreels she had seen, that perhaps these people might object to her ministrations, but she couldn't have been more wrong. She felt she never wanted to see another bandage or smell the acrid aroma of ammonia, and although the crowd of curious black faces had thinned there were still several women and children sitting in the waiting room. They had a dogged determination, these people, she thought, shaking her head blankly. The patience never to give up, no matter how long they might have to wait. Only the children showed any signs of irritation, and then only the older ones. The younger children suckled at their mother's breasts when they were hungry, and crawled happily about when they were not, but the overpowering scent of humanity was gradually giving Helen a headache.

'That's enough for now,' declared Morgan at last, as Helen was ushering an old man from the surgery. 'Close the door and lock it. We can use the other door into the house.'

'Oh, but——' Helen gestured feebly towards the patients still waiting. 'I mean, what about—them?'

'I'll deal with them later,' replied Morgan, getting to his feet and slamming the door himself. He turned the key in the lock and then began to remove the white coat he had worn for his examinations. 'You've had enough for the moment, and I could surely use a cool lager.'

'That sounds appealing,' sighed Helen, removing the coat he had lent her. She had had to turn back the sleeves, and tie a piece of string about the waist to give it some shape, but she had been glad of the protection. 'I didn't think they'd approve of a woman.'

'So long as you're wearing a white coat, you look like a nurse to them. Besides, you've had some experience of hospital work.'

'Well, yes—but mostly out-patients.'

'That's all these people are.' He pushed back the hair from his forehead with an impatient hand. 'Come along. Just leave the coat over the chair.'

Helen put out a hand to him as he went to unlock the door which led into the body of the house. 'Morgan . . .' She hesitated. 'Morgan, about last night——'

'Forget it,' he advised her brusquely. 'I have. Come on. I want to lock the door behind us, just in case anyone takes it into their heads to raid the surgery.'

Helen doubted anyone would, but she passed through the door obediently and then walked dejectedly along the hall towards the kitchen.

There was no sign of Kori or Andrea when they reached the kitchen, so Morgan helped himself to two tins of lager from the fridge, handing one to Helen with a tall glass. Himself, he drank from the can, and after watching him for a moment, Helen did the same. The lager dribbled down her chin, but it was deliciously cold, and very reviving.

When it became apparent that he could not avoid the issue any longer, he said: 'You said something last night about needing to talk to me. What about?'

Helen wiped the lager from her lips. 'It—it was about Andrea, actually.'

'Yes?'

He wasn't being very helpful, and she glanced desperately about her, seeking for words of inspiration. 'I—we—we had a talk.' She paused. 'About—about the reasons for me being here.'

'Yes?'

'Oh, Morgan! Stop saying "yes" in that tone!' Her lips trembled and she pressed them together to hide the small betrayal. 'I—I guess I made a mess of it. Somehow she's got it into her head that—that maybe you're not satisfied with her the—the way she is.'

'Go on.'

He finished the lager in his can and watched her with narrowed eyes, and her legs gave out on her. Seeking the refuge of a chair, she continued: 'I—I think she's very—self-conscious about her appearance.'

'I know that.' His voice was curt. 'Is that all you have to say?'

'No. I mean—well, maybe. Morgan, I honestly didn't think——'

'Oh, don't worry.' Morgan tossed the empty can into the waste bin. 'You're not responsible for Andrea's hang-ups. Her mother holds that distinction, I think.'

'Her—mother?'

'Yes, her mother. Pamela. My wife.'

'Your—ex-wife,' she interposed softly, and was startled at the sudden anger in his eyes.

'Where did you hear that? Oh, God—Kori, I suppose,'

'No!' Helen swallowed with difficulty. 'A-actually, Andrea told me.'

'Did she?' His lips twisted. 'Oh, well, you had to know eventually, I suppose.'

'Yes.' Helen bit her lip and got to her feet again. 'I'm sorry if—if you'd rather I didn't know, but—well, Morgan, you have to accept it sooner or later. I mean, it's happened to hundreds of people, and just because it's happened once it doesn't mean——'

'What the hell are you babbling on about?' he snapped furiously. 'What are you trying to say? That you sympathise with me? That you believe I still care about that disastrous relationship? My God, you couldn't be more wrong. When I signed the form that meant I was free of Pamela, I was relieved, do you hear that? Relieved! God, how relieved I was!'

'But——' Helen was trying confusedly to absorb these new facts. 'But——'

Morgan moved then, coming round the table towards her, thrusting his face close to hers. 'Oh, you poor fool!' he exclaimed cruelly. 'I know what you're thinking. You thought the reason I had told you that there could be nothing between us was because I was married, and then, when you discovered I was divorced, you told yourself that I must be suffering from some romantic delusions of a love gone sour! God, it would be funny if it wasn't so pathetic! Did you really think I wanted to marry you? Did you honestly believe that if I'd made love to you last night—and God knows, you asked for it—I'd have been obliged to do the honourable thing by you?'

'And—and wouldn't you?' she asked, forcing back the tears that threatened behind her lids.

'No.' He shook his head. 'Helen, I've said it often enough, goodness knows! Don't you believe me? Can't you accept that I don't want to marry *anyone*?'

Helen felt numb, but at the same time she felt a resurgent charge of anger against him. How dared he stand there and shout at her that he didn't want to marry her? How dared he treat her like some dreadful harpy who wouldn't take no for an answer? It didn't matter what she had thought, what she had believed. He was only guessing. He couldn't know for certain what dreams she had nourished.

'You really have some opinion of yourself, don't you?' she got out now, summoning every ounce of stamina to defend herself against him. 'And such old-world charm! Well, let me tell you, you have the mind to go with it! Do you honestly think that I'd expect marriage from you, just because we'd spent the night in bed together? How old-world can you get!'

'You told me——'

'I told you what?' she overrode him. 'That I didn't go in for that sort of thing? That Barry had never touched me? Did you believe that? Now who's naïve? Oh, Morgan, England's not what it used to be, and we girls know exactly how to have our cake and eat it!'

His hand stung across her cheek, and her gasp of dismay was echoed by the girl who, attracted by the raised voices, had come to stand in the open doorway.

'Daddy!' she choked in horror, as Helen pressed her palm to her stinging flesh. 'Oh, Daddy, how could you?'

Morgan stared at his daughter as if he couldn't believe she was actually there, and then he looked at Helen again. 'Oh—*God*!' he muttered savagely, and brushing past Andrea he left them.

CHAPTER NINE

NRUBI was quite a sophisticated town by Osweban standards. Its buildings were clean and reasonably modern, and it was possible to buy practically anything in the stores that lined the main street. Many of the store-owners were Asians, Indians and Pakistanis, with a fair smattering of Chinese among them. These people lived in the larger houses set on the outskirts of the town, but not far from Nrubi the African villages were as primitive now as they had been fifty years before. However, there was little antipathy between the races, and Helen's impression was that generally speaking they were a contented people.

Her own contentment had never materialised, although strangely enough the antagonism between herself and Morgan had achieved what gentleness and straight talking could not. Andrea had become her friend, her protector almost, and while Helen went through agonies over her feelings for the girl's father, she was able to console herself with the bitter knowledge that Morgan's purpose for bringing her out here had been achieved.

Since that terrible row they had had the morning after her arrival, she had scarcely spoken to him. Oh, they exchanged politenesses, of course—*Good morning* and *Goodnight*, and an occasional *Pass the salt, please*, but little more than that. She supposed she ought to be grateful he had not ordered her back to England regardless, but the more she thought about it, the less of a deprivation that appeared. It was all very well to tell herself that she had come here for Andrea's sake, and truly she had begun to like the girl for herself, but if she was completely honest she would have to admit that with Morgan's final rejection, the bottom had dropped out of her world. She had wanted to run away then and hide, conceal herself until she could draw the shreds of her torn emotions around her. But instead she had been forced to behave as if the matter was of no consequence. And she had won Andrea's admiration.

The girl had been so sweet. Perhaps witnessing someone else's humiliation had made her realise that she was not unique after all, that beauty and personality could just as easily be spurned. Perhaps it had reassured her that rejection was not always motivated by physical characteristics, but much more by a condition of the mind.

Whatever her private feelings, during the past two weeks Andrea had taken up a defensive attitude towards her father on Helen's behalf, and after a few tentative conversations, the two girls were slowly developing a genuine companionship. As yet, Helen was still wary of overstepping that tenuous bond, but gradually Andrea was beginning to show an interest in Helen's clothes and the perfumes on her dressing table evaporated more quickly than could be blamed on the heat. Judging by the aura of rose petals that surrounded Andrea sometimes, Helen guessed she found the toilet sprays irresistible, but she never complained. The child had had so little encouragement in her life so far, and Helen was simply relieved that their relationship had given her that freedom.

Helen's ability to drive had proved a boon. An elderly Fiat had been resurrected from its resting place in the yard of the garage in Nrubi, and with Morgan's permission the two girls had taken short trips into the surrounding area. With Andrea, Helen had discovered the falls which fed the stretch of water behind the villa, and learned that Hawk's Drift was in fact the name of the water and not the house. It in turn ran into a river which tumbled and splashed its way down to the plain to join the swamp-edged waters of the Tsinga. They visited Dushombi, with its round thatched dwellings, gazed awestruck at the massive rocky outcrops which were said to be the relics of that ancient subterranean upheaval that had torn the savage fissure of the Great Rift Valley, and visited a farm where mangoes and pawpaws were grown. Helen had been persuaded to taste the fruit, but although she had found the mango quite pleasant, the pawpaw she decided was an acquired taste. They even explored the ruins of a city which was believed to have been inhabited by the Persians. Standing in the forest, surrounded by tall trees, it was very eerie, and the local tribesmen insisted that it was haunted. Pushing her way between the creeper-clad pillars that were crumbling into dust around her, Helen was quite prepared to believe it.

The night before Andrea's birthday, however, Helen knew she would have to speak to Morgan alone. She had known, of course, that the girl's birthday was at hand, but coming into the kitchen unexpectedly that morning, she had surprised Kori in the process of spreading icing over a fluffy sponge cake, and found it was nearer than she had supposed.

'This is kind of you, Kori,' she exclaimed, admiring the efforts he was making to cover the cake before the sugar melted. 'Did Massa Morgan ask you to do this?'

Kori finished what he was doing, and hastily put the cake away in the refrigerator. Then he turned with some indignation. 'Massa not know!' he declared firmly. 'Massa prob'ly forget birthday.'

'Oh, surely not, Kori!' exclaimed Helen in dismay. 'He—wouldn't!'

'Massa very busy,' said Kori, putting his dirty dishes into the sink, and Helen sighed.

'I know that.' It was true. Since Morgan's return, he had scarcely had a day off, and while she was glad to avoid the inevitable difficulties his presence would create, she was concerned about his health. So far as she knew he had had no more attacks like the one she had witnessed, but as she saw so little of him, how could she be sure? She was sure a town of Nrubi's size should have more doctors, but although she knew there was an Asian doctor actually practising in the town itself, so long as Morgan was available, people were prepared to make the trek to the villa. In addition to which, Andrea had told her her father had a laboratory adjoining his surgery where he was making a study of tropical diseases, and Helen guessed he spent any free time he had in there.

But Andrea's birthday was something special, and she determined that whatever kind of reception she might get, she would have to speak to Morgan about it. For herself, she had already chosen to give her a necklace of her own which Andrea had particularly admired, and intended to combine it with a length of jewel-bright poplin in a particularly attractive shade of blue. She hoped Andrea might permit her to make her a tunic suit in a style she chose, but until she knew what kind of reception the material would get, she was making no plans.

Her opportunity to speak to Morgan came that evening immediately after dinner. Andrea disappeared as she usually did to get the coffee, but when Morgan moved to make his usual departure for his surgery, Helen asked if he had a moment to speak to her.

'Yes?' His voice was wary as he stood behind his chair resting his hands on the back. 'What do you want?'

'Not here,' exclaimed Helen awkwardly, glancing round, afraid that Andrea might come back and overhear them. 'I mean—privately.'

Morgan straightened, his eyes assuming the hard glint she had come to know so well. He had never apologised for his actions the day he had slapped her, and the memory of that always lay between them, like some ugly chasm.

Looking at him, Helen tried to keep her own eyes as guarded. But it was difficult when the sight of his lean hard face and lithe muscular body made every nerve in her body tingle. It was impossible to dissociate these thoughts from the memory of his knowledge of her body, too, and she knew that no matter how he treated her she would never be able to repulse him as he had repulsed her.

'I don't think that's a very good idea,' he said now, his voice as hard as his eyes. 'If you have anything to say to me, I suggest you come right out and say it.'

'I—can't!' Helen's face blazed with colour. 'Morgan! Please! It's important.'

He thrust his hands into his pockets with obvious impatience. 'Oh, very well. Come to the surgery in fifteen minutes. I'll speak to you there.'

'Thank you so much.' She couldn't keep the bitter sarcasm out of her words, and he nodded as if it was nothing more than he had expected, and left the room.

Getting away from Andrea was less easy. Eventually, Helen lied and said she had a headache, and the girl made no objections when she said she was going to her room.

The surgery door was ajar when she reached it, and she pushed it open tentatively and slipped inside, closing it softly behind her. There was no sign of Morgan, but the door to his inner laboratory was open, and even as she hesitated, he came to the laboratory door to speak to her.

'Well?'

Helen sighed. It wasn't the most auspicious opening and she never found it easy to broach personal topics with him. 'I-it's about Andrea,' she ventured at last, and he made an offhand movement of his shoulders.

'Is it?'

'Yes.' She paused. 'It's about—tomorrow.'

'Her birthday. Yes?'

'Oh, you know!'

Morgan's mouth turned down at the corners. 'You didn't seriously believe I didn't.'

'Well, I—Kori said——'

'Oh yes? What did Kori say?'

Helen shrugged. 'Just that—that you'd been busy. That you—could forget the date.'

'Indeed? Well, I haven't. Was that all you wanted?'

Helen pressed her lips together. 'I suppose so.' She linked her fingers together. 'Do you know Kori's made her a cake?'

'He usually does,' retorted Morgan laconically. 'But we waive the party.'

This last was said with obvious mockery, and Helen's teeth clenched. 'That's all right then, isn't it?' she declared. 'I'm sorry I troubled you.'

He inclined his head politely, and she had no choice but to walk to the door. However, as she reached it, she turned again.

'Morgan . . .'

'Yes?' The wariness was back in his tone.

'A-Andrea and I are getting along very well together.'

He relaxed slightly. 'Good.'

'I wondered . . .' She caught her lower lip doubtfully between her teeth. 'I wondered how long—that is—do you still intend to send her back to England?'

'Yes.' It was a clipped definitive.

Helen expelled an unsteady breath. 'I don't think she'll want to go.'

'You'll persuade her.'

'Me?' Helen was astounded.

'Yes, you.' He took a couple of steps towards her. 'You

don't want to stay here indefinitely, do you? I'm sure you're becoming bored already by our simple life.' He ignored her indignant protest, and went on: 'If you can convince her how much happier she'll be with all the advantages of western civilisation, I think eventually she'll want to go back with you.'

'But *why*?'

Too late, Helen realised she had overstepped the bounds of polite conversation, and Morgan's next words reinforced that belief. 'Whatever I decide for Andrea is no concern of yours!' he commented coldly. 'At the risk of repeating myself yet again, I must point out that you are here to do a job of work, not offer opinions!'

Helen's lips tightened. 'You love humiliating me, don't you, Morgan?' She pressed a hand to her stomach where the meal she had just consumed was churning sickeningly. 'You enjoy making me feel small.' And when he still didn't respond, she added: 'I don't think you care about anyone or anything!'

'That's another opinion, is it?' he demanded harshly. 'What makes you think you have the right to criticise me? A little tramp like you!'

It was as if he had slapped her again. Helen's face mirrored the pain he had deliberately inflicted. But when, blinded by tears, she groped for the door handle, it was flesh and bones she found, long hard fingers that gripped hers so tightly she winced.

'Oh, God, Helen,' Morgan said in a strained, tormented voice, holding both her hands in his. 'It's no good, I can't go on like this. Helen! Helen, I'm sorry, I'm sorry.'

She looked up at him through the blurring mist of tears. 'Morgan?' she breathed, half questioningly, but his face was descending to hers and the probing warmth of his mouth was more potent than any words. With a groan of satisfaction, he gathered her close against him, and all the torment of the past weeks was forgotten in the passionate urgency of his desire.

'You—you've been so horrible to me,' she choked, when he released her mouth to bury his face in her silky curtain of her hair, and she felt his assenting nod. 'Why did you pretend you didn't care about me? Why did you get so angry when I tried to talk to you about it?'

'Women!' he groaned with resignation, drawing back to rest his forehead against hers. 'Why do they always want to talk at the most inopportune moments?'

Helen moistened her upper lip, an unknowingly provocative gesture. 'It's not unreasonable, is it? After—after the way you've behaved?'

She was half afraid her words would instigate further antagonism between them, but they had to be said. She couldn't pretend these past weeks had never happened. She had a slimmer figure to prove it, and it wasn't fair that he should think he could change his mind without explanation.

Now he sighed and said: 'Put it down to my uncertain temper.' His lean mouth was cynical. 'I'm a selfish swine, as you've said.'

'No.' Helen's eyes were troubled. 'No, it's not just that. Morgan, I want to know the truth. How do you really feel about me? Did you really bring me out here just to be a companion for Andrea, or—or was there something more?'

His eyes darkened. 'That's a crazy question, and you know it,' he muttered, and to her dismay, he released her.

'Why?' she persisted, trembling a little. 'Why is it crazy? Don't I have a right to ask?'

Morgan thrust frustrated fingers through his hair. The dark blue silk shirt clung to the muscular contours of his chest, and his action stretched the buttons to their limit. Dark corded pants exposed the powerful length of his legs, but Helen's eyes focussed somewhere between his waist and his shoulders as she waited for the axe to fall.

'All right,' he said at last, and the words seemed to be torn from him. 'All right. You do have the right to ask, and God knows, I want to tell you. Of course, you attract me. You always did. Lord, you know that.'

'Do I?'

'Yes. Yes.' His eyes glittered with impatience, but whether with her or himself she didn't know. 'You know what you can do to me. That's why I've tried to hold you off.'

'But why?' she breathed, hardly daring to take this in. 'Why hold me off? You—you know I love you——'

'No!'

'Yes.'

'Then I wish you didn't,' he said with cold finality, dashing her hopes once more.

'I see,' she whispered, but her efforts to appear calm seemed to infuriate him.

'No,' he contradicted roughly. 'No, you don't see at all. Oh, Helen, it's impossible for me to explain——' He broke off, pressing his balled fist into the palm of his other hand. 'God, I wish this had never happened! If I'd not been so concerned about Andrea, if I'd never gone to England . . .' He shook his head. 'If we'd never met . . .'

'I'm sorry.'

The tremor in her voice seemed to torture him, and almost against his will, she felt, his hands reached for her again. He hauled her close against him, moulding her body to his, making her overwhelmingly aware of just how deeply she did disturb him.

'You see,' he said, unbuttoning the neckline of her simple cotton tunic to caress her bare shoulders with his lips, his breathing hoarse and shallow. 'I want you. I need you. I lie awake nights imagining how it would be if you were in the bed beside me, and wake in the mornings sick to my stomach because you're not.' He bent his head lower to kiss the soft curve of her breast, teasing the nipple with his tongue and flooding her body with sensual warmth. 'I want to make love to you,' he breathed, 'I want to possess every part of you, and I want you to possess me . . .'

His words ceased abruptly as his mouth sought hers, forcing her lips apart and taking its own possession. It was a shattering experience; an intoxicating, drugging lethargy made her limbs curiously weak, and when his legs parted to draw her nearer, she surrendered utterly to the sensuous demands of his body.

'Not here,' he managed to say at last, drawing back to look down into her bemused face with eyes glazed with emotion. 'Let's go to my room. We'll be more comfortable there, and besides, I can't see enough of you like this.'

Helen's lips parted softly. 'Nor me you,' she confided, and a faintly mocking smile crossed his face.

'At least I don't have to teach you what it's all about, do I?' he remarked dryly. 'The sight of a man's naked body holds no fears for you.'

'I—why—Morgan——'

A sudden knocking at the door interrupted her incoherent efforts to try and explain that he was suffering a misapprehension about her. With misgivings, she remembered her stupid boast that she was an emancipated woman, that his ideas were old-fashioned, that he would not be the first with her. Was it possible that Morgan was only giving in now because he thought she was experienced? Because he expected her to have taken all the necessary precautions to avoid the possible complications?

The knocking at the door was suddenly a respite, an opportunity to consider and to think. But right now, with her emotions aroused and vulnerable, it was difficult to feel anything but dry-mouthed disbelief.

'God!'

Morgan's oath was followed by a reluctant drawing away from her, and as he thrust his shirt back into his pants and endeavoured to conceal the physical evidence of his feelings, Helen hastily drew her tunic back on to her shoulders. She turned away to fumble the buttons back into their holes as Morgan opened the door, and the sound of Kori's voice was almost a relief. She had been so afraid it might be Andrea.

'You there, Massa sir,' he said, and Helen guessed he would be looking past Morgan, trying to see if she was with him. 'Boy here from village. Say someone bitten by mamba.'

'Oh, *Lord*!' Morgan brushed a weary hand across his forehead. 'What village? Where's the boy? Did you get his name?'

Helen turned as Kori was nodding vigorously. 'His name Masawa, Massa sir. He come from——'

'Gabura. Yes, I know.' Morgan's mind was clearing. 'A

mamba, you say.' He glanced helplessly at Helen. 'The most venomous snake in Osweba.'

'Is it?' Helen was still very shaken, and the brooding tenderness that crossed Morgan's face at that moment didn't help. 'I—will you have to go?'

Morgan's mouth tightened. 'Yes, I'll have to go,' he agreed. Then he turned to Kori again. 'Get me some ice from the freezer and put it into a flask, and then find me a length of that leather you use to tie your sandals.'

'Yes, Massa.'

Kori hurried away, and Morgan turned once more to Helen. 'I'm sorry,' he said. 'I don't know how long this will take. I may not be back before morning.'

Helen nodded. 'I understand.'

'Do you?' His tone was ironic. 'I wish I did.' Then he went past her into the laboratory.

Helen followed him doubtfully. 'Will—will whoever it is die?' she asked, and he gave her an old-fashioned look.

'Not if I can help it,' he replied shortly, and she felt rather foolish.

'I'm sorry, I didn't mean to imply . . .' She glanced round helplessly. 'Is there anything I can do? Do you want me to—to come with you?'

He shook his head, unlocking a glass cabinet and taking out a bottle. He studied the label for a moment and then put it into his bag along with a hypodermic syringe and supply of dressings. Helen watched him for several seconds, then, half relieved by his reply, she asked:

'What will happen? I mean, does venom usually induce unconsciousness?'

'Not in this case. Spasms, convulsions, vomiting; sometimes even paralysis. It depends how serious the bite is.'

'But it is lethal?'

'It can be. Not all snakebites are deadly, of course. It depends on the snake. Unfortunately the mamba is probably the most dangerous.' He closed his bag and it locked, automatically. 'Its venom attacks the central nervous system, you see. What we call neurotoxic. Some venoms affect only the area around the incision. They cause poisoning, and left unattended, gangrene will set in, but ultimately they're less likely to be fatal.'

'Ugh!' Helen couldn't prevent a shiver of horror. Then a thought occurred to her. 'You won't—that is—the snake won't still be around, will it?'

'With any luck, they'll have killed it,' commented Morgan flatly. 'If not, rest assured, it will be long gone. It's wary of finding its way into the stewpot.'

'They wouldn't!' Helen stared at him aghast.

'They might,' he retorted wryly.

Helen refused to think about this. Instead she said: 'Be careful, won't you?'

He came towards her carrying his bag in one hand, lifting a leather jerkin off a wall hook with the other, pushing his arm into the sleeve. 'Do I detect a note of concern?' he asked mockingly, and her lips compressed.

'You know you do.'

His eyes darkened for a moment with remembered emotion. Then they dropped down the length of her body before returning to her face again, turning her skin to crimson. 'I tell you what we'll do,' he said, coming close to look down at her. 'Get Andrea to pack some things and we'll go down to the coast for the weekend. We'll leave in the morning, as soon as I get back. I could do with the break—we all could.'

Helen trembled slightly. 'A-all right.' Time enough to worry about the sleeping arrangements after he had gone. 'Drive carefully.'

'I will,' he assured her softly, and dropping a searching kiss on her mouth, he left her.

CHAPTER TEN

HELEN slept badly. When she did manage to fall into a fitful doze she was plagued by terrible dreams of hooded snakes rearing their ugly heads, and when she awakened she was soaked with sweat, her heart hammering like a drum. Her ears were alert to every rustle around the villa, and once she was awake she lay for ages listening to the night sounds with a disturbing prickle along her spine. She shed her nightgown in search of coolness, and then lay worrying that Kori might come in in the morning and find her naked. She kept imagining she could hear the station wagon returning, and with nerves stretched to fever pitch, she wound the sheet closely about her, shivering with fearful anticipation.

She still did not know what she would do if Morgan came. Could she turn him away when she loved him so desperately? Could she deny him the one thing she had encouraged him to take? And what would he think of her if she did? Would he believe her if she confessed she had lied about her relationship with Barry, or would he think she was teasing him again and take her without the saving grace of tenderness?

She didn't know what to do—what to think. Until that moment in the surgery when he had taunted her about knowing what it was all about, she had been prepared to give him her body unreservedly, but what would he think of her when he discovered she was still a virgin? Would he be pleased or angry? Anxious or accusing?—blaming her for deliberately deceiving him. Whatever his feelings, whatever lash he was flaying himself with, it seemed obvious that marriage did not figure in his plans for the future, and knowing her as he did, he might suspect she was hoping to trap him into a relationship he did not want.

Of course, she could deny this, but what if she became pregnant? He was a doctor. He would know immediately if anything was wrong. And how could she acquire the necessary immunity here when she had no means of obtaining the drug or indeed any knowledge of what drug she ought to take?

It was an impossible situation and that, combined with her anxiety for Morgan's safety, did not make for relaxation. Instead, dawn found her wrapped in her thin cotton dressing gown, seated at the window, waiting for the sun to gild the rushes that grew tall and straight at the water's edge.

If only her problems were as simple as Andrea's, Helen thought, remembering with a pang that today was the girl's birthday. She had been so excited at the prospect of a trip to the coast, but her information that Morgan owned a two-bedroomed shack at the beach had only added to Helen's uncertainty. Two bedrooms! One for Andrea? She shook her head helplessly. What was she going to do?

For the first time since leaving England she wondered whether she had done the right thing. Not about walking out on Barry—that had been inevitable from the minute she laid eyes on Morgan—but for coming out here with him, for allowing such an ambiguous situation to develop. Her parents would be horrified, she knew, if they suspected what she was contemplating, but wasn't her love for Morgan the most important thing after all?

Thinking of her parents reminded her that apart from a card from Nairobi she hadn't written to them since arriving in Africa. She hoped they weren't worrying about her, and then decided that so long as Morgan was in touch with his father, they would know she was all right. The elder Mr Fox was bound to have kept in touch with the Raynors. He was that kind of man.

The unmistakable sound of an engine suddenly filled the air and panicked a handful of wild geese into reckless flight. It brought Helen to her feet, too, and hardly considering the scarcity of her attire, she left her room to hurry along the passage to the hall. The door was locked, but Morgan had a key, and she was standing there, hands clasped tremulously, when he came in.

He looked exhausted but triumphant, and when he saw

her, his lips twisted in lazy appraisal. 'That's what I like to see,' he mocked. 'My woman waiting for me when I get back.'

His *woman*! Not his *wife*!

Helen forced a smile. 'The man?'

'It was a woman, actually. And she'll live. I got there in time.'

'Oh, thank God!' Helen was fervent.

Morgan sighed and dropped his bag on to the floor. Then he looked steadily at her. 'Did you tell Andrea?'

'Wh-what about?'

'Going to the coast. What else?'

'Oh! Oh, yes.' Helen wrapped her gown more closer about her, and then realising how revealing that was, loosened it again. 'Yes. Yes, I told her. She was very excited.'

'Good.' Morgan's eyes had narrowed during this display, and with an almost offhand gesture, he said: 'I need some tea. Hot and strong and sweet. Then I'll get a couple of hours' rest before we leave.'

'I'll make it.'

Before he had time to protest, Helen had darted ahead of him into the kitchen, and when he came in to slouch wearily against the table, she had filled the kettle and was setting it on the hob. Clattering cups and saucers, she wondered if she looked as nervous as she felt, and then decided that she probably did. There was a certain cynicism in his glance, as if he knew what she was thinking, and relief vied with an aching longing to offer to go to bed with him.

By the time the kettle boiled, he had washed his hands and face at the sink, sluicing his neck under the tap. Then he seated himself at the table, and stretched his legs to rest on its rim.

'Would you—do you want anything to eat?' she asked, steadying her hand as she poured milk into the cups, but Morgan shook his head.

'Only tea,' he essayed dryly. 'And bed. In that order.'

She nodded, spilling some of the milk on to the draining board, and with an exclamation, he swung his feet to the floor and came round to her. His hands at her waist were hard and compelling, and she didn't want to resist when he drew her back against him.

'Relax!' he ordered huskily, rubbing his beard-roughened jaw against the side of her cheek. 'I know what you're thinking, and I'm not a complete fool. I've had time to think, too, remember?' He gave a short laugh which had little of humour in it. 'Do you think I haven't guessed that you must have been lying to me? No woman who's as experienced as you claimed to be could act like a startled doe every time I came near her. It's all right'—this as she started to protest—'I forgive you. Fortunately, no harm has been done. You ought to be grateful to that mamba. It saved you from a fate worse than death.'

Helen swung round in his arms then, staring up at him mutinously. 'Stop teasing me, Morgan. All right, so I haven't—slept around. That doesn't make any difference to us.'

'Yes, it does.' He let her go, pushing her firmly away from him. 'Pour the tea. I need it.'

Helen pressed her lips together, but she moved obediently to the teapot, lifting it with careful precision. Already she was regretting her eagerness to confess, and asking herself what he would have said if she had denied it.

'Hmm, that's good.' Morgan cradled his cup between his hands, his features revealing his tiredness. 'It was one hell of a night. The woman was having a screaming fit when I arrived, and half the village had gathered round her hut. Even the local witch doctor was there, and he and I have never seen eye to eye. Fortunately, the woman's husband cared more about his wife than he did about old Elopi.'

Helen listened in silence, her face mirroring her earlier indignation, and presently he lay back in his chair and regarded her broodingly.

'Stop it!' he ordered sharply. 'Stop feeling sorry for yourself. It wouldn't work, and you know it.'

'Why wouldn't it?' She didn't waste time pretending she didn't understand him, and he sighed.

'Because I can't marry you.'

'I know that.'

'Oh, you do?'

She flushed. 'You've said it before.'

'So I have. Okay, so what are you saying? That you want to be my mistress?'

Helen bent her head. 'Yes.'

'God Almighty!' He thrust back his chair and got to his feet. 'You know what you deserve, don't you?'

Helen forced herself to look up at him. 'No.'

'Then you should.' He shook his head. 'Did no one ever give you a good hiding when you were a child?' He spoke roughly, but she sensed he was curious rather than angry. Then he sighed. 'Helen! Helen! You're only making things impossible—for both of us.'

'Why?' She got to her feet, unafraid now. 'I know what I want.'

'Do you want to be sent back to England?'

Her eyes clouded. 'No.'

'Well, I know what I want,' he muttered, turning away, but when she took a step after him, he looked over his shoulder and added: 'Sleep, Helen. Sleep! Only sleep.'

When he had gone, she sank down weakly into a chair. It was useless, she thought despairingly. Whenever she felt she was getting close to him, he put her aside, showed her that whatever it was he felt for her it was not the all-consuming emotion she felt for him. So why couldn't she accept that, and be thankful he was not like any other man, who might have taken her love carelessly, and tossed it aside when the affair was over without a second thought. The truth was that deep inside her she didn't believe him when he said he wouldn't marry her—couldn't marry her. She always had the feeling there was something else, something he was holding back, some reason that made him step beyond her reach. But what could it be? Her mind went over all the stories she had read—the mythical reasons why one or other set of lovers could not be joined in matrimony. All she could think of was the stigma of some terrible disease, an inherited thread of insanity, or some incestuous relationship unknown to one of the partners. Yet none of these things seemed to apply to them. So far as she knew, there was no insanity in Morgan's family. His father was one of the sanest people she knew, and Andrea had no hysterical tendencies, just a highly-strung nervous system. And as far as incest was concerned ... Well, it was ridiculous to think about it.

She sighed. Obviously she was wrong. Somehow she would have to accept that, or her life wasn't going to be worth living.

Even so, when she was sure Morgan would be asleep, she left the kitchen and made her way along the corridor to his door. It was barely six-thirty, and not even Kori was up yet. The handle squeaked as she turned it, and her breath faltered in her throat. But she need not have been concerned. Morgan was sound asleep, sprawled carelessly across his bed. He had not even bothered to take off his clothes.

Irresistibly, Helen moved nearer to the bed, looking down at him emotionally. He looked younger asleep, as many people did, the lines relaxed around his nose and mouth. The short stubby lashes were tipped with gold, bleached by the sun like his hair, and she thought how strange it was that ultra-violet light could lighten hair and tan flesh with equal intensity. Morgan was very tanned, and remembering Barry's pale flesh, Helen couldn't help but compare the two.

She extended her fingers almost involuntarily towards him, and then withdrew the gesture. She couldn't disturb him, no matter how much she might want to. He needed the rest, and at least this weekend she would have plenty of time to talk to him. *To persuade him?* Somehow she doubted she would be able to do that.

She was emerging into the corridor again when Andrea's door opened. It was so early, and Andrea was usually such a late riser, that Helen had never expected to encounter the girl in such ambiguous circumstances, and it was with frustration she felt the betraying colour deepening in her cheeks. All of a sudden, her wrapper was scarcely decent, and the conclusions the girl must be jumping to were only too obvious.

'Andrea!' she forced herself to say with assumed assurance. 'You're an early riser!'

The girl tied the knot of her dressing gown tighter, and then said, almost offhandedly: 'I guess I was excited because we're going away.'

'Oh, yes.' Helen's smile was strained. 'And of course, it's your birthday! Many happy returns!'

'Thank you.' Andrea moved her shoulders awkwardly. 'Did—er—did Daddy get back safely?'

Suddenly Helen realised she didn't know what the girl was thinking at all. 'I—why, yes. About half an hour ago.'

'I know.' Andrea cleared her throat. 'I heard the station wagon.'

'Oh!' Helen breathed more freely. Then she gestured to the door she had just closed behind her. 'I—er—I was just making sure your father was resting. He—well, he needs the sleep.'

Andrea nodded, and when Helen made a reluctant move towards her room, she joined her. 'Are you looking forward to going to Charlottesville?' she said, her tone as casual as ever. 'You'll like the bungalow. Oh, Daddy calls it a shack, but it's really just a single-storied cabin. It's right on the beach, and the water is really beautiful.'

Helen listened with some relief. Obviously Andrea was prepared to believe her visit to Morgan's room had been as innocent as she had said. If she had heard the station wagon, she must also have heard her father come to bed—alone. Yet Helen couldn't help wondering what her attitude would be if she ever discovered the depths of their relationship. She wasn't possessive, not really, and she had befriended Helen when she thought an injustice had been done, but contemplating a more permanent relationship was something else.

'Come in,' she invited, when they reached her bedroom door. 'I've got something for you.'

'For me?' Andrea was clearly surprised. 'What?'

'A birthday present,' declared Helen, firmly putting all thoughts of Morgan aside and concentrating on his daughter. 'There you are. What do you think?'

Andrea was touched by the gift of the necklace. 'But it's

yours!' she kept saying, as she fastened it round her neck. 'I couldn't take it!' as she preened herself in front of Helen's dressing-table mirror.

'It's yours now,' insisted Helen, smiling. 'It suits you. It's a young pendant, especially for someone of your age.'

'Well, if you really mean it . . .' Andrea obviously wanted to keep it. 'And what's this?'

This was the parcel of cloth Helen had bought for her in Nrubi. She had added a length of hand-embroidered braid and some silver buttons, and while Andrea admired the material, she explained what she had in mind.

'But I don't sew at all,' exclaimed Andrea anxiously. 'I mean, I can mend hems and put on buttons, but that's about all.'

'That's all right,' replied Helen easily. 'I can do it. All I need are your measurements. I've got the cotton.'

'There's an old sewing machine somewhere,' mused Andrea, frowning, and Helen exclaimed delightedly.

'We'll get Kori to turn it out, then,' she declared. 'Just as soon as we get back from Charlottesville.'

Andrea nodded, then a look of regret came over her face. 'I wish . . .' she began, and then broke off, folding the poplin back into its wrapper.

'You wish what?' Helen had heard that wistful plea. 'Andrea! What do you wish?'

Andrea smiled. 'Are you my fairy godmother?' she teased. 'Oh, it wasn't important. I'd better go and get dressed. I still have some packing to do.'

'No, wait!' Helen wouldn't let her go like that. 'Perhaps I am your fairy godmother, who knows? Tell me what you wish, and I'll tell you if I can grant it.'

'You can't,' declared Andrea, shaking her head. 'I was just wishing the suit was already made, so that I could wear it this weekend.'

'I see.' Helen felt a resurgence of excitement. 'You mean you'd like something pretty to wear?'

Andrea hunched her shoulders. 'I'm not a pretty person.'

'No.' Helen was honest, and Andrea looked up at her half defiantly, pushing the spectacles up her nose. 'But you could be very attractive,' she added firmly. 'If you'd let someone give you some advice.'

Andrea bit her lip. 'You.'

'If you'd let me.'

'What could you do?' There was a trace of woodenness in Andrea's tone, and Helen guessed she was half regretting her decision to confide.

'Well ...' Helen studied her thoughtfully. 'You don't make the best of yourself. I mean,' she hastened on, before Andrea could object, 'being tall is an advantage, not a disadvantage. And being slim these days is a most desirable state. You can't go bra-less with big ... well ...' as she saw Andrea was beginning to smile, 'we won't go into that.' She paused. 'What you really need are pants suits and soft, feminine dresses. Not those awful cottons, like the African women wear. And wearing your hair in a braid is childish. If it's too hot to wear loose all the time, have it cut, to shoulder-length. You'd be amazed how different you'd look with short hair.'

Andrea expelled her breath on a sigh. 'You really think so?'

'I know so.'

'Daddy's never sugested I have it cut.'

'Daddy doesn't have to put up with it.'

Andrea giggled. 'You know, you have a point.'

'There you are, then.' Helen hesitated. 'Do you have a swimsuit?'

Andrea shrugged. 'Yes.'

'What's it like? Bathing belles of 1949?'

'What do you mean?'

'Well, is it a two-piece suit? A bikini?'

'Heavens, no! Daddy wouldn't like me in a bikini.'

'I think he would, if it suited you. And believe me, Andrea, you'd look good in a bikini.'

'Would I?' Andrea was doubtful. 'I have such long legs.'

'At least they have some shape. Be brave, Andrea. Take my word for it. I wouldn't ask you to do anything I didn't think was for your well-being.'

Andrea nodded. 'I believe you.' She scuffed her toe

against the rug beside Helen's bed. 'I like you, Helen, I really do. I didn't at first—you know! When we met. But that was because——'

Again she broke off, and although Helen wanted her to go on, she didn't feel she had the right in this case to force her. Instead she said lightly: 'I guess, as there was just you and your father, you were suspicious of another woman, hmm?'

'Yes. That is——' Andrea moved her shoulders in a helpless gesture, 'I—I guess I was afraid you'd be—you'd be like my mother!'

'Like your mother?' Helen repeated the words blankly. 'I'm sorry, I don't—understand——'

'Daddy didn't tell you, then?'

'Tell me? Tell me what?'

'Oh, no, I can see he didn't.' Andrea bent her head. 'I expect he thought he was protecting me.' She flicked absently at the bedspread. 'It's the sort of thing he would do.'

'He loves you, Andrea.'

'I know that.' The girl nodded. 'I don't know what I'd have done without him.' She paused, as if considering what she was about to say, and then she burst out: 'She took me with her, you know! My mother. When she went away with Rolf Havastad. Not because she really cared about me, just because she wanted to hurt Daddy.'

'Oh.' Helen absorbed this cautiously. Then she said: 'Andrea, do you think you should——'

'Yes.' Andrea lifted her head. 'Yes, I think you should know. I know you like Daddy—I've seen the way you look at him. I think you should know what happened.'

'All right.' Helen couldn't deny her curiosity. 'But who is Rolf Havastad?'

'He's an engineer. He came from South Africa, to work for the Osweban government. Uncle James introduced them, actually.' She gave a rueful smile. 'I don't think he ever forgave himself afterwards, although, as it's turned out, I think it was for the best.'

'And—your mother took you to South Africa?'

'Yes.' Now Andrea's face assumed a solemn expression.

'We left one morning after Daddy had gone out to answer a call. My mother left him a note, telling him she was running away with Rolf. I had no choice in the matter.'

'And how long ago was this?'

'Oh, about eighteen months, I suppose. My parents hadn't been happy for a long time before that. I can remember my mother meeting some man in Charlottesville when I was about nine or ten, and I expect there were others when I got older and she didn't have to bother taking me with her. She never wanted me along. I wore glasses, and I don't think she liked admitting that I was her daughter. She was quite beautiful, you see.'

This little speech was delivered so dispassionately, Helen felt an overwhelming urge to comfort her. But comfort would not restore Andrea's confidence. Only time and encouragement would do that.

'So—but she took you when she left your father?'

'Yes. Like I said, I think she only did it to hurt Daddy. Rolf didn't want me around. He never liked me, and I *hated* him.'

Helen could imagine her feelings. At thirteen, Andrea would have been old enough to understand exactly what was going on. It was the most vulnerable age for a girl, and if this boy-friend of her mother's, this Rolf, had ridiculed her, it might well have done irreparable damage.

'But your father brought you back,' she ventured now, and Andrea inclined her head.

'Yes. He tried to bring me back straight away. As soon as he found out what had happened, he flew to Cape Town to see my mother. But she refused to let him take me, and the laws being what they are, she succeeded in hanging on to me despite all his efforts.'

Helen shook her head. It was a story she had heard and read time and time again. But never so poignantly as Andrea was telling it now.

'Go on ...'

'Well, I fell ill. You see, I was so unhappy, I—sort of forgot to eat, and eventually I couldn't eat. There's some disease—I don't know what it's called ...'

'Anorexia nervosa,' put in Helen gently, and Andrea nodded.

'That's right. Have you heard of it? Well, nobody really knew that was what I had until I caught this chill. My mother and Rolf were out a lot of the time, and I was left with this old black woman called Naomi. But she used to spend her days drinking Kaffir-beer, and half the time she didn't know where I was.' She sighed, her eyes clouding with remembered pain. 'Anyway, as I say, I caught a chill. I used to go down to the beach on my own and one evening there was a terrible storm. I got soaked, and when I got home, Rolf was so mad because I'd ruined his dinner party that he made me sleep in the hut outside.'

'Andrea!'

'It's true.' She half turned away, and Helen sensed that it still upset her to talk about it. 'I—I was frozen in the morning—Cape nights can be so cold. I had a high fever, I think. Anyway, my mother was forced to call a doctor, and he diagnosed pneumonia.'

Helen's hands were clenched listening to this appalling tale. No wonder Morgan had been glad to be free of his wife! He must have felt like murdering her for what she had done to his daughter.

'So . . .' Andrea's voice was a little shaky now. 'Daddy was sent for. One of the doctors in the hospital had worked with him in London, you see, and when he saw the state I was in, he cabled Daddy.' She shrugged. 'I don't know everything that happened. I know there was a terrible row. But the authorities were more prepared to listen to Daddy with the evidence of my illness behind him. Also—also my mother and Rolf were having arguments over me, and I think she realised that if she wanted to keep him, she would have to let me go.'

'And are they married now?' asked Helen.

'I don't know. I don't care. I never want to see her again!' And finally Andrea's voice broke.

'Oh, darling, don't say that!' Helen had to defend the woman, even though she had noticed that throughout her narrative Andrea had never once called her 'Mummy'. Always 'my mother'. So cold, so formal. 'She is the woman who bore you, you know. That must mean something.'

'Not to me,' said Andrea in a muffled voice, rubbing her eyes childishly with the backs of her hands. 'Not to me.'

Helen said no more after that. It was enough that the girl had felt able to confide in her, and somehow she guessed she was the only person Andrea had told, apart from her father. No wonder the child hadn't wanted to go to England, no wonder Morgan was so concerned for her future. She was so incredibly vulnerable.

'Well,' Helen said now, after Andrea had dried her spectacles and blown her nose, 'this isn't exactly the way we should be celebrating your birthday, but later today ...'

'What?' Andrea sniffed and stared at her.

'Well, we should reach Charlottesville some time this afternoon, shouldn't we?'

'Yes.'

'Yes. So I suggest we do some shopping, hmm? And first on the list is a bikini.'

'Oh, Helen! I can't wear a bikini!'

'You don't expect me to wear mine on my own, do you?' demanded Helen teasingly, and ruefully, Andrea gave in.

'But only if Daddy approves,' she insisted, and Helen allowed her that small condition.

CHAPTER ELEVEN

MORGAN'S 'shack' turned out to be a wooden building set among palm trees at the edge of one of the most perfect beaches Helen had ever seen. Compacted white sand ran down to the water's edge where, when the tide receded, crystal-clear pools of rock coral invited exploration. Situated some distance outside Charlottesville, it was completely private, and what it lacked in amenities it more than made up for in beauty and solitude.

The cabin itself consisted of two bedrooms, as Andrea

had said, with a living room, and kitchen-cum-dining room at the back. There was no bathroom, only an outside shower, fed by an overhead tank which had to be filled before it could be used, and the smallest room of the house contained only a chemical toilet. But there was plenty of fresh water from an underground spring, which Andrea explained was why her father had chosen to site the shack here.

They drove down to Charlottesville later in the morning, after requesting Kori to keep his cake refrigerated until their return, and after lunching at the Yacht Club, Helen and Andrea went shopping. Morgan had produced a silver charm bracelet for Andrea's birthday present, but he was more than willing to finance their shopping trip, and Helen felt embarrassed when he pressed a roll of notes into her hand.

'You can pay me later,' she said, planning on using the international credit card he had suggested she acquired before leaving England, but Morgan was firm.

'Spend as much as you like,' he advised her shortly. 'I may not be a wealthy man, but I'm not a poor one either. Andrea's been needing some clothes for ages, but I don't know much about these things. Get whatever you like.'

So Helen had reluctantly agreed, and after a time she found she was enjoying herself immensely. The stores that lined Bay Street were not as comprehensive as those one might find in Oxford Street, but they were sufficiently modern to allow her to choose the most suitable garments for a girl of Andrea's age. In no time at all, they had bought jeans and tee-shirts, corded pants and sweaters, tights and shirts, and several sets of underwear.

'I've never worn a bra before,' exclaimed Andrea, fingering the scrap of nylon lace that matched some lacy panties. Then she giggled. 'Gosh, I feel quite grown up!'

In a store catering for teenagers, Helen found the dresses she wanted for Andrea, loosely fitting smocks, with scalloped necklines and embroidered skirts. Their fullness only hinted at the slenderness of her figure, and high-heeled sandals gave her height and unexpected allure.

Andrea had shed her spectacles to try on the dresses, and

now she looked at herself in the mirror with startled eyes, hardly daring to believe that that slender young girl with the long curving legs and cascade of silky hair was really herself.

'I—I look—I look——'

'Very attractive,' declared Helen dryly. 'So don't ever let me hear you putting yourself down again. Do you see that young man over there—the manager?—he even has his eye on you. And I've changed my mind about your hair—we're going to keep it long.'

Andrea made no demur. So far as she was concerned, Helen had performed a small miracle, and she was humble with admiration.

They had arranged to meet Morgan at the Yacht Club at six, but it was only a little after five-thirty when they entered its cool portals. Andrea's name was sufficient identification, but the steward looked long and hard at the two young women, the one so dark and the other so fair.

'Why is he staring at me?' Andrea asked in an undertone, after they had handed over their packages for his safe-keeping, and Helen smiled.

'I expect because he hardly recognises you,' she remarked wryly. 'That smock really does things for you, and those sandals surely are an improvement on plimsolls.'

Andrea made a sound of delight. 'They do give my legs some shape, don't they?' she murmured consideringly, and Helen nodded.

'Heels always do.'

'But I always thought a high heel would make me look too tall.'

'Tall, yes. Too tall, no. Don't be ashamed of your height, Andrea. I'm taller than you are, and I wear heels. Why should you worry? Your father's well able to give you a few inches.'

'I know.' Andrea sounded as though she had just made a wonderful discovery. 'Oh, Helen, this has been the best birthday I've ever had!'

'Good.' Helen was pleased. It was time Andrea started

having some fun in her life.

They were entering the lounge when a vaguely familiar voice hailed them:

'Helen! What a surprise! Why didn't you let me know you were in Charlottesville?'

Helen turned and found James Oneba threading his way between the tables towards them. Immaculately dressed as usual in a light fawn lounge suit, he looked big and handsome, a supremely confident man, with an air of command.

'Helen!' he exclaimed again, as he reached them, wringing her hand with obvious warmth. 'How good to see you again. Is Morgan with you? Why haven't you given us a call?'

Helen extracted her hand with difficulty, and then made an apologetic gesture. 'We only came down this morning,' she protested. 'We haven't had time to contact anyone. We've been shopping.'

James shook his head. 'I forgive you,' he smiled. Then he glanced briefly at the girl by her side, before performing a swift double-take. 'Good lord! It's Andrea, isn't it?'

Helen could have hugged him. She was almost sure he had recognised Morgan's daughter immediately, but knowing women as he did, he had guessed that some favourable reaction was demanded.

'Hello, Uncle James,' murmured Andrea shyly, and he took both her hands in his and surveyed the transformation with evident admiration.

'My dear Andrea, you look delightful!' he exclaimed sincerely. 'The dress—it is perfect. You look at least—sixteen! A young lady, no less.'

'You really like it?' Andrea's voice betrayed her lingering uncertainty, and James nodded. 'Do you think Daddy will like it too?'

'I'm sure he could not fail to do so,' James assured her, squeezing her fingers before releasing them. Then he turned back to Helen. 'But where is Morgan?'

'I'm not sure.' Helen moved her shoulders doubtfully. 'He said he would meet us here at six o'clock.'

'It is some occasion, then?' enquired James, frowning.

Then he pressed a hand to his mouth. 'Good lord! It's the eighteenth, isn't it? Your birthday, Andrea. Oh—happy birthday, darling.'

He kissed her cheek and then clapped his hands. 'I know—we must have a celebration. You must all come to my house for dinner this evening.'

'Oh, Uncle James!'

Andrea was clearly excited at the prospect. She obviously saw it as an opportunity to show off her new clothes, but Helen wasn't sure Morgan would approve.

'I don't know ...' she began, but James was forceful.

'You are staying overnight, aren't you?' he demanded, but this time Andrea replied.

'We're staying at the beach house,' she explained. 'Helen hasn't seen it yet. We had lunch in town.'

'Ah, I see.' James drew them into the lounge as he spoke, directing them to the table he had been occupying where several young men rose politely to their feet at their approach. 'But it will be dark before you get there anyway. What do a few more hours matter?'

Before Helen had a chance to reply, he was introducing them to his companions, three of his aides from the Ministry. They were all well-dressed, intelligent young men, younger editions of himself, and watching them with Andrea, Helen guessed that this was exactly what she needed—attention from the opposite sex.

They all seated themselves around the table, and while one of the young men was despatched to fetch drinks for the girls, the others spoke casually to Andrea. Watching her, Helen saw her intense shyness being forced aside, and when the conversation came round to swimming and sailing, she spoke quite unselfconsciously.

'She is growing up,' said James's low voice near her ear, and she turned to find he had taken the seat beside her. 'Don't worry so much on her behalf. She's Morgan's daughter. She will make out.'

Helen forced herself to relax. 'Is it so obvious?' she asked ruefully, and he smiled into her eyes.

'Not to everyone,' he assured her gently. 'Now, tell me: how is Morgan?'

'Morgan?' Helen glanced round, then realising their exchange was not being overheard, she added: 'He's fine. Tired, of course, but otherwise ...' She frowned. 'Why do you ask?'

James shrugged, and drew back in his chair. 'I can see you are not suffering from any dread disease, although I do believe you have lost weight since I last saw you. And Andrea is obviously blooming. Can I not ask about my good friend's health?'

The words were said with a smile, but there was an underlying note of gravity which James was trying hard to disguise. It troubled her a little. It was all too reminiscent of her thoughts on the reasons why Morgan refused to consider a permanent commitment, and she was tempted to ask James why he thought Morgan was so adamant.

But of course she couldn't, and instead, she said: 'I think this break will do him good. He's been working very hard lately.'

'Morgan always works hard,' James agreed regretfully. 'Maybe if his marriage had worked out ...' He shrugged. 'Who knows? I suppose he's told you about that.'

'He hasn't. Andrea has,' replied Helen quietly, and James looked impressed.

'You know, she's never talked about that before, to anyone.'

'Yes.'

'She must like you very much.'

'I hope so.'

'It wouldn't be difficult for her to love you,' he continued softly. 'You're a rather—lovable person.' And then, as her cheeks flamed, he added: 'But I expect Morgan's told you that, too.'

'What have I told her?'

Lean fingers descended, one hand on Helen's shoulder, hard and compelling against the flesh exposed by her sundress, the other digging into the fine material of James's collar. It was Morgan, right there behind them, and Helen was unutterably relieved when he caught a glimpse of his daughter at that moment, and her shy expectancy sent him round the table to her side.

'Well, well!' he remarked, drawing her to her feet so that James and his aides were forced to rise, too. 'What a pretty dress!'

'Do you like it?' Andrea was anxious, but she needn't have been.

'I like it,' he agreed, his eyes dropping down to the high-heeled sandals. 'You make me feel quite old.'

Helen crossed her legs, and smoothed her skirt with distrait fingers. Now she was more nervous than Andrea, and not even James's encouraging squeeze of her hand could rid her of the feeling of impending disaster.

James sent one of his minions to get a drink for Morgan, and Morgan himself took the chair nearest his daughter. It was across the table from Helen, and she had the feeling he had seated himself there deliberately to observe her every movement. James reseated himself beside Helen, his arm familiarly along the back of her chair, but if he hoped his support would relax her, he couldn't have been more wrong. She knew Morgan so well by this time. She could see the disturbing glitter of his eyes. And she knew he thought she had been discussing their relationship with James.

'I have just been suggesting to your daughter and Helen that as it is Andrea's birthday, you should all come to my house for dinner this evening,' James said now, spreading his hand expansively. 'You know how pleased my family always is to see you.'

Morgan's mouth turned down at the corners. 'I don't think so, thanks all the same, James.'

'Why not?'

'Yes, why not, Daddy?' Andrea turned to him eagerly. 'I'd like to—well, I'd like to show Mariana my dress.'

Morgan's eyes met Helen's coldly. 'Do you want to go, too?'

Helen flushed. 'I—I——' As she sought for words she couldn't help thinking that dinner at the Onebas' would at least provide a respite for Morgan's anger to subside. 'I think—it would be very nice.'

'You see!' James was triumphant. 'How can you refuse?'

'How indeed?' agreed Morgan dryly, but no one was deceived by his apparent acquiescence.

The drive up to the Onebas' house was accomplished in virtual silence. Helen was glad to be occupying the back seat, particularly after listening to Andrea's thwarted attempts to make conversation with her father. Eventually she too fell silent, and Helen quelled her automatic exclamation of remembered delight at the floodlit beauty of the building.

Before dinner, they were all invited to shower and change in the rooms they had occupied during their previous visit, and as Helen extracted the case that contained her garments from the station wagon, she felt relieved that she had decided at the last moment to bring a gown suitable to the occasion.

Surveying the enormous bathroom, she looked with wry uncertainty at the bath before deciding to use it after all. Why not? she argued with herself impatiently, as she shed her dress and flimsy underwear. She might never get another opportunity, and it was magnificent.

It looked even more magnificent when it was full. The four mixer taps, each shaped like a silver tiger's head, issued a steady stream of crystal clear water into its depths, and when she plunged in it was like having her own private swimming pool. She gurgled with laughter as she played about, her problems melting beneath the concealing foam of the lotions she had added to the water, and submerged her whole body beneath its satin-soft canopy.

She had not locked the bathroom door. She had not felt the need to do so; and she was so absorbed with the novelty of the bath that she did not hear the door open or anyone come in, until the cooling draught of air from the bedroom aroused her to the awareness of someone standing by the bath, looking down at her. Her gaze travelled up over booted feet and mud-coloured Levis that clung revealingly to the powerful muscles of their owner's legs, to a bare, brown chest, covered lightly with fine, sun-bleached hairs. Then her eyes dropped again, and she sank lower into the water, trying to hide her foam-coated body from his gaze.

'What do you want?' she demanded, her voice higher than it might have been had she had some warning of his appearance, and flinched as Morgan lifted one boot and collected a smear of foam on its toe.

Then he said broodingly: 'What has James been telling you about me?'

Helen tried to make light of the situation. 'Was it necessary to come into my bathroom to ask me that?' she exclaimed. 'Couldn't it have waited until later?'

'No, damn you, it couldn't,' he retorted angrily. 'And how was I to know you'd be in the bath? I took a shower. I imagined you would do the same.'

'And would it have made it any less embarrassing if I had?' she asked, indignation colouring her tone, and he pulled a wry face.

'Embarrassing?' He shook his head. 'Helen, I do know what a woman's body looks like. I know what your body looks like. Remember?'

She coloured then, avoiding his eyes. 'Must you be so callous?'

'Callous?' He sighed. 'Helen, you still haven't answered my question. What was James saying to you?'

She shrugged. 'This and that.'

'Helen!'

'Well! It's true.' She looked mutinously up at him. 'I notice it doesn't worry you that he seems to find me attractive!'

'James?' Morgan chafed at the distraction. 'James finds all beautiful women attractive. However, I doubt he'd get seriously involved with anyone who didn't share his religious beliefs.'

'Well, thank you!'

Helen pursed her lips and with another sigh, Morgan squatted down beside her. 'Helen,' he said, more gently this time. 'Helen, don't be a fool.' His hand probed her jawline, smoothing the damp hair back from her shoulder. 'I'm not made of stone. Watching you like this is the purest kind of torment I know. Now, please what were you and James talking about?'

Helen sniffed. 'I don't remember.'

'My God!' Morgan stared at her. 'You really are a selfish little——' He bit off an epithet, his mouth clenched impotently, and in spite of the warm water, she shivered. 'What am I supposed to have told you? That's all you need to remember. Or have you forgotten that as well?'

'Oh!' Helen brushed her lips with a thoughtful finger. 'As—as a matter of fact, he expected—that you might have told me about your wife!'

It came out with a rush and she sat regarding him anxiously afterwards, glad that she had not had to lie to him.

'About Pamela?' Morgan frowned. 'What about Pamela?'

Helen bent her head, not at all sure she ought to discuss Andrea's confidence with him. She wished now she had not said anything to James, but she had had the suspicion that he was about to discuss it with her, and somehow she hadn't wanted him to talk about Morgan's marriage.

'Oh, well ... if you must know ...' She looked up at him with rueful reluctance. 'Andrea told me about—well, about what happened.'

'Pamela's taking her to Cape Town?' asked Morgan, with ominous quietness.

'Yes.'

'But she's never spoken about that before.' His mouth tightened. 'Are you sure it wasn't James who told you?'

Helen was indignant. 'Of course I'm sure.' She shifted uncomfortably. 'Is that all?'

'What did she tell you?'

'Oh—just about being ill, not being able to eat.'

'And Rolf Havastad?'

'Well—yes.'

Morgan's jaw was taut. 'I nearly killed him, you know. Did she tell you that?' He expelled his breath with remembered vehemence. 'When I saw what they'd done to her ...'

Helen gazed at him understandingly, her love for him shining in her eyes, and as he encountered her stare, Morgan's anger faded, to be replaced by emotions of a different kind.

'Aphrodite!' he murmured, his fingers exploring her nape. 'I must go and get dressed.'

'Must you?' She rose beneath his hands, aware what the sight of her body was doing to him.

'Yes,' he said thickly, but almost involuntarily his fingers were stroking her breast, and she stretched up to touch his lips with hers.

'Helen,' he muttered achingly, his mouth against hers. 'Helen ...' Then with a groan, he kicked off his boots and uncaring of his clothes, he slid into the water beside her.

His hand behind her head was all that kept her afloat beneath the liquid sweetness of his kiss. His arms gathered her fully against him, and for the first time, she understood what it was like to be kissed and caressed without the unnecessary encumberance of clothes.

'Beautiful!' he breathed, his hands touching every part of her. 'But I knew you would be. So cool and calm on the outside, and so warm and passionate within.'

'I don't feel very cool and calm,' she confessed, winding her arms around his neck. 'Take off the rest of your clothes ...'

'God, *no*!'

That was when he surfaced, releasing her abruptly and clambering out on to the tiled rim. His hair was soaking like the rest of him, and the Levis clung to him like a second skin.

'Morgan ...' she pleaded, resting her arms on the side of the bath, chin resting on her hands. 'Morgan, you can't go like that.'

'Do you think I don't know it?' he muttered half impatiently. 'God, I must have been out of my mind!'

'Or your senses?' she suggested softly, and a wry smile twisted his lips.

'That's right. You go to my head——'

And then, as if he disliked the metaphor, he unzipped his

pants and stepped out of them, hauling on the towelling bath robe that hung behind the door before turning to face her again.

'I'll go. I'll explain these somehow.' He indicated the soaking Levis in his hand. 'See you at dinner.'

The evening was an anti-climax after that. Sitting opposite Morgan at the dinner table all Helen could think of was the sensuous feel of his body against her, the tantalising caresses of his hands, the bulging strength of his thighs. She wanted him so badly, there was a physical ache inside her, and she knew he was avoiding her gaze for the self-same reasons. But it wasn't fair, and no amount of self-delusion would make it so.

Her gown of black crêpe silk had attracted a satisfying amount of appreciation. Plain though it was, it accentuated the rounded curves of her body, and the honey-gold tanning of her flesh complemented the chestnut streaks in her hair. But although Andrea had expressed her admiration, Morgan had scarcely spoken to her, and it was left to James to assure her she looked most desirable.

When dinner was over, however, Morgan insisted that they would have to be going. 'I'm not at all sure what Kori's packed in the way of food,' he said, 'but whatever it is, it needs unpacking tonight. And there are beds to make up, and water to draw ...'

'Why not stay here?' suggested James at once, but Morgan shook his head.

'No, thanks.' For the first time since dinner Morgan looked at Helen. 'We want to go swimming in the morning, and we'll have to leave again in the late afternoon.'

Convinced he couldn't change their minds, James gave in with good grace, and they left amid a chorus of farewells, and the friendly chatter of the children.

'They're nice people,' said Helen, involuntarily, glancing back out of the window, and Morgan silently agreed.

Despite the fact that it was late when Helen finally got to bed, she was awake almost at first light. The bedroom she was sharing with Andrea had windows that opened on to the side of the house, and moving stealthily so as not to disturb the girl, she ran across the composite floor to take her first real look at Selena Beach. Andrea told her she had named it that, after the first doll Morgan had ever bought her.

Below the cabin, the sand sloped away to the curve of the beach. At this hour of the morning, the sea had a greenish-gold haze to it, and the horizon shimmered before her entranced eyes. There were seabirds squabbling at the water's edge, but her attention was caught by something climbing rapidly up one of the coconut palms nearer the cabin. It was a monkey, only a tiny thing, with reddish fur, and patches of white on its undersides. Helen was so astounded she let out a small exclamation and then clapped her hands to her mouth, afraid she must have disturbed Andrea. But the girl still slept soundly and Helen was forced to enjoy the unexpected discovery alone.

She wondered if Morgan was awake. But after last night she shrank from the impulse to find out. He had made it very clear after their arrival at the cabin that so long as they were here, he would do nothing which might disturb Andrea. It had made Helen wonder whether this had been his intention all along—to gain some breathing space, knowing if they stayed at Hawk's Drift it would be only too easy to give in to their mutual attraction.

To begin with, she had been charmed by the beach house, and she still was, up to a point. But the vain hopes she had cherished of spending hours alone with Morgan had not materialised. Andrea was constantly with them, and when she went to bed, Morgan went to bed too.

The bedrooms were small and functional. There were two beds in this room, and one in Morgan's. Helen guessed Morgan and his first wife had used this room in the old days while Andrea slept in the other, but the night before there had been no question of Andrea sleeping alone. Besides, Helen knew she herself could never do anything to hurt the girl, and while a small voice inside her taunted that she and Morgan would not have needed two beds, she had determinedly put such tantalising thoughts aside.

Even so, it would have been nice if Morgan had been more friendly. His withdrawn manner had deterred even the most innocent overtures, and Helen had gone to bed feeling very much the interloper.

But it was morning now, and irrepressibly her spirits were rising. The sea beckoned in all its untamed beauty, and without stopping to worry what Morgan might think, she stripped off her nightshirt and dived into her case for her bikini. It was a scanty thing of brown striped cotton, held together with gypsy hoops, and fringed with russet braid. It had been part of her trousseau and had never been worn, and she hesitated a moment before putting it on. Then the desire to submerge herself in that green-gold ocean overcame her misgivings, and she quickly fastened the rings in place. A swift brush of her hair and she was eagerly opening the bedroom door, glancing back half regretfully at Andrea, who still snoozed on. Should she wake her? But no. These few minutes were for her alone, and she intended to enjoy them.

The outer door of the beach house was not locked, and she went down the steps lightly, halting only when a huge sand crab rose blindly in her path. Her skin prickled at the sight of those waving pincers, but she guessed it was more afraid of her than she was of it and side-stepping, she continued down to the water's edge.

The shifting eddies were cool to her toes, but soon, as her body temperature adjusted itself to the water, she realised they were quite warm. This made her braver, and she skipped further into the gentle waves, suppressing gurgles of delight when they lapped about her knees and thighs. Down through the water, which was crystal clear, she could see a varied assortment of plant life, and even small fishes, darting in and out of the grasses.

She waded in up to her waist and then, shivering slightly, she plunged into a slow crawl. The water was extremely buoyant, and only the minimum effort was needed to keep afloat, but she swam strongly through the waves, enjoying the rare freedom of movement.

She saw nothing unusual. No sharks braved the ragged

ramparts of the reef that was exposed at low tide, no devil rays or barracudas came to disturb her peaceful idyll. The only company she had was the seabirds wheeling and crying overhead, and the tiny shoals of coloured fish she could see when she turned on to her stomach, and swam a little distance underwater. The cathedral-like silence and magical beauty of that underwater scene enchanted her. There was so much to see and she wished she could explore the reef. But that required equipment and technical skill she did not possess, so she contented herself with the calmer waters of the lagoon.

She had reached shallower water where she could walk ashore before she saw Morgan. Wading up out of the water, pushing the soaking hair back out of her eyes, she saw him squatting motionless on the sand, watching her, his only attire a pair of frayed denim jeans, cut off just above the knee. Immediately she was selfconscious of her scarcity of attire, and impatiently aware that she had forgotten to bring a towel. Not that she really needed one. The sun was already burning on her shoulders, and in no time at all her swimsuit would be dry.

Morgan rose to his feet as she emerged from the water, and came down the sand to meet her, his bare feet making prints on the packed coral sand.

'Hi,' he said civilly. 'I guess you enjoyed that.'

'Oh, yes.' Helen made an instinctive gesture to cover herself, realised how suggestive it would be, and pressed her palms tightly against her thighs. 'The water's gorgeous! I couldn't wait to try it.'

'Obviously not.' Morgan inclined his head, chewing on the blade of grass he had between his teeth. 'I thought you might have waited for me to join you.'

'You?' Helen stared at him defensively. 'Why, I thought you were still asleep.'

Morgan shrugged. 'I didn't do much sleeping last night.'

'No?' Helen's throat felt suddenly dry. 'Why not?' She paused. 'Weren't you comfortable?'

'If you mean by that, was the bed comfortable, then yes, I guess you could say it was.' His eyes held hers intently.

'If, on the other hand, you mean, did I sleep easily, knowing you were just on the other side of the partition, then no, I wasn't comfortable at all.'

'I'm sorry.' Helen refused to run the risk of being accused of taking too much for granted. 'Never mind,' she added, turning to shade her eyes and stare towards the reef. 'We'll be back at Hawk's Drift tonight. And no doubt your work will compensate.'

There was silence for a moment and then Morgan shifted his weight from one foot to the other. 'Is that an attack—or a defence?' he asked softly, and despising herself she glanced sideways at him.

'I never know,' she conceded unevenly. 'But I know I have feelings, too, and I don't think they can stand any more bruising.'

'Ah, Helen!' He ran restless fingers through his hair. 'What am I going to do with you?' He shook his head. 'Do you know what James said I should do last night? He said I *should* marry you. How about that? After—after everything, he thinks I should marry you!'

Helen's heart was palpitating rapidly. 'I see. And—and of course you told him that you couldn't.'

'There was no need to tell him that,' retorted Morgan enigmatically. Then he heaved a sigh. 'He's crazy! I told him so. But when I'm with you ...'

'Yes?' Her heart almost stopped beating.

'... when I'm with you, I find it incredibly difficult to behave sensibly.'

Helen licked her dry lips. 'Is that so important?' she ventured. 'Behaving sensibly, I mean? Doesn't everyone deserve to act madly sometimes?'

'No, not everyone,' replied Morgan flatly. 'Sometimes—sometimes there are—circumstances that—preclude that kind of madness.'

'Oh!' Helen's heart plunged. 'And—and James doesn't understand this?'

She didn't even know what they were talking about, she thought wildly. But so long as they were talking, there was always a chance ...

'James sees things—differently,' he conceded slowly. 'But James is a hedonist, and hedonists don't always think before they act.'

Helen's lips trembled. 'Hedonism,' she echoed softly. 'It sounds a pretty good doctrine to me.'

Morgan stared at her for a long, disturbing moment, and then strode towards the water's edge, kicking savagely at the ripples. He had thrust his hands into the pockets of his denims and was staring tight-lipped towards the heavens, as if praying for guidance. Then he turned, and although Helen couldn't read the expression on his face, she guessed he had come to a decision.

'All right,' he said, walking back to her with slow deliberation. 'All right, I give in. I can't hold out any longer. God knows, it's what I want—what I need!' He reached for her urgently, drawing her close against the hard male strength of his body, finding her parted lips with his. 'Marry me,' he said against her mouth. 'Marry me—as soon as I can get a licence.'

Helen's limbs gave out on her, and she sank down weakly on to the sand, overbalancing him and bringing him down beside her, half crushing her with the weight of his body. 'Mmm,' he breathed, burying his face in her hair. 'You know what I'd like to do? I'd like to make love to you here on the sand, with the seabirds crying overhead and the sand crabs looking on.' He drew back to smile down at her. 'Do you think they'd observe us as we observe them? Do you think they'd know what we were doing—and why we were doing it?'

'Oh, Morgan ...' Helen pulled his mouth back to hers and then, against his lips, she whispered: 'I'll marry you whenever you say. You know that, don't you? But please, don't make me wait till then ...'

'I won't,' he promised huskily, and suddenly the prospect of returning to Nrubi was charged with excitement.

For several satisfying minutes there was silence between them, then, as if unable to sustain her nearness without possessing her completely, Morgan reluctantly drew back to stretch his length beside her, eyes closed. Helen rolled on to her side and lay looking at him, scarcely daring to believe that this was really happening. Morgan had asked her to marry him. Whatever there had been in his past, whatever misgivings he had had, he was prepared to try again.

'Darling,' she ventured at last, causing him to open his eyes and gaze at her through the thick stubble of his lashes. 'You won't—change your mind, will you? Not again?'

Morgan's tawny eyes flickered for a moment, but he shook his head. 'No.'

'I'm glad. I couldn't bear it if——'

'Leave it, Helen, will you?' Morgan's air of relaxation vanished and he jack-knifed into a sitting position. 'Look, I think it's time we went back and wakened Andrea. She'll be sorry she's missed an early morning swim, and besides,' he added determinedly, 'I'm hungry.'

All through breakfast, Helen expected Morgan to tell his daughter he was going to get married again, but he didn't. It was as if after making the decision he wanted to forget all about it, and she was hurt by his casual manner towards her.

Andrea appeared to notice nothing amiss. She had still been in bed when they returned and she said she would rather have breakfast before going for a swim. They ate on the verandah that overlooked the beach, Morgan having prepared a meal of scrambled eggs and coffee on the tiny Calor gas stove. Helen had offered to do it, but he had told her he could manage, and she had spent an agonising few minutes in the shower, rinsing the salt from her body with water that had become ice-cold overnight.

They drove back to Nrubi in the late afternoon. Helen was sorry to be leaving so soon, but the prospect of the night ahead filled her thoughts to the exclusion of all else. It didn't matter if Morgan was offhand with her. She knew it was only a façade. Beneath that mask of curtness was a man of passion and strong emotions, and she was confident that soon all their troubles would be resolved.

It was dark when they reached Nrubi, but there were lights in the villa. Then, as they reached the turn-off to the house, they heard the voices—shrill, excited voices that, incoherent as they were, spelled trouble of a very different kind.

'Kori!' muttered Morgan savagely, slamming on the brakes and thrusting open his door. 'My God! What's been going on?'

His words were not unwarranted. The entry to the house was strewn with broken furniture, cane chairs from the courtyard patio, torn cushions and tumbled rugs, all combining to make a terrifying introduction to their return.

'Morgan!' Helen was right behind him. Andrea behind her, exclaiming at the damage, but Morgan turned and ordered them back to the car.

'God knows what's happening,' he declared grimly. 'I'll find out myself, but you stay here.'

'Morgan!'

'But Daddy——'

Both the girls protested at once, but he was adamant, and they were forced to turn away and clamber back into the station wagon. They watched with misgivings as Morgan picked his way between the rubble and entered the house, the noisy clatter of voices hardly subsiding as his presence was made known.

'What do you think has happened?' exclaimed Helen, unable to remain silent, and Andrea shook her head.

'I don't know. If I knew who it was, I might be able to hazard a guess, but as Daddy insists on keeping us out here ...'

Helen fretted anxiously. 'Do you think there's been a robbery? Do you have much violence out here?'

Andrea frowned. 'Not really. Just tribal things mostly—one man taking another's woman, that sort of thing. Wait a minute——'

She broke off abruptly and Helen stared at her dry-mouthed. 'What is it? What have you thought of?'

'Bosumi!' declared Andrea dramatically.

'Bosumi?' Helen had heard the name, but she couldn't remember where. 'Who is Bosumi?'

'Do you remember the day you came here?'

'Do I not?' Helen's tone was dry.

'Yes, well ...' Andrea coloured, remembering her part in it, 'do you remember the woman who was here? The woman with the baby who was constipated?'

'Of course,' Helen nodded. 'Morgan said she was *Bosumi's* woman.'

'That's right, she was. *Is!* And maybe Bosumi's found out she spent three days here. Perhaps he's come to get even with Kori.'

'To get even with Kori?' Helen felt she was being particularly dense, but she couldn't understand this. 'Why would Bosumi want to get even with Kori?'

'Oh, come on.' Andrea gave her a wry look. 'Don't you really know?'

'Oh!' Now it was Helen's turn to look discomfited. 'I see. You mean Kori—Kori and the woman——'

'—slept together, yes.' Andrea agreed impatiently. 'People do, don't they?' She tipped her head on one side, holding Helen's eyes with her own. 'All the time.' She paused, as if waiting for Helen to say something, and when she didn't, went on: 'Anyway, that's my theory. The baby was Bosumi's son, after all. Pushing all that witch doctor stuff up inside it can't have done any good, and *three* days ...'

'Oh, no!' Helen remembered the bloodstained floor of the surgery. 'You mean——'

Andrea nodded. 'You see, Kori's apparently got this irresistible charm for women, and working at the house of the Massa doctor gives him a sort of—status.'

'I see.' Helen shook her head. 'But that's it, isn't it? Living here, working here, he must have known what she was doing was wrong!'

'He wouldn't care,' replied Andrea airily. 'So long as he was getting what he wanted. Men! Honestly, they're so selfish!'

'Your father's not selfish,' pointed out Helen quietly, and Andrea made a rueful grimace.

'I know.' She paused. 'You care about Daddy, too, don't you? I guessed you did yesterday, when we were talking, and then—this morning ...'

'What about this morning?' asked Helen anxiously, but Andrea only moved her shoulders in a reluctant gesture.

'I saw you,' she said softly. 'I think you must have wakened me when you went out of the bedroom. Anyway, I lay for a while, then I got up, too. You'd gone into the sea by that time, but I saw Daddy standing there, watching you. I was going to go and join him, but something, I don't know what, held me back. Then you came out of the water, and I could tell by the way you talked together that you were not talking about me.'

'Oh, Andrea!'

The girl smiled. 'Don't look so worried. Oh, I don't deny I was envious at first, but then I thought—why shouldn't Daddy have a chance for happiness, too, and I know you're not like my mother.'

'Andrea ...'

Helen didn't know what to say, but Andrea was looking towards the house again, her eyes dark and anxious. 'I've just remembered something else,' she exclaimed worriedly. 'Bosumi is huge, easily seven feet. If either Kori or Daddy were attacked by him, they wouldn't stand a chance!'

'Oh, God!'

Without thinking, Helen pushed open her door and got out again, running towards the sound of the voices, uncaring that Morgan had insisted she stay in the car. She could hear Andrea coming behind her, and together they burst into the living room of the house, coming to an abrupt halt at the sight that confronted them.

There were four men in the room, and the woman Helen vaguely recognised as having seen before. One of the men Helen guessed it must be Bosumi as Andrea had suspected, was standing near the window, one brawny arm around Kori's neck. But it was not a friendly gesture. In his other hand he held a short-bladed knife, the kind of knife a hunter might use, and this he held menacingly close against Kori's distended throat. Whether he had adopted this attitude at Morgan's intervention Helen didn't know, but the fact remained that Kori was in a very dangerous situation, and a grotesquely-scarred individual, dressed in exotically patterned robes, was obviously urging Bosumi to finish what he had started.

'Elopi!' breathed a horrified Andrea behind her, and Helen recognised the witch doctor's name. The witch doctor who had little time for Morgan.

Morgan himself was apparently endeavouring to persuade the woman to get Bosumi to let Kori go. The woman was crying, which accounted for the shrill cries they had heard earlier, and she persistently covered her face with her hands and shook her head, as if refusing to listen to him.

Helen and Andrea's eruption into the room aroused Elopi to a frenzy. He started hopping around, screaming what Helen felt sure were obscenities, gesturing at them as if they were involved with the long, pike-like spear he was carrying. It was like a scene from a nightmare, thought Helen disbelievingly, realising that Morgan looked almost as angry as the witch doctor, but much paler.

'Will you get out of here?' he snapped furiously. 'I told you to stay in the car. This is no place for women!'

'But what's happened?' exclaimed Andrea impulsively. 'Why is Bosumi here? What is he going to do?'

'His son's dead!' retorted Morgan coldly. 'Now, will you go away and leave this to me?'

'But, Daddy——'

'Andrea!'

Morgan glared at them, and Helen realised he was more concerned for their safety than his own. There was no guarantee that after killing Kori, Bosumi might not turn his anger on the other witnesses to his crime, and years of working with psychologically-scarred people had shown Helen how easily a disturbed mind could be persuaded. If nothing else, Elopi was obviously a convincing advocate, and he had his own reasons for wanting to get even with the white doctor.

Yet how could they depart, leaving Morgan to handle this alone? The odds were high, three against one, for Kori looked terrified out of his wits and incapable of helping himself. If only James was here, Helen found herself thinking, realising he was the only person they could turn to. But he was far away in Charlottesville, and no miraculous rescue bid was about to be mounted.

'Morgan, is there anything I can do?' Helen risked his anger yet again. 'Could I talk to—to her? With Andrea as interpreter.'

Morgan sighed. 'Helen, can't you see how explosive this situation is?' he demanded in a low voice. 'Don't you think I have enough to do trying to persuade them to release Kori, without you and Andrea getting involved?'

Helen hesitated, then she said: 'I think we are involved, don't you?' She made a covert gesture towards Elopi. 'If we leave now, he'll think we're afraid of him. Just imagine how that will sound to Bosumi.'

'Oh, Helen ...' Morgan pushed back his hair with a weary hand. 'What a homecoming!' Suddenly, a wry smile touched his lips. 'I think if Bosumi doesn't kill Kori, I will.'

It was a relief to see him smile, and Helen responded, refusing to give Elopi the satisfaction of seeing exactly how anxious she really was. She was anxious for Kori, of course. He was cheeky at times, and arrogant, but there was no real harm in him and he didn't deserve to die for taking what the woman had obviously been prepared to give. And she was anxious for herself and for Andrea, most particularly for the girl, who was just beginning to gain a little confidence. But most of all, she was anxious for Morgan. She could see certain familiar signs about him—the line of sweat on his forehead, the deepening lines beside his mouth, and the intense weariness that was draining every scrap of colour from his face. They were signs of the headaches that plagued him with such disturbing regularity, and she longed to break up this crazy fiasco so that he could get some rest.

Yet something told her that they were nearing crisis point. The woman was still shaking her head, crying hysterically, and Helen realised that her tears were more for herself than the baby. If Bosumi could be persuaded to let Kori go, he might begin to doubt her part in the affair, and unfaithful wives could still be beaten. Kori himself seemed frozen with terror, making no attempt to defend himself, his lips moving in a silent prayer. Bosumi's broad face bore an expression compounded of anger and uncertainty. Although he was such a big man, he was not naturally aggressive, but like all ponderous people, his anger, once aroused, was slow to diminish.

Maybe without Elopi's constant tirade, he would have accepted Morgan's explanation of the woman's shared guilt and left without violence. If he could have been persuaded that Elopi's medicine was what had killed the child, his anger might even have taken a different course. But the old witch doctor was enjoying his brief resurgence of power, and abandoning his attempts to make the woman see sense, Morgan approached Bosumi himself.

'Daddy!'

Andrea's cry was involuntary, but Helen silenced her with a frowning shake of her head. Instead, the girl gripped her arm tightly, and together they watched as Morgan held out his hand, apparently appealing for the knife.

Elopi screamed, Bosumi reacted automatically, and the knife, jerking against Kori's throat, sent a stream of blood running down his neck. But as if the sight of blood revolted Bosumi, he dropped the offending instrument, and Kori slumped against the window, clutching his throat and uttering incoherent whimpering sounds.

'It's all right, Kori,' said Morgan, in a strangely strangled voice. 'It's only a pinprick. You'll survive.'

Then he bent to pick up the knife, but instead of doing so, he slumped full length on the floor and was still.

CHAPTER TWELVE

THE South London Hospital was in Chelsea. It stood on the Embankment overlooking the grey waters of the Thames, rain-dark now as the gales of November drove relentlessly across the country. But inside the hospital there was light and efficiency, a professional team of people moving competently about their duties, doing the jobs for which they were so well qualified. There was a convincing sureness about the way they performed those duties, a reassuring ability of purpose that was only shattered when something went terribly wrong. The hours Helen had spent in the waiting room at the hospital had taught her to recognise that break in composure, the compassionate turn of phrase that prefaced news of a distressing kind, and she had turned her eyes aside from other people's grief and prayed for the strength to accept whatever was to happen with fortitude.

It was strange waking in the mornings and finding herself in a hotel bedroom in Kensington. It was strange hearing the muted roar of London's traffic outside her windows, instead of the protesting squeal of the goats being driven down to the village, and even stranger having to wear warm pants and sweaters and a leather coat to face the weather, and not the thin cottons she had worn in Nrubi.

And yet, in other ways, it was not strange at all. On the contrary, at times she felt it was so much longer than a week since they had left Osweba, and it was as if her whole life had been flowing towards this point since the day she first met Morgan.

Recalling their departure from Charlottesville was like turning a knife in an open wound. The pain of those hours after Morgan had collapsed was still too sharp to contemplate without agony, and there were times when she wondered how she had succeeded in driving the sixty-three miles from Nrubi to James Oneba's house.

It had been a terrible experience. Her father's apparent seizure had sent Andrea into hysterics, and even Kori had started moaning and rolling his eyes and entreating all the ancient spirits for help. It had been Bosumi who had helped her, surprisingly enough. Morgan's unconscious state had stricken his woman dumb, and ignoring Elopi's disgusted admonishments, he had knelt down beside Helen and showed that he wanted to help her.

After a swift examination, Helen had realised that this was no ordinary faint. She was no doctor, but she suspected his condition was more that of a coma, and no amount of hand-chafing or face-slapping was going to bring him out of it. She felt so helpless at that moment. Andrea was no use, and besides, she was too young to know what to do. There was no one in Nrubi she could turn to except perhaps the Asian doctor, and she doubted his ability to cope with something so serious. There seemed only one solution. She would have to drive Morgan to Charlottesville—to James. He would know what to do.

With Bosumi's help, she got Morgan into the back of the station wagon, and bringing Andrea to her senses with a sharp word about her selfishness, she got her into the seat beside her. It was only as they drove away that she realised she was leaving Kori to face his fate alone, but somehow she sensed Bosumi's anger was all done.

The journey to Charlottesville seemed endless. She didn't know the road, and in the dark her headlights seemed totally inadequate for the conditions. Andrea sniffled into her handkerchief beside her, occasionally, on Helen's instructions, making sure her father was still unconscious. Once a huge elephant reared up in the headlights ahead of them, and only then did Andrea seem to recover her composure.

'*Stop!*' she ordered hurriedly, and stepping on her brakes Helen wondered why the sight of that great mammal no longer had the power to terrify her. It was curious, she thought, waiting for the rest of the herd to cross the road. All things were relative. Compared to her fears for Morgan, the dangers eloquent in meeting an elephant head-on were minimised.

After that, the two girls spoke together in low voices. Suppressing her tears, Andrea wanted to know what Helen thought was wrong with her father, while Helen acknowledged with cold realism that her emotions were frozen, numbed from the moment Morgan collapsed before her. She had reassured Andrea with platitudes, quoting all the possible causes of unconsciousness, avoiding the most serious probabilities never once mentioning her own fears of a coma. It was possible she was wrong, and there was no point in frightening the girl unnecessarily. Nevertheless, it was a heavy burden for her to carry, and when the lights of the capital appeared ahead of them, her strength almost gave out on her.

Andrea directed her to James's house, although Helen suspected she could have found her way there unaided. It was strange how necessity sharpened the senses, and she turned into the gates of the Oneba house without hesitation.

It was only then she realised how late it was. The flood-lights had been extinguished, and only a small light glowing over the entry signified that anyone was still up. And even then, she might be wrong. That light could stay on all night.

'It's one o'clock!' exclaimed Andrea, as if reading her thoughts. 'What if Uncle James is in bed?'

'Then he'll have to get up, won't he?' retorted Helen, with just a trace of hysteria in her voice, and pushing open her door, she got out.

In the light from the opening door, she looked into the back of the station wagon. Morgan lay motionless, and her heart wrenched with sudden pain. He looked dead, and clenching her fists, she opened the rear door and laid trembling fingers over his lips. A faint warmth stirred against her hand and without another word, she closed the door again and turned towards the house.

A servant answered her repeated pressure on the bell, but he fell back aghast as she brushed past him and entered the hall with Andrea close behind her. She felt a moment's impatience with the girl that she had not stayed with her father, but then compassion stirred within in. Morgan was like a corpse, and Andrea was only fifteen.

'Who's that?' she asked the girl, indicating the anxious servant. 'Does he speak English?' but before Andrea could answer, footsteps sounded on the marble stairs, and James's irritated voice could be heard, obviously demanding to know what was going on.

'Uncle James!' It was Andrea who attracted his attention first, but when he saw Helen his face changed, and an awful greyness crept over it. It was then she knew that he suspected what had happened. That he *knew* what was wrong with Morgan.

'James, Morgan's sick!' she got out chokingly. 'He—he's in the car outside. I—we—we came to you. We didn't know who else to turn to.'

James came the rest of the way down the stairs, fastening an embroidered dressing robe about him. Judging by his bare feet, Helen guessed it was all he was wearing, but that didn't prevent him from striding swiftly across the floor to the door, issuing curt orders to the startled servant, and stepping outside to see his friend for himself.

Bidding Andrea to wait, Helen hurried after him. He went straight to the station wagon and swung open the door, staring grim-faced at the man lying on the rear seat. He said something in his own tongue, a bitterly vehement imprecation, and then he turned to Helen.

'What happened?' he asked, and in as brief a few words as possible she outlined the events following their return to Nrubi.

'You know what's wrong with him, don't you?' she exclaimed at last, half afraid that Andrea might come to join them and thus prevent her from asking him outright. A dozen half-remembered incidents—glances exchanged; words spoken, as she thought, without meaning, were coming back to her, and it was no indiscriminate judgment she was making, but an intelligent assessment of circumstances which hitherto had seemed unconnected.

'Yes. I know,' agreed James quietly, his voice heavy with emotion. His arms went about her, and for the first time she made no resistance. 'I promised I would never betray his confidence, and I never have. But I always thought he was wrong, and now it seems it's out of his hands.'

Helen shifted restively. 'What's out of his hands? James, please! Don't waste time. Tell me what's wrong. I have to know.'

James's hands gripped her shoulders firmly, and the faint light from the car showed the lines of strain around his mouth. 'Morgan—Morgan has a—growth. Here.' He touched his head lightly. 'What you call a—tumour, yes?'

Helen's knees trembled. Her palms felt damp, but her

body felt cold, and an awful ache was beginning to make itself felt just behind her temples. She swallowed, but there was little saliva to lubricate the parched dryness of her throat, and her lips parted as if to suck what little moisture there was from the air.

'You—you mean—a brain—tumour,' she got out at last, and James inclined his head. 'But—but why wasn't he in hospital? Why hasn't he been operated on before this? How long has he known about it?'

The words quickened to incoherency as she spoke, and James's hands on her shoulders tightened steadyingly. 'Calm down,' he advised gently. 'One question at a time. Morgan wasn't in hospital because he didn't *want* to be in hospital. He hasn't been operated upon because he never intended to have the operation. So far as knowing about it is concerned, then I guess the time runs into months rather than weeks.'

Helen shook her head disbelievingly. 'But—but why?'

James sighed. 'You think I did not ask him that? Of course I did. His answer was always the same—he could not bear the thought of becoming any less of a man, of running the risk that is always involved, that of losing his faculties. He did not want to become a vegetable, and as such, Andrea's responsibility for the rest of her life.'

Helen quivered. 'Andrea doesn't know either.'

'No.'

'So that's why he wanted Andrea to go to England. Why he wanted to persuade her to leave.'

'That's right. His intention was that she should be far away before the crisis point came. Unfortunately, he seems to have misjudged the time left to him.'

'Oh, God!' Helen blinked rapidly, her breathing no more than a shallow gulping of air. 'Oh, God!' She glanced round at Morgan's still form. 'But—but surely they'll operate anyway.'

'He expected it to be too late for that. Or perhaps he hoped to die on the operating table.'

'*No!*' Helen tore herself away from James to stare mutely at the man she loved, the man she had hoped to marry. She drew in a tortured breath. 'Was that why—why——'

'—why he refused to marry you?' asked James. 'Oh, yes,' as she looked at him, 'I knew all about that. And of course, you are right. He dared not run the risk of you finding out.'

'But—but he did ask me,' she exclaimed, twisting her hands together now. 'This morning, on the beach. He—he said—he said you had told him he should.'

James's eyes glistened. 'Oh, the fool!' he muttered, emotively. 'The blind fool! Why in the name of Allah did he not tell you the truth? As soon as he knew he cared about you—and he did—why did he not take Marsden's advice and admit himself to the hospital where he works?'

'Marsden?' Helen had heard the name before.

'Yes—the brain surgeon he saw while he was in England. A most accomplished man. His diagnosis was that with immediate surgery there was every possibility of him recovering completely.'

Helen remembered the day Morgan had spent in London, the day before she had met him in the town and taken him to the flat ...

'And—and this man, Marsden, said that?' she stammered now, tripping over her words in her haste to find a grain of hope. 'Then—then couldn't he have the operation now? Is it possible for Marsden to be flown out here to operate?'

'I think not.' James shook his head, and her spirits plummeted. 'Osweba is just a small country. Our hospital facilities are improving all the time, but I doubt we could offer the kind of equipment Marsden would demand to work with.'

Helen clenched and unclenched her fingers. 'Then couldn't we take Morgan to London?' she appealed. 'It's not too late. He's still alive. Why couldn't that be done?'

James frowned. 'It could be done, of course, although I do not know whether Marsden will agree to take the risk when it is over a month——'

'Risk? What risk?' Helen was impatient. 'Morgan's going to die if he doesn't have the operation, isn't he? Would you rather he died without trying to save him?'

James's face darkened. 'You know I love Morgan——'

'Then help him!'

'His instructions were to avoid surgery for as long as possible——'

'To hell with his instructions!' Helen was almost beside herself. 'I'm his fiancée. I love him. And I don't care if he's only half a man, so long as he survives!'

James hesitated. 'If you were his wife ...' he ventured softly, 'no one would argue with you.'

'His wife!' Helen stared at him. 'But—but how—we don't have a licence.'

'I am a minister of the Government,' he declared proudly. 'I can arrange for a licence to be issued. The marriage would be valid only here in Osweba, but a licence is a licence, and by the time the British authorities have investigated its validity, Morgan will already have had the operation.'

'Oh, James!' Helen could have hugged him. 'Could we? Could we?'

The Osweban air force jet, used by its Prime Minister on official occasions, brought them to London. James had certainly exerted his authority to the full, and the ambulance that was awaiting them at the airport cut all formalities to the minimum. Helen, still bemused by the ring on her finger, had paid little attention to the ceremony of it all. She only wanted to get to the hospital and meet Howard Marsden, who had responded without hesitation to Oneba's cable.

The hardest task she had performed was breaking the news to Morgan's father. He, too, had been summoned to meet them in London, and in the quiet of her hotel room, Helen explained the circumstances leading up to her almost morganatic marriage to his son. Andrea had been with her, a strangely adult Andrea, who had shared her anguish and her grief, and who no longer behaved as if her own happiness was the most important thing. She had been shocked to the core to learn what her father had been keeping from her, and although neither James nor Helen had discussed

Morgan's reasons with her, she had guessed his motives for herself.

Meeting her grandfather for the first time was an emotional experience for her, but overshadowed as it was by her father's illness, there had been no time for shyness or recriminations. They were all one in their sorrow, and Helen did not know what she would have done without Mr Fox's quiet strength.

James had accompanied them to London, but although he had had to return almost immediately because of government commitments, he was in touch constantly, and had offered encouragement every inch of the way.

'Mrs Fox?'

A young nurse was standing by the bed offering her a cup of tea which she took gratefully. She had lost count of the cups of hot sweet tea she had swallowed since she first came here, but their warmth was always welcome. She had never taken sugar in tea before; she had not cared for sugar in any hot drink. But these days, it had become the only sustenance she could stomach.

The nurse lingered as she sipped the tea, and Helen glanced absently at her watch, noticing with sudden dismay that it was almost six. She must have slept for over five hours. *Five hours!* The remembrance of the previous day's events came rushing back at her, and she turned anxious eyes up to the nurse's face. Morgan had had his operation the day before, but at midnight Mr Marsden had insisted she must get some sleep or she would crack up, too. She had not wanted to leave Morgan's bedside, but he was still unconscious, and she had been offered this bed in an adjoining room so that she could be there as soon as he wakened.

The nurse took the cup from her unresisting fingers, as if she had been waiting for just this purpose, and as Helen's nerves stretched to breaking point, she said gently:

'Your husband is conscious, Mrs Fox. Would you like to see him?'

'*Conscious!*' Helen felt a choking lump in her throat.

'He's conscious?' She trembled. 'The operation was a success?'

'Yes.' The nurse smiled. 'Absolutely.'

'Oh, my God!'

The hot sweet tea welled into her throat and she had to force it back, as she pressed a hand to her breast. Morgan was conscious! He had survived the operation. Whatever happened now, he was not going to die, and she thanked God for that release. But how would he react when he discovered what she had done?

The legs she lowered to the floor felt unreliably shaky, and she put a nervous hand to her hair; as if her appearance was of any importance!

'Are you all right?' The nurse was looking at her with some concern, but Helen managed to nod her head, wondering if her pants suit looked as creased as it felt. It was a silly anxiety, but somehow it was so important that Morgan should not be disappointed in her.

'Come along, then.'

The nurse led the way out of the tiny side ward and along the stark corridor to Morgan's room. Even at this hour of the morning, the lights were burning brilliantly, and the bustling heart of the hospital was already beginning to throb. It might be dark outside, but inside a new day had begun, and Helen prayed that it might be the same for her and Morgan.

The lights in Morgan's room were muted, just a lamp beside the bed that highlighted the hollows of his pale cheeks and drew attention to the swathe of bandages about his head. But his eyes were open, those curious tawny eyes that could take all the strength from Helen's body and leave her weak with emotion.

There was a nurse seated at the foot of the bed, but she rose at Helen's entrance, and the nurse who had accompanied Helen said quietly: 'You may stay five minutes. No longer,' and both nurses went out together, leaving them alone.

Helen moved clumsily towards the bed. She didn't know how conscious Morgan really was, whether he would remember what had happened, whether indeed he would recognise her. It astounded her when he lifted one brown arm from where it was lying on the green coverlet, and extended it weakly towards her.

'Oh, Morgan ...' It was enough to send her rushing forward to grasp his hand, dropping down on her knees beside him, pressing her cheek against the cool skin of his knuckles. 'Oh, darling,' she choked. 'How are you? How do you feel?'

'Helen,' was all he said, but there was a wealth of satisfaction in the word, and he drew his fingers from hers to touch her hair, her face, the parted softness of her lips.

'You're going to be all right,' she breathed unsteadily. 'Do you know that? The operation was a complete success.'

Morgan closed his eyes in assention, and then opened them again as she drew nearer, tentatively stretching her fingers to touch his cheek. The action drew attention to the gold band on her third finger, and she would have withdrawn her fingers again if his eyes had not lighted upon it.

'The ring?' she murmured with trepidation, in answer to his unspoken question. 'I—you gave it to me. It—it's our wedding ring.'

A frown drew his brows together, and anxiety flooded her being. 'You—you asked me to marry you, remember?' she stammered. 'We—we were married five days ago, in Charlottesville.'

'Married?' he said huskily, and she nodded, wondering what she would do if he despised her for taking advantage of the situation. 'Married!' He licked his dry lips, and then his expression grew disbelieving. 'You married me? Knowing ... knowing ...'

'Of course,' she whispered unevenly. 'Did you think I'd let a thing like that stop me?'

'Oh, Helen!' For a moment he just looked at her, and if she had ever had any doubts about whether or not he loved her, they were all dispelled in that disturbing moment. 'My wife,' he breathed, with evident satisfaction, and closed his eyes again.

Helen was alarmed, but the nurse coming back into the

room at that moment just drew her to her feet with a finger against her lips.

'He's sleeping,' she said softly, 'that's all.' She smiled. 'Whatever it was you said to him, he seems very content, doesn't he?'

Helen knew what she meant. There was still the faintest trace of a smile on Morgan's lips.

Eight weeks later, Helen came down the steps of the beach house at Selina carrying two tall glasses of iced lager. As she had spent several weeks wearing nothing but a bikini, and sometimes not even that, her skin was tanned a honey-brown, and the inches she had lost during those ghastly days in England, waiting for the results of Morgan's operation, had all been replaced. She looked fit and well, and extremely happy, and she was.

Further down the beach, Morgan was stretched out in the shade of a beach umbrella. Since they had returned to Africa, he too had recovered completely, and the lines of strain which had marked his illness had all been ironed away. His hair, too, was slowly growing again, but Helen teased him unmercifully about its baby softness. Yet, like the rest of him, it was getting stronger every day, and soon she wouldn't be able to torment him on that score.

Dropping down beside him on the rug, she saw his eyes flicker open with evident reluctance. 'Lager,' she announced, holding out the glass, and lazily he propped himself up to take it.

'What time is it?'

'Almost twelve,' she replied, sipping from her glass and then putting it aside. 'We have to leave at six. Do you feel up to it?'

'No,' he said, and then, seeing her anxious face, he put his own glass aside and reached for her. 'Having dinner with James reminds me only too well that our time here is limited,' he told her softly, unfastening the bra of her swimsuit and tossing it carelessly aside. 'Mmm, I love you, but why do you wear that thing? Why do you wear anything?'

Helen responded to his kiss with helpless urgency, her

limbs melting beneath the sensual onslaught of his touch. No matter how many times they made love, they still couldn't get enough of one another, and Morgan's wish of making love in the open air had been fulfilled a score of times.

But now she pushed against his chest until he supported himself on his hands over her, and said huskily: 'Do you really feel all right?'

'Perfectly,' he agreed with a mocking smile.

'Then——'

'I know. I have to make the effort. Particularly tonight as my father and Marcia are here, not to mention Andrea.' He nodded. 'It will be good to see them all again, but I'm glad you didn't want to live in England.'

Morgan had recuperated at the Foxes' home in York. Despite the irregular circumstances of her marriage to his son, Mr Fox had insisted that Helen stayed there, too, and over Christmas she had even made her peace with Barry. Perhaps the fact that he had a new girl-friend had made the difference, or perhaps it was the seriousness of Morgan's illness. Whatever had prompted his change of heart, Helen had been glad of it.

Her own parents had looked on her marriage to Morgan as inevitable. Her mother had even gone so far as to say that she had known it would happen all along, and it had been simpler not to disabuse her.

For Andrea, there had been time to get to know her grandparents and her father's brother and sister. Contrary to Morgan's expectations, Susan got along quite well with her young niece, and in no time at all she was teaching her to dance, and suggesting she shopped around for more sophisticated spectacles.

'You can get such dreamy specs these days,' she exclaimed, sounding as if she wished she wore glasses, too, and Andrea's confidence, boosted by Helen, gained in strength.

It had been Helen's suggestion that she and Morgan should get married again in the church where she and Barry had planned to take their vows, and on a cold January day, wearing the wedding gown she had once hoped never to see again, Helen had become Morgan's wife for the second time.

Their honeymoon had been spent here, at the beach house; four weeks of doing nothing except sunbathe and swim—and make love.

But now it was getting near the time when Morgan would have to begin to take up the threads of his career again. Not at Nrubi, however. James had been a tower of strength, and through his efforts a substitute had been installed at Hawk's Drift, and Morgan was to spend the next couple of years doing the job he had never expected to achieve—that of researching into tropical diseases. James had put the facilities of his not-inconsiderable laboratory at Morgan's disposal, and a grant from the government was enabling Morgan to work in Charlottesville. Already a house was being prepared for them, and as a final gesture of his gratitude that Morgan should have chosen to come back to Osweba, James had flown his parents and Andrea out for a holiday. It had been Helen's decision that they should come back to Africa. Morgan had given her the choice. It would not have been difficult for him to find a post in England, but she knew his heart would not be in it. For better or for worse, Africa was in his blood, and somehow she thought it was in hers, too.

Andrea, however, would not be staying. She had voted to return to England with her grandparents and complete her education. She would come out to Charlottesville for holidays, and a long talk with her father and stepmother had assured them that she did not resent their happiness. And Helen knew that the bonds that had been forged between them during Morgan's illness would not easily be broken.

Morgan was nuzzling her neck now, his tongue making tantalising forays along her shoulder, and she gave herself up to the ecstatic pleasure of his lovemaking. There was plenty of time for talking . . . the rest of their lives, in fact.